HEATHENS AND LIARS OF LICKSKILLET COUNTY

A Novel

Derek Berry

PUBLISHING

ISBN 978-0-9840142-7-9 paperback
ISBN 978-0-9840142-8-6 electronic book
ISBN 9781941416006 audio book
Library of Congress Control Number: 2015931865
ISBN: 0984014276

PRA Publishing
P.O. Box 211701
Martinez, GA 30917
www.prapublishing.com

Printed in the United States

Praise for Heathens and Liars of Lickskillet County

"A haunting, humorous tale of teens negotiating the fiery labyrinths of love and hate in the South. Berry's timely, contemporary voice is engaging and entertaining."

-Kelly Owen, author of *The College Chronicles Novel Series*

"A multi-layered satire about coming-of-age in a small town in the wake of a divisive murder that somehow manages to both celebrate and savage the contemporary South. Berry is an impressive writer."

—Anthony Varallo, author of *Think of Me and I'll Know*

DEDICATION

To the weird kids. To the ones who wanted to be anyone else. To the ones who grew up and then fell in love with who they have always been.
For Adam Strong

Patrick:
Thank you very much
Welcome to Lickskillet.

Stay awhile.

Derek Berry

[signature]

ACKNOWLEDGMENTS

Thank you first to my friends who took the time to read this manuscript when it was still a manuscript and not a novel. In particular I'd like to thank Laura Cox, Tess Dooley, and Matthew Harberg for their commentary and critiques. Thank you especially to Matt Harberg for not thinking it was weird that your freshman college roommate would stay up into the wee hours of the morning writing a book.

I would like to thank my editor Ben Scolaro, who managed to see a glint of greatness in the book and helped shape the manuscript into something truly publishable. Seriously, editors are the "Dumbledores" of the literary world—they magically make your writing so much better.

I'd like to thank my publisher, Lucinda Clark, who has provided gracious guidance and assistance to my writing career. Without her, this book wouldn't even exist. She took a chance on me, and for that I will be forever grateful.

I would like to thank Roberto Jones, who provided me with both artwork for the cover of this book as well as impromptu therapy sessions on his couch. He has on more than one occasion saved my sanity.

I would like to thank my family for letting me stay in my room for hours at a time writing and for buying me a laptop when I was only twelve because I spent so much time on the family computer working on various fantasy books.

I want to thank my writing peers as well, whether journalists, fiction writers, or poets. This includes Kendall Driscoll, Matthew Foley, Catherine Zickgraf, Paige Padilla, Iva Cierra Reed, Marcus Amaker, Khalil Ali, Fresh, Annalise Eberhard, Paul Allen, Laura Cox, and basically every writer and poet I've met. Each one of the people named has influenced my writing and career in very important ways, and for that, I thank them, though there too has been dozens of others at slams, conferences, and readings who have shaped me.

Lastly, I want to thank my english educators for teaching me to write real good.

"We are what we pretend to be, so we must be careful about what we pretend to be."
Kurt Vonnegut, *Mother Night*

CHAPTER 1
DECLIN OSTRANDER

I need to shave, I thought, rubbing my chin as I leaned into the rearview mirror. Sparse hairs covered my neck, encroaching on the soft edges of my jaw, looking more like a hand-knit scarf than a beard. But maybe I could grow a beard out, the facial hair making me look older, more mature. Girls liked guys who were more mature—that was why they went gaga for hunks on motorcycles. Or maybe they preferred boy-band aesthetics: shaved legs, faces, and chests and astronomically high-pitched voices. My expertise in what attracted or did not attract teenage girls matched my knowledge of interplanetary astrophysics.

Nil.

Exhaling firmly, I pushed the mirror askew and settled into the passenger's seat. "Stop touching the mirror. I'm trying to drive." My father glanced at me, beating his palms against the steering wheel to a static-garbled hip-hop station I knew he hated. "When was the last time you shaved?" Insert dramatic sigh and eye rolling here—I couldn't let him know he had caught on to this insecurity.

At a new school, you had to make a good impression, both for the teachers and the students. The first secret: arrive early and talk to the teacher—no one did that, not any kid at a new school. But if you arrived before the other kids showed up, you wouldn't look like such a loser, and the teacher might favor you for however long you stayed in that town. When you move to a new city every six months, you tend to adopt a short-term mind-set. You need not make a lasting impression, but you could score a few easy A-minus grades.

Once the hordes of students enter the classroom, assume the role of passive zombie. Years of firsthand research have concluded that participating in lessons does not lend good fortune to your social life. Become an actor, a liar.

Chew your pencil and your nails; crack your knuckles; doodle meaningless designs, nothing too outlandish; text underneath your desk to all the friends you pretend exist; cross and then uncross your legs, and then cross them again; stare out the window; if you have glasses, clean them every few minutes with the collar of your shirt.

Don't question this advice. I was a champion liar once, a professional "new kid."

At one school in Mississippi, I wore an eye patch and spoke with a Spanish accent. Told everyone I had been training as a bullfighter all my life, until the tragic accident during my first match. Bull tore right through my eye, I told them. A miracle I even lived, actually. Before I fought, I had held such promise. They called me "the Cyclone" once, but now they only called me "the Cyclops." I moved to America for the shame of suffering such a loss.

We arrived in Lickskillet after the fact, as we arrived in every town. Always the outsiders, arriving in the wake of tragedy, and people looked at us as if we were carpetbaggers. Whether it was a lynching or a gay suicide or a burning cross, we came. Summer almost over, downtown brimmed with people, a mix of teens and retired couples.

To lie so spectacularly, you needed rules.

I could not lie outlandishly, unless I never needed to prove myself. For example, you should not attempt to convince the natives of Miami that you are a talented surfer; in rural West Virginia, this lie would be permissible.

I created lies to make myself seem more interesting because even being a new face in a small southern town became boring. How could you expect to make any friends?

As the radio station fizzled and crackled and finally my father turned the radio off, I recalled the past few years. A flaw in the system: something I needed to refine. Though lying often made me interesting, it did not necessarily make me attractive.

In Tulsa, you've seen a mob murder and have been relocated by the Witness Protection Program.

In Columbus, you've lived in the Australian Outback with the Aborigines.

If you only ever stay in one place for a few months—the length of a hate-crime trial—it was easy to be someone new.

In Lickskillet, I was nobody. For now, driving through town, I was only Declin Ostrander, son of a lawyer who worked for the Knights of Southern Heritage.

If no one knew who you were, you could be anyone.

A week before we arrived on a muggy August morning, a jogger took the running trail in Golden Oaks, zipped inside her nylon warm-up suit, plodding along with new running shoes. These health nuts, the retiree runners—they're going to be pretty disappointed to outlive all their friends. I was too young to care about immortality. I planned on dying long before I was old enough that people would shrug and say, "It was his time."

Running with an iPod in one hand, this old lady didn't even see the body dangling there. Tied up in a tree that stood at the end of someone's backyard, he hung from a noose and swayed. At five thirty in the morning, this woman was fiddling with the play menu so she could listen to a Sir Mix-A-Lot remix. Her head bumped into a pair of heavy shoes.

These sorts of incidents—they always occurred just before we arrived. Suicides, murders, lynching, arson—in a southern town like Lickskillet, there was really only one sort of people to blame. You couldn't have a cross burning without referring back to the Ku Klux Klan—you know them best as the racist organization that killed black men in the Reconstruction South and rebelled against the civil rights movement.

My father knew them as clients. He worked all sorts of cases for any groups that were blamed "with prejudice." The Ku Klux Klan. Confederate American Pride. Neo-Nazis. The Confederate Hammerskins.

The Knights of the Southern Heritage often hired my father, claiming that their group supported American values, not racism. That whole pack of bullshit. Like deep down inside they weren't ignorant bigots, afraid of the big bad modern world.

Whenever something like this happened, there was bound to be a court case. My dad drove around to these small southern towns, representing their better interests. This time, we landed in Lickskillet.

We lived off the litigation of tragedy, drove town to town paying for gas with a sack of silver coins, nourishing our lives with strange fruit.

The people on the street walked with the tenseness of Atlas's lower back. They kept flashing peace signs as a form of hello. Imagine everyone's grandmothers gathering for the Sunday bridge game and trading recipes for kale and tofu wraps. Jeans rolled up past ankles. Politeness strutted the streets like a western gunslinger.

In a town where a sinister and likely race-related crime had just occurred, Lickskilletans were trying too hard. Just for the record, I could hear people outside referring to neighbors as

African Americans and Latinos. "Why, Gonzalo, my great Latino friend—you're Dominican—how about dinner with my family tonight—after we finish the lawn, of course?" Chuckling.

In the midst of a murder, Lickskillet was trying to reinvent itself. The Knights of Southern Heritage also tried to reinvent itself, to become a protector of Protestant values, as if a new slogan could fool anybody. But that was the idea—everyone was constantly becoming someone or something new, and so what if my way tended to be more direct?

"It's all about marketing," my father would say. "Whatever you market yourself as, you can be."

Accents helped, and so did good stories. Read plenty of books.

Be ready with a story if someone asks you why your parents made you live in Africa throughout your childhood without making you learn English. Just say, "Click-cluck-cluck."

Someone will ask about what your father does for a living. Tell the truth, because in a few weeks, what people suspect will be in the papers. If anyone asks about your mother, don't feel obliged to answer.

Make it something interesting if you choose to lie—don't just say that she's not around anymore. Tell people she died in a skydiving accident or was devoured by rabid sharks. Anything but the truth.

You'd actually be surprised how easily I could convince the people of Boise that I grew up in Africa—just click your tongue a lot.

What's your name?

Click.

Where'd you come from?

Click-cluck.

Do you speak English?

Clackety-click.

The truth was that people around America didn't know enough about each other to call me out, and certainly not enough about the world.

If you started to hate yourself, it didn't matter. It wasn't as if you needed to continue to be yourself. You could always be reborn the next time some teenage lesbian was murdered by a hate group that may or may not have been the Ku Klux Klan. In a few months, I would be a brand-new person.

A new racism. A new city. A new house. A new you.

⊷⊶

I scrunched up my face and pressed my cheek to the window.

"You hungry?"

"Sure."

No matter where we traveled in America, there were greasy burger joints. Any town in the South, we could order sweet tea. Always some restaurant boasting "Kuntry Kookin'" and the same chain restaurants charging roughly the same prices. Across states, you'd be surprised how everything seemed exactly the same. Every new adventure just another old memory. There were minor differences, yes, but we could remind ourselves where we lived because every town had a McDonald's.

We ordered simple burgers and sat in silence. This kid across from us was maybe eight years old, sitting with his father, iPod earbuds drooping from the sides of his head. They sat eating, but not really talking. This kid just listened to his music, staring placidly out into space while the father read the sports section of the newspaper. And I kept thinking, So, that's a family.

Maybe a couple of years ago, we were like that. After we lost my mother. Driving from town to town, silent at the dinner table. Perhaps we were still like that.

Before he worked for racist organizations, my father worked for a drug company, repping for pills. We lived in Virginia, in a house with a wraparound porch. In a town like that or in a town like Lickskillet, people never forgot who you were. After we became momless, my father decided we needed to move.

Maybe that was how it worked with grief—that change healed things. If you altered your entire life, got a nice shift in scenery, you would be living a new life. Your past might have never happened.

As I ate, I studied the brand-new LED-lit screens, milk cascading into fancy coffee cups, mountains of whipped cream forming from nothingness. The way the menu looked, McDonald's could have been a classy place. Exactly what I meant by change going on. Everyone could rehabilitate their image: if a fast-food company could make itself look like a snazzy coffee shop, racist hillbillies could make themselves look like Protestant white knights. Everyone was trying to become something new.

Eyes clung to us from the other tables. Outsiders, the faces said. The yuppie dad and yuppie son, come to protect the rights of some racists who allegedly lynched a man who once was mayor. A man who beat up Francis Jameson and then hung his body from a tree in an upscale neighborhood. All of this happened; then the Knights called us.

After we finished eating, we drove to our new house. This time the house was a suburban cookie-cutter stand-up. With two windows and white trimmings, like every other house on the street. I had already seen it in the brochure, and believe me, it would be your dream house. Mine too. Everyone's little dream home, packaged and shipped in pieces for you to assemble. Straight from your nearest IKEA.

The moving truck had already come and gone; the movers had unloaded our boxes of clothes and belongings in the foyer and left. What we owned totaled to ten cardboard liquor boxes. Moving around so much, we didn't have time to accumulate junk, to let old toys pile up in the attic and old clothes sit in dank trash bags in the garage. Whatever seemed too old or too unused, we threw away or donated. My father and I didn't value many possessions beyond the essentials.

We were puppets with our strings cut.

As I trudged upstairs to unpack, my father answered his phone. "Burned down? Last night? Shit, I didn't even—of course, I can be there in about ten. We just got to the house and—an emergency? Yes, I understand. I'll see you soon, Mr. Rutgers." He closed his phone and called, "Declin, I have to run downtown. Just make yourself at home. Remember, school starts in two days here. We might be staying all year, so—anyway, I have to go."

Just like that, he was already gone. I walked through the empty house, trying out the appliances. Flushing the toilet over and over again. Washing my hands in the sink. Everything worked fine.

In my room, I unpacked the fin off a surfboard I'd crashed on the beach. The eye patch that had covered my "bad eye." We had only stayed two weeks there, so I never had to show them the hole underneath where my eye supposedly wasn't. I laughed at that story, to myself: the Cyclops.

A few months, my father had said. We never knew how long we would stay anywhere. When we left, it was sudden. We arrived and departed in flurries of wind, on the whims of men I had never met before.

The television turned on, but it was pointless to watch, since we hadn't had our cable hooked in yet. Instead, I walked outside into the small patch of corn-yellow grass that we called a yard. Up and down the street, the houses were identical. Anywhere in America, in any town or city, in any little suburb, that was where I was. Everywhere and anywhere.

To reach downtown, I'd only have to walk for ten minutes. Locking up the house, I started off. In such a maze of sameness, I might have gotten lost.

A story—I needed a story. Not a surfer, not a bullfighter, certainly not someone who spoke no English. Something simple, enticing. Popular, certainly, with many old friends I could pretend to miss. From California, but not too far north—in the Bible Belt, "Yankee" was the worst name you could call someone.

Charismatic, funny, and well known. I had a girlfriend named Meredith who was very attractive, though not the most attractive girl in the school. Still, so attractive and kindhearted, it broke me up inside to end things when I moved. No one could console me. But if some girl tried, I was not exactly going to stop her. Or tell I was still a virgin at eighteen—that'd be a death sentence.

As I kept walking, I smiled to think of this version of myself, this wonderful, vibrant derivative of Declin Ostrander. Keep it simple, I remembered, and pretty soon I would be on my way.

CHAPTER 2

ARON KING

The first time I realized that these people were not your garden-variety racists was when the police found a body hanging from a tree. National news stations covered our small town, and for once, we were significant. My father knew the man they hung—Francis Jameson, a prominent black politician who had recently finished his term as mayor and looked now to return to real estate. Alongside Rutgers Realtors, Jameson Houses Inc. had developed thirteen different subdivisions and crammed them with American-dream houses.

For a month or more, we were semi-famous for this murder. News anchors stood in downtown, stealing glances over their shoulders as if bracing for hurricane weather. Talk shows dissected the political discourse, called Jameson a martyr and the man who killed him a monster. They arrested Matthew Pepper, one of a redneck brood of ginger-headed hicks. The television channels connected him with a group called the Knights of Southern Heritage, whose online home page appeared again and again on the screen. I found it difficult to wrap my head around the idea that latently terrorist, racist organizations had websites stocked with family-friendly slogans and beautiful photography of white families playing in sprinkler systems.

The second instance that jarred me out of twenty-first-century reality—that era when people weren't supposed to murder each other for their skin color or for whom they wanted to marry—was when they burned down the old haunted house.

Maybe it wasn't long after we first met Charlotte that everything in our lives began spinning out of control. Of course, we lived in a town suddenly notorious for this year's premier hate crime, but our lives went on as normal. After all, local tragedies couldn't shock us out of complacency any more than events halfway around the world. Given the choice between tsunami, earthquake, and lynching, the citizens of this town would clamor for anything other than peace. Calm and stability were boring.

Maybe I'm moving too quickly. It might be better to tell a story. Even if this town was dry for excitement like Egypt was dry for water, we lived for stories. Everyone had a story for everything—why the city collected garden gnomes and why Golden Oaks was at a higher elevation than the projects and why the Rise and Shiner Café hosted Roller Derby matches and why Julian Branch died in a car accident two summers before and why so many people from up north laid roots in Lickskillet to work at the local nuclear power plant and why the haunted house was haunted. These were stories we told ourselves to remind us where we came from, our own versions of history. As for Blaine and me, we wanted to become stories as well. We wanted to become part of this town's mythological past, so that once we left, we might live on. We might be self-made legends.

Let me back up.

When we were still kids living on the block together, Blaine and I dared each other to sneak into the haunted house, which we still called "haunted" even after we stopped believing. Years later, we still broke into the house to drink or smoke. The house screamed with every step you took, the wood old and yielding. No wonder we'd been scared shitless as kids.

Lickskillet's resident haunted house stood atop a hill just outside downtown. You could see the house from a mile away, sitting on the knoll stewing ominous and dark and Gothic. There had once been a Catholic church at the foot of the hill, and the graveyard encroached onto the grounds of the house. The church had been knocked down; the house had not.

When we were kids, we weaved through the crumbling tombstones and climbed up through the first-story window. Then we ascended the grand staircase, where most of the steps had caved in. It was to the attic we had always dared each other to go, since the old kids frightened us with stories of a made-up murder that had once happened there. It was to the attic we climbed still.

Blaine opened a small cigar box where he kept his spliffs in a neat row. Plucking one out, he held the tip against the moon's light to examine it.

The house screeched, a banjo out of tune, as I crossed the room.

Crack.

My foot dropped into a hole as the floorboard collapsed beneath my heel. Pausing, I balanced on one leg and swung safely away.

"I've made a new hole." The attic floor was riddled with holes where the wood had given way under our weight. Dust coated my mouth and dried my tongue. I swallowed, but it was like chewing on cotton balls. All my saliva just got absorbed, turning my mouth into rough concrete.

The wallpaper was sickly yellow and alive.

We smoked, breathing out through the broken windowpanes, dashing our ashes down onto the house's front steps. "Remember coming up here on your birthday?"

I nodded. "You scared the shit out of me."

My mom had come down to visit from New York. She bought me a new bicycle, which had really pissed off my dad. A week after she left, the bicycle mysteriously disappeared. My dad had the bike compacted, I suspected. So rare for her to visit, and the nerve—he couldn't handle being outbid for my attention and love.

Because I was turning ten, Blaine had decided I was man enough to climb into the attic alone. We usually ventured in together, calling back to each other. Whatever lived here wouldn't attack as long as there were two of us. I boasted that I could go in by myself because I was three months older. I wasn't some wimp.

I would enter the attic alone. The ghosts would not touch me; they were afraid of me. They were ghouls in sheets; I was the night incarnate. Or as Blaine worded it, half night incarnate.

Were the ghosts envious or merely sympathetic? Jealous of pumping blood or anxious over our uncertainty, clucking their tongues, shaking their heads?

Blaine waited outside while I crept onto the porch. I opened the door slowly and stepped inside. The foyer seemed much darker than before. All cliché and full of cobwebs, which was what frightened me most. I had seen far too many horror movies about haunted houses to ignore the obvious signs: the creaking floorboards, the creepy religious art, and the discolored wallpaper that looked like dripping pus all screaming, "Get the fuck out of here."

The house infected me with worry, a sense that what I knew was not right, that at any moment the wooden teeth would crunch together, entrapping my body. I trembled, brushing a cobweb from my path and letting the sticky string dangle off my elbows, my fingers. The moon winked its eye twice; light fractured, extinguished, reborn. There was no red pill—no options for escape

But I was ten and proud and wanted to prove that I was manlier than Blaine. I climbed the stairs, avoiding the step second to the top, since it groaned so loudly every time you walked over it you would piss your pants. On the top floor stood sculptures on pedestals that lined the corridor to the attic door. I never realized how strange and sick the figures appeared until I walked past them alone. One depicted a white marble man who looked like Atlas, only the earth had grown too heavy and now crushed him, his crooked fist reaching from under that tectonic weight.

The story we told: a man lived here at the start of the twentieth century. He was a very rich recluse who had inherited his money from his Yankee father. When he moved to Lickskillet to escape the crowds in the cities up north, he built a beautiful Gothic mansion. After his death, the city refused to destroy the one-of-a-kind house because Lickskillet was a town that lacked a wealth of prestigious buildings.

This rich recluse married a young, frail woman, whose health did not permit her to go outside. No one saw the couple for several years as they roamed their sprawling mansion. According to local legend, he locked her in the attic because she had gone mad. She grew vicious and spiteful, so whenever he brought food, she lashed out. She attacked him. Until he finally stopped visiting. Until one day, the house began to reek of death.

We told each other this story, huddled under blanket forts. We told it lurking in the cemetery. We told it as we tramped up the spiraling staircase that led to the attic, that made us choke on dust and feel claustrophobic with its low, pitched roof. On my tenth birthday, we snuck out, and I ascended the stairs just as the recluse had years ago.

When he reached the top, it was said he paused. He called out her name. "Linda?"

She was just a frail girl of sixteen.

They found him, his guts spilling across the floor. His head was missing, but they found it later poised on the weather vane, decorating the roof Vlad Dracul–style.

Blaine swore that his head ended up downstairs on a dinner plate, but the way I heard it, it was staked on the weather vane. If you walked up to the attic and called her name, you could invoke her spirit and anger her enough to attack. But only if you were alone, we figured, since we had once tried it together and nothing had happened.

On dark nights, like the evening I turned ten years old, locals claimed that you could see a light flickering upstairs. They said Linda still lived in the house, though the light likely came from the flicks of lighters belonging to teenagers smoking pot.

I reached the attic door and grasped the handle. I cleared my throat and called, "Linda?" Something shuffled loudly on the other side of the door. Just my imagination. I opened it and stepped through.

"Give me your soul." A black shape blindsided me, knocking me to the floor. I screamed and clawed at Blaine's face, throwing him off of me. I had always been stronger. He crouched on the floor, shaking with laughter. "I—I climbed the wall. You can climb up to the windowsill."

The window he had opened years ago had been shattered. The kids today had grown bored with the idea of haunted houses. Maybe our horrors entertained us in a way this new generation would never appreciate, having more refined fears than our own. They couldn't be bothered to come into the place, so we used it as a hideout to drink and smoke. Protected by the malevolent spirit of Linda.

We finished smoking and left the haunted house for a party at Cass's place. We climbed into Blaine's Mustang, which was a shade of yellow the manufacturers described as "canary," though I thought it looked more liked "mustard." Maybe even "puked-up vanilla pudding."

Blaine rattled on as we drove down the street. "You know, we have to work on our prank techniques," he began. "Practice is essential. You know why I'm excited to be a senior—besides getting out of the armpit of the South?

"The senior prank. I mean, do I have ideas? Once this year is over, we're going to be legends. Twenty years from now, they'll whisper our names. You know what they did last year? Stole the doorknobs from A-Wing. I mean, that shit was hilarious, but it'll be forgotten. We won't ever be forgotten, will we?"

I laughed and nodded. We were immortal. Believing this did not take much effort, not when you were friends with someone like Blaine.

Driving down the road, he glanced sporadically in every direction but settled into a smooth acceleration interrupted only by the rusting stop signs to which he paid little attention. Cass's house wasn't too far away, and I didn't worry about Blaine driving high. He could fly an airplane stoned if he wanted.

We rode through downtown, deserted at night, and I beat on the hood to the rhythm of the music Blaine blasted from his speakers, which was mostly just a deep, rumbling bass. But it thundered through my lungs and made me feel alive.

We were bad, and we were dangerous. We smoked pot and drank liquor and drove all night to reach the beach before morning. Then we would dance on the dunes until dawn before passing out under some empty house's porch. Our fantasies ran amok.

We never went to the beach, but we told each other stories about these made-up events Monday morning. We would tell each other we were too drunk to remember the memories we had made up, and then we would help each other regale our forgotten tales. We dreamed that we lived lives far more exciting than we actually did, but even the most boring of events could become epic if recited by Homer.

"You know, Blaine, I was just thinking about what you did when we were ten. When you scared me. That was fucked up."

"It was fun to watch you squirm. Aren't you supposed to be tough? To be thug? You're the whitest black guy I know."

No one ever seemed to let me forget this. I fired back, "And I suppose the blackest white guy, too?"

He didn't answer.

"I thought you were a ghost," I said.

"Or a demon," he added.

"Or the devil."

"Maybe I am the devil." He grinned manically and began speaking in a hissing voice. "Yes, I am Lucifer, Lord of Darkness. Fear me! I have come to liberate you from the bonds of earthly morality and your fear of death. In my story, we will all be heroes of sin. That's what's wrong with the Bible, in my opinion. It's one-sided."

"I'm not sure you grasp the Bible." It made me uncomfortable that Blaine was an atheist. I was raised in the church, and even though I didn't always enjoy going to Our Holiness Pentecostal Church with my family, I still believed in God. I wanted to believe that there were forces of good in the universe, but for Blaine, the concept of good and evil was far more fluid.

"No, I totally understand the Bible. Everyone is the good guy in his own story. I'm sure if Satan rewrote the Bible, it would read a lot differently. End differently, too."

We reached the gate. Cass lived in Golden Oaks, a wickedly rich suburb where every house was an estate on which a team of gardeners worked all through the spring and summer.

The security guard was an old woman with cleavage banging against her knees and gray hair coming out her nose. She waved us through after checking a list on her clipboard. That was what made Cass's parties so exclusive—that she lived in Golden Oaks and you needed special permission to get past the gate. So Cass could invite exactly whom she wanted. No freeloaders or lousy freshmen ever showed up. Still, most of our high school came to mingle and drink at her mansion. And almost all of the Exeter boys.

At this party at the end of the summer, I met Charlotte.

Charlotte sat on Cass's couch in a tight jean skirt, legs spread apart, begging for my eyes. Her fishnet stockings were torn from her thigh to an unknown destination under the denim, and her nose ring glinted in the dim light of Cass's living room. Cass had outfitted the room with fake strobe lights that grazed our skin in fatal, slow swoops.

I could tell you that I was fairly drunk, but not really—I had a thing for girls who wore tops low enough that you could see the blue veins through the skin of their pale breasts.

Understand right off that this story does not end well for me. This girl was the imaginary number squared—her solution: to make everything negative, laboring under radicals.

I wasn't the type of guy who allowed girls to leave a toothbrush at my place, mostly because I still lived with parents, but also because I didn't make commitments. I didn't want a girlfriend or fiancée or even a lover. I thought Charlotte and I were akin in this belief.

After the party winded down, we talked; she laid her head across my chest, and I didn't care, because she was quiet.

"Where's your friend Blaine?"

"I don't know. He's probably smoking outside or trying to hit on Cass or—something. I'm not sure I care."

"Maybe he went home with a girl. Too bad for you."

"Blaine?" He loved to talk about his dating game, as if he pulled a different girl every weekend night, but there were only a few girls in Lickskillet to actually hook up with. Those that eventually did sleep with guys, even just one guy and even if he was her boyfriend, were deemed whores by the other boys. Of course, if they continued not to have sex with anybody, the boys would call them prudes. In a place like Lickskillet, a girl couldn't win.

Blaine had broken up with his six-month girlfriend back in March, and he had been unclear about whether he actually had sex with her. Maybe he just got to third base. I, on the other hand, had hooked up with two different girls. The first girl I dated for a few weeks before we slowly got bored with each other, and the second girl I met in New York while visiting my mother. I realized slowly sitting next to Charlotte that a new opportunity had arisen.

I looked up through the bleary scene in Cass's living room. Empty Solo cups littered the floor, the keg had run dry two hours ago, and wafts of pot floated in from upstairs.

"Are you OK?" I asked Charlotte.

She shrugged, struggling to keep her eyes open. "Just tired. Maybe we can get away from the noise."

"Well, sure." We slinked off of the couch and linked arms as we ambled out of the door onto the porch. "Where're you from? You don't come to school here."

"I used to go to Exeter, but I got kicked out. I should be going to Lickskillet High this coming year. I'll be a junior." Nodding mutely, I gestured toward the road.

"Didn't drive myself. Is that a problem?"

"Come here." She dragged me toward her own car. "Maybe we can go swimming."

As we drove, I tried to gauge whether we would actually have sex.

"Why did you get kicked out of Exeter?"

She shrugged. "You know, stuff. They don't like anybody to be interesting in a place like that. They're all stuck-up, and I guess I look—different?"

"I think you look great," I said, though my voice was strained.

"What's the new school like?"

"Huh?"

"Where you go?"

I lolled my head. "It's not so bad if you don't mind swimming across campus when it rains. Or that you can't use laptops. The classrooms really only have one outlet each because the place was made into a school in the fifties. I—where are we headed?"

"I know a place. This country-club pool—very exclusive. Only retired folks go, but my grandparents have a membership. It'll be deserted this late at night. I—I have a key." She jangled a ringlet of brass keys, which I cupped in my hand for a moment before nodding.

Once we unlocked the gate and undressed, we came together, groping like clumsy, blind beggars.

Sometimes, life could be like a vacuum of consciousness. Like I'm not really participating but looking in from outside through a smoky lens. Watching my actions as if on reality television, except I have some control over what happens. Still, so detached—light and confident but detached. Oddly alive, yet almost dead.

I had electric veins and ionic eyeballs. Like my heart was hooked up to a car battery, except the energy kept flowing the wrong way.

Charlotte swam toward me, her breasts bunching together inside her polka-dot bra. Her skin smooth, like an alabaster pool float. Gliding effortlessly through the tide she made. Because it was past midnight, we could not turn on the lights, and I could see only her gleaming whiteness. Like a polished cameo button from a soldier's coat, fallen in the grass of a blood-sodden battlefield—that was her body in the deep end.

At the moment, I wanted to believe that it would never matter to me that I was mixed black and she white, but such facts always mattered. In the South, you couldn't escape your own skin, no matter how hard you gritted your teeth and claimed it didn't matter. My white friends always used to joke and call themselves color-blind, congratulating themselves on their friendship with me, until I began reminding them I was the only friend of color any of them had. I was a token they wanted to slide into life's slot machine to win the thousand-ticket prize for being oh so tolerant.

During the nineties, sitcoms featured predominantly white casts—whole troupes of stereotypes including nerdy, funny, and brawny white males who dated ditzy, professional, and aloof white females on and off. There was always one black guy, usually the intelligent comic relief who embodied a muted masculinity and never dated the white girls. He existed more or less as proof of diversity that didn't actually exist. At Lickskillet High, I was *that black guy*, and I wanted to be anything else.

Floating beneath the fabric of stars, we waited. Her kiss tasted like a cigarette, because though I knew how unhealthy her lips might be, I still smoked. We rushed in a fit, like when you have a complete freak-out. A sob-into-the-pillow freak-out, the ones even I had. Breathing into pillows too hard because you couldn't deal with what was happening. We kissed just like that, with the intensity of a meltdown, as if each of us searched with our tongues for a secret moon in the other's mouth.

And suddenly her bra was flung out of the pool, dangling on the head of a collapsible chair. Naked under the stars, trying to replace memories with mental pictures of her body. Mental pictures I'd later try to thoroughly shred. Both of us were so detached from the moment, from the notion of romance, that we didn't need anything more.

Both of us—we were refugees of love, trying to find something better.

Of course we never handled it well. Of course what began in the water never worked out, but nothing ever seemed to. That night, I brought her to my lips, took a nice long drag, and breathed the smoke back into the night.

I grew up half-black in a nearly all-white community. No one treated my father and me any different until they found Jameson hanging in Golden Oaks. Ms. Malbury, bent over like a wheelbarrow racer, crept up our porch steps toting a steaming green-bean casserole. Smiling with her mossy teeth jutting over her wrinkled, chapped lips. My father answered the door, confused at first, but then accepting the casserole, nodding, and thanking her. When she finally hobbled away from our house, he slammed the door, scraped the casserole into the trash, and stored the glass container in the dishwater. "She sends her condolences," he mumbled. This was only two days after the mayor died. We were not related to him, but my father did know him from work.

A week later, Charlotte texted me, and I tried to remember whether I had given her my number.

Charlotte: Hey, sorry for not contacting. I've been busy.
Me: That's fine. What's up?
Charlotte: Nothing interesting. Doing anything tonight?

Blaine and I were supposed to meet Cass at the Red Hole in a grand farewell party. While I texted her, we were en route to the haunted house, to smoke beforehand.

Me: I'm busy.

I didn't want to build our onetime hookup into anything more serious. In a year, I would leave for college and would never be able to maintain such a relationship. Falling in love was a bet I couldn't afford to make.

Outside the haunted house, we hopped out and scaled the gate, sprinting across the overgrown lawn, bounding up the porch steps, and ascending to the attic staircase.

Blaine passed me the cigar box as he stumbled into the attic. Inside, we breathed a rotten smell, the stench of death. Linda, the sixteen-year-old wife, had died here. Had somehow become a monster. Or maybe she had simply waited and then murdered her husband. Butchered him and then escaped. You could feel that she was still here. She looked just like Charlotte with her jagged black hair, unnatural and ugly in a beautiful kind of way. I imagined Linda up in the attic, naked and pale in the moonlight. We would fuck, and then she would tear out my throat with her teeth and leave my head perched on the weather vane.

I was the marble man trapped underneath the world. Collapsed, the earth crushing me. The weakling Atlas. Once you're dead, you can't even hold up yourself, much less the world.

We smoked two spliffs together, sitting on the boxes in almost silence. "Damn shame about what's happening to the Red Hole. You hear?"

"I've been there and seen it. The whole place is crawling with government employees." He said the word *government* as if it were venom in his mouth.

"We're supposed to say good-bye tonight." I breathed deeply until my throat burned with smoke. I coughed violently, doubled over, and beat my chest. Sometimes, I couldn't get rid of the cough. When I smoked too much, my lungs grew weak. B l a i n e paused. "Do you remember Cass's party? I—do you hear that?"

"Hear what?" I asked.

"It's like a trombone. Or a piano. They sound so much the same."

He was pretty far gone. I snatched the spliff away and smoked deeply, greedily. And then I heard it too. Only it wasn't music. It was a scuttling.

No. More like a scratching. Nails dragging slowly across the wood.

I stood up. Slowly approached the walls.

"You hear them too. They're inside." Blaine smiled as he picked up the joint I had dropped, sucking the smoke up into his eyeballs. Only he looked like he was growing horns with that sly smile. The devil, I realized. I thought, Blaine is the devil. Actually Satan.

I backed away from my friend until my back grazed the wall. And then I heard them. The rats scurrying in the walls, scratching at the wood, trying to break free.

"Calm down, man," Blaine said.

"No, you calm down. There's—they're trying to get at us." Blaine tried to hold me back, but I was stronger. I lunged at the wall and beat on the wood until my fists became a bed of splinters. "Get back, you rat bastards. Get away from us before we— I'll smash up every one of you. I know you're in there."

"Nothing—"

Dashing across the room, I clutched a heavy book that rested on top of a box and hurled it through the wall. The wood cracked loudly. I screamed.

The rats poured out.

Blaine screamed as well, leaping onto the windowsill. I had nowhere to go, though, so I stood my ground as a mob of rats swarmed from the wall. Like all the rats in the house had decided at once to attack us. They did not attack, though, only brushed past my feet, taking refuge in the empty boxes and open cabinet. Hundreds spilled through the hole I'd made, fleeing the wall. I leaned down, snatching them up one by one. Flinging them back toward the wall.

But for each rat I deterred, another twenty scratched at my shoes. One tried climbing my leg, but I swatted it away. I leaped over them, smashing them beneath me. With each leap, their bones cracked, the fur running red. Climbing onto the table, I crawled free of the rat horde. Then the last of the rats disappeared as if the floor had not been a battleground. It was then that I smelled the smoke.

⫘⫘

We were bad. We were dangerous. Only death and fire were worse and more dangerous.

Blaine kicked at the windowpanes, the glass shards falling through. When I reached the window, I pushed the frame right out of the wall. It fell, the last of the glass shattering against the ground. Peering down through the window, we saw where the fire had started. A cross flamed brightly just in front of the front porch, and there were words written around it, flaming letters we could not discern.

"We have to jump out." Blaine pushed me toward the new gaping hole. I could see the entire house now. The front porch had collapsed on itself like the jaws of a dead dragon. The entire first floor burned, ready to give out. We would be buried in ashes.

The school year had just begun. Scouts would be searching for me on the field. I was supposed to get a scholarship to rocket me out of this hick town. Somewhere where my sport was appreciated. Where no one called me white or black, just accepted that I was like the fucking creamer half-and-half.

"I'm not going to jump. I'll die. And my leg—I'll break my leg."

Blaine must not have heard. He climbed up on the sill and leaped. I held my breath. He tumbled down onto the grass. For a moment, he didn't move. But then a groan rose. He had survived.

I backed away from the window. The stairs. Maybe from the second floor, I wouldn't get hurt. I reached for the door.

"Ahhhhhhhhhhhhhh!"

When I pried my hand away, it was too late. Red blisters sprouted over my pale palms. The pain overwhelmed me. Even without my hand on the metal door handle, it felt as if I had immersed it in boiling water. Stumbling toward the door, I reached out my burning hand. Maybe it was on fire, I thought. My mind thought too slowly. I was still too high to function. The floorboards cracked beneath me, and suddenly I was falling, falling.

My head hit the arm of a sofa, flaming pieces of floorboard falling on top of me. Toppled to the floor. Flames leaped from the walls. I crawled across the floor toward the entrance, my sight growing dim. The front door opened, and I could see Blaine again standing above me. I felt him tug at my arms just as everything went black.

<hr />

My father was pissed that I had been taken to the hospital to treat my burns, since he claimed they were not so serious. Only my arm looked grotesque, like it'd been baked. The doctors told me it would clear up eventually, that perhaps the skin would fall off and come back. But my arm wasn't too burned. The right hand, however, would need to be bandaged and rubbed with a special salve until it healed. My father was angry only about this. He never asked what I had been doing in the haunted house. Maybe he thought it was Blaine's idea of a dare.

Blaine had broken a pinkie and badly sprained his ankle, but he was happy that he was alive. Throughout his career of stupidity, he had suffered much worse.

He visited me the morning I woke up.

"We were really high. I don't even—"

"The house was on fire."

He nodded. "There was a cross burning in the front. They were saying it was the Knights—you know those racists who meet at that church? They didn't know anyone was inside, but they wanted something to burn. On top of the hill, everyone could see their big letters. Could see their cross. It was eight feet tall, that cross. Made by hand. The firefighters who came, the police officers—they kept talking about the message. Took me a while before I saw it. They spelled it out in the grass on the hill with kerosene. I don't think they even meant for the house to set fire. It just did."

"What did it say?"

Blaine pointed up through the window. The hospital faced the hill that rose beyond the downtown area, just where the Pepper land began. The letters were burned into the side of the hill. The ultimate billboard. "You see, it's got to be them. See what it says? 'Get out of our town.'"

CHAPTER 3
BLAINE MOREAU

If you want me to blab about all the bad things I've done, first you must understand that I'm not a reliable narrator, but I'm a damn good storyteller. I fancy myself an agent of change, the catalyst of adventure, and summarily the antithesis of sobriety. I guess my side of the story starts at Exeter Academy—this insanely preppy school in downtown, in case you couldn't tell by the designation "Academy." But anyways, I was sitting in the lobby waiting for an admissions interview.

I sat on an apple-green divan feeling broken and lousy for what might have been eternity. Having stayed up till four in the morning the night before, I could not fathom another all-nighter. Needed something to keep me awake, keep my eyes peeled wide open. Staring at my hands, I let my mind wander. Couldn't stop shaking, dammit. Always so jittery. Anxiety tasted so bitter.

My parents hoped for a scholarship. I just hoped that I wouldn't vomit all over the headmaster. The pills kicked in. The room shook underneath me. I sat thinking, Shit, shit, shit.

Everything in the place was so unreal; the pills made the academy trippy as hell. I counted forty-two sconces along the corridor that led me into the central lobby. They called it a parlor, though the room looked like the lobby of some fancy hotel. With marble floors and a lit fireplace, for fuck's sake. Those sconces. On Halloween, I bet they lit torches in them.

Why the hell should anyone have torches in a school?

I couldn't sit still, so I read about this painter called Albrecht Dürer on Wikipedia, which I know (according to only a hundred English teachers) isn't the best source of info, but you might be surprised how much you can learn on the Internet. Blew me away that we sat around with these devices in our pockets capable of summoning any knowledge created in the history of humanity and we just used this gateway to eternity to laugh at cat memes and watch amateur porn.

I was getting jouncy when this secretary who was some pornstar look-alike came to ask me back.

When the headmaster sat down to speak with me, he delicately licked his lips. My hair always made a bad impression. He watched me watch him. "Blaine, is it?"

Across his desk on a bronze strip stood the headmaster's name in bold letters: Rupert Leopold Peregrine IV.

"Yes," I answered.

He cocked his head, waiting for me to mutter, "Sir." I began to wonder whether I smelled too much like pot. Maybe he thought it was just some noxious new cologne: Cannabis Sativa by Polo Ralph Lauren.

"I'm here to talk about attending the academy," I said, sitting up straighter.

"Of course you are. Well…I've been looking at your transcript. What happened your sophomore year? Your grades suffered."

"Not all. Not in—"

"Algebra. Yes. When it comes to the calculating art of mathematics, it seems you're talented. But do those talents overshadow

a severe lack of discipline? You realize you've been given a gift?"
He adjusted his glasses and attempted a laser-beam stare, the
sort adults assume when trying to operate authority.

"Well, my parents—"

"At Exeter, we expect the best from our students. We pride
ourselves on producing the finest young gentlemen in the South.
And women—them too, of course. If you presume to become a
part of our tradition, I'd like to see some shaping up. Your disci-
plinary records are not—ah, outstanding."

I admired his confidence, speaking with the voice of a man
sleeping with his secretary.

"I'm aware I've suffered a few altercations. I've missed a lot of
school, but—Lickskillet High did not challenge me as I am sure
Exeter will. Besides, my condition…"

That was my pocket ace. What no one understood, no one
could presume to explain. I only had to mention my condition to
garner immediate sympathy: my brutal gift.

"Yes, as you do display the abilities of—well, a savant, I believe
we can arrange to help you pay tuition. What does your father do
for a living?"

I was a little offended, both by the designation "savant," which
implied that he attributed absolutely no work to my academic
success, as well as his question about my father's work. "An electrical engineer."

He snorted. "Not a perfectly useless job, no. Is he also gifted
then? In all varieties of math?"

"He needs to be for his job—good at math, I mean. He's ef-
ficient in the typical sense, but he's nothing like me. No one is."

He was impressed with my confidence as well, judging by
the way he smiled. "Now, let's get down to the official interview,
shall we, Blaine? Most boys at our schools have clear goals for
their futures, ambitions. Some will become prominent doctors,
judges, politicians. We have graduated award-winning authors,

US senators, and even one actor who went on to have a lucrative career in shampoo commercials. We do not often give full scholarships, so I want to know exactly what you mean to do with the experience we will give you."

"Well, hopefully, a high-school degree—"

"But we don't just give degrees here. We give you tools for your future. And your future—what do you foresee?"

Bad decisions. Drug addiction. Homelessness.

If we were talking short term, I might have said smoking a few spliffs in a crumbling haunted house with one best friend before trying to have sex with my other best friend.

"Well, I'm not exactly sure. I suppose something with math—"

"Of course, of course. Engineering or—why restrict your gifts to one area when you could be making an impact on so many people?" he asked.

"Yes, why?" I shifted uncomfortably.

"One more question, before I let you go." I tried hard to concentrate on him, holding in a vile eruption of vomit. "If you could be any animal, what would you be?"

I stared a moment, wondering whether he had really asked that question. The sort of question online guides will claim interviewers might ask. "I would be a tiger." He did not register my answer, staring intently still at my transcript.

"Ehhmhmm." With a wave of his hand, he ended the interview. "We will be contacting you by the beginning of the school year."

"Do you mind if I show myself around the school? I've never seen it."

He sucked on his teeth until he made a popping sound. "I'll call someone in to escort you around. Don't want you to get lost."

While I waited, he called in one of the students, who stood like a foreign sentinel at the door until I followed him. When we exited into the lobby, he looked right through me. "Do I know you?"

"Do you? My name is Blaine."

"You bought some weed from a boy named Cory not long ago, in front of the library. You're not exactly an inconspicuous person."

"You know Cory?"

"He goes here. All the Swag Boys do. And you want to go here as well, right?" I nodded. "Good, I'll show you around. This is what we call the parlor. It's meant for us to hang out here, but who hangs out inside of their own school? We go into town for that—walking distance. You might want to see the classrooms, but they're much like normal ones. Only better. You'd like to see the dormitories? Yes? But if you live in town—by the way, my name is Cain."

"Cain. Good to meet you. So, this place looks nice, but it's a bit stuffy. Doesn't that get a bit cramped? Or even a bit boring?"

He laughed. "Do you enjoy drugs, drinking, sex, Blaine?"

"You have no clue."

He sighed. "Look, somebody's got to take the moral standpoint here. We can't all go on being so hedonistic. Then there's nothing to compare ourselves to. Then immoral becomes normal. And then what will we do to be badder than the rest? There will be nothing we can do. Don't just let everyone take drugs, have sex, and listen to rock 'n' roll. What will people think of us then?"

"Maybe nothing. Maybe that just makes you normal."

"The absolute worst thing to be."

"You could be dead," I replied.

"If only. We try to have some fun here, Blaine. But don't come in expecting to be badder than the rest of us—just because you've been to a public school. We get those types every year, kicked out for drugs or fighting, whatever, expecting us to be something softer."

Irked at his air of superiority, I attempted to change the subject. "What do you do, then, for fun?"

"For fun? Personally, I butcher small children and murder invalids. I burn kittens alive." He paused and then chuckled. "I'm just kidding. Blaine. I'm sure you'll find that you fit right in. By the smell of you, I think we have similar interests."

Next to Cain, I didn't look like I could blend in here. He stood with perfect posture, smirking, wearing a blue blazer, the lapels bordered in red. He wore his hair slicked back, neat and formal. Every bit the sort of boy the headmaster wanted to churn out of this place. But by the way he talked, Exeter was all about appearance.

As we walked back through the lobby, he muttered, "Well, I hope to find you here once the school year starts in a week. Even if not, I'm sure we will see each other again."

"Will we?"

"Count on it."

Outside, I tore off my tie, stuffed it in my pocket, and unbuttoned the first two buttons of my shirt. How the Exeter boys could stand wearing blazers around everywhere, I had no clue.

I would not be attending this pretentious fucking school, not with its uniforms and dormitories and sconces on the wall. Not with guys like Cain trying to intimidate me as if he and his measly Swag Boys were an actual gang.

Lickskillet High was perfect for me. Students could sleep in class, cut class, and smoke in the restrooms if we opened the windows. Naturally, we were not *allowed* to do such things, yet we had always done them. A guy could breathe freely at Lickskillet.

I suddenly felt sick. The stupid pills.

Doubling over, I began retching into a rosebush, trying my best to make the worst sounds possible. Outside of the headmaster's window. When I finished, I wiped the vomit from my mouth and stumbled away. Pills made the ground move sometimes, which made it difficult to walk. Vomit sounded like car horns.

I started feeling pretty lousy. Once you throw up, you can't feel too high anymore. Back at the house, I had a small stash of weed to stoke the euphoria, but we were supposed to smoke that later, when Aron and I visited the haunted house before Cass's party.

Cass threw the best parties, since she lived in a house bigger than Exeter Academy. In Golden Oaks, you were liable to think you were partying in LA or at least in a non-rural part of South Carolina.

She always bought too much alcohol, so we could never finish it. We never worried about smoking all her drugs because she supplied us (especially me) with bags of the best. She could afford it, she said. Once, she even had a connection for Molly, but she used the drugs with her boyfriend before sharing any with me. Since then, I searched for Molly and for whatever came by, though Lickskillet was dry for hard drugs—save for meth, which I would never touch.

I drove a yellow Mustang that I'd parked downtown. A measly downtown, to be sure.

Never being able to snatch enough sleep, I felt drowsy driving. I could hardly keep the car going in a straight line, so I stuck up my thumbs, telling myself to keep the road between those thumbs and I'd be fine.

Driving even slightly high, the amygdala took over. I surfed down the road as if on a roller coaster. After an eternity and half a second, I was home.

My parents were both complete crackpots with fine intentions. Ever since learning about my gift, they'd been entering me into math competitions. Already before my senior year had begun, they pushed scholarship applications toward me. Memorize pi to the hundred-thousandth digit. Explain the properties of zero. Speed-trial multiplications. The applications were stacked high all around my room, ready to be used as impromptu rolling paper.

Summer wasn't for planning for the future but instead deconstructing it. As far as I cared, the world could end before I ever started school. That would have been more than fine with me. A comet could have come down to smash our town to bits, and that would have been fine.

We couldn't be certain working so hard would pay off, so we didn't work. We smoked and drank and stayed up too late and slept in all day. Sometimes, we spent entire days in the hot sun, reading obscene books and telling each other shocking, half-truthful stories. We weren't sure what might last and what might not.

In our temporal little universe, with our fleeting ideas and dreams, wearing new faces every day, we could take nothing for granted, not even death.

I bent down to pick up a condom wrapper that had fallen just short of our new recycling bins. They stood every fifteen feet. We would feel better about throwing away our shit if the city promised to recycle it, but I suspected everything would end up in the same place anyways.

The adults of this city had adopted strange habits. Like wearing homemade jean capris. And fedoras. And tie-dyed bandanas. Just a week earlier, I overheard my father say he would learn to play the didgeridoo if only he could find the time.

Maybe they were shocked by Francis Jameson's death and wanted to figure out a way to feel young again before they died. Maybe they wanted to seem as little southern as possible, to remove themselves from the possibility of racism.

Our parents had to do that: pretend that when they were kids, they had never gone to all-white schools. That they had been part of the protesting rallies against segregation, against war, against everything my own generation mildly disliked. Every parent swore they had smoked weed and gone to Woodstock, not that they wanted us to follow in their footsteps.

Our parents recounted false miracles and quoted each other each time they said, *those were different times.* Everything was different. Living the way we did, it was no big deal, they told us. Only it very much was because our parents had never lived these made-up lives. Enough to make me wonder whether I would be doing the same thing in thirty years, swearing I followed a deep code of ethics.

When I was your age, I had morals. What kind, I'd never say, just that I had morals. I recycled and never called anyone a faggot, I'd say. And somehow, that would seem like enough. One day, everyone would stop talking about any kind of tragedy, and that, in a sense, was our option of silence.

Even now, we were silent. Every person reacted. Whether we were teens who chose to smoke green in shambled haunted houses or adults who decided that their midlife crisis would require a late onset of hipsterdom. Evidence everywhere.

Maybe we needed change, real change, the sort that starts down in your soul and creeps up your throat like a parasite. This town got boring over the years. Live in any place for your entire life, and you begin to wonder whether or not you're in purgatory. With daily eight-hour trips to hell, also known as public school.

At least now, we could experience something exciting. Something life changing, even if only superficially. Something that we could pretend was bringing our community closer. That would bridge racial lines. As if 70 percent of black citizens in Lickskillet did not live in just one area of town, secluded. That place we were told not to go simply because they were government projects, because there were drug raids and shootings there.

If it bothered you, you paid too much attention. Better to feign blindness. Color-blind was our school's initiative, as if that

ever helped anything. Now we had this one little explosive murder to help us pretend to care. Over the next few months, I anticipated rallies and fund-raisers and a lot of hushed talk. We
wanted change. Of course we did. We had to make the guilty
suffer so the rest of us could become saints, and we could return
to our beloved silence. We would make the guilty suffer, and the
rest of us could be saints. And then we could return to beloved
silence.

CHAPTER 4

CASSANDRA TERRIES

W e could not let go of the landmarks of our past. Some of us still kept stuffed animals beside our beds and told ourselves we didn't need them. But we needed to remember. We preserved relics of our youth because already we could not recognize ourselves, our changing bodies and morphing minds. Already, we looked like adults and wanted to be adults but still felt so young. We had already forgotten small pieces of our pasts, the whispered lullabies of childhood that had been drowned out by every year of junior high we spent listening to screamo music through giant headphones. When I was in sixth grade, before I grew boobs, I used to listen to music that sounded like trash-can lids banging together because my parents hated that music— they were radio DJs and thought themselves progressive. I didn't want to be progressive, just different.

We didn't want to destroy the Red Hole, but the only alternative that existed would be to watch it demolished by machines. How impersonal a destruction, we thought. If our past must perish, we should hold a funeral. Tonight would be the last night at the Lickskillet swimming spot, that place fondly remembered as the Red Hole. The boys mounted the yellow bulldozer to dive off into the muddy waters. As Justin climbed the machine, he called out to me.

"Cass, watch this. I'm gonna do a flip."

I watched. I held my breath.

He swung his arms in wide arcs, like some immense condor preparing to take flight. His feet left the yellow roof, and he floated. My imagination flashed violently in the few seconds before he splashed into the water.

What if he struck shallow water and broke his arm? Justin was his arm, the premier quarterback at Lickskillet High who had already received two scholarship offers from private colleges.

What if he broke his neck? Just like that, his future could end. Our future could snap bloodily on the night we tried to bury our past, his blood mixing with red clay. A few days before, the machines pushed mounds of clay into the water and dyed our swimming hole a dark maroon. We arrived tonight to destroy the Red Hole ourselves, so that no one else could destroy it for us.

Splash. Justin's head bobbed to the surface, and he laughed. I took a swig of vodka and winked at him. He emerged shirtless, his chest streaked with red mud.

"That was incredible," he cried.

I nodded my agreement, though the image of his limp body floating in that pool of red persisted. He clutched my arm, leading me toward the forest. As we disappeared into the tree line, his friends whistled and jeered. But I didn't care. He was mine. Each Friday night in the fall, he would swagger across the field with his football helmet cradled beneath his arm. He would tip his head up and point straight at me. I felt so wanted, and when he looked at me like that, his smile a gulf crammed with firecrackers, I knew no one else in the school could feel so good. I was Cass, Cleopatra—the lover of Caesar. Everyone looked at me and knew I'd be happy, and I enjoyed their piteous jealousy. If nothing else, I was Justin Ferrara's girlfriend, and who could ask for a better life than that?

⊨⊨

I collected my underwear from the grass and wondered where my friends had gone. Blaine and Aron had promised to arrive an hour early after smoking pot at the local haunted house. They still liked to break into that place, though I wouldn't set foot in the mansion. The house would fall apart soon, its wood crumbling to dust. I tried to stir Justin from his after-sex doze, but he only grunted.

"We need to go to the Red Hole. Everyone's getting here."

"Just, I'll be there." He turned onto his side away from me.

As I dressed and walked out of the woods, I rubbed my arm. The bruises still ached. When I emerged from the forest, other teenagers from Lickskillet High had arrived to pay tribute to the place where we had made so many bad decisions.

Our holy and untarnished hideaway would become a housing development, an upscale community for yuppie retirees. Where the trees now stood would lay a sidewalk where elderly joggers would rig along their strangled Yorkies in successive 6:00 a.m. parades. Even now, no one dared skinny-dip in the muddy water where we once had swum naked, where our parents had once swum naked, and where our grandparents had once swum naked. Each generation pretended to forget the backwoods secret as they grew older, leaving this secret place of sins as inheritance to the next crop of teens.

Now the water mixed with red sludge. A wooden barrier blocked the road to the hole, and everyone parked a half mile back to walk down. We tried defacing the machines, tried throwing rocks at them in the hopes that dents could defeat progress.

Soon, they would build fences too, begin laying down concrete foundations, and drain the hole. For those of us who stayed in Lickskillet, our children would have to find new places to drink and smoke and fuck. The places of our youth were all changing, all ruined. These places we had known were leaving us.

We gathered the shovels and formed a semicircle around the hole, bowing our heads. We prayed to the nights of cigarette smoke, toxic tequila shots, and shedding our clothes. We dug into the ground and dumped the dirt into the water.

Each mound of red clay made the hole less swimmable. Each mound of red clay ruined our past. We could not let outsiders corrupt the holy sacraments of our town, so instead we destroyed the Red Hole ourselves, each crunch of clay a memory of a night dissolving, a photograph's dissipating smoke. We stood for a moment in silence, revering our loss, our parents' loss, and our children's loss. Here, everything got passed down—the clothes and the land and brittle hospitality. We each gave away our pasts because we could not live long enough to enjoy them and would exist in the eternal cycle of mortality. Though even now we thought not us, not me, no, not me. Everyone else could die, but we never would—how unthinkable.

≈≒ ≒≈

Justin rested his hand on my thigh as the cars departed into the night, some swerving at the hands of drunk teens.

"Not now. Wait till we get home."

He sighed and put the truck into gear before driving away from the hole. But I wanted his hand on my thigh, his hand everywhere, his lips everywhere, wanted embrace and gush and embarrassment.

"Turn left."

"What?"

"Just turn left. There's a police block up there. They'll know you're drunk."

Blue-and-red lights blinked, illuminating the sky, and above them stood blinding spotlights. Like an alien spacecraft had crashed downtown.

"They won't. I—I'm good. I'm straight."

"Just turn." He turned off onto a side street. We would take a detour to reach Golden Oaks.

"We can smoke at your house, right?" he asked.

When we reached the outside gate, I told Justin to roll down the window and allow me to do the talking. He could hardly drive, much less carry on an intelligent conversation. Even sober, Justin served his conversation in grunts and outdated pop-culture jokes. "Cassandra Terries. I live on—"

"Of course, Ms. Terries." The plump old guard raised the arm guard. "Go on right through. Are any more of your friends coming tonight, Miss?"

"No, just us. For tonight, that is."

"Have a good evening," the guard replied.

Justin jerked the car forward, almost colliding with the rising arm guard. The radio cut to commercials. "Coming up, the number-one chart topper," a male voice blared from the radio. "Courtney, did you hear about Philip Weaver? Nasty divorce."

Next came a female voice, equally chirpy. "Well, Robert, she's a model, and he's a B-list actor who was arrested for—"

I slapped the radio button and sighed. "I absolutely hate listening to my parents. Why would anyone? They're fucking annoying. It's bad enough I hear them talk about celebrities at home nonstop."

"Nine months, and you won't have to. You'll be on the sidelines cheering me on. You won't have to worry about any of that because we'll be far away."

Smiling only made the invisible ring feel tighter on my finger.

Justin parked in the garage. My house stood grand and empty. We tumbled out, him so drunk he could hardly walk. With his arm around my shoulder, he stumbled into my kitchen. He toppled forward onto the hardwood floor. He crawled onto the couch before passing out, and I wondered how we had survived the drive home if he was so drunk. Maybe he was just pretending so I wouldn't talk to him.

Taking off my shoes, I tiptoed across the room. Somewhere in the house, a machine emitted shrill beeps. As I passed the couch, I stepped soft on the hardwood. I didn't want to bother him.

Whenever I walked through the halls, I could only hear my own footsteps. If someone were to press their ear to the basement door, they might hear the machines pumping below. Even a rattling breath. Upstairs, we could hardly hear him down there. I didn't want to think about the man in the basement. Switching on Norah Jones, I swayed drunkenly in circles.

When I was younger, I demanded to be a princess in a ball. Instead of buying a stupid, cheap Halloween costume, my parents paid a woman to make a dress just for me. With a little corset at the top and a long flowing pink skirt that flew up in the air whenever I spun a graceful dance. I wore a tiara and high heels, even though they killed my little ankles. For a small while, I was royalty, destined for this fantasy life.

Finally, I fell against the sofa and leaned back, closing my eyes.

⊷⊶ ⊷⊶

"Fuck." The alarm's persistent cymbal clash woke me, and I rose from the couch grasping for a clock. Justin no longer slept on the couch—had disappeared in the early morning. The beeping came from downstairs. The basement. "Fuck."

Bursting through the basement door, I nearly tripped down the stairwell. He lay in the corner, convulsing. His medicine was in the case next to his bed. Somehow, Grandfather tumbled out and crawled away, managing to rip off his respirator. I filled the vial with a clear liquid and delicately slid the needle onto the end before approaching him. His mouth hung open, strings of spittle stretching across his cracked lips. I leaned over his body, pinning his shoulders to the floor.

The medicine disappeared. He stopped shaking, folding into himself like a skeletal bird. We would one day all rely on chemicals to keep us alive, though most days we consumed chemicals to die faster. I carried him back to his bed and rearranged his robe so his wrinkly body wouldn't show. My mother would be furious if her dad were seen pissing himself in the basement.

The convulsions were getting worse. They came more often now, but my parents refused to allow him into a nursing home. Before he got so sick, he had fought adamantly to stay away, to stay free. I looked around our dismal basement where he had a bed and a fuzzy television. Was this freedom? After the grit and the shatter and the tongue kiss of living, what I had to look forward to: these memories becoming jumbled, incomplete, and meaningless.

"Stupid," I muttered aloud as he fell asleep. I should have given him his medicine the night before, before I went out to the Red Hole. We could have lost him too, just like I would lose the hole and the summer and everything else. He began snoring.

Sometimes it seemed easier to just snuff him out with his pillow. Press it over his face long enough to stop his breathing. But this was the man who had made everything possible—who had financed this house and my future.

My grandfather had once been both a dignified and horrible man. Martin Darry ruled the music world. He signed jazz quartets, rock stars, blues singers, Motown wailers, pop-punk rebels, and piano virtuosos. Made them famous, sculpted their pedestals.

And now nobody remembered him and could hardly remember us. My parents kept my grandfather's will in a state-of-the-art safe in the living room, but he existed as our secret investment in the basement. A rotting apple peel, shriveling and shaking.

When I turned on the television, he sat up, muttering, "Fucking Polacks coming through the street again. Shaking and banging up all manner of—Susan, why are you in the office?"

"Susan?"

"Get the fuck out of here, you stupid bitch." His voice sounded so childish. "This is no place for you. What if—my wife—get out—"

"Yes, Grandfather."

I rushed up the stairs as he flipped through the channels, still muttering. "Too many Jews work in this business, I tell you. And worse, you get some of those slimy Italian types, think they own—"

His voice faded. Closing the door behind me, I walked up to my bedroom. I could no longer hear him. Music blasted loud through the house. I needed more sleep. I needed to pretend I was alone in the vast, empty house. I needed to feel alone.

Already, I felt the future slipping, something too vast that I thought I could fit into. But at least I still retained a future, a past, a sense that now was now and would be five minutes ago five minutes from now. I hadn't gone crazy, not yet, and I wondered if, decades from now, I would be mourning the Red Hole. Grasping at a past, desperate to reclaim some part of myself I could recognize. Unable to remember even my own name.

CHAPTER 5

DECLIN OSTRANDER

"Declin! Everyone, Declin's here." A cheer went up from the swarm of partygoers. One of the boys I met at school grabbed me and pulled me through the crowd. "Cheers for Declin! Does everyone know how incredibly hot his girlfriend was?"

"Yeah, I'm still trying to get over it."

"Well," the boy said, "we threw a party just for you. Look around. All this is for you. You're so cool."

"Yes. Well—"

"I hope you brought swim trunks." He led me through the house into the back, where more teens leaped drunk into the clear pool. Fortunately, I was already wearing my swimsuit, though I did not remember putting it on. Several tanned and impossibly beautiful girls lounged in a bubbling hot tub. I climbed in.

Leaning against the rim, I took a sip of champagne. "This is a fine vintage," I said, toasting the girl beside me. They circled the tub, topless under the bubbling surface. "When I moved to this town, I had no clue all the ladies here were so—exquisite. Want some more, Whitney?"

Whitney leaned close, pressing her breasts against my arm. I poured her a glass and settled my arm across her shoulder. "It's a beautiful night. I'm so glad to spend it with you, Declin."

"Me too," whispered Alicia.

"Me too," said Candy.

"Me too," said Tammy.

"Well, ladies, don't fear. There's plenty of me to go around. And we have until morning here under the stars. I guess we can all be comfortable together—oh, look, are those my swim shorts floating there? I suppose so. Come here, gorgeous."

Whitney said, "Declin, you're going to be late."

My dad said, "Declin, wake up. You're going to be late."

I turned over, folding my arm over my face to protect my eyes. "Leave me alone. I don't want to go. I mean, they wouldn't even—"

"Best make a good impression, eh? Come on. Get up."

I clambered out of bed and dressed while my dad rushed around upstairs. His first day too, defending Matthew Pepper. When I climbed out of the shower, dripping over the new carpet, I greeted a deserted house. Fifteen minutes until school began. My schoolbag empty except for some pencils and one notebook, I stumbled out the door and began trekking down the street. Classes started at eight o'clock.

The girls at Lickskillet High probably were not all tan and did not swim all night topless in hot tubs. Or have stripper names. Walking through downtown, though, I retained high hopes. I just wanted to be attractive, to be wanted. Having a girlfriend for just six months might be nice. Getting laid would be even better. Moving around so often, I had never done more than kiss a girl.

Last year in Huntsville, Alabama, I once tongue kissed a girl named Francesca in her car at the mall. This experience of trading spit constituted the extent of my sexual experience. In each city, you hear fresh stories about wild parties, about exactly what teens do at them. But I had been to dozens of parties across the Southeast: still a virgin.

Maybe my intensely interesting personality intimidated females, or perhaps with their extra X chromosomes came the inability to observe Declin Ostrander's true sexiness.

＝＋ ＋＞

Downtown, I again experienced Lickskillet's cultural upheaval. I passed middle-aged businessmen wearing cloth shoes made in remote Indian villages, carrying recyclable cups of free-trade coffee, and reading anarchist, anti-consumerist pamphlets that some college stoner probably printed in his basement.

Smack in the middle of the other buildings stood a quasi castle. Tall and white with impressive columns and heavy doors, standing across the roundabout from the library and courthouse. Exeter Academy, my dad told me, attracted brilliant students from across the nation, being one of the most prestigious private schools in South Carolina. When I asked whether I would be enrolled there, he just laughed.

Lickskillet High wasn't as prestigious or even uniform; it attracted no exceptional students, but plenty of cockroaches of record-breaking size. Four blocks from Exeter Academy, it existed in a field, an archipelago of detached buildings bearing hodgepodge architecture and atmosphere, each new wing having been built in different decades during unique design eras.

The last building, though, had been constructed in the seventies, making Lickskillet High more or less a patchwork stucco piece of shit, an assortment of drab army barracks. The inclusion of outhouses would not have surprised me.

Not the worst public school, though, certainly not in South Carolina. Some of the cities we lived in were actually less like modest hamlets and more true-to-the-core redneck Nowheres.

Towns where orthodontists went bankrupt on account of there being only so many teeth per capita.

The sorts of towns where no one had ever heard of smartphones or the Democratic Party or anal sex.

———

I trekked across campus through waves of students, navigating the school like some intrepid Magellan. In my first-period class, I sat down in the center of the aisle. No one else had arrived, except for a redheaded girl who ground her pencil into pulp with the sharpener.

Recite the story; make sure you don't forget it. Do not forget who you are, who you pretend to be.

There was a girl once, a beautiful girl with blond hair and deep-blue eyes—all that romantic shit—and a 36C bra size. We had been in love. I debated getting engaged to her. But I needed to break it off upon moving. Would they find engagement exciting or was that too common in this state? Did teenagers get engaged? I couldn't be sure.

Regardless, I had been devastated after our love's tragic, sudden displacement. I was the sort of heartbroken that Ryan Gosling's beard symbolized in the second act of *The Notebook*. But any females who chose to soothe my pain—I would not turn them down.

Pretending to be another person, to be different from you, was all about relativity. To be more attractive, smarter, better than the next guy, I only needed to compare myself to the right people. Standing next to the proverbial "other guy," I could be Brad Pitt or Albert Einstein. As long as I didn't try to compete with the preexisting high scholars, I could seem semicoherent. Compared to Hui Jin—sure, I was a dumb ass, but just put me up against anyone named Bubba. Suddenly, I was a genius.

Rednecks: perfecting the bell curve since 1865.

I arrived entirely too early. Bells rang, and students bustled, and another student entered the room. He barged through the door, pointing at me. "I spy with my little eye something metaphysical. Ah, intruder from the black castle. Who do we have here? A tomato to my lovely matador, perhaps?"

He was a tall boy with blond hair slicked back on his head with gel, his cheekbones sharp and protruding. He wore a black leather jacket, even though it was over ninety degrees outside.

I answered him. "Ah—I'm Declin Ostrander." He cocked one deranged eyebrow.

"Dillon! Ah, well, your acquaintance has been made, hasn't it? And in the meantime, the entire world has tilted, sending us spiraling at thousands of miles toward the sun that will likely obliterate us."

"Um, who are you?"

He lowered his voice so it sounded like he was revealing national secrets. "Call me Blaine. And watch out—the tomatoes are watching."

His eyes bulged, red lines sparking across the whites like tributaries on a map of hell.

Only after the entire class arrived, thirty minutes into the first period, did the teacher, Mr. Pearson, arrive. He entered swinging a mile-long veil of black dreads, knotted on his head in an intricate style, waterfalling down his back: Medusa snakes writhing and curling. "Sorry for being late, kids." He began to scrawl *American History* across the board.

"We'll start today with a basic discussion about what topics we'll cover throughout the year, and then—"

The bell rang, shrill, persistent.

As we stumbled out of the door, I grabbed Blaine by his shirt. "Where is Ms. Schall's biology class?"

"Ah, we're headed to the same place. Come, Mr. Tomato. Follow me."

I had no choice but to chase him through the packed halls. This next period, I would have to be ready to meet more people, lie to them. Lying became a chemistry experiment, a unique reaction that could combust at any moment. Each lie you told increased the entropy of the universe, the randomness of events multiplying. Until you had to tell more complicated lies. They were catalysts—basic chemistry.

As we pushed outside, sprinting across the campus, I found my hot-tub angel.

Underneath the skimpy pines, I glimpsed her for the first time. Awe-inspiring and almost as attractive as my made-up girlfriend. She floated across the gum-frescoed sidewalk like a girl from a dream and then dissipated into morning as dreams tend to do.

⊨+ +⊨

In biology, I shared a table both with Blaine and the serial pencil sharpener from American History. Another boy arrived, breathless. A tall, light-skinned black boy who simply mumbled, "Morning." Blaine responded by trying to fight him.

Ms. Schall, a warthog-esque teacher sans tusks, ordered us to intimately get to know each other. I fixed my hair, cleared my throat, and watched the others expectantly.

"Well," said our newest member, "my name is Aron King. I play soccer, and I guess I'm fairly good. My dad is a lawyer, going on about the Francis Jameson case day and night. That's it, probably."

Blaine's chest swelled as he sang, "Dragons don't fly at midnight because the moon absorbs all of their power. And if that happens, they can't breathe fire anymore. If that happens, they

51

can't enjoy fine campfire s'mores any longer. Which would be quite sad. And even though sadness tastes like blueberries, I hate blueberries."

The redhead girl. "My name is Pepper. You can call me Pepper."

Finally, all eyes turned to me. What if I started hyperventilating? When you first began to lie, it felt like ascending the first slope of a roller coaster, and you wondered if you still might want to get off.

"My name is Declin Ostrander, and I only just moved here a week ago. I love the town. Very—humble place. Not as big as where I lived in California, but nice enough. And clean. I guess what you should know about me—I can't surf, even though I lived in, as you know, California. I used to be really popular. Very much so. Everyone liked me, and I hope everyone will like me here too. I like to think that I am quite likable, and while modern psychologists would pinpoint this as self-serving bias, I think there is ample proof of my amiability.

"And I had a mega-hot girlfriend named Scarlett—I mean Meredith—who was very, very—well, hot. With pretty big—well, she was a 36C, which some people say is pretty impressive. Not that I only miss her breasts. I miss her as well. We had to break up, which drove me to suicidal levels of depression. Except not actually suicidal, but close enough that you should all be concerned. That's all."

I smiled, quite satisfied with slipping this information so subtly into my introduction. "Well," said Aron with a long sigh. "Isn't that fucking intriguing?"

⇌⇌

Next I had an advanced literature class in the oldest building on campus. The classroom reeked of mildew, the rotting walls covered in inspirational posters with pictures of Albert Einstein and Oprah Winfrey. The ceilings had begun to cave in, and as I looked around, I could find no electric outlets.

"You're new here."

"Oh so observant. Everyone says that first thing and—oh." As I turned, the elusive rainbow fish appeared again. The dream girl. "I'm Declin."

"I'm Cassandra. But call me Cass. Only my mother calls me Cassandra."

"I'll remember that. Did I tell you—that, um—I'm from California?"

"Really? My parents moved from out there. Where did you live?"

"Oh—oh, California."

"No, no. What *city*?"

"City? Oh, you know—we moved a lot. All over. Anyways, is this class—it's boring to talk about school, isn't it?"

"Basically." She smirked. "You don't even know what to say, do you?"

All I could think was—she's speaking to me, to me, to me, to me. "Well, you—do you get out much? I mean, is there much to do around here? Parties and—" My voice faltered like a limestone foundation built above the sea during an earthquake.

"Whoa, you're getting ahead of yourself there, Declin. What, you think you can come in here mumbling and stumbling and start getting drunk? You've got a lot to learn."

"I—I—well, OK. I just—"

"I know. I know. Well, you'll like it here. Or not." She seemed to consider it seriously for a moment. "Probably not."

Class began, and throughout we kept stealing glances at each other. Mr. Brantley, an exhausted young teacher, ranted for the next hour on why Hemingway was so important to our lives. "Did no one read what I assigned over the summer? I mean, does no one even know the name of the narrator? Come on, this is idiotic." He gave up, raising his futile fists to the sky. "Ah, read silently for the next fifteen minutes. Good luck." He slumped into his desk, mumbling.

I tried to read, but every time she looked over her shoulder at me, more than my heart fluttered. This was the girl who would make me the most popular guy in school. Cass.

Soon enough, guys would clap me on the back and say, "Hey, that's Declin! That really cool guy who fucked Cass. He must be so interesting and awesome." When I applied for a job one day, the first thing my potential employer would read from my résumé would be "had sex with Cass." Upon reading that, I suspected, they would hire me on the spot. Maybe even give me stock options or make me vice president of the company.

Sex didn't seem so important. Sex seemed just a little thing, a simple act, and a small amount of pleasure. Mechanically, it didn't seem very complicated. But I was in high school; sex was more than that. Sex was everything. The pinnacle of human experience wrapped up inside the body of another. The only place I wanted to be was between the sheets, and though admittedly I had not yet ever seen a girl naked, I imagined it would be the highlight of my formative years.

⇥ ⇤

At lunch I sat down with Blaine and Aron. Blaine kept mumbling things under his breath, and I surmised he might either be crazy or have a serious drug problem. We sat, Aron looking very serious, Blaine floating somewhere in a haze, when a girl approached us. Everything about her seemed petite except for her breasts (and don't criticize me for noticing this, because you would notice it too), which looked like two bowling balls set upon her chest.

"Who is this?" I asked.

"This? Well, this is my girlfriend, Charlotte. She's new here. We met this summer."

Another new girl? She looked exotic with her jet-black hair and *Rocky Horror Picture Show* costume and dangling bat earrings.

Blaine suddenly spoke up. "Our kites were meant for thunderstorms. Mine thrums with static electricity, a skeleton in the sky."

Aron smiled, turning away from his girlfriend. "Well, Dillon, tell me more about yourself."

I ran through the same spiel I had in biology class. This was how I embedded my own false memories into their brains, making truth out of fiction. I told stories again and again until they became memories for me as much as for them. I was not Declin Ostrander, son of KKK lawyer. I was Declin Ostrander, man-about-town, Don Juan–esque and hip.

One day, we would be mythologies. We would be cave paintings. Our kin would unearth our interred bones and question their legitimacy. We would survive only in the tales told by old men who insisted we truly existed. All would name them wrong, senile. The legend of us would be far greater than our story, no sordid memoir of utter truth but biased for romantic eyes. May they paint us as heroes or gods and not wicked beasts, as was nearly always our custom.

I spun these tales to reddening ears until they simply accepted them.

After lunch, the day sped by, and my lies became easier. The catalysts of lying. Once I told one, it became easier to tell more until I had told so many, the lesser ones seemed divine truths. In Spanish after lunch, I even told lies in another language, which wasn't difficult to do because I wasn't sure even my teacher could actually speak Spanish fluently. Spending three months as the matador, "the Cyclops" had vastly improved my vocabulary.

Then came Statistics, in which I mapped out charts of how easy lies became the more often I told them.

⚊⊹ ⊹⚊

In Psychology, a boy named Elijah Rodriguez told me that I sat in his traditional seat, so I moved. He approached me with large eyes behind bottle-thick glasses. I politely moved, mostly because he knew my name without me telling him. Perhaps the rise of Declin Ostrander had begun.

After an hour of watching a movie with a teacher who possessed questionable knowledge of psychology, I slipped out into the hallway.

No matter what school I went to, no matter where, the end of a school day still held the same cathartic relief, filling my lungs with air after they'd been compressed too long.

⚊⊹ ⊹⚊

Despite the concussion, I remembered a little of what happened next. Justin Ferrara crossed paths with me for the first time, his hulking presence ominous even three hundred feet in the distance. Later I would learn of the conversation he had with Cass, how she had implicated me as a romantic opponent, how he'd finally reacted.

She—Cass—spotted me from across the courtyard. She waved at me, at which time I noticed she was clinging to a boy's arm. Whatever he said, he was angry about it. His name, I would later learn, was Justin Ferrara, and he could bench thrice his body weight. Like an army marching into a Russian winter, she walked toward me. She stopped a few feet away, said something I probably misunderstood.

Then came the boy staggering, his body embodying hurricane gravity. "Cass, is this your—"

"Wha—da—you doing?"

I blinked.

"You talking to her?"

"I—"

"Declin, he's drunk."

"It's the middle of the day?" Then his face loomed, his fist a shadow plummeting into vision. Then nothing.

⇥ ⇤

In the black space of shuddering dreams came lips, her body. Her mouth, hard against mine, felt stiff and persistent.

⇥ ⇤

I woke through an ether of confusion on a hard bed. My vision blurred, and the world played "Red rover, red rover, send Declin back into unconsciousness." Cass's face hovered above mine, and I smiled at the thought of kissing her. When I tried to tell her this, I said, "Gagoushagaga." She nodded.

"Is he awake?" A man's head floated alongside Cass's. "We need to get him out here. Can you take him home?" The man looked to Cass.

"Yes, Principal Reiser. Sure. If you want. But I don't even know him."

The principal rolled his eyes and then peered down at me. "Boy, what's your name?"

"Declin?"

"So the concussion isn't so bad." He smirked at me. "You've got your little friend to thank for that."

"Who?"

"The little guy. Where'd he go?" Reiser nodded to Cass, and she shrugged. "You—what the hell were you doing?"

"Me? Doing what? He hit me. Where is he?" I sat up suddenly, peering past the curtain. But only the gaunt principal, a beefy security officer, and Cass stood in the room. "Justin punched me."

"We know exactly what happened," Reiser growled. "Only your first day, and you're getting in fights. Justin would never—he's an exceptional student."

"But he—"

Cass broke in. "He's not lying. Justin started it. You can't suspend him; he just—"

"Detention, then," said Reiser with an air of finality. "Consider yourself lucky." He exited the room, the security officer following him outside.

I fell back against the bed. "Detention? Seriously?"

Cass shivered. "I'm sorry."

"What do you mean?"

"He just—I was taunting him. I told him that I was kidding. But I—it doesn't matter." She fell silent, her face concave. How could someone so beautiful be so self-conscious?

"How do I look?"

"Fine. Elijah saved you from—whatever. From Justin. He's just—you don't understand him. I know you don't know him. He's really a good guy, just sometimes he gets—sometimes he acts different. I don't know why."

I couldn't ask.

"Do you want a ride home?" She helped me climb out of the bed and then led me down the hallway. "Detention's not so bad. My friend Blaine's going to be in detention as well. It can't be so bad if he likes going so often."

Once in her car, I tried again to place my memories correctly. "So, what happened? Why'd you kiss me?"

"Kiss you? Are you sure you're OK?"

"I'm—I thought—well, I remember—what happened?"

She grinned. "Maybe you were dreaming. Were you dreaming about kissing me?"

"No, I just—you know. I don't really remember."

I reached behind my ear and felt a pulsating welt that Justin's fist had conjured. She chuckled, and I turned away, sucking in my breath. "Don't worry about it. Maybe you don't remember events well." Of course not. As if there were anything to remember. Just the same towns, the same houses, the same lies. If anyone ever asked about my experiences, what my actual life had been like, I couldn't tell them, hadn't experienced anything special. There existed no worthy memories. "That boy helped you up. He said he was your friend. He—well, he gave you mouth-to-mouth."

"Oh."

"But we didn't know what to do. I should have stopped Justin, but I couldn't. And that boy—he did."

"Who?"

"I said his name was—Eli?"

"Elijah? He was in a class with me—he—what happened?"

"You know people just stood and stared. That's called the bystander effect, you know. Too many people see an accident, and nobody wants to help. Well, this kid helps you up and gets the security officer to carry you to the nurse's office." She glanced at her mirror. "What street do you live on?"

"Just north of town."

"Everyone lives just north of town, kid. What street?"

After digging a piece of paper from my pocket—on which I had scrawled my new residential information—I gave her directions. "So, that was your boyfriend?"

She laughed again, and I wasn't sure whether I had become the butt of her jokes. "I guess he's my boyfriend."

"You guess?"

"I shouldn't have said that. You know how it is in relationships, though—you get together like you're two high-school sweethearts, and everything's going perfect, and then, well—things are different. Your expectations are too high."

I had no clue, but through a swift nod, I conveyed that I did understand—hopefully engaging in the secret communication of head nods that only two people who have shared a special experience may perform.

She looked at me for a moment. "So, you met anyone yet? Here?"

"I've met you. Also, you mentioned Blaine, but he—"

"He's a close friend of mine."

I stifled my remarks and then said, "Yeah, great guy. Ah—"

"It's OK to just ask. Go ahead—ask."

"Ask what?"

"You want to hang out with us."

"I mean, sure, if you want to, but I wasn't—what do you mean?"

"You're new in town. You want people to show you the ropes. I understand. And I'll say, Declin, of course you can hang out with us. I'll give you a tour of the town—just you wait."

I scoffed. "Here? Bet there's a lot to see. What do you do for fun around here anyways? It's so—"

"Stifling? Small? Yeah, I know. Maybe you'll have to wait and see what we do for fun around here. Maybe you'll be pleasantly surprised. And what about you? What you do for fun? Tell me about the enigma that is Declin Ostrander."

My lies perched on the tip of my tongue, preparing to trampoline into her ears, but my voice caught. "Well, I—I guess I'm into, you know, anything. Everything. I just don't want to be bored."

Her car slowed as we approached my house, and she raised her palm to deliver a hearty high five. "Yeah, no one does. See you around, kid."

Around ten o'clock that night, my father stumbled in, ragged and exhausted. He dropped a sack of fast food on the kitchen table, and I ate greasy burgers with him. "How was your first day at school?"

"Here? Well, it's much different and much the same. I can't really tell yet. But I guess—I guess I've made some friends, maybe."

"That's good. That's great, Declin. Right." He fell asleep at the table with a french fry half in his mouth, poking out like a cigar. I wandered upstairs to my bed and began to dream of Cass between the sheets.

CHAPTER 6

ARON KING

My body: a punching bag with the stuffing poking out. Only a true asshole like Goodman would have evening practice the day before school began. Running up and down bleachers, doing squats and sprint cycles. All body-wracking, bone-numbing exercises. My alarm squawked and blinked at seven, so I unplugged it and fell back to sleep.

When I woke again, the house was deathly quiet. I missed my first-period history class. But I could still make it to school. The shower water felt freezing. I dressed and snatched food from the fridge before heading out. I lived near Blaine, in a crowded suburb with twisting streets crammed between downtown and the walls of Golden Oaks. A demolition crew had set up shop on the haunted hill, where they were preparing to knock down the flame-gutted house.

The doctors released me from the hospital the day I woke up. I had not stayed there long. After asking a few questions about why we'd been in the house (just as a dare, we said), the doctor discharged me. The words on the hill had blackened, singed into the brown thatch of grass. "Get out of our town."

We had known that some racist outcasts lurked among us, but not until Francis Jameson died had they ever done anything so dramatic. The arson could not be directly blamed on the Knights of Southern Heritage, my dad said. "The law is strict, yet fair." He was full of these bullshit aphorisms. "Justice. Justice is the only thing we can count on. Without it, we're all blindfolded, stumbling in the dark." But Justice—she was blind too.

Lickskillet High campus sprawled huge but was poorly maintained. Separate sections stood far from each other, loosely conjoined departmental wings with mud and trees in between. In the center of these long, brick buildings was our cafeteria, small by half since the school population had exploded since they last remodeled the school. Which was in 1954, when it had been changed from a prison to a high school, a fact never lost on its students. Since then, the city added new buildings without renovating the older ones.

The parking lot brimmed with cars on the first day of school (students generally chose to show up for at least the first day), and I had to park on the outskirts of the football field—a dismal patch of unshaven grass and uneven white lines.

As I approached the buildings, students began to flood out of the rooms. I joined the mob, letting myself ride the tide to a biology class that I would share with Blaine this year. He sat at the table farthest back, lolling his head back and forth. "Morning."

"How dare you intrude my skull? First period...a giant tomato hit me right in the face." He stood, lifting his arms, clenching his fists, and assuming a boxing stance. "Put your dukes up. Your dukes. Fight me. Fight me." He threw a punch, which I ducked before pushing him back onto his stool. "My right mind? I left that at home. I'm wearing the wrong one—the left one. The wrong pants, too. What is the world but a blinking fire engine?"

"Are you OK?"

He looked up at me soberly. "What do you mean? Fine as fireflies."

"Are you on drugs?"

"I respect your hypotenuse, and your thesis is correct."

When I sat down beside him, Blaine kept quiet but kept licking his lips. Our teacher, a flighty woman with a bullfrog face and nervous giggle, hobbled to the front of the room and started writing. "My name is Ms. Schall. Biology is—please write this down because this might be on our final exam—the study of life. Do you have that? Good, we're almost done for today." She wiped her brow.

After an hour of painful interrogation among the students, the bell rang, the great migration commencing. Strange to see old friends, now emboldened and tanned by summer, nodding at me as a stranger. Over the summer, if we didn't keep in touch, we put up walls. We built invisible force fields around ourselves. We returned to our social circles, believing ourselves so much better, so much more mature than during our junior year. "I've changed," we'd want to say, be it through new shoes or a new haircut. "I'm not the same person you knew before summer. I'm an adult now, and I do adult things. We've outgrown ourselves." Every year, the same blight of perceived change. The same virtual makeover.

In the restroom, students had already begun to write obscenities on the walls. What a time-honored tradition. Messages scrawled back and forth between rivaling gangs. Misshapen dicks drawn everywhere. Defacement: public entertainment in its most private form. A voyeuristic form of insight into the mind of the rogue artist, who could be simply a shy exhibitionist.

Why not draw the Mona Lisa in a bathroom stall? A beauty in a setting of crude animal acts—was it still beauty? Not many Mona Lisas on the walls, but still, I figured that would be nice. Even a little poetry would be appreciated.

2 B or not 2 B. Dat is da ?
No one appreciated beauty around here.

⇥ ⇤

When I stepped out of my next class, she appeared from no-where. My throat constricted. I should not have felt so guilty but remembered that I never texted her back.

"Aron, I've been waiting to run into you."

I stopped. "Hello, I haven't seen you since—ah, how are you doing?"

"Well, I might need help finding this class—um, Chemistry? I'm taking the class with Mr. Um."

"Who's that?"

"No, I just can't pronounce that name. Karesstorvots."

"Oh, you mean Krestovoz. Yeah, just follow me." I led her through the corridor, looking forward. "Sorry I never contacted you back. I know you want to hang out, but that night, I didn't—well, what I mean to say is—well, all I want to say—"

"You're not interested?" She nodded sagely. "No, I know."

"Not interested? I wouldn't say that. You're hot. I mean, what we did was fun. I would love to do something like that again, but I thought it was just a onetime thing. It wasn't serious."

"Yeah," she said. "It wasn't that serious. It's just, well, I thought maybe we could get to know each other before deciding that."

"Look, I know you must be lonely and want a boyfriend, but I'm not boyfriend material."

"Well, we can't even be friends?" She pressed close to me, her hand brushing my junk through my pants. I stiffened. I couldn't handle this. "You were interested the other night."

"I guess you can come to lunch with me if you want. I'll intro-duce you to some people."

I felt sorry for her mostly. Her heart was a Ouija board, auctioned off to ghosts.

⇒⊹ ⊹⇐

As part of the county soccer team, I attended practice nearly every weeknight and most days on the weekend. To become part of such a team, you had to be the best. To coach such a team, you only had to be willing. You needed only a lot of free time and a silver whistle. We had Goodman.

While we ran drills on the field, he sat in a lawn chair, massaging his bulging paunch that his shirt failed to fully cover. Lounging with a beer can in one palm, he shouted incomprehensible orders. Some of us would be picked up for the state team. We would travel all over the nation and play. Colleges would see us, recruit us, and pay us money to play for them. I would be drafted. While learning law like my father. That, anyhow, was the plan.

We carried our plans, our hopes, with us. Nothing could be more accurate. Our futures were already foretold. We knew what we would become, mostly. But then, we had no clue.

After practice, I drove back home, half-asleep. The house empty. Ms. Malbury had left a pie on our front porch, and I stole it upstairs before my father arrived to throw it out. For dinner, I cooked pasta for myself, since my father worked very late. Ever since Jameson had been murdered, he had been working overtime at the courthouse. Every lawyer in Lickskillet was scrambling to snatch up the case. As I ate my pie and the pasta, I thought of Charlotte.

Nothing could be more binding between a boy and girl than oral sex. Already I had gone out to coffee with her once, and I wanted nothing more than to have sex with her. I couldn't stop thinking about her naked. I thought about what I said at lunch, about her being my girlfriend, not just a friend. Stupid, stupid.

She was like a succubus, luring me into hell. The thought made me shudder. Her eyes lined so thickly with black, her eyes so dark, so dull. Looking into them, I saw only lust and flickers of anger. This might last forever, might keep going on until I knocked her up, put a ring on her finger, and bought a house. But forever couldn't last for eternity. In high school, the longest anyone could hope for forever to be was maybe two weeks. This thought alone angered me as well, that I knew somehow she wanted me as a boyfriend as an exotic fetish. My blackness excited her just as much as her whiteness excited me.

Suddenly I felt light-headed, like I needed to run and forget. Sometimes, I felt trapped in my skin, not that I was embarrassed of either heritage. I loved my father, and my mother as well, but I regretted that they had ever gotten together. If they had known that they would grow bored with one another, that he would become used to her whiteness and she his blackness, that they would just stop loving each other, then why had they made me? I didn't belong anywhere, with anyone, as if the one-drop rule applied both ways. The white kids at school provoked me because they thought maybe if they hung out with me, some gangster would wear off onto them. Blaine was different, of course. We grew up together. But most kids at the school considered me either too white or too black to befriend. These were the same kids who muttered under their breath that it would be unfair how easily I could receive scholarships because of my mixed race, because yes, being mixed seemed so damned easy. Then the black kids thought I constantly tried to one-up them, that I thought I was better than them. That somehow, because I played soccer, my athletic abilities were worthless.

Conversely, teachers used to pat me on the shoulder and congratulate me for how damn articulately I could speak. Damn right I could articulate myself. Fuck that. If I wanted to spit slang, I would do so, but if I wanted to wax poetic, I would speak that way as well. And I wouldn't let some young girl eroticize that idea of me; you had to fuck me for me, not for my skin or for the sake of telling your friends about it.

Thinking of this, I tried to stop worrying. Eventually, she would grow bored with me. Maybe I would get to sleep with her as collateral, but nothing serious could ever possibly come of that.

CHAPTER 7

THE JOURNAL OF ELIJAH RODRIGUEZ

September 5

The worst part about using the toilet at public school is that when someone walks in, I can't keep going. The stream just stops.

Last year, most of the teachers allowed me to go to the restroom during class to avoid these awkward run-ins, but this year, I have to run in, make sure I'm alone, and then sprint for a stall. Even alone, I still can't use urinals; I'm working on it.

I'm in the stall, and I've even started a steady stream. I'm reading the words on the walls, the back-and-forth Sharpie gang fights, and the accusations of whoredom of most of the varsity cheerleading squad. The door bursts open, and I just stop. Library silence. I wait until the intruder begins his own urination, which happens for him miraculously fast, before I flee back into the hallway. I have to wait an entire hour before going again. This is why I hate public school, Quentin.

Is it still weird that I'm calling you Quentin? I know I am supposed to call you "dear diary" or "dearest diary" or "deepest friend of mine," but my dad says diaries are for homosexuals. That's why I started calling you Quentin—it's almost like I'm talking to a friend, not a book. My dad thinks growing up in the United States has softened me, but to be fair, he only moved to the United States when he was eleven years old.

Junior year should be much the same as sophomore year except academically much harder. The first week wasn't so bad, but others say that the workload will get much, much worse. I dread that more than Sauron dreaded the destruction of the One Ring.

Today, I'm writing to you because I have not written in more than a year. Flipping through the pages I wrote when I was a sophomore depresses me. My understanding of grammar and proper syntax was dismal. It would be very embarrassing for some future humans or even a future alien race to locate this diary as the final artifact of our era only to discover that our ability to write was subpar. Sometimes, I think the only reason people may read this is because they found it on some archaeological site. Or maybe it's just some dusty little book in a box in my parents' attic that tax collectors will find and burn along with the rest of our junk.

This year, I have also begun my newest initiative to make friends.

I may have made friends with Declin Ostrander, the only new kid at our school besides the freshmen, but I don't think he really knows my name. On the first day, he roared into the school, talking to everyone as if he belonged there. He claims to be from California.

During the last period of my first day, I spoke to him. "Declin, you're sitting in my seat."

"Oh, well, how—this is the first day of school. Do you already have a seat?"

"I sit in the same seat in every class. Front row, third from the left."

Very amiably, he stood up and offered me the desk, moving one row back. "So, are you OCD or something? Why do you need that desk?"

"It just provides the optimal learning experience."

Declin shrugged. "Ah, so you have cheated me out of the optimal learning experience. Well, be damned."

"I'm sorry. I hope I can make it up to you."

He laughed it off. "Maybe. What's your name?"

"Elijah. My name is Elijah Rodriguez."

"And you know my name? I guess you don't get a lot of new kids at this school, then?"

"No, not really. Only old people move here. They come from up north to retire. But never anyone with high-school kids. Most of the people here grew up in this town."

We shared a psychology class. On the first day, our teacher showed us the film *One Flew Over the Cuckoo's Nest* and fell asleep at her computer. Then class ended. Things became interesting for me, and I believe that on that first day I may have embarked on a fatal journey.

I only witnessed the punch. Justin Ferrara—he was six feet tall, muscled as a gorilla, stinking of booze. That first day of school would be the first time I ever spoke to this Goliath. After a few moments of raucous shouting, Justin launched at Declin, clocking him on the side of the head. Down went Declin. Cass screamed at him, clutching his wrists, but he struck her as well, pushing her away.

"Stop. Stop." Something happened, but I'm not sure what— I stood over Declin in front of the seething quarterback. "Don't—stop."

Justin shuddered and then slapped his forehead. "Who the fuck are you? I will crush your fucking teeth into the cement and then curb stomp your faggot ass, if you—"

"Justin, please, don't, don't." Cass sobbed, pressing herself against his chest. "Please, don't." Justin watched me for a moment, spit on the ground, and then stormed off in the opposite direction.

Officer Winkler and Principal Reiser appeared from the hallway, rushing toward us. I dropped to my knees, lifting his ankles. "What are you doing?" asked Cass. I didn't know her well, but I knew her.

"Blood to his head. Is he breathing?" She shook her head. I spread his mouth open and breathed into it. If my father saw me doing this, he would probably disown me, but I learned this sort of flimsy first aid in the Boy Scouts before I begged my father to quit. Maybe he'd be proud.

"Get off of him. What happened here?" Reiser stood over us, pulling me to my feet.

The students had formed a wide semicircle around us, though the population had dispersed since Justin stormed away. One shouted, "They got in a fight."

Reiser stood over me, clenching his fists. "You got in a fight?"

"I—no, I was trying to help. I—I'll leave." Winkler slung Declin over his shoulder and began bustling into the hallway. I turned to Cass. "Sorry."

"It's fine. You—you did well. Is he your friend?"

I didn't know what to say. "I have a class with him—that's all."

She nodded. "Me too." She followed Winkler and Reiser into the school, and I hesitated. I wanted to follow. Turning my back to the school, I hurried to the sidewalk, my head bowed, and then walked home.

＝≕┼ ┼≍＝

The next day, Declin did not appear in class. On Wednesday, however, I spotted him in the back of class in Psychology. He nodded politely. When class ended, he tapped on my shoulder. "Elijah, I wanted—I just wanted to thank you about the other day. I heard what you did."

"I didn't really do too much."

"I owe you a favor, you know that?"

But I didn't want a favor, only someone to talk with me. I nodded.

For the rest of the week, eyes followed me around campus. People whispered about what I had done. But I didn't want to be that boy who stood up to Justin Ferrara. Maybe I just wanted to be no one. I wanted to be invisible, not so vulnerable in the wilderness of this school.

When I write again, I will tell you more, but for now, it is late, it is Friday, and I have only two chapters left in the latest Neil Gaiman book I'm reading.

CHAPTER 8

BLAINE MOREAU

I tapped his shoulder and asked, "You just got here yesterday. What are you doing here?"

Declin turned in his desk, very serious but blushing. "You didn't hear? I taped some guy's buns together."

"Wait, what did you do?" The proctor, a draconian teacher with bulldog jowls, shushed us. I whispered again, "What?"

Declin faced forward. "It was a joke. *Breakfast Club* reference. What about you? What are you doing here?"

Shrugging, I mumbled, "I know exactly what I did wrong. I got caught."

The first day I met Declin, I spoke Dr. Seuss *Looney Tunes* babble, the sort of tripe strung-out opium addicts blab about through blurbs on online blogs. But sometimes, you have to act crazy around people you don't know—maybe they're crazy too, and it's better off to establish the dominant insanity, for safety purposes. Also, if a person hangs out with you when you're spitting venomous slang wrapped in bacon, doesn't hardly complain about your queer use of verbiage, and even sticks around, that person might become a decent friend.

The first two hours in detention flew by as they always did because we were forced to do schoolwork. But we never had to work all day. Given such leisure, we tore through classwork and homework and future projects. Bent over like skeleton scholars transcribing the end times, we wrote tirelessly until nothing else presented itself to be written. Then each of us, one by one, became overwhelmed by morbid boredom that tasted awful. Like synthetic cheese, the sort individually plastic wrapped by the slice.

Then six more hours with a novel and under-the-breath mumbles. Would turn out the novel you snatched from a rogue bookcase would not actually deliver you from boredom. Probably because it was not a novel at all but instead a Spanish–English dictionary. Even considering that you could learn enough to take a spring-break trip to Cancún, the entire experience probably turned out pretty fucking dull.

Nausea overcame me along with the droll feeling of boredom.

If I swam, I could hear soft tones, piano-like notes drawn out. Eating curry, I saw a haze of red. But with boredom, nothing happened. My condition was unprovoked. I felt the void, the abyss that I stared into, while it stared back at me.

The boredom gnawed at me. My eyes drooped heavy as corpses. Three days without sleep had taken a toll. I needed entertainment, anything that might keep me awake—even as my head brushed the desk, our prison guard sprang up with greater agility than anyone could have expected, grasped the back of my necks, and pulled me out of my stupor.

"This is detention. Not daycare," she said, marching back to her seat with smug piety.

I hated Declin for chuckling, though I might have done the same thing. I only needed to sleep, to collect myself.

I remembered the tin of pills in my pocket. Pure, pharmaceutical narcotics, without the enzymes that slowed down the release of codeine into the body's system. Just pure hydrocodone, ready for consumption. I tapped Declin's shoulder again and passed him one. Generosity—my ultimate nature. One might have done him in; I needed four.

With a strange look at me, Declin slipped the pill into his mouth. As if he knew what he were getting himself into. Even I didn't accept drugs from strangers. But here he was, fresh and eager to prove himself bad and dangerous, just as we all tried to be bad and dangerous.

From around the classroom, animals stared down at us from posters, posed behind motivational quotes from saints, presidents, and Oprah Winfrey. A lion turned to stare at me, throned regally on golden plains, the quote hovering above set in bold, dazzling font.

The animals turned and watched. Their eyes followed me, and I slipped into a chaotic high before I realized what I'd done. No true hallucinations here, but a fine, ethereal high that cured my boredom.

Boredom: our natural state, our default. For our entire teen lives in Lickskillet, boredom was true evil, our archenemy, the Darth Vader to our Luke Skywalker. We tried everything to absolve ourselves of this carnal sin. Most drank heavily, even idiotically. Which was the best way to drink, with the high possibility of death. Most of the boys drank beer, challenging each other to gulp down more until all had passed out. Girls preferred liquor, mixed or straight. And then everyone, roaring drunk, would smash boredom against the walls. Would take off boredom's clothes or pass out on boredom's lawn.

Marijuana was our new vogue—joint rolling became as common a social skill as driving or shooting a spitball. Once kids started smoking green, the floodgates opened for Woodstockian levels of experimentation. For me, this meant experiencing extreme forms of my condition.

Our ailment was our failure to stimulate ourselves. This town cultured an illness that festered hot and rotting in each of us. A convulsing itch that we scratched until our skin burned raw and our eyes went bloodshot. Thrown into a cycle of ecstatic highs and dull lows, we lived a constant war.

We chucked eggs at houses, gave car rides to hoboes at two in the morning, snuck into the Red Hole to smoke and skinny-dip, drove out in cars to abandoned thickets of forest and coaxed young girls to blow us, and didn't give a fuck about what lay ahead. Or maybe that was just me. Sick of ambition and my fate dangling at the whim of deadbeat parents.

"Blaine, get up."

"What?"

"The bell rang. Didn't you hear it? School ended. You've just been—sitting there."

And so I had, clutching the yellowed dictionary. I wiped drool from my mouth and shuffled numbly out of the room.

———

When I was seven, collecting fragile sticks in my backyard to make a wigwam like we learned how to at school, I found out that a punch to the face tasted like white-lemon Italian ice. The same flavor sold out of the truck that drove around the neighborhood, playing its jingle in broken intervals, the song feeling like gritty sandpaper rubbed across my tongue.

Being a synesthete, I didn't *not* feel or taste or hear what I felt or tasted or heard, but I did feel and taste and hear more. So, being seven and being punched in the jaw by Justin Ferrara still hurt; it just also tasted like white-lemon Italian ice.

When I told my parents that Justin punched me in the face and that it tasted just like the Italian ice sold out of the ice-cream truck that sometimes came around, my parents shrugged and sent me to my room. They didn't freak out until I spit two teeth and a wad of blood spittle onto the kitchen table. They must have thought I had a concussion or had gone crazy from the punch, because they kept talking about how my brain was messed up as we drove to the hospital, me still babbling about white-lemon Italian ice.

Turns out, there *was* something wrong with my brain. Something different.

The doctor sat me down to ask me about who hit me and whether or not it was my parents.

I told him, "Justin Ferrara punched me."

He asked, "Why?"

I told him, "I don't know. He's an asshole." My parents still thought I had gone bat-shit crazy from being punched, so they didn't even get mad about me cursing.

He asked, "Did it hurt?"

I told him, "It tasted just like white-lemon Italian ice, the kind—"

He suggested to my parents I have an MRI, that I might have suffered brain injury. That's when we found out about me being a synesthete. As I lay under the shifting machine, my parents bent over a screen, reading my increased brain activity. Whispering regrets like, "Wait, I've heard about this. Don't some geniuses have this? I never thought he was so smart."

"His brain," the doctor muttered. "It's working overtime."

Of course the condition didn't work like that, didn't inject me with a sort of superior intelligence; sometimes, the colors made mathematics simpler, but they complicated all else. My parents never understood that what progress they saw as inevitable actually took hours of studying, of humdrum work.

After that trip to the hospital, my parents enrolled in me in special programs meant to enhance my "natural intelligence." If I could become a math genius, I could be a chemist or a nuclear physicist. The doctor explained I might have trouble comprehending abstract thoughts. I might never be the president of the United States, but to become a doctor—that was possible.

Synesthetes see things differently—take a math equation for example. A normal person sees an x variable, but I feel it—x is a cold breeze creeping up your arms. Imagine every word you read and every number you process becoming a physical object, almost. Numbers create a landscape you only need to navigate. It's difficult to explain, really. All I knew then was it made me different.

And sure, there are different sorts of us too: some people see music as color, others hear noises in memories, some see people as colors or auras, and others feel textures as tastes. But in me, all these get mixed up, an amalgam of already-hybridized sense. I was a special sort of synesthete, one that actually benefitted from the condition beyond the constant visual trips—I could use the patterns. Most of us were terrible at math, distracted, but somehow the combinations of sense switching caused a spark in genius that I only needed to cultivate.

This all occurred because I had been collecting sticks in our backyard and I reached through the slats in the fence to pick up a stick from the Ferraras' grass. Maybe there had always been a seed of meanness in Justin. Seeing me pick up that stick, he exploded. Barreled at me, a dog realizing that red dots originate from laser pointers, now too indignant not to react.

Thrashing through the fence, he tackled me into an anthill. Without hesitation, he drew back his arm and slugged me right in the jaw. Sometimes, I think maybe he did give me brain damage.

Numbers had personality, I discovered. The more I began to understand the condition, the more I learned to use it. Nines, I recognized, were dark, mysterious. Looking at the nine, for me, was like standing in a stone corridor filling with mist or smoke. Six made me hungry for seafood, like having a huge buffet in front of me.

I learned to look at a set of numbers and know what didn't belong. Math became less arithmetic and more mind pioneering. But experiencing so many senses, I wondered what other pains might feel like. At nine, I broke my fingers with a hammer in my dad's garage. That familiar Italian-ice flavor seemed drowned out by the throbbing pain; whenever I screamed, I could see red lines dance across my eyes like flitting birds. I began to experiment a lot with what different sensation combinations I might experience: I had a unique opportunity to live like no other person on earth.

Add drugs to that equation.

———

The weekend arrived full blast, a cold breath filling lungs after a week of drowning in school. Two of those days I spent agonizing in detention. Each day, I spent the final two hours with a math tutor, a tireless ex-professor whose words and knowledge I devoured so fast we would soon not have much else to teach each other. Synesthesia had its perks, certainly. Three months, I guessed, before I would surpass even this genius. Nearly all my classes were oriented around mathematics, and I hardly ever went to those.

A few more were necessary (biology, American history, literature), but the school placed me in what it deemed "special education," not because I was slow but because I was too quick of a learner. Except with English and history, I understood everything with the effort of reading a gum wrapper. In my senior year, I would learn more advanced functions of math, but beyond that—I was free to do whatever I needed to with my gifts.

Friday pushed numbers and equations and summations off a cliff.

We stood on the precipice of a weekend. The abyss stared back.

When darkness fell, I picked up Aron and his new girlfriend in my Mustang. They stood on the corner, folded together like origami. When she climbed into my car, she blew me a kiss and said, "Evening, Blaine," as if she'd known me her entire life. What a fake—you had those kind of girls who talk very loudly in public about how much money their parents made or that concert in Charlotte they could afford to attend or how they totally almost gave a blow job to the bassist or how they, like, loved to party. They had started dating recently, though I recalled Aron expressly stating his intention to never date her. Made me sick, that he was just dating her for sex.

Cass called off Friday night. First weekend of the year, but no parties to go to. We called everyone we knew, asking who would go with whom and who had weed to smoke or sell. Buy that, hit that, snort that, trade that. My stash had somehow depleted over the course of the first week. I blamed elves.

We wandered like a murder of sad crows searching for a dead feast. Around midnight, we found other lost souls at the Red Hole, soaking their feet in the puddle that had once been our swimming hole. I parked the car and switched off the lights. If they noticed us, they did not stir, sitting side by side. We climbed out, and I called, "Cass, what the hell? Called off the party, did you?"

"They drained it," Cass said.

Aron held loosely onto his rag doll of a girlfriend, stumbling from the car. "Where's Justin? Why aren't we all at your house?"

Cass shrugged. "The parentals are throwing some lavish cocktail party in the garden. Bunch of drunk industry players. I'll go home to find them passed out on all the sofas. Last time I stuck around, some coked-out freak tried to grab my tits, and I had to break his nose. Adults are wild animals."

"I didn't know you knew Declin, Cass." I smiled at him. He grimace-smiled back. "How'd that come about, that you two made—um, each other's acquaintances?"

Declin looked to Cass and back to me. "Boring story really. Cass has been showing me your local landmarks. So this," he said, gesturing to the pathetic muck around him, "is what you do for fun? Your cure for boredom?"

"I admit it did look nicer at the beginning of the summer. Must have stretched two hundred feet across. Perfect for swimming in. Water like the Bahamas. Clear and blue. And now it is ten feet across, muddy, surrounded by mounds of slimy red clay. So what? Things fall apart."

"The neighborhood where we moved—they have a lake. Not a real lake, but a nice alternative. Manmade pond pushed way back behind all the houses. Has a little beach and everything. If you want to party, we can go there."

I nodded. "Yes, let's show your new friend what we do around here for fun."

Cass's car took the lead, Declin directing the way. She drove a sleek Audi her parents bought her for her sixteenth birthday. After driving through a labyrinth of houses that looked suspiciously similar, we came upon the lake, wide across as the Red Hole had been. Charlotte lifted her head from Aron's neck and pulled a bottle from her oversize purse. "I brought rum."

I felt restless, jouncy, ready to prove myself. "Don't think we're boring. We do just as much as you do—where is it you're from? Wisconsin?"

"California."

"Close enough." We walked to the edge of the lake, sitting in the grass. From our vantage point, we could see the smoldering remains of the haunted house. "Damn, Declin, have you heard about that?"

"About what?"

"We almost got burned alive inside that house. Do you see? That hill in the distance—that's where it stood. Aron was there too."

Aron launched into the story about our night escaping the haunted house, and at certain parts, I laughed and jested. "Rats? There were no rats."

"There were rats. Tons of rats. Hundreds."

"Maybe one rat."

"Dozens."

Aron fell back into the steady beat of spinning a yarn, when I broke in again. "Wait, wait, Aron, the smoke didn't make you pass out."

"It did."

"We got out of the house, and then you passed out."

"I don't remember leaving the house. I don't remember. I was unconscious, remember?"

"No, no, that's not what happened. You were pissing yourself—you were imagining things, conjuring your own horror. No, the house didn't actually fall until much, much later, even after the fire trucks had shown up and distinguished the fire. The only reason it fell was because the place was damned close to collapsing in the first place—the fire helped it along."

"Well, that's not how I remember it."

"I mean, you tell a good story, but you make me sound like an asshole. You make the whole affair fucking macabre."

"Macabre? What kind of word is that?"

"So what? I used a word. Macabre. Macabre. It's a word—that's what sort of word. Fuck you."

≒⋕⋕≓

We grew restless again. "Cass, start up your car. Remember last winter? New Year's Eve, downtown? We all felt so alive. Let's do it again."

Cass laughed. "Didn't Aron think he broke his leg?"

Aron scowled. "So? I was serious. We could have—"

"But there's less pavement here. Let me give it a try. Cass, you drive. Wait till you see what fun we have here." Patting Declin on the back, I clambered onto the roof of Cass's car. She started the engine, and I clutched the car rails. "Surfing. Let's go surfing."

We were the agents of youthful delinquency. Mission: fuck shit up.

Cass roared off down the dirt road that circled the lake. My body slid down the length of the car, but I held on. She twisted around the first corner, and my legs jumped up. One hand came loose, but I gripped the rail again even tighter. Then she slammed on her brakes. I nearly flew forward but did not. "See, Declin? Now that's excitement. I bet I could stand." Gingerly, I climbed to my feet. "Go, go, go."

For a full second, I managed to keep my balance, sailing through the air, my feet planted. But then Cass jerked the car, and I toppled backward off the roof.

Pain in my mouth and a jolt through my back. I cried out. The taste of blood and white-lemon Italian ice.

⇒┼┼⇒

A ministering angel hovered above my face. "Blaine, are you OK?"

I groaned, rubbing my eyes. "Man, what happened?"

Aron laughed. "Dude, you totally wiped out. That was gnarly."

Sitting up, I looked around. "Did I black out?"

"For a few minutes," Declin put in. "Maybe this isn't such a good idea."

"Well, it's late enough for us to return to my house if you'd like. Sound good?" Cass herded us off of the grass and into our

84

respective vehicles. She grabbed my shoulder. "Aron told me a few days before school that you might have a hookup for Molly?"

I shook my head. "I wish."

I walked away, pressing my hands against a tree.

"Maybe I can find some. I'll text who I know." Once I climbed into the car, I frantically scrolled through my contacts. Surely someone I knew sold Molly. Though I had never tried it personally, I knew it made users erotic, sexual. And if Justin were gone for the night, the only person I would have to compete with was this new kid.

Declin climbed into the car after me. "Can I get a ride with you, then?"

"Buckle up. Or don't. We're a wild crew." I smiled manically and stomped the gas pedal, lurching after Cass's car. "Biology, right?"

"Huh?"

"Nothing. I don't want to talk about school anyways. You spend all day there, and people still talk about it." I paused. "'Course, I'm a hypocrite."

"Right, yeah, that makes sense."

"Uh-huh. So, I heard about you getting punched."

Declin's face grew bright red. "Oh, yeah, I guess people are talking about that. I mean, I didn't know she had a boyfriend. He just came out of nowhere."

"I'm not judging you. Most guys would do anything to get with her."

"Do you have any interest? Anyone at school you're seeing?"

I grew quiet, contemplating my tumultuous love life so far. Junior year, I dated an airy stoner girl on and off, though she wasn't too interesting. Mostly sat in my bedroom and smoked, and occasionally we'd have sex. But we broke up at the beginning of summer when she began her year abroad in Italy, citing that she "wanted to keep her options open."

"Naw. I don't want to date anyone; I don't want to get tied down to this place." I jerked around a corner, and Declin smacked his forehead against the dashboard.

"Ouch."

"Anyways, the only females who interest me are Lucy, Molly, and Mary Jane."

⋙ ⋘

Once we reached the house, Aron and Charlotte retreated to one of Cass's bedrooms. I sighed at this dramatically, to publicly embarrass him, at least for Declin's sake. Or Cass's, who might have been under the impression I could date whomever I wanted but chose not to.

After we settled in, Declin began drinking warm wine from a crystal glass a guest had left on the table. We slipped through the quiet house as if we were ghosts as some of the guests still chatted downstairs or in the back garden. Cass assured us that as long as we stayed upstairs, we wouldn't disturb anyone. I wanted to smoke with Cass, and Declin squirmed when I offered but accepted. The kid reminded me of a lemur, the way he twitched. Declin took everything seriously, like each question was a test and at any second we might cast him out like a leper.

"Do you think you could really get Molly?"

"Shit. I don't know." Sitting up straight in her bed, I checked my phone. A prospect—some kid who had sold me weed before. Cheap but low quality. His name was Cory, and he was one of the Swag Boys, this local gang of rich boys who attended Exeter Academy. But Cory had texted back simply, "Moon rocks."

⋙ ⋘

"You have to go. I'll stay here, but here's some money..." Cass scavenged her parents' bedroom with casual disregard for her noise levels. "Fuck, I know it was here somewhere." She tossed a necklace aside from a shelf and then slid open a drawer that she rifled through violently.

"I can get a good deal, I think." I didn't know this, but I felt a little nervous that if getting the Molly seemed too difficult, we would never do it. We had to try it tonight, I kept thinking.

Declin and I raced down the stairs once I received Cass's money, and we slipped purposely past rooms where some of the party guests still drank and talked. Most of them had either left by midnight or passed out in various bedrooms. Though only four people lived in Cass's house, they had eleven or twelve bedrooms, depending on whether you counted the closet with a pull-down bed.

Once in my car, I began coordinating a meet-up time with Cory. What I absolutely hated about being the friend with whom everyone facilitated their drug orders was coordinating with drug dealers. Unless you could establish a schedule, buying the same amount on the same day every week, you would have to haggle a price. Then came the dilemma of meeting to exchange money for the partying assets. There were manners, rules, guidelines, declarations, and codes to observe when engaging in illicit business, and these were never fruitful elements.

A dealer once met me outside of a gas station, sitting with his younger brother in the car, wearing sunglasses while smoking a joint. He hung the joint out the window, and even as I climbed out of my car on the opposite end of the lot, the scent wafted to me. Suddenly, I felt odd that I too didn't think to wear sunglasses, but I didn't need to—I wasn't high—but then should have I arrived high? Did the dealers not take me seriously because I still checked the intersection for police cruisers before approaching their car?

I paid them twenty dollars for a bag of stems and seeds; they peeled away, and I felt odd, as if I had done something wrong, as if I had ripped them off.

Two years later, and I still hated the logistics of buying from shady characters and shifty strangers. One needed to text in code and learn endless inane slang, constantly clambering for definitions of every other term.

But Cory had been profoundly discreet, even though I blasted music in the library parking lot.

"Is this the place we're going?" asked Declin once as we pulled in to the trailer park on the outside of town.

"Don't worry," I said. "This place is fine. It's past midnight, anyways, and most people will be asleep." Even as I said this, I listened for voices or gunshots.

"Why would this guy want to meet out here?"

"Who knows? Just stay in the car."

Parking the car, I cut the lights and sprinted to the trailer window. Cory had said to go to 23A. A moment later, an acne-ridden face popped through the window. "You the kid looking for Molly?"

I was in shock he called me *kid*, since he looked maybe fifteen years old with his impish grin. "Cory sent me here."

"Hundred bucks for a gram."

I paid him a stack of Cass's money, and he palmed me a tiny baggy and then shut his window tight. I climbed back into the car and dropped the baggy on Declin's lap.

"You said you were getting a gram? This looks so tiny."

"Don't worry about it."

"How do you even know it's what he says it is?"

"Don't worry about it." I shrugged for emphasis.

When we arrived back at Cass's, exhausted, Declin suddenly announced, "Shit, it's past one, and I was supposed to be back by midnight. Blaine, can you take me home?"

"Well, if you'd told me that when we were speeding across town, I could have—look, just wait another hour. Or two. I'll take you home in two hours. Your dad's a lawyer, right, and he's probably asleep by now, so as long as we can get you back before he wakes up, we can tell him you came back at midnight. Simple— don't worry."

I brushed past him and scampered upstairs to where Cass had nearly fallen asleep. "Want to do this now?"

"I don't know. I'm tired, actually. I didn't think about how tired I'd be, and I mean, where have you been?"

"We were only gone twenty, maybe thirty minutes."

"I've been bored out of my mind, and I almost fell off the roof. We shouldn't smoke up there." She leaned back onto her bed, closing her eyes. "You do it first, then."

After a moment, I began to scrape crystals of the MDMA onto the surface of my cell phone, which was flat enough to collect the drugs. Then I divided the small pile into smaller lines, thin and only two inches long each. I rolled up a dollar bill railed the small line with excessive nasal force like I had seen in the movies. Like being shot right in the head, and then you're careless—you feel like you'll never truly die.

After fifteen minutes, the Molly really kicked in, and I began dancing to the dribbles of music still flowing up from downstairs. Cass did not move to stop me; she had fallen asleep. Declin wandered in, and I offered him the drug, shaking his shoulders and shouting. "Come on. Holy fuck, please, you have to."

But he looked at me like I was a raging gorilla at the zoo, a fucking solar eclipse.

"No, I guess you don't exactly have to. But you could smoke and drink and maybe stay up with me? Then I'll drive you home. Come on. Cass fell asleep and Aron must have driven himself home." I gestured toward the window, and stepped out onto the roof. Declin followed, settling atop the ridge leaning against the chimney. "Thanks for coming out here. I don't mean to be so insistent, but I don't want you to feel bored. That's the worst thing."

"There's a lot worse than being bored, Blaine. Like being dead or arrested or fired from your job."

Licking my lips, I felt a surge of new energy. "No, Declin, not for me."

"I mean, she's a little needy, don't you think? They're both fucked up. She follows him around like he's king of the universe, and he treats her like she's a pet, a very attractive pet. It's completely fucked, the whole thing. I mean, what's she expect to be, the quarterback's wife right out of high school?"

"Well, I couldn't say I know her, but it can't be that bad. You can't be that vapid and be in a relationship so empty."

I rolled my eyes, but it worried me, the prospect, that maybe that was what she wanted. "You don't understand anything about the weirdness of this town. Man, living so close together, everyone's up everyone's ass. And I know fakeness when I see it. You ever watch your parents talk to each other like they're fucking robots? Like they absolutely despise each other?"

"My mother's dead."

"Oh, well, that's how it is, and who wants that? They try to convince us that that's what we want, to be miserable? That's all she thinks, that she can be happy somehow. If she can hold on to that jerk. I just can't believe that's what everyone's aspiring for. It's a bullshit idea, a future that doesn't make any sense." I held my face in my hands. "Sorry, I get overwhelmed." The combination of synesthesia and some of the drugs I took caused my wires to get even more mixed up. Nothing I said made sense, and I would begin rambling.

90

"Don't worry about it. She died on an expedition up Mount Kilimanjaro. Went up the wrong time of year and didn't pack the right gear, froze to death up there." He gauged my reaction. "She was an adventurer, really exciting."

I knocked the ashen bud in the bowl, shifting the green to the middle. "Well, friend, that's pretty fucked up, can't lie. Everything's pretty fucked up."

He only nodded, looking at the door. "What time is it? Shouldn't we go? I was supposed to be back by midnight."

Checking my watch, I shrugged. "You're already pretty late."

⚔

We stumbled out of the door, darting into the back garden spotted with colorful rosebushes and passed-out sound engineers. Hopping over their crooked legs and vomit-splattered faces, we found my car. The sun peeked boldly through the trees. "It's already six in the morning. We'll never make it. When did it get so late?"

""Don't worry about the time." I still felt incredibly blazed from the marijuana we'd smoked, but I closed my eyes and tried to concentrate.

Collapsing against my car, I burst into a fit over the fact that I'd just said, "Pipe down," and then I climbed into the car. While Declin jackhammered in his seat, his head flailing while his fingers accosted the car clock, I tried to find the perfect music playlist for the occasion.

Settling on a series of classical piano pieces, I drove out of Golden Oaks while Declin flung his arms in the air, apparently distressed. I tried to remember whether I had ever truly cared about coming home in time, or at all. As far as my parents were concerned, as long as I kept up decent grades in school, they didn't care what else I did. Sometimes, I felt incredibly lucky to have so much freedom, but sometimes I felt numb.

"Why the piano? I mean, this isn't what you're supposed to listen to at parties."

"But as you've pointed out multiple times, it's certainly morning, and I don't know what else would be appropriate for morning." A winning smile, the sort a maniac gives his victim before lopping off the guy's limbs.

I skirted to the curb beside his house at a quarter to seven. Declin dashed up the lawn and disappeared into the house. After a minute or more, I turned off the piano music and drove the few blocks downtown.

Downtown, all the recycling bins were empty and the coffeehouses quiet. The streets singing silence, I walked atop them as if they were tightropes. Sometimes I tasted how this town felt to those who walked the streets before me. I could almost see the faded colors of their big cars, the Bel Airs and first family sedans, roaring up and down these streets. Ghost teenagers racing each other in the dark.

Walking past these stores, I wondered what they had once been, who once had owned them, and what had happened here. Who were these nighttime specters jovially haunting me, following me and joking and making plans for futures that had come and gone? What adventures had these leather-jacketed seraphim embarked on? Had they plunged headlong, suicidal, into the workplace machinery or struck out alone and poor to freeze on empty boxcars headed west? And would I join them one day, another former resident of this town, howling about my stories, my loves, my life?

Though the morning was cool, it was never too bitter a cold. I walked two blocks. I could have run the distance naked.

I felt invincible, and I would keep pushing forward. Keep living, living, living until I was no longer living. And if I died, well, then I would simply be dead.

CHAPTER 9

ELIZABETH PEPPER

I huddled in the bushes, carefully pulling a tick from my arm with my teeth. The makeshift bow I had made the summer before lay underneath a burrow full of briars. My small hands could reach back through the prickly bushes and retrieve it. Not as tall as a full-size bow, but slender. Supple and carved from birch, gleaming white in the moonlight. Standing above the briar, I drew the string taut. Good. I was ready to hunt.

The pine trees rose around me—stark, barren protectors, Matty told me when I was still little, like pickets in a fence or battlements for a castle. They kept the bad people from finding us, from making all of us leave.

A deer would be good to kill. Even a rabbit. Anything to hold up in front of my face to claim as my own. I needed to kill something. Daddy always talked about how no one should hunt unless they intended to eat their kill. Just because we *would* eat what I killed, it didn't matter, not this time; *I* hunted to kill. To put bullet to brain and be blooded. My brothers had all killed something—even Charlie had before he died. Matty killed his first doe at eleven. I was almost eighteen.

Daddy talked often about the ritual of the first kill. Everyone, every Pepper, came together to celebrate. They skinned the deer in the same shack every time. Daddy's job, as our father and protector of all of us, was to smear blood onto our faces.

The blooding rite.

Everyone said this was tradition. How things had always been. Daddy said, a long time ago, that God deemed we had to wear the blood to allow the animal we killed to live on in us. We wore the blood streaked across our brows out of respect. We obeyed God this way. We also never wasted a kill.

We killed what we intended to eat. We understood the true meaning of death, which could come only from necessity, not anger or revenge or cruelty. We were made thankful and killed only animals that had lived wild and free. A life in a cage, on a farm, was not true life. Daddy said we should not consume it. Only life could give life.

Eighteen. Never blooded. Matty used to tell me it was fine since I was a girl. He said it wasn't my job to kill. I had to cook. But Matty was gone, locked away for something he didn't do.

Soon, everyone would be gone and scattered far away from here. I would have to learn to hunt or die. Shuddering at that thought, I remembered Daddy was still in our house talking to Mr. Ostrander. We had not yet been torn apart. Not yet.

⊯ ⊰

What happened was that someone killed a black man and when they found him hanging from a tree, they thought maybe Matty murdered him because the man had been sleeping with Matty's girl, but they weren't together anymore though sometimes were. Maybe Matty got real mad, but he never killed anybody before, so now Daddy had to drive down to Charleston and ask his boss if he could borrow money to hire a lawyer.One of Daddy's friends from Newberry, a Klansman like Daddy, recommended a law-yer who once helped him in a court 'cause one of theirs beat up his sister's girlfriend. The man never went to jail. Daddy says maybe the lawyer can help Matty out too so they won't kill him and he won't have to go to jail. When the lawyer came down to Lickskillet, Daddy said, "Now, Elizabeth, you stay outta this. You don't talk to this man—he's a strange man, and I need you work-ing." But I liked cooking, so I stood up in that trailer with all that steam and chemical burn.

That first day, with the truck from the rental company, Roscoe Ostrander turned down the dirt road beside where we put out a painted sign that read *Pepper.* The pine trees bent over the dirt road like jagged claws. At the end of the road stood half a trailer, the shutters browned and tattered, weeds springing up around the perimeter. This was where I cooked.

Mr. Ostrander did not seem like a nervous man, certainly not prejudiced, but climbing out the truck, I could see he felt anx-ious. He felt uneasy probably the same reason all other people felt uneasy. The yard teemed with odious energy, ready to split apart the earth.

I crouched on the stool to my desk, peeking through my blinds as he took in everything he saw. Don't blame him for be-ing a bit put off by everything—it was the same reason I wanted to leave as soon as I could. Rip the bags out from under the floor-boards where I keep them and just light out for somewhere new. But I never had gone anywhere new before.

Stepping out of the truck, Mr. Ostrander jumped at every sound. A bark. Pit bulls. Eight of them bounded into the yard from behind the dilapidated trailer, mouths slobbering long strings of spittle, eyes shining hungrily. He leaped back into the cab of the truck, pulling the door closed as the dogs slammed against the metal exterior. Eight hundred pounds of rabid flesh pounding at the window. Roscoe had kept the window halfway down, probably to cool himself off (I ain't never been in a car here with AC)—now apparently a mistake, as dog muzzles were poking through. Jockeying for a position, gnashing their teeth, pawing at the door. Each scratch emitting a metallic screech.

A gunshot.

A bullet: an alloy of lead, tin, and antimony.

One of the dogs slid down the car door, smearing a trail of blood across the handle. Seven pit bulls whimpered, scampering back behind the house. Daddy stepped out and walked over to Roscoe's car.

I tried to think of how Mr. Ostrander felt, being attacked by our dogs—not really *our* dogs, though they hung around here often. Just a pack of dogs that other people had left behind in the woods, dropped off by the sides of desolate roads the county over. Now they ran through the woods in wild fury, snapping at rabbits and assaulting strangers.

Mr. Roscoe, seeing my daddy, would wonder who this man with a gleaming white scalp crowned with sparse red hair approaching him was. I knew that some people sure thought Daddy was strange. Mr. Roscoe climbed out of the passenger's side of the truck, peering uncertainly underneath at the dead dog.

"Dogs—they're wild. They're nuts. Damn." Daddy carried a shotgun over his shoulder, shaking his head. "So, who the hell are you?"

"Well—well, before your little tribe of Cujos attacked, I—I'm Roscoe Ostrander."

"Like that dumb ass from *Dukes of Hazzard*." Har-har-har.

"Yes, exactly. Mr. Pepper? You're Matthew's father?"

Suddenly Daddy's face sobered, his little mouth tightening. You never were supposed to really mention Matthew around him just yet, because he was still mighty sore about it. He clasped his hands together over his protruding stomach and said, "So, you're who they sent then?"

"I just—I want you to be aware, sir, that your son was a member of the Knights of Southern Heritage. Not sure if you're—ah, familiar with the movement. My employers told me all about what happened. They sent me here to represent Matthew in court, to the media, to talk to people about him. To prove that he's innocent. That they're—you know, decent people and that whole thing?"

"You really think he's innocent?"

My daddy had a habit of asking uncomfortable questions; I bet at this point Mr. Roscoe's spit was drying up like his saliva glands were dammed with concrete. "I mean, I don't know him. What do you think?"

"Mr. Ostrander, Matty is my son. Of course I don't think he did it."

"In a few weeks, a trial will begin. I hope you know what we're in for. Do you?"

"They think my son killed that black man. He was the mayor, you know? A couple years ago, he was the mayor. Young black mayor—we were mighty progressive." Mr. Roscoe grimaced. I knew he was looking my daddy in the eyes, those eyes that threw you off, eyes that glinted with intelligence surpassing the realm of a trailer park. Here in the woods, no one expected to find that. "You know, he was the one who wanted to put recycling bins downtown, but no one wanted them. Once he died, they—well, they put those bins in. And he wanted to develop more land, and you know, he kept asking to buy land from us. Wasn't just a mayor but also a real-estate agent. Wanted to fill the whole woods with damned suburbs."

"You weren't fond of him, then? And Matty?"

"That's the problem. We may have had cause to hang that bastard up, but we didn't. And Matty didn't, I know, even if—even if, well—"

We lived here, our entire family. After our first trailer, where Matty, Daddy, and I lived, stood dozens of others spotting the sticks. My whole redheaded family lived back there, crammed into clearings with their dilapidated trailers. Like we were trying to guard something very special, just us, the Pepper tribe. And to tell the truth, we were.

Most of my family were never too smart, but Daddy told me that Matty and I were different.

See? I said "Matty and I" because that's how we were taught in school; I wasn't half-bad at English but I was especially good at chemistry.

My teachers used to say, "Boy, you Peppers sure do know your periodic table," and we did. Even my daddy knew the enthalpy delta for a reaction between carbon and carbon dioxide to yield carbon monoxide. Even Daddy could explain chemistry.

"Well, I hope I don't run into any of those dogs again." Mr. Roscoe nudged the dead dog beside his truck, eyeing the spiked collar. "You said they were wild?"

"Every dog around here is wild, Mr. Ostrander. Sometimes, those neighborhood mutts from the suburbs join in with the wild dogs. Once they're out away from their homes, it don't matter, do it? Who's wild and who's not. Deep down, they're all wild."

—◄+◄+►—

One morning, a few days before the Ostranders arrived, Dylan argued with my father over hiring a lawyer from the national Knights organization to handle the matter.

The trailer shuddered as Dylan's truck approached. He sprang out of the chasse, his eyes burning like firecrackers. "Papa Pepper, I got a word for you."

No answer echoed from within our house, so Dylan barged in. I climbed out of the kitchen window and crossed to the house, standing on tiptoes to watch Dylan whip my father off his feet.

"Get your hands off me. You're angry."

"We should be angry. The enemy is winning."

"The enemy? Who?"

"Liberals. Blacks. Usual bunch—they're sending that damned corporate lawyer to help us, but that's bullshit—you'll see."

The summer before, when Dylan began to conduct much of the family's business with outside pushers and dealers, Daddy made him an honorary member and also a sort of official head of security for the local chapter. In the Knights of Southern Heritage, people's roles meant something. In this family, your role lasted till you croaked.

"Are you referring to me appealing to the national organization to send one of their men? I thought it best. If they believed their image could be hurt—"

"They would distance themselves as far away from this court case as possible—you know that. Now they're going to send some pussy faggot to come talk about how backward we are, how Matty didn't know better."

Daddy paused, placing the book he had been reading facedown on his lap. "Are you questioning my leadership? What would you have me do? Let the state provide some unbiased lawyer, throw him to the wolves? My boy's innocent—they're sending a professional to prove that."

"Even among our own kind, they're working against us. Maybe even on the plantation, there are some—dissenting voices. We must not fear reproach or anger. Ours is an order of moral purity, and if we taint that with the teachings of some—some outsider, then we cannot stand as one. Already, we're no longer a nation but instead an occupied territory. The enemy is in control. Think of Elizabeth. What would happen to her if she began to stray? Think of what kind of thinking you're exposing the children to."

My father stood, pressing his fingers against Dylan's chest. "I understand your concern, but there are more important things to consider. My son—"

"What about your son? What was he worth anyways?"

"Look, I've lost a child before. I can't lose another."

"So?"

"Charlie. When he was thirteen…I wasn't in the truck when it flipped. I let Matty drive the damn thing to the store."

"And look what happens when you give responsibility to him. Just because he's your son doesn't mean he knows what's best for this family. Not like I do."

"Oh, I know what you think is good and decent for the family. I know you contacted the man out from Charleston. Well, now we're gonna do things my way—we're gonna—"

I ducked as Daddy looked over Dylan's shoulder at the window where I stood. Fretting over whether he had seen me, I raced back into the trailer to finish the latest batch.

⊱⊱ ⊰⊰

Matty still sat in the prison in Columbia, where we tried to visit him as often as possible, but it was hard because he was on trial for murder. Never kill unless necessary, my daddy told us. Surely to hang that man on the tree was not necessary; why couldn't that be evidence enough? When I told Mr. Ostrander that, he shook his head and said, "No, that won't work."

One of the feathers on the arrow I had strung hung loose. I released the string, and the arrow veered to the right, detoured by the botched fletching. Matty told me I missed first of all because I used real feathers to make homemade arrows when I should have just bought arrows from the store with the money I had saved up and secondly because I needed to spend money on a gun, not a bow. My family members were protective of their guns, and no one used one that did not belong to him. But I was saving that money, saving up for college maybe. I worked hard, earned money, and would pay for more than a gun.

The squirrel I had been aiming for scurried up a tree before I could notch another arrow. Matty also told me that if I was dead set on making my own bow, I needed to use english yew, which was stronger and not so springy. Only I didn't know tree types as well as him; I suspected no english yew grew on our plantation.

The land we owned where all the Peppers lived we called the Pepper Plantation, which most people in Lickskillet assumed was a throwback to the days when southerners owned slaves. But no, we called our place a plantation as an inside joke: my cousin Dylan grew crops, though we were not supposed to actually talk about those. He talked sometimes about expanding his private venture, but Daddy didn't think that was a good idea.

When it began to get dark, I stashed my bow back underneath the briar and walked through the woods to our house. Among the trailers on the plantation, my father and I (and Matty before he got arrested) lived in a house. Though slightly ruinous, it was home. Because Daddy didn't want the house to smell like chemicals, we had to do the cooking in the trailer out back. Everyone agreed I had some fantastic affinity for cooking.

I walked inside, where Daddy and Mr. Ostrander talked very seriously around the table. "What have you been up to?"

"Yass, well, the business is very delegate." Meaning *delicate*, probably, or maybe not, depending on whether he knew what a delegate was. Mr. Ostrander just smiled and nodded nervously, wiping sweat from his brow every few seconds.

"Daddy, I need to work on some chemistry."

"It's dark out, yass. Go ahead, then. Just be back soon."

As I walked out to the trailer, I considered this. They would hold their meeting tonight, forming a firelight halo in the secrecy of the woods. These pines protected us, Matty would say. But Matty was gone, and he was the one they would discuss, how to set him free. Or maybe they would not. Maybe Mr. Ostrander would never find a way to set Matty free. They would fry Matty in a chair, and his eyeballs would pop out, and his skin would sizzle like bacon.

They never included me in these meetings. Never told me what happened, as if what I thought simply wasn't important. Maybe not.

Crush pseudoephedrine tablets into a power.

When they held the meetings, they suited up in white before driving out in trucks to the clearing. Sometimes, they burned a huge pile of wood and stood around it, sometimes chanting. But that seemed superstitious and too childish in the light of recent events.

Mix powder with solvent to separate out unnecessary substances.

Whenever everybody went off to the monthly meetings, I was supposed to look after the children. Daddy didn't want me going to the meetings or having anything to do with the Knights. Some other people from the community would show up and park in front of our house, and then truckloads of white-robed men would ride off into the woods. They waited until they reached the clearing to put on the pointed hats and hoods, though those were only formal and seemed childish sometimes too.

Then bubble hydrogen-chloride gas up through the liquid so it becomes crystallized.

I was supposed to stay at home and work on this science project, an exhaustive use of chemistry. It seemed to be getting too hot, the fumes too strong, so I considered moving the project out into the woods so the house wouldn't smell so sour.

But it could probably wait. I finally laid all the materials out on the kitchen table and walked outside where my little cousins Jem and Louisa were standing. Barefoot and smiling.

"Jem, do you think you can look after your little sister?"

Jem was eight, and by eight, I could handle myself fine. When I turned ten, Daddy even let me cook, but only under his supervision.

"Maybe? Can we eat something?"

"Let me go get you something." I stepped inside.

I removed slices of bread from a flimsy plastic sleeve and dropped them onto the counter. Though I should not have put the food near the rock on the stove, I didn't care. A peanut butter and jelly sandwich would do, but last time I went shopping, I couldn't afford grape jelly. After I gingerly scraped mold from the slices, I spread peanut butter across the bread.

Leaning out the trailer, I called, "A sandwich?"

"Peanut butter and jelly."

"We only have peanut butter."

The meetings were supposed to be secret, supposed to be very important. Because I wasn't a member, I wasn't allowed to go. But then again, my dad let Mr. Roscoe go, which was completely unfair. I imagined, though, that Mr. Roscoe hadn't been completely comfortable with the idea of coming along to one of their meetings. Mr. Roscoe didn't like to take risks. He rode off in the back of my daddy's pickup truck.

I tried to imagine everything Mr. Roscoe feared. He probably feared many fates, likely including being slingshot from the back of a pickup truck, splattered across the pavement, and peeled off a day later by a road scraper. He seemed the sort to be very afraid of a lot of things: congenital diseases, black beetles, shards of glass, cramped spaces, lofty heights, drunken clowns, Nazi zombies, clandestine meetings, legal obligations, city officials, home-brewed beer, Magic Markers, people with Mohawks, and supposed white supremacists. Seemed to be a mighty fearful man.

Walking inside, I closed the curtain in the kitchen so that Jem and Louisa wouldn't see my project. All those chemicals lying about could be dangerous for kids. I needed some sort of disguise, the Knights uniform—that way I could walk in there with my hood pulled up, and nobody would know. Scavenging through my father's closet, I pulled out one robe that was ashy gray more than white. I found a matching mottled hood.

Most of the Pepper kids were homeschooled, because people liked to pick on us at school. Mostly, they sat around watching television or learning a trade. The kids weren't so smart around here, so I was considered a genius. Not that I didn't love them.

Not all the families living on the acres of property were actually family either. But move in here, and you were considered an honorary Pepper. We lived all together, all very close together. We prayed together. We ate Thanksgiving meals together. We partied together. We survived together. We died together. I gave Jem and Louisa sandwiches and dashed into the thick of trees.

When I was deep enough into the woods to be invisible, I pulled the robe over my clothes, the hood over my head. No wonder people thought we killed Jameson, the robes making us look like Klan members. We're not racist, Daddy said, just proud.

No one would recognize me. Generally, the women didn't wear the costumes, but I had not grown anything close to resembling breasts, so I doubted anyone would notice.

I could see the mass of white, billowing above me like a great sheet in the wind. The men stood in costume, forming a large circle, flanked on the perimeters by their women.

The Knights stood in the trees, watching for intruders, but no one seemed to notice when I stepped into the ranks, staring around through the stark eyeholes. I supposedly knew everyone here. I couldn't identify anyone at all.

The only normal-clothed man was Mr. Roscoe, who cleared his throat and stepped into the circle, glancing about as if he were stepping into a ring of jackals. A banner bearing a Knight's flaming sword fluttered above their anonymous faces.

Daddy spoke.

"Good evening, brothers, sisters. We have a visitor in our ranks." The eyes that bore through the slits into the fiery dark glared at Roscoe. "He is our friend. He came here to help my son, Matty. As you all well know, Matty is accused of killing a man." Hisses from the crowd. "Puts a mighty bad mark on our integrity. We don't believe in murder or in hurting anyone. And as Mr. Ostrander here says, it hurts our marketability. Who will take our cause seriously when they believe we are merely racist bigots?" Daddy raised his arms to stop the whispering, circling around slowly.

Mr. Roscoe stepped back, swallowing.

Daddy spoke up again. "So, we're going to do something about it. We of the Knights stand to protect Protestant values, and our values are coming under question here in Lickskillet. How much we value tolerance in this group—that is what people question. They think because you're all white, all Republicans, that you're bigots. We're not murderers.

"Mr. Ostrander, our lawyer sent from corporate—he's a got a right fine plan to get us out of this fix. And once everybody sees how we're not so bad, maybe Matty—he'll be saved."

Usually, these meetings dissolved into hearty barbecues, the men drinking Busch Light in the forest around the blazing bonfire. Pushing up their masks, they sipped and talked late into the night.

Tonight, the men seemed tenser. Their wives wore faces marked weary and bruised. Their wives who didn't mind that their husbands wore white masks and carried gaudy torches. Their wives who didn't mind their husbands' militant attitudes—who still kissed those husbands, although jagged whiskers scratched their faces. Their wives who understood. Now they peered with muffled consternation at some man who drove like a carpetbagger from town to town, cleaning up messes. Mr. Roscoe.

"What has plagued this organization for years is its public image." He tried to smile slyly, but ain't nobody was buying his jokes. "What do people think of when they hear the Knights' name? Not of white knights or protectors. No, they think of cross burnings and lynching, all of those things of old. The things perpetuated by groups you have nothing to do with. That ain't who you are, right?" Mr. Roscoe felt the burn of every stare, the furrow of every brow grasping at him from afar. "We need to strike down the slander. The Knights of Southern Heritage needs to *show* this city that it can be accepting—that we are in no way racist. And I know how. Maybe—we—maybe, well—I have a plan—"

"Spit it out already."

"Well, it's just—I know what we—"

"And?"

"Ah, maybe we should take action. Yes, something to, uh, show them." Silence persisted. "Maybe we can accept a black member."

"What?"

Even Daddy sputtered and gawked. "Roscoe, you know we can't—"

"Why, sure we can. Is there anything in the rules—"

"I'm pretty sure there is."

"Then we'll break the rule."

The Knights stood on their haunches, ready to strike, but Daddy raised his arm. "Calm down. We'll talk over this in private. We're not going to—we have to—we'll see. OK? How about that?"

Mr. Roscoe and Daddy stumbled out of the ring into the trees, and we were left standing dazed, staring down each other. I thought, If that's the answer to freeing Matty, if Mr. Roscoe really thinks it works, then—then good. I held my breath for them to return, for whatever plan Mr. Roscoe concocted to work. I held my breath for the family not to fracture apart.

They returned. My daddy shook his head and tried to wave down the cries. "Well, maybe we should try it. Maybe—"

But then the ranks broke, and the men charged forward. Outrage.

"No blue-belly nigger ain't gonna—"

"We'll string up his ass before he puts on the armor of knighthood."

Dylan led the rebellion, shouting, "He panders to the enemy! The enemy!"

Daddy, smart as he could be, pushed Mr. Roscoe away and roared, "Dammit, stand back! Don't act like a pack of wild animals." All quiet. "Look, sure, we want to protect our rights, our interests, our businesses. But that's not the only reason we come together so often. We're a family of sorts, got it? We stick together. And when one of our own—my son, mind you—is in trouble, we stick by him. You know, Matty didn't hurt anybody. But there is a cruel plot in this town against him and against us. Against my—my boy, innocent as a mockingbird. So, please, let's just try."

I couldn't see how the Knights could accept any black man into their group, in the same way you wouldn't expect the sea to cover the mountains. Just wasn't natural—that was what Matty might say. But I was thankful they'd try for my brother's sake. As the men moved to open their ice chests, I slinked back into my forest to return home.

⊶ ⊷

My secret outing made me feel more grown-up for some reason. Almost as if I'd been allowed to see behind the fold of secrecy my daddy kept. Nearing midnight, I wondered how long it would take for the Knights to return to the plantation. They usually stayed out late, but Mr. Roscoe's idea had startled them. There would likely not be any celebrating, only somber hung heads and quiet voices.

Back at the briar, I lifted the bow to eye level. As if God wished to mark this night for me as the night I passed into the terrible realm of knowing secrets, he shined a ray of silver moonlight through the pines to spotlight a single deer. He stood majestic just feet away, seemingly watching me, so much a part of the forest I could not take in his sublime nature.

I drew the bow back; the deer did not flinch. *Twang.*

The arrow struck the deer in the chest. The deer stumbled and fell, jerking slightly with the arrow protruding out of what I guessed was his heart. Tomorrow morning, it would hang upside down in the skinning shack. I needed no one's help to clean this kill, even if it took all night. Leave them to secrets and costumes and foolish plans. Someone needed to act—someone needed to find out what really happened to Jameson that night. I could do it. I could find whoever killed that poor man and strung him up in that tree, could help set Matty free.

Gingerly walking toward the deer, I looked into his eyes, black and blank. I ran my hand along its antlers, counting seven points. I leaned down and dipped my finger into his wound. Smeared blood across my brow.

CHAPTER 10

THE JOURNAL OF ELIJAH RODRIGUEZ

October 23

"Elijah, Elijah, buy one of these bracelets." The girls sat behind a fold-up table on which lay piles of braided bracelets, vibrantly colored and designed. "It's for charity," the girls chimed. "With every bracelet you buy, the money goes to some woman in South America who made it. See, this one was made by Juanita. Is that your cousin—or?" They laughed.

"What?" I drew closer to the table, rubbing a bracelet between my forefinger and thumb. A tag with a small biography and a picture of a smiling brown woman was hanging from the latch. Juanita. "What do these do?"

"You wear them, duh." One girl held up her wrist, her arm striped with the Latin American bracelets. "If you actually cared, you'd buy one. Come on, buy one. We're raising money for our tennis team."

"But doesn't the money go to these women?"

"Some of it, sure. Just buy one. You could save someone from poverty." She said this very matter-of-factly. "Just five dollars. Be a savior."

"I don't have any money."

"But—what do you mean? Come back. Whatever. We're only selling these for *your* people, anyways."

I lowered my head and stepped into the school.

———

I sat at lunch alone. Two shadows loomed over me. These moments change lives, Quentin.

"Elijah?"

This was from the soccer star, a black boy with sullen eyes and teeth that gleamed as white as a wolf's. "Yes?" They knew my name, and him saying it made me squirm.

Blaine leaned down. "We wanted to invite you to Cass's Halloween party."

Looking up at both of them, I asked, "Why?"

For a moment, Blaine said nothing as if to denote that it was a very good question. "Why? We just want you come, OK? Wear a costume."

For three years, neither Aron nor Blaine had so much as spoken to me. My suspicions about their intentions were well founded. "I've never been to a party before. I—"

"Of course not," said Blaine. "So come to one before you die of boredom. Or of a rogue bullet ricocheting off a cop car. Or dysentery. We're giving you—well, an opportunity to be social. We can show you a good time."

I nodded. "I think I would like that."

A party—a real party just like everyone talked about with drinking, drugs, and topless girls having orgies—maybe sans orgies. "But why me?"

Blaine turned and began talking to Declin Ostrander, ignoring me. Aron said, "When you stuck up for Declin, that was cool. Justin could have kicked your ass, and you saved a few of his teeth. I'll tell you that."

"I just didn't want anything bad to happen. I only told the truth—that's all."

Aron nodded and then looked too long up and down at my table. "Do you like eating alone?"

"Not particularly."

He didn't ask why because I suspected he knew. Of course he knew. I looked more like a fifth grader than an eleventh grader, so tiny and skeletal. I wouldn't even hang out with me, maybe because I spoke about fantasy books too much, maybe because I hardly spoke at all. Or spoke to girls, for that matter, because what woman would want this weakling as a warrior? Aron knew all this, and his face told the story plainly.

"Come eat with us. Sit down here."

Although I said nothing, I had a swell time. They spoke fast, shouting over each other to tell stories. Always about what had happened and what would happen. Every story fascinated me. Aron trained for playing college sports every day, Blaine talked about the cool people who would come to the party, and Declin even joked Halloween might be fun since he wouldn't fear Justin trying to kill him with me there.

Their conversations strayed to the strange, yet were compelling in the most absurd ways.

"In the world of phallic foods, the banana is king."

"What about hot dogs?" asked Aron.

"They're manufactured." Blaine shrugged. "Bananas naturally represent the male genitalia, making their phallic symbolism all the more significant."

It made me feel happy in a strange way, almost as if I belonged.

⚒⚒

I never wanted to make any real connections, not with people. When I was younger, I invited kids from school to my house, but my father freaked them out. Too volatile and strange for them, my father, who delighted in calling my friends homosexuals, pansies, girly boys. When he grew up a second-generation migrant in the seventies, these slurs saved him from becoming the butterfly pinned beneath the bullies' microscopes. They attacked the openly gay kids, the flower children wearing crowns of roses, the outsiders. In high school, my father joined the football team, beefed up—he told me that nobody could talk down to a man. To be a man was the most important thing.

At sixteen, my father heard someone call him a spic for the first time, and whoever said the word couldn't speak again for four months with his mouth wired shut. All my life, I knew that I lacked the masculinity he embodied, missed something. Needed bigger muscles, a stronger reserve, but as I grew older, I never tried to fight my dad, never struck back. He worked as a police officer for the Lickskillet department, carried a gun that he only showed me when he was drunk.

At thirteen, he enrolled me in the Boy Scouts, but the white boys never talked to me, so then he put me in a Hispanic troop. Nobody talked to me there because I couldn't speak Spanish. When I turned fifteen, he joked about throwing me a quinceañera. Every year since, he forced me to try out for football, but not this year—he had given up. "You're never going to be a Puerto Rican. You're never going to be a man."

CHAPTER 11

DYLAN PEPPER

I drove up to Lexington, somewhere near the state capital where Matty was rottin' in a concrete block. Shit, I stayed there once crammed inside a "juvenile detention center" for six months, fifteen years old maybe, 'cause I set fire to a trash can in the school bathroom and blackened the stall, and that all happened after I took off from home, stopped talking to my parents. Taught me to avoid adult prison. Fuck that—you fuck with those skinheads in prison, and pretty soon they'll be stabbing you in your sleep. Sometimes, I sent Matty packs of cigarettes hidden in thick novels, only 'cause Papa Pepper forbade me to use the Holy Bible.

Parked between two little cars, a Prius and a MINI Cooper, which hood would I step onto when I climbed out of my truck? Looked through the windows—the man should have been there. I hoped I picked the right Waffle House. Inside, I slid into a corner booth. I read the menu.

Being inside the trailer all day made my eyes fuzzy, and the lights hurt to look at. Strange place, these posters all around you like they're from the 1950s: World's Best Chili, Sweet Southern Sweet Tea, Fresh Grilled Burgers. Old photographs and smiling cooks. Ain't no cooks smiling here.

Man I was s'posed to meet—he worked for some important people down in Charleston. They needed a supplier, so told my friend who was a trucker who helped us ship meth across state lines. Motherfuckin' King of Cannabis, they called this guy. Bigtime. My leg kept jumping something fierce, like a rattlesnake kept biting my toes.

The menu kept stickin' to the table 'cause it was covered in syrup. When I tried to pull it up, it tore right in two.

"Red hair and stupid," said a voice above me. I looked up to see a tall, muscular, bald man slide into the booth across from me. "That's what they said you Peppers looked like. You must be the boy I'm looking for, eh?"

"Lemire?"

"That'd be me, but don't say my name too loudly. When you get to be guarding a man like my employer, there's not a shortage of bastards who want to slice off your dick and feed it to their dogs." He paused. "Well, who the hell are you then?"

"Pepper. Dylan Pepper."

"Hm, yeah, you Peppers sure do know how to be in the news. You're not related to—?"

"What's important for you is that we own hundreds of acres of land, but we live on only three acres of it. The rest is forest and fields, perfect for crops. Sure, family's tried to grow crops before but nothing quite as profitable as all that—and we're already cultivatin' a few acres. We could expand the operation. Friend tells me you need a new supplier."

"A few hundred acres? You think that's a lot?" He snorted. "What makes you think we need help from you?"

A waitress waded through the Waffle House kitchen toward us. "I know that the cartels have been attacking your shipments. It ain't safe to keep bringing crops from South America, not if the Mexicans are going to sic pirates on you."

He nodded, crossing his arms. "And what if they sic pirates on you?"

"Morning, honey. My name's Darlene, and I'll be taking y'all's orders. Know what you want to drink?"

"Coffee. Black."

"Water please."

She strutted away, swinging her ass as she retreated behind the counter.

"Look, kid. I appreciate your enthusiasm and all, but I didn't agree to meet you because I think you're going to supply us with pot. We got that. But there might be other ventures we need help with."

I shifted in my seat and studied the tattoos on his arms. I wanted to look intimidating, but I felt like I was shrinking. "Rock? Meth?" Lemire nodded silently. "But—what we've got— that's a small-scale operation. We sell locally, maybe to a few cities around here, but—"

"But it's a market my boss might be interested in. Look, kid, you'll want to think about this. Your cousin—his name's Matthew. He's in trouble, right?"

"He—he didn't do anything. He didn't killed that man."

"Doesn't much matter, does it? What is it your uncle's leader of? The Ku Klux Klan?"

"We're the Knights of Southern Heritage—we—it's not that important, ya know?" I felt vibrations kick through my knees.

The man set his jaw tight and placed his fork gingerly beside his plate. "Matters to me, you know. Knights of Southern Heritage don't sound like nothing so innocuous as you been hopin', boy. Press is having a field day with it. You're all a bunch of hick racists, conspiring in the woods."

"All right, honey, here's your coffee. Y'all know what you want to eat?"

"I'm not hungry."

Russ Lemire ordered a chocolate-chip waffle, and then Darlene shuffled away again, and he lowered his voice. "The man I work for is a powerful man. He has friends everywhere, even down in your little shit hole of a town. You understand what I'm trying to say here? I think we can talk about growing marijuana all day long, but next time we talk, tell me a little bit about your little business."

But Elizabeth, Matthew's little sister—she was the best at chemistry. No one else could cook meth better than dog shit. Only she'd be headed to college in a year, leaving us. "I don't know if I can."

"And I don't know if they'll fry that cousin of yours." He smiled. "Fine, don't worry about it. Tell me about your ideas, about the pot fields."

"Then you do need a new supplier?"

He grunted. "You're not wrong about those Mexican cartels. Ever heard of the Zetas? Those fuckers leave heads in bathtubs, would skin me or you alive if they knew about this. That's what we're up against, you understand?"

I settled my face until I looked as menacing as possible. My scar sometimes made me cringe. "But they don't know the Peppers. They don't know who they're up against."

"That's bold talk from a kid. They shoot your fuckin' redneck head off." I could swear the greasy bastard almost smiled. "I just want my fucking waffle."

Darlene arrived with his chocolate-chip waffle, and we went quiet. He smeared butter over the waffle and filled each square pocket with sticky syrup. "How do you get away with it? Pay off the cops? What?"

I perked up. "That's the best part. There's a Sheriff Jones who we know through the Knights of Southern Heritage, and he knows the judges in town."

"If he knew the judges, why wouldn't he help get your brother off?"

Because he thought Matthew was guilty—I couldn't say this. "It's a state case, a felony. He doesn't know the judge ruling, has no power."

"Then you do need help?"

"I thought we were talking about growing pot?"

"We are. We supply most of the Southeast. Your contribution—it'd be good to cultivate farms stateside, as long as it's safe."

"The city officials are under our thumbs."

They were leery of us at best. Carl Jones was only friendly because I sold him drugs in high school and helped him lose his virginity to Becky Schuler senior year. Once we ruled this town because we had members of higher class in the Knights of Southern Heritage. Barnaby Rutgers himself even wore a robe with us at one point, though he parted ways with us two years before, and now he wanted to put one of our own under a bus. He left 'cause Papa Pepper told him we couldn't outright scare the Yankees away—that man hated Yankees more than anyone I ever seen hated anyone. He thought 'cause he didn't own all the new subdivisions, all these new housing developments would cut into his business. 'Cause he'd have to compete with Francis Jameson, and now that he was dead, he wasn't even so thankful as to keep our boy out of jail.

"And your family is OK with this?"

"My family? This is what we do."

Papa Pepper never exactly said he wanted business with the man from Charleston 'cause we didn't need more attention, but he didn't know what was best for the family. For the family.

"That's a good thing to hear," Lemire said. He stuffed the last bite of the waffle into his mouth, chewing like he was some fucking cannibal.

CHAPTER 12

CASS TERRIES

I heard about what Justin did from Claire, three days after the fact. Cody told Claire because they hooked up that night. Jane told Cody when they left to drink outside. No one knew who the girl was, just some stranger from another school. They said she was a foreign exchange student from Sweden or Nova Scotia or Liberia or something. Jane was a pudgy girl with lymph nodes that exploded annually. She invited Justin and me to her party, though I declined. Apparently, she heard the girl from Timbuktu and Justin fucking upstairs, and three days later, I found out.

I carried a stack of fashion and lifestyle magazines into the front lawn. My parents were on a three-day trip to Atlanta, probably snorting lines of coke with the drummer from High-Velocity Kettlebells. Magazines wielded a glitzy authority, mocking me with Photoshop and advice columns. I swooned at the pictures of men's chiseled abs. I read the horoscopes religiously.

But too long, I realized, I placed my faith in *Cosmo*.

I would stop taking quizzes that meant nothing, printed on the back of an ad for lip gloss, because I no longer needed their questionnaires to form an identity from multiple choice.

Are you really in love?

Will you and your boyfriend last forever?

Who will you date next?

What do your shoes say about you?

Should you date your crush?

What type of unicorn are you?

Which *Breakfast Club* character are you?

As if some magazine could ultimately decide who you were, predict who you might marry or what job you'd get one day. All this bullshit seemed less reliable than the horoscopes crammed near the back with the advertisements for preteen breast enhancements.

The day after Justin cheated on me, or rather the day after I discovered he had, I carried my magazine collection from my room to my backyard and torched it. Every hotness scale blazed. Every list of best celebrities' hair combusted as if all the hairspray consumed by these coiffed styles were approached with a match. I watched, smoking my last cigarette.

Questionnaire: Will you ever be happy?

I cried. Our gardener sprinted across the lawn with a bucket sloshing with water, hoping to put out the flame. But I wanted fire, wanted the cliché symbolism of the phoenix to burn me anew, to bear me into beauty from ashes.

⚔

I tried to ignore their stares. For three days, so many people had known his secret. I did not. Last Friday, they had looked upon me with respect—she was Justin Ferrara's girlfriend. Her parents were rich and semifamous. Her future was so enviable. Even now I could only refer to my past self as "she," because I wasn't his girlfriend anymore. We were dating, but only the night before had I realized how little he cared. But I didn't show that pain, staring straight ahead at the whiteboard. I waited for class to end so that I could confront him, extract the truth from his own lips.

Before I knew what happened, I thought everything we had gone through had been worth it. I never wanted to have sex with him, not the first time, but he threatened to leave. I didn't want him to leave. Ever since that first time, I still yearned for him to look at me like he did when I took off my clothes. Two years ago, he told me he loved me, kissed down my neck onto my breast. I believed him. Too often, I believed him. Now our conversations felt hollow and mechanical, and even sex felt impersonal. He wanted to do it from behind, and maybe he just didn't want to look me in the eyes. Maybe all this time he had been squeezing his eyes shut and imagining someone else. The bruises on my arm ached, reminding me that none of this had been worth it.

I found him standing alone outside the weight room, checking his cell phone. Outside the large gym doors, I tapped him on the shoulder. "Cass, you're—"

"How could you?"

"What—what are you—listen, the bell—I've got to get to class."

"No, stay." The bell rang, and others seeped out of the hallway until, finally, we were alone. "I want to talk." We backed against the brick wall. "Is it true?"

"Is what true?"

"What they've been—don't think I'm stupid. You've noticed. You know what everyone is saying. About you and that girl."

He pushed me back against the wall, kissing me full on the lips. I tried to push him away, but he pinned down my arms. Every time I struggled, he held tighter, making me feel so—good. This was what I loved, how he controlled me. But this was what I hated, the loss of control. Finally, I pushed him away. "Don't touch me, you—bastard."

He lunged at me, his fist clenched. He looked from his left to his right and grimaced. He almost hit me. Almost. But he would not, not if other people might see.

I swatted at his chest, pushing him away, but he was a statue, stoic, unmovable. "It's over. I'm done with you, you fucking—asshole!"

When I pushed him this time, he stumbled back, knocking the door open. It slammed against the wall and brought abrupt silence to the gym. We stood awkwardly in the doorway, every eye on us. "You will regret leaving me if you do," Justin mumbled. "You will."

"Fuck you." I marched forward and slapped him across the face so hard that my hand left a red, five-fingered mark. As I strutted away, I knew I had won a small victory. But it was really over now. My gut still boiled with indecision. There was no going back.

⇒⊹ ⊹⇐

"I'm sorry."

That's what Justin told me the first time he hit me, just snapped, his arm flailing against my face. He told me he hadn't meant to react so angrily, kissed me better, told me how horrible he felt.

"I'm sorry."

Justin told me this again the first time he popped my eardrum, and I bled onto the emergency-room floor.

"I'm sorry."

The first time he fucked someone else—we were juniors then, and he sobbed for hours. He begged me to never leave.

"I'm sorry."

When my parents saw the bruises, I told them I had fallen from trees, had tripped. Especially after we started having sex, rough sex, I began tripping more often.

"I'm sorry."

I felt afraid he'd kill me, and I never thought anyone could hurt me. South Carolina, the state where I was born, ranked first in women killed by men in domestic relationships. I grew up dreaming myself very lucky.

"I'm sorry."

I told him after he socked Declin Ostrander in the face because I mentioned on the first day of school that I could sleep with him, that I could leave Justin if I wanted to. If only I wanted to, he'd never see me again.

"I'm sorry."

Every morning after, in his truck outside of my house, honking his horn. Blaring, cycling through the suburban air with the insistent rhythm of fists, always inside each house the rhythm of fists, the makeup never enough to cover the marks. I could remember seeing the same bruises on my mother. The truck horn sounded brash, interrupted my own silence with the eruption of mumbled apology. "I'm sorry. I'm sorry. I'm sorry."

After a while, Justin stopped apologizing. He never said, "I'm sorry," but only sulked when I would not sleep with him. After a while, I stopped registering that phrase at all, because his anger became normal. Men, my mother would say, always acted a certain way, that masculine enigma—they couldn't help themselves.

Blaine grew up in the house next to Justin. I befriended Blaine because he liked cool things like frogs and ice cream and video games. The girls at our elementary school liked to play this game called MASH, where you would choose who you would marry and what house you would live in. Justin used to ride his red Schwinn up and down the block, and we watched him. Aron used to come over as well, and the three of us grew up together. Even now as we drifted apart, they were my best friends. During sophomore year when I started dating Justin, I spent more time with him than my friends. I thought the people who talked to me at parties or came to my house were also my friends, but after I broke up with Justin, only Aron and Blaine remained.

Blaine told me I should get back at Justin by having a party on Halloween. I agreed, though I knew his real motivations were to simply get fucked up. The party could serve as vengeance against him—everyone would come except for the lonely quarterback, drinking alone.

═╬═ ╬═

Each year on the final Wednesday of October, Golden Oaks hosted an Autumn Gala, an occasion for the men to dress in tuxedos and compare their wallet widths, their low scores on the green, and the size of their wives' breast enlargements. A competition in pretentious ego.

Our mothers wore expensive jewelry our fathers bought for them after much coercion and oral sex. They drank wine so expensive you could sell a bottle to pay for a midlife-crisis Porsche.

All of this was very classy until each adult got roaring drunk and began telling stories of youthful debauchery while each teenager (and there were few enough of us) covered his or her face in traditional embarrassment.

We left at half past six, piling into my dad's Jaguar for a three-minute drive. The country club loomed above the Golden Oaks houses at the top of our lush golf course (eighteen holes complete with ponds, bunkers, and stone bridges). The clubhouse itself stood three stories tall with imposing columns. Looked like the White House. An American flag flew lonely from the pole at the top of the gabled roof.

In the circular parking lot out back, valets were parking the cars. Fucking valets. We climbed from our car and entered together, my parents flitting to their friends. They clutched at each other's necklaces and commented on how they each felt fat, to which the others would coo, "No, you look amazing." I gawked at the champagne bottles, the pink pastel polo shirts, the erect nipples of neighborhood cougars, standing in the corner with my arms crossed. My parents expected me to find company at the party, socialize with the children of Lickskillet socialites, but most of the teens were intelligent enough to stay home typing into iPhones, not trapped here with me in the seventh circle of hell.

Everyone except for Cain Rutgers.

"Cass, you look great."

I grunted.

The Rutgers, one of the few names everyone knew, were one of the fifteen Lickskillet families, who had lived in the town before the northern invasion into the suburbs (circa 2000s), before smart engineers moved in to work at a nuclear power plant not too far away (circa 1970s), and before the rich Arthur Walter built the famous gnome museum. Walter, like many other rich New York transplants, arrived in Lickskillet to treat his tuberculosis. For some reason, the town had been renowned as a health spa. Every winter, they enjoyed the balmy climate of Lickskillet, some staying in a lavish hotel downtown, and then returned home for the scorching summers. Only a few of the original families remained, the ones who owned the railroads and the textile mills in Coketown and the cotton plantations. The Rutgers family had known the Terries for more than eight generations.

"I hear you and Justin broke up. Sorry to hear about that." He sidled beside me, a rotten cologne wafting from his collar.

"Are you sorry?" I paused. "How's Exeter? Every year, my parents want me to go to Exeter, but then I remember I have to deal with pompous little boys like you."

He laughed, pretending not to be offended. "You obviously don't know me at all."

"Enlighten me."

We picked up glasses of wine from the unsupervised booze table before sliding outside. On the patio of the clubhouse, old couples sat drinking and talking very loudly. In the distance, we could see the golf-course greens stretch for miles. The wall that separated Golden Oaks from the rest of Lickskillet was in the distance.

A barrier for petty thieves and poor kids on Halloween. In a neighborhood where ex–Ponzi schemers gave out hundred-dollar bills to faceless ghouls in ratty white blankets, kids peeping out of eyeholes, we needed a wall. Else, all the kids in Lickskillet would come armed with plastic orange jack-o'-lantern buckets to fill up. Who needed candy when you could get money? But this was our special treat, the reward for those lucky enough to be born on this side of the wall. The day after Halloween, we traditionally visited Walmart to stock up on Skittles and Reese's.

"Too bad you don't go to Exeter. We have a good time." He smiled. "You know, we're the last southerners."

"I'm not a southerner."

"If you're born in the South, you're a southerner. Don't act like you aren't proud. We're not hicks or rednecks. We're not the Peppers. We have a past."

"I don't wanna just be another daughter of the town, though. I don't wanna be just another tree rooted in the South. I want to grow out."

He shrugged. "You know, my father hates them."

"Who?"

"The others. The northerners. For so long, we did just fine. Dad says before the engineers came, at least the Yankees were rich. And the blacks. All came down and lived in camps to build that power plant, and now—they're everywhere. They're ruining this town."

"I don't think—whatever. Maybe we should get inside."

He growled, almost imperceptibly. "Whatever."

I tipped back the champagne glass and swallowed. Inside, the men had abandoned their tuxedo jackets, and the sinks were sprinkled with random white powders.

>==+= =+==

I stripped off my dress and hung it delicately in the closet. In my underwear, I walked to the bathroom and removed my makeup, staring at myself. Damn, sometimes I looked good. Sometimes I looked terrible. I pushed my boobs together and then let them fall again. Sighed.

The bruises under my arms, spotting my rib cage, had begun to heal. But the long scars slicing against my thighs still shined red. From when I thought I was pregnant with Justin's kid. The night before going to the doctor, I regretted this traitorous skin, this haven for mistakes. How arbitrary the body, how cruel its indecencies. Wrecked joints squelched and shrieked like nails on chalkboard. How our bodies could betray and forgive.

Imagine how the Virgin Mary felt when the archangel Michael first told her she'd bear a child, even if she'd never had sex. How people would stare. That night I carved my shame into my legs, hoping people would stare. If I were pregnant, at least I hadn't carried something as intangible as the Holy Spirit, Mary's body no longer her own, bearing a heavenly destiny.

I couldn't live in this body anymore, couldn't stand it, because you could never be happy with your body. Never live up to the standards of Photoshop, embody every beauty tip. My nose would always be too large, and if I fixed my nose with plastic surgery, then I would need to fix my lips. If I fixed my face, my liver might give out, and all the remodeling of this flesh-and-bone house would go to waste. Some days, I wanted to break the mirror, and other days the mirror courted my stare for hours. We could not choose to live in anything else but these bodies, though we wanted something better. We prayed to never be named holy, to never face the wrath of a man's love blooming in our bellies. We wanted to choose what was sacred for ourselves.

⚊⟨⟩⚊

The day before Halloween, I had delivered the list of names to the guard, the name of every student at the high school save for Justin's.

I got dressed. Five o' clock: four hours and counting.

My grandfather still lay in bed, shuddering. "Grampy," I called him. "Are you awake?"

He sat up and looked right at me. "Cass, I'm so tired. Can you help me up the stairs?"

"Outside? Do you want to go outside?"

"No, dammit. I want to go to the kitchen. Let me cook you something. Waffles? You like waffles?"

He stumbled off of his bed and clutched onto his bedside table. Today, he at least knew my name. "The stove is so—dammit, Rosa. I told you to cook some waffles." Maybe he didn't remember, the memories jiggling in and out of place like a loose tooth. He swept all of his belongings off the table with his coat-hanger arms. He began preparing waffles, maybe. I did not stop him, immediately. Just watched.

I took his arm, pulling him back to bed. "You're not in the kitchen. You're in your bedroom."

"I told you to book us a five-star hotel, and we end up in this piss hole? By God, I ought to—"

"Grampy, it is OK. *Wheel of Fortune* is going to come on soon. Come on."

He smacked me away and began to scream. "Don't you treat me like a child. I know who I am. I know that you're my grand-daughter. Don't think I would ever forget that. You treat me like

I'm some sort of insane person. I started out from nothing and made it big. I made something out of my life, so don't you treat me like I am still some kid. You hear me? I deserve a little respect."

"Of course, Grampy. I'm sorry. It's just sometimes—your condition."

"You think I have a condition? You people are crazy. The sanest man in this house. Now, you listen here." He pulled me in close, his bony fingers perched on my chin. "Don't end up like your mother. She's a whore. I can't believe I ever married her. I mean, she ran off and left me with you. But don't think I—I know what you and he do up there. I know you snort blow all day long, and listen, back in the day, in Hollywood, we ate that for breakfast. But honey, don't end up like your mother. That's the curse in this family.

"No, honey, you're going to be more than a pair of great legs for some jackass construction workers to whistle at. You can be like me."

The thought terrified me.

"Look around this place. Isn't this the grandest place you ever did see? Ain't it? What got me here? Hard work. I had a dream, and I followed it, and—God, I really am—I am old."

His face sunk, and then his body collapsed. "Leave me alone," he said. "Just—just turn on the damn television. I thought—thought I was at my office at the studio. I thought we were—you were—"

He stopped talking and started trembling, staring up at me with watery eyes that were almost a milky white. I turned on the television and left him to watch it.

The party, the party, the party—I had a huge night to prepare for. He would survive for one more night in his craziness, his dream world. Maybe that was how we were meant to exist: the past, present, and future were all one, shifting forever. Transcending how normal people live to exist in a way no one else can possibly understand. As I ascended from the basement, I hoped—I hoped that the patients of Alzheimer's were really just time travelers of the mind—that was it. That was all.

I waited. Blaine showed up first with more green than I'd ever seen before. We dispersed marijuana into wooden chip bowls, set around the house. "Are you feeling all right?" Blaine's face hovered toward me, and suddenly his lips collided with mine. I wanted to jerk away, but I let him kiss me. I did not kiss him, but I let him kiss me.

"I'm feeling—well, fine. Who's this you brought along?"

The boy who had been sitting with us at lunch had come with Blaine, had sat down on the couch and stared, mouth agape, at the black television screen.

Blaine smiled. "Oh, you're going to love this. Remember this guy? Elijah Rodriguez. Meet him again, new and improved. This time, higher than a comet." I breathed heavily, wiping his kiss from my lips.

As the boys shambled off, I waited in the foyer. The rest arrived in flocks, wild and flailing and young. We wanted transformation, yearned for new skin. We would breathe in the night until it changed our DNA, until it changed our lives.

CHAPTER 13

DYLAN PEPPER

The boy knocked on the trailer door. "Come on in." He entered and slouched against the wall. Little shit, this fuckin' kid. Y'all don't even know what sort of snobby-nosed Yankee-spickin' shit-for-brains they breedin' today.

On top of that, his father Barnaby Rutgers even hated the culture that made the kid, and the kid pretended to be on board with our business. Talked about the need to sustain southern values, family values, whatever, but the kid couldn't till land worth shit, couldn't shoot a gun, couldn't nothing. Only thing he was good at maybe was sellin' drugs.

"Smells like piss in here, you know that?"

"Shut up, little fucker. You want me break your damn teeth 'gainst the wall? What you want? Another ounce?"

He shrugged. "Well, I know there's a party coming up. I figure I can go by, sell pot there. Maybe push some others drugs if you need."

"What? You think your friends want to try meth?"

"Not really." His face grew pale. "But I mean, you think I should start selling that?"

I scratched my head. Maybe this kid knew too much about what we did here—maybe he was too close. I watched him closely. "Not sure. That what you wanna start doing? Playing the real game, selling some real shit?"

"Well, maybe if you can brew up a batch, I know a few crazy assholes who might try." Cain paused.

I led him into the kitchen, pulling out a bag of marijuana and a hefty scale. I began weighing drugs for him. "I don't particularly care whether you sellin' shit or not, but we're thinking about expanding the business. We want to see how the rock sells on local markets, before we start sending this shit to Charleston."

"Expanding the business, huh? And is there any room for— eh, promotion?"

Licking my lips, I stared him down. "No offense, but you're not really the type of guy I need."

"I can be—fearless. I can do anything."

I pressed my face to his, wanted to seem all intimidating and the like. "You see this scar? When I was in a detention center at age fifteen, they held me down and wanted to cut off my dick. But they carved this beauty mark into my face. And that—that made me hard inside. That made me ready for the shit it might take. You think you could handle that, pretty boy? Come here. I'll give you a little beauty mark."

He swallowed. Good—he was afraid of me. I needed people afraid of me.

Pushing a stack of bills across the table, he reached for the marijuana I had dropped into a ziplock bag. "Come by the night of the party. I'll hook you up."

"'Course. I'll be here, then."

"Don't fuck this up."

Bleary. Cain shuffled in the kitchen, smashing impure meth with a tiny hammer. "This looks like shit or something."

"You'd be surprised what people will smoke. All right. Throw it into the bag."

A few paper bags lay on the table, holding ounces of meth, a few with marijuana inside, drugs Cain meant to bring to the Halloween party once he left my trailer.

He had bought an ounce of Molly from Augusta and mixed in the meth, planned to sell more.

Someone knocked loudly on the door, and the kid ran to answer it. He spoke with someone at the front door and then returned.

"You said you wanted me to find customers?"

CHAPTER 14

BLAINE MOREAU

During the summer before my senior year, I worked odd jobs for loose money, pocket money—cleaning pools, selling drugs, cutting lawns—but perhaps my most lucrative business began with my grandmother. She was the typical elderly invalid, scuttling around with a tennis-balled walker and curling-ironed hair bouncing on her head as she talked. Her mouth jowly and toothless. Handing me her ID and papers to go down to the DMV and file for new tags.

When I arrived at the DMV, after an hour and half's wait, they did not even ask for the ID and gave me the tags right away. As I drove home, I thought to myself, if only people would pay for that service. Turned out, people would.

At first my business attracted ladies too engrossed in reruns of *Jeopardy!* to bother waiting in line, but soon, it expanded beyond that. Working moms, harried suits, stoned neighbors, and anyone with high blood pressure would fork out some cash so that I could suffer through their DMV prison sentence for them.

From thirty minutes to four hours, the wait differed depending on what days I went. You could not underestimate how lazy everyone was or how much they hated the DMV, but I loved the DMV: this made me even more money than laminating fake IDs or making and selling my own moonshine. If while at school I was lazy, when it came to making dough, I was the most innovative bastard alive.

Already, my ingenuity made me highly superior to the other low-life scum from Lickskillet High. I would go on to do wondrous, impressive things. Our senior prank would trump every other prank for decades. Life would treat me like the king I was.

To cure boredom while waiting inside, I stole copies of the *New Yorker* from a dentist's office next door. The place we called the Solar/Polar Molar, because it was cold enough in the summer to freeze your nipples and steaming enough in the winter to be used as a sweat lodge.

At the DMV, every face was red with frustration, everyone's fingers tapping impatiently. The very seats inspired an itching discomfort, a forced anxiety that overwhelmed. And then me with my feet propped up while reading a poem about butter or irony or Muslim culture. If this were hell, I would make money through eternal damnation. Cash payments to tolerate others' tortures. I was a fiscally sound masochist.

One day in late July, around noon when Cass's parents spoke on the radio about celebrity gossip, I drove to the edge of town where the government-subsidized housing stood. Like a labyrinth of poorly constructed woodsheds. I drove out to houses to pick up IDs and necessary papers. You'd be surprised how many people would part with their Social Security card for three hours if it meant not having to wait in a line.

The man who answered the door could have rivaled a walrus in weight. He squinted at me from behind too-tiny wire-framed glasses. Disgust tasted like cat food. He invited me in to wait as he searched for his insurance card. He wore a T-shirt (collar stained with mustard) for a black metal band I had never heard of, and I guessed that the duck wielding a chain saw was their logo. His house smelled like death, armpit, and urine. Pizza boxes, emptied microwave-dinner trays, and crushed energy-drink cans littered his kitchen.

I could not precisely pin him as either a quiet, socially inept weirdo who never grew out of his middle-school awkward phase or as the type of weirdo who jacked off to anime, paid a Norwegian woman to post "I Love You, Baby" on his Facebook wall once a week, and criticized porn for its lack of realism. Likely the latter.

Once he gave me money and papers, I dashed out of there before I ended up in a pit, him lowering down lotion in a bucket, ordering me to rub myself with it or else I'd be hosed down.

The next time I saw this man was in the driver's seat of a vomit-yellow Gremlin. Elijah climbed out of the passenger's seat and waved good-bye. Jabba the Hutt paid me no mind and drove off.

"Who is that guy? If it's your dad or brother—"

"No, the Dragon Master isn't my brother. He's just my friend."

Shit you not, this was what he actually said. "What the fuck is a dragon masturbator?"

"The Dragon Master. That's what his friends call him." Elijah turned flamingo pink, which sounded like nervous laughter behind your back. "His real name is Nick, though."

"And he's your friend? He's probably a registered sex offender, you know."

Elijah said again, a little defiant, "He's my friend."

"Right. Well, maybe that's part of the reason you've never been to a party before. Because you hang out with grown men who call themselves the Dragon Master. I give up."

"Well, what do you want me to do?"

"Ever smoked marijuana?"

"No. That's—"

"You've drunk alcohol, right?"

"I've tried it, but beer tastes—"

"Come on, kid. You've got to learn to live, you know? Just trying to be a good teacher is all. I'm in charge of making sure you have a good time, so we're going inside the house first."

My mom and dad were having their weekly date night, during which—I imagined—they would compromise to go see a mediocre movie (though my dad would want to see anything with Bruce Willis, and my mom would want to see anything with Katherine Heigl, but because it would lead to bickering, they would settle on a movie that was half romantic comedy and half action starring B-list actors and would be disappointed but not altogether displeased); then, they would go out to eat somewhere my dad thought was too expensive and my mom thought cheap, like Applebee's, where my dad would complain about the prices and get drunk enough to actually look at the waitress's tits; then, they would drive home slightly pissed off at each other; they would lie up in bed for about an hour, my dad expecting obligatory sex and my mom reading some shitty romance novel meant for preteen girls; then, both exhausted, they would fall asleep almost touching each other, but not quite, the silent expression of what could have been love.

"What about the party?" Elijah asked.

"It's only six. The party won't even start till—well, we're going to leave in an hour."

Inside, I collapsed onto a couch, feeling the tube of pills in my pocket. I stood up very suddenly and produced the pills. "Here, hold on to this." He took one from me, staring dumbly. "Go ahead, try one."

He popped one of the codeines into his mouth and struggled to swallow. Leaving him alone with the pills, I made myself a bowl of cereal and dialed Cass's number. "I have everything. Everything we need for tonight. Got to tell you, the sucker who sold to me was a hardcore—Cass, Cass, are you listening? Well, OK, I understand. I will talk to you later then."

When I reentered the living room, the boy had pocketed the tube of pills and sat on the couch, engrossed with the blank television. "Well, that's just fucking dandy." Hilarity sounded like a marching bagpipe band playing KISS.

After an hour, I dragged Elijah into my car and drove to Golden Oaks. As I predicted, not a single vehicle sat outside of Cass's mansion. When I walked inside, I set the marijuana on the table for her to admire. Before now, even I had never seen so much in one place.

"You brought. Oh, I'm so happy, I could—"

She paused, her breathing heavy. Her lips floating closer. The kiss sounded like fireworks and tasted just like that—a kiss. Wet and sweet and passionately tongue-tied. We broke apart, and I was sucked back into reality. I kissed her, and she kissed me, out of gratitude or—something more. My entire body tingled with anticipation. I was totally going to get laid tonight.

"Blaine, what's wrong with this kid?"

Sometimes, when someone absolutely breathtaking kisses you, you forget that other people even exist. In Elijah's defense, a lot of people probably often forgot about his existence, I would bet, including his own family. He was so quiet and meek he did not attract any unnecessary attention to himself.

"Oh, you're going to love this. Remember this guy? Elijah Rodriguez. Meet him again, new and improved. This time, higher than a comet." On the ride over, I had watched him push at least four pills through his trembling lips. Finally, he was getting the right idea. Tonight would be absolutely fantastic with this kid around, tweaking out. Though I feared he would pass out before the party even started.

We stood there for a moment, all three of us eyeing each other. I wanted badly to kiss her again, throw her over my shoulder, and carry her off to bed caveman-style. But there were still hours of polite party talk to slough through before we could shed our clothes, so instead I set about placing the weed in salsa bowls. Like the fucking Martha Stewart of drugs.

⇥ ⇤

As the paragon of animals, we had reached the stage in evolution where we had become so perfect, so capable of angelic activities with endless faculties, that we needed to ingest poisons to slow down evolution. As humans, we were required to now rewind our progress. Over generations, we had grown too complacent in making informed decisions, so we drank and smoked so that we could return to our animalistic roots.

I stubbed out the last of the third joint in Cass's fancy glass ashtray, and I could feel myself drifting. Shooting off in the night, spinning and spinning. What a fantastic feeling. Had there been more? Had I said more? Had we danced? Did I say anything the entire night or simply sit there, breathing smoke?

The night flew by too quickly, all raised bottles and laughing faces, rushing, rushing, rushing like a ship plunging willingly down a whirlpool. Declin had stumbled around earlier, dressed as something—a robot in clunking metal, or, no, he looked more like a knight. Either way, he was an idiot: no one wore actual costumes to high-school Halloween parties.

Rain began to pour.

At some point, I glimpsed Elijah making a pyramid out of bottles. I fell into Cass finally. I kissed her neck on the couch, running my hand over her leg. She laughed, so drunk, so disoriented. I knew she wanted this too. I thought, Fuck Justin and his overcontrolling ass, because she's mine now.

We wandered onto the porch. "Blaine, Blaine, we need to talk."

I brushed my face against her cheek, trying to kiss her again, but she turned away. "No, I'm serious."

138

"What?"

"We're out of drugs," she said. "Can we get more?"

"Oh—that. How?"

"Well, apparently the wind from this storm was so strong, the marijuana was blown into the yard. No one has been able to find it."

"In a second we'll go out and get more—don't I—I should be thanked for—well, my services." We collapsed onto the swinging seat on her porch, and I snaked my hand down her dress. My right hand rested between her breasts, and I could count time to her thumping heart. Being turned on felt a lot like floating into space without a suit on, suffocating while getting the purest view of the entire earth anyone had ever had before.

"I don't want—"

"It's more than that. I don't just want sex, though—while I'm high, let's make it clear I want sex—but I want more. I want love. I mean, I want you." I didn't know what I was saying, words spilling out forcibly like drunk vomit.

Joy leaked out of her eyes. "I want to tell you something, but promise not to get mad." I nodded. "I don't think you know what you're doing, and neither do I."

"Why?"

"You're crazy. So am I. You think if you fuck enough girls, you'll be happy. It's pathetic. Your life will make sense if you fuck this girl or that one. If you get drunk tonight or the next or the next. Me, I'm worse. Under the impression that I can marry into happiness, piggyback into the promised land with some jock loser. Who the fuck thought up that sick joke? I've been going around, thinking—the next dress I buy, I'll be happy. Everything will be perfect. Everyone will like me and love me, and I'll never be lonely. Don't you realize it never works out that way?"

Part of me felt immensely offended and the other part impressed. "That's harsh. At least you see through all the bullshit."

"Maybe. Sorry to go off like that. I'm just—I'm riled up about everything going on. This party is a joke too. Maybe it was a mistake."

I leaned in and tried to kiss her, instead grazing her cheeks with my lips, but somehow, I still felt pretty damn romantic. "Maybe some good will come of this, you know? Maybe if we—well, we'll see. Keep drinking. We can see." She smiled at that.

The door crashed open, and Declin, apparently drunk, stumbled through the door. "Good," Cass announced. "We need to go get those drugs, don't we?"

Through a blurred series of events, I eventually sat in the backseat of Cass's car with Aron. Declin drove, Cass beside him. I tried to tell Declin why we needed more drugs, though I did not exactly know myself, requiring me to embellish on some details.

Downtown flashed by us, and I directed with astute commands, "The second left past that building that is slightly taller than that other red building, the one with the awning. No, there!"

After leaving downtown, it was a smooth drive to the Pepper Plantation. Everyone in town called it that, even the Peppers, a queer bunch of people who had some serious drug connections. I bought green from a shady Pepper named Dylan who had an unsightly scar that stretched from his forehead to his chin. With such facial damage completing a truly creepy look, Dylan could do nothing but illegal work. His very face screamed sinister.

After a few minutes, we drove past a wall of trees. Each sounded like low tuba notes, playing the *Jaws* theme song. We pulled into a clearing, quiet and dark except for the torrential rain. I climbed out, trying to orientate myself. Dylan lived alone in a mobile home sporting a yellow pop-out awning. After half crawling through a brush, I spotted it leaning against a tall oak.

I could hear dogs barking savagely in the distance. The forest opened up its cragged mouth and swallowed the trailer whole.

Damn, I thought. Where am I? The drugs, the drugs, the drugs. Shit, shit, shit. Soon, I collapsed before the trailer, on my knees— a desperate penitent. Praying, Our Drug, who art in this trailer, hallowed be thy name, give us this day our daily highs and forgive us our stupidity as we forgive the stupidity of others.

The door opened. "Dylan, it appears you have a visitor." A boy helped me to my feet and slapped me lightly. "Are you OK?"

He wore black pants and a black V-neck, his face shining in the absolute darkness. "Cain," shouted Dylan from inside, "who is it?"

"My name is Blaine. Dylan knows me. I need to buy drugs."

The boy named Cain laughed at that and then let me drop. I crumpled against the trailer, staring dumbly at the sky. "Dylan, he says he wants to buy drugs. Don't worry—I've got him under control." Suddenly he looked at me more closely. "We've met before, haven't we?"

"I—I don't know."

"Yes, at Exeter. You came to visit the school. Well, that's interesting."

I just nodded, not knowing what to say.

Cain disappeared into the trailer and came out a moment later with a brown paper bag. "Three hundred for this batch."

"All right." Unthinking, I dug bills from my wallet and handed them over. I only needed to make it back to the car, then back to Cass's, and then into Cass's bed. I imagined what she'd look like naked.

"You should not have woken up Dylan, kid. You'd better scram."

I took the bag from him, thanked him, and sprinted back to the car. My clothes were soaked.

"What did you get?" Cass snatched the bag away, opening it. She made a strange face and then closed the bag again, handing it back.

We pulled out onto the main road again.

"I think he was angry about being woken up. But I swear that whole family is crazy. I suppose that's a good asset, though, for a drug dealer. But still, damn. The whole family is crazier than those fucking dog whisperers on TV. You know the—what the hell?" What was I even saying?

"Dammit," Declin said. "Why can't he turn off those lights?"

Behind us, bright lights flashed through the back windshield.

"Fucking idiot." I rolled down the window, propped myself on the sill, and leaned halfway out, screaming, "Fucking idiot!"

We raced down the dirt road, and the truck behind us flashed his lights, bright, low, off, bright, low, off. Like a bastardized Morse code.

Twisting around: "Who the fuck keeps flashing their lights? Drive faster."

I tapped Declin's shoulder, and he sped up. If I were not too fucked up to drive, I would be gunning near a hundred. When we finally reached the outskirts of town, we stopped. A screech. The truck behind us barely stopped short of our bumper.

Cass turned around, sticking up her middle finger. "What is wrong with this asshole? Get out of here."

The truck door opened.

Our car roared, lurching forward. We sped through downtown, a comet through the night.

The truck's light flashed on and off. The driver beeped his horn. I rolled down the window again and yelled, "Fuck you." The driver revved the engine. Cass slumped down in her seat, crossing her arms.

Declin peeked through the rearview mirror and whipped his head around. Rain slapped the windshield.

I punched his shoulder. "Look at the road, idiot." We turned a corner, but as soon as we flipped on the signal light, the truck's signal flashed also. "He's following us." Our car sped forward, and I held on to Cass's shoulder, howling. "Declin, the light. It's yellow. Stop, stop." Declin began to slam on his breaks. "No, we can lose him. Go, go, go."

The light flashed red. Declin floored the car. A flash of lights from the side. I glimpsed the truck, some heavy eighteen-wheeler, before I heard its horn. It rattled toward us, daunting and speeding. The sound of metal on metal made my head explode, every sense screaming brashly.

Such an intrusive, screeching sound.

Flashes of white.

Cayenne peppers shoved in my nostrils.

White-lemon Italian ice.

Blood. The taste of blood.

CHAPTER 15

THE JOURNAL OF ELIJAH RODRIGUEZ

October 31

I am writing this because it is my last will and testament. Please, if my parents find this, don't read it, and if you do read it, don't share it with anybody. Especially do not read it aloud at my funeral. I'm not sure I could ever survive that.

My insides burn like there's a sparkler fizzling out in my gut.

Just because I died of a drug overdose, I'm not a bad person. It wasn't my fault. If you're looking for anyone to blame for this tragedy, blame a boy named Blaine.

Because he handed me an orange tube and said, "Here, hold on to this." I held the bottle of pills gingerly, weighing it in my hands as if it were a bomb. "Go ahead. Try one."

To be fair, he asked me to try just one, not six. Or eight. Or however many I swallowed down, slipping further into oblivion. I apologize because I swear I'm normally more eloquent than this, but when death comes barking at your door, it's not easy to even hold a pen.

I might die. My insides hurt so bad, I'm sure I might die.

Not the worst death, I know. Still, it seems pretty nasty. I could have tripped in the forest and impaled myself on a rogue stick. Instead, I'll curl up on the floor of my bedroom, waiting to fall asleep, and then choke on my vomit. I would prefer lying in pine needles, a stick through my gut, trying to figure out how to reassemble my intestines, rather than my intestines waging war against my failing senses.

I would prefer to be crushed by an ice-cream truck, the strawberry ice cream melting and mixing with my blood in the cracks in the asphalt or hit by a projectile exploding piece of toilet. That would be a whopper of a death. It's only that drugs are not the most glorious reason to die—Elvis died of an overdose, didn't he? Of course there are worse ways to die, but given a choice, I'd choose something my dad would not be totally pissed about.

Maybe I need to explain further, just in case.

Start at the beginning.

⊷⊶

Perhaps you can also trace this blame back to Aron, who's a senior. He's this mixed kid who is intensely talented at soccer. He invited me to Cass's Halloween party, which is where I took the drugs in the first place. Or you could blame Cass for throwing a party that might inspire nonpartygoers like me to sample random pills from an orange tube.

Both of Cass's parents work for this big radio station, which is probably why they allow her to wear a nose ring and to have her name tattooed across her back. My parents are not radio jockeys like Cass's, so I could not wear a nose ring even if I wanted one. My dad said nose rings make you look like a homosexual. How he said it was exactly like that, in a matter-of-fact way, not so much derision as observation.

Sitting upstairs on my bed, I can hear them both snoring in unison; they sound like a euphonium duet, which is strange because they always complained about the other's snoring, refusing to admit to each other their own poor sleeping habits.

My father Robert worked as a police officer. He worked the night shift, running down drunk drivers and responding to calls at homes, telling kids to turn down music or go inside their houses. Often, during the daytime, we could not make much noise, but on Saturday night, they're both home.

Before the party, I was supposed to go to Blaine's house, which is where he gave me the pills, but before I went to Blaine's house, I went to play *Dragon Sphere*. Yesterday was a Saturday.

Dragon Sphere, Quentin, is probably the best game ever invented—like *Dungeons & Dragons* but with more dragons. We all went to Nick's house and sat around a board, rolling dice. Then Nick would draw a card with a scenario we would have to solve. For example, this afternoon, while crossing Weltschmire's Pass, an earthquake caused rocks to fall upon our crew, crushing much of our food supply and trapping us in the ravine.

Nick acted as the dragon master; his job was to make up extra rules and judge what we could or could not do. Though I'm not sure *Dragon Sphere* required increased complexity, the dragon master also made the scenarios more difficult. "Adversity teaches the mind," the dragon master would say. Naturally, he added dragons.

"Maybe we can use the boulders as cover," I suggested. "That way, while we figure out a plan, we won't get scorched by fire."

"Good plan, but the boulders aren't big enough to deflect the flame."

Josh rubbed his chin, on which he was beginning to grow a goatee. He tipped his fedora back on his head, which made him look really cool, and said, "Maybe we can try climbing over the rocks."

"The rocks have built a wall too steep to climb. If you do manage to climb up, the dragon will burn you alive. It's flying overhead, waiting for you to starve so it can cook you with its breath and have a nice snack."

Greg sighed. "Well, what if we fight the dragon and then double back? We left that village of elves not long ago, so maybe we can go back and restock on food."

The dragon master smiled, and, it seemed to me, his teeth were almost pointed. "But you have no more gold either. Not that it matters. This dragon burned down that village and—"

"OK, well, you can go fuck yourself." Greg stood up and started to leave.

"You can't leave, Devil Dwarf. You're stuck in a ravine."

Greg marched through the house. "We're not in a ravine. We're in your fucking basement, and it's not like you even have any Hot Pockets left. You're too lazy to even order pizza. That would help us in that ravine, if that dragon could pick up a pepperoni pizza. You're the worst dragon master ever. There are always dragons."

"In *Dragon Sphere*, there's bound to be dragons."

"Not in every single scenario, Nick."

"Please, call me Dragon Master."

"I'm not calling you fucking Dragon Master, you freak." Greg stormed out the house.

Josh also stood up, gesturing. "I'm sorry about that, Dragon Master. He's new to the game, you know. He doesn't—"

The Dragon Master cut Josh off. "It's fine, really. Some of us can think on a higher plane than others. Never allow your friend to return to this realm, and all will be well."

"Of course, Dragon Master. I think he was just a little bit pissed off about being a dwarf."

When you first start playing *Dragon Spheres* (I started playing eight months ago, while Josh and the Dragon Master have been playing since the game's inception), you choose what character you will be. Simply shuffle the cards and pick them up until you find a creature card. Usually these are added to scenarios to make them harder, but at first, you use them to figure out your identity. Of course, most creatures have special abilities. I am a wizard, level three, so I can at least use some elementary spells. Josh is a woods elf, and Greg was a devil dwarf.

"Well, if you die," said the Dragon Master, "you'll have to start this mission over."

"Can I use a water spell to erode the rocks in our paths? Just enough to carve out a passage so we can go under the rock pile instead of over? Josh can use his camouflaging charm to make us blend in with the rocks, and we can escape from here."

The Dragon Master paused, either furious or exhilarated. "I will allow this."

When we finished the game (we died after Josh stepped on a magical land mine that caused lava to erupt from the earth and scorch us alive), Josh went home, and I asked the Dragon Master whether he could drive me to a party.

In the car, he said, "A party? I guess you can't hang out with a bunch of losers like us, huh?" He chuckled but seemed to be only half-kidding. I wondered if he had ever been invited to any parties.

"No, it's just—"

"I understand. I went to a lot of parties back in high school as well. We did drugs and drank, yes. We did everything you did. In fact, you—you remind me a bit of myself as I was back in high school. You're smart. That idea about erosion—that was a good move. Perhaps one day you will be a dragon master too."

I shrugged. "I'm not sure because I guess I still have a lot to learn, you know?"

"Of course. It's not the easiest task in the world to play God."

He halted in front of Blaine's house, and Blaine walked out toward us. "Be careful whom you befriend, Blue Wizard. Some people will use you just because they think they can."

His words make some sense now.

Fast-forward through an hour of sitting around Blaine's house, after he handed me the drugs. I took two because at first I thought it was a candy. Then, after realizing they were pills, I wondered what they might do. I had never taken drugs before, and at least these were only pills, so they didn't seem so bad. I mean, if people took them because they needed them, they wouldn't kill me, right? I took another because the first didn't do anything.

By the time we began driving to Cass's, I felt slightly light-headed.

I'm a junior, I think I should mention, because Aron and Blaine are both seniors. No one really suspects me to be hanging out with seniors.

No one really expects me to do anything on a Friday night, because no one expects much of anything from me. My parents expect good grades, but it's not like anyone else cares.

Take Justin Ferrara for example—he's our quarterback. People expect things from him. On a Friday night, Justin does not question whether or not he will walk onto the football field to throw a football. He never wonders whether he should go to practice or not; it's his routine. His routine: to walk onto the field with the white lights blazing down. The war paint on his face already peeling. The grass crunching beneath his tread. Clutching a football in his right hand, his fingers bent around the frayed white laces. A routine.

No one asks Justin whether or not he would like to play football either. It's expected that he will arrive at practice and run onto the field at games, bursting violently through the banners reconstructed each Friday afternoon by a dedicated cheering committee. Every Friday night, he bursts through, barreling through the tunnel of band students who stand with trumpets pointed to the darkening sky, clarinets poking toward the ground. He runs, because he is expected to run. He runs, because the crowd expects him to run. He also does not question the necessity to run.

To arrive every Friday night, score touchdowns, win the game. His parents expect him to win a major football scholarship at a prestigious school. And maybe to you that sounds monotonous. But glory once a week? That sounds like a pretty solid routine to me. I would like for people to expect me to triumph.

I guess I'm still alive, so maybe I should tell you about the party. The pills have maybe calmed down, because I can see everything almost clearly. The visions died away.

⇒╬⇒

Golden Oaks simply feels like a richer place than the suburbs where we live, which is strange, considering we are only separated by a wall. The grass here makes our lawns looked sunburned. The golden granite holds the promise of heaven. Each bedroom light is a beacon to divine loneliness.

I popped another pill, for good measure. They were small circular pills that tasted sour if you kept them in your mouth too long. You had to swallow quickly before the pill turned bitter.

After waiting at Cass's house for maybe an hour, I went outside. When I climbed back onto the front porch, I saw that more people had slipped inside via the back entrance and garage.

I hovered for a few minutes in the doorway, where we could see that the party buzzed inside. I mean *buzzed*, because that's what it seemed to do: music shook the floor; vibrations trembled through the air around us. Writhing bodies in the next room erupted with those violent vibrations, those gleeful undulations of teenage ecstasy. I'm not sure if the pills had yet kicked in, but it sure seemed like it. Every breath was conscious, every step a stumble.

I guess I could describe the party as a rave, but Blaine said that you need better drugs for a rave, and my dad said only homosexuals go to raves. Immediately, Blaine pushed me into the mob of dancers, and, well—I danced. I danced, and the bottle of pills rattled in my pockets, but we danced to that too, because it sounded like maracas.

I liked the way we danced, because it gave us a sense of purpose—we were all one entity, swarming and leaping and shaking our bodies.

And the great thing about it was that everyone was drunk. And not mean drunk like in the movies when someone's dad hits a kid. But nice drunk, friendly drunk. So drunk or stoned that it didn't matter how we danced, so we could dance anyway we wanted, flail about, shake our hips, swing our hair around our scalps, twist our feet, do the robot, dance like our parents, or jump up and down. Because I don't really know how to dance, I pushed myself into people, being jostled by bodies. Except I didn't know what to do with my hands, rather than hold them near my chest or above my head. Otherwise, they kept swatting against girls, and I don't think the girls noticed, which made me feel even worse. And being so close together, well, people kept accidentally swiping my crotch. It's embarrassing, but the entire time, I was turned on.

If you are reading this because you're from the future and found this, I should explain that *turned on* means sexually aroused. I guess I shouldn't use so much slang.

I was dancing with Cass. As I came to, I realized that I was, in fact, dancing with Cass. She pressed herself up against me, which was awkward at first, but then I put my hands on her hips; somehow, it was all right. I should probably explain that Cass is the most beautiful girl I have ever met, and the hippest too. Only, I don't think she even knows that my genitals were practically resting on her name tattoo. Moments later, she stumbled into the arms of some other guy.

This was when I began feeling very strange, because I had taken maybe six pills. And the room started spinning. I walked into the kitchen where there was a pyramid of vodka bottles stacked on the counter and an ice chest full of beer. Sitting down on a stool, I began drinking one of the beers, but it tasted like what urine might taste like if refrigerated.

No one was in the kitchen. Everyone danced in the living room. And I strayed, alone with a can of fizzing beer that I wanted to pour down the sink, except it seemed like too much of a waste.

I may have sat there an hour. Things began to get soft, like a cloud had sidled into the room. And in the cloud, things didn't make sense.

I found myself on the ceiling. Drafty up there, the fan blades spinning so close. The ripples in the ceiling kept moving above or beneath me—whichever.

I egg dropped—*thud*—to the hard tile, so I crawled to the plush carpet. I lay on the outer orbit of the dancing circles. Stroking the carpet as I lay. Crippled, curling up like an anorexic fist. Crippled, my abdomen writhing like a yoga trainer on speed. Crippled, realizing I was dying.

Looking back, I can't even tell you how many I took, the events now presented with such a circular chronology. Blaine disappeared at some point that evening, swallowed whole by the drunken masses.

Tiny white circles in the palm of my hand. Pop. Swallow before they get too bitter.

Here in my bedroom, there are still a couple rattling on my floor, possessed by some wicked spirit to keep rolling back and forth. A floor pendulum, the bottle rolling back and forth. Overdose. I thought that maybe when I died, it'd be better than this. Only, I can't really be dying. I just thought so before. I feel a little better now, I admit.

I walked home somehow, after leaving the house and I think throwing up in Cass's front yard. All those lights that were on before were now put out like smoking campfires started by lonely cowboys. I caught myself a few times as I looked for the wall, but finally I found a place where the branches of a tree allowed me to climb over it—*thud*—down across the other side, staring straight up into the sky, at the stars. Maybe that was when I came to terms with my mortality.

It began to rain then, and somehow I dragged myself home, wondering whether I could call the Dragon Master to pick me up this late. Drops of water streamed down my face, and I could taste the sky.

Now I am home and writing this journal entry and feeling sort of stupid. I write a lot of things, because it helps me make sense of everything I think.

I write poetry sometimes, when I'm feeling very serious. Somewhere, I read that it helps relate all of your problems, but for me, it just makes them seem even less tangible. Because sometimes I can't seem to put anything into words. So instead of writing about how I feel, I write about something else.

But I also read that I need to write something real about myself, that writing the opposite of how I feel is just like lying. That's why I started this journal in the first place. Mind you, it's not a diary but a journal, because my dad said only homosexuals write in diaries. But Ernest Hemingway wrote a journal, and he's certainly not homosexual because he hunted quite a lot. And not just deer or doves like people do here, but elephants and lions and rhinoceroses. Downtown, they hold these monthly poetry readings, but I have never gone, because I don't really think what

I write is good enough. It's confusing even for me, so I guess no one would even get it.

My father shuffled in late tonight, after responding to a call. Even on Saturday nights, called out to deal with some drunk-driving accident. I could hear them talking earlier, but I was too tired to listen.

Maybe I won't die. Maybe I might go to sleep.

CHAPTER 16

DECLIN OSTRANDER

Even with seven months to go, we already anticipated summer. For the Lickskillet kids, summer meant no responsibilities and preparing to go to college. For me, I wasn't sure what that meant. School days became a series of pointless conversations that seemed to obscure rather than highlight the facts. Class became circus for highly opinionated students, the teachers acting as impartial referees who refused to deny even the strangest, most backward ideas for fear of being sacked.

"Global warming?" our biology teacher said, her face blanching. "Well, there is an argument for and against that. What do you think?"

To encourage everyone to have their own opinion, you were not supposed to oppress them with yours. The only way to be truly open-minded was to not think at all. A few kids threw around theories that sounded patently untrue, and then the teacher shrugged and labeled the theme "too complicated to fully appreciate."

In American History, a comment about legalizing marijuana sparked an hour-long debate, and when we asked our faux-Rastafarian teacher to decide the battle, he swallowed and dropped the chalk. "Well, I mean, there are—well, there are two sides to every argument. You've got to realize that. And I mean, no one side is right. So I suppose you must look at both sides and decide for yourself."

During the second quarter of biology when Ms. Schall turned the page with trepidation and then announced that we would be discussing Charles Darwin's theory of evolution, someone from the back whispered, "My dad says evolution is bullshit."

"Well," said Pepper, "it's not. Not Darwin's theory anyways. He wasn't the one that said we evolved from monkeys. In fact, he promoted natural selection. The notion of one species turning into another, like a ladder, is ridiculous. That's not how evolution works."

"Still bullshit."

"Stop saying that," barked Ms. Schall, who held a dry-erase marker with incredible concentration, as if predicting its supposed trajectory toward Blaine's head. "We're going to discuss this—like the adults we all are. Mr. Ostrander, what do you think?"

"I—I don't know. I'm not really sure."

"How can you not have an opinion?"

"It's just that I can't really make up my mind. About Darwin, I mean—natural selection. I guess it makes sense. What's your opinion?"

"Frankly, I'm not sure. The school wants me to remind you that evolution is only a theory...or maybe that theories mean something. Anthony, your hand is up?"

"Well, Darwin was a Satan worshipper. The devil told him all this science crap to confuse us."

"Darwin was a self-proclaimed Christian, actually. Maybe we should talk about his theory."

"But I don't want to. I don't really care."

"We didn't come from monkeys, I heard," said another girl. "I heard we came from fish. Like, we used to have gills, and then we grew legs, and then we were cavemen."

"Adam and Eve were not goldfish," someone else said.

"Well, you could be wrong."

"No, you're so wrong. Just shut up. Just—seriously, shut up. If you're going to say something that stupid, then just shut the hell up."

"I told you—don't say that. And *no one* is wrong."

Pepper's hand shot up. "How can no one be wrong? I mean, either Adam and Eve were goldfish, or they weren't. They couldn't both be *and* not be goldfish. Only one person can really be right."

Ms. Schall shook her head again. "No one is wrong."

※＋＋※

Barnaby Rutgers sat on our couch, his legs crossed too high up the thigh to be comfortable. My father bustled in with a tray of iced tea. Strange, since he never drank tea. I wasn't even sure he was capable of making it. To make proper iced sweet tea, I was under the impression one needed some special southern grandmother voodoo, or else its drinkers would make the same polite but disgusted face Rutgers made upon drinking that indicated he had just sipped Yankee poison.

"This is Barnaby Rutgers, Declin, head of the New Citizens Welcome Committee."

"Sorry it took so long to come see you. We have quite a number of new citizens who have moved here in the past months. That's why the committee was made—to make sure people migrating to our beautiful town would feel welcome. In fact, Francis Jameson founded it—how progressive. Do you feel welcome?"

Welcome? I maybe didn't feel particularly *un*welcome.

"Yes, well, I'm very busy. I haven't been able to enjoy the town as much as I would have liked to. I hear you have the largest collection of unique garden gnomes in the world."

"Very happy to say that, yes." Every word Rutgers spoke seemed slathered in barbecue sauce. "Though Portland is trying to beat that record for some damned reason. But you know, I bet we'll win out in the end. Always do. I think you'll come to find that Lickskilletans have a few core values: hard work, dedication, and justice."

"Yes, well, that's what I'm here for. Justice," my father said.

My father could drone for hours about how Klan members were just like normal people or how the Knights were not racist so much as closed-minded, how they worked hard and deserved respect just as much as any other Americans. But then again, he had won very few court cases for these groups.

"Yes, well, Francis Jameson needs that. Justice, I mean. The way he died was not only cruel but also unjust. And the tragedy hurts the image of this town. Did you know that, in the past decade, the population of this town has doubled? People from up north have wised up and moved south. Cheaper gas and cheaper taxes. Nice quiet towns like Lickskillet to retire in, not that Lickskillet is quite that quiet anymore. A body up in a tree—that could scare away people who want to move here—who might make this town better.

"And Mr. Ostrander? I'm afraid I'm not just working closely with the prosecution. I am the prosecution."

"Really? Yes, well, I agree about Lickskillet being—"

"You wouldn't be saying that Matthew Pepper is actually guilty, no? I mean, hell, I figure his whole family is crooked. I'm not saying he's guilty. As far as I'm concerned, he's not. Only, we do need to flesh out the details of what happened that night. For your sake and his, maybe you're right." He smiled. "So, I'm not here as a lawyer. I'm here to make you feel at home, like you can come to me for anything you need. How do you like the town so far?"

"Well, I've only seen the inside of the courthouse. I think Declin has been pretty impressed with the school. Right, Declin?"

I nodded my head.

"Well, I think everyone welcomes you. Most people, anyways. Before you came, we had a bit of a problem with an arsonist. Burned down one of the town's most historic buildings."

My father, uncomfortable, smiled. "I heard about that when I arrived. That must have been a shame. I'm a sucker for historic buildings."

"Whoever burned it down also set a cross aflame—not implying anything here, but you do know that the Klan burns crosses, not that the Klan burned this particular one. Not that anyone here in town is connected to the Klan. There was something written on the hillside, burned into the grass.

"Of course we got rid of it—so unsightly. Only, I can't help but think maybe it had to do with your coming. As if certain people in the community—maybe they, being a more proactive people than me, despised what you stood for. For the Knights, I mean—and perhaps they wrote the message if not the Klan themselves. It does seem rather coincidental that this all happened a week before you arrived."

I remembered that first week at school, when some kids had whispered about the haunted house burning down. Before being torched, the residence served as a local landmark and public drinking spot. Aron and Blaine even claimed to have been in the house when it burned down, though most people did not believe them. With our generation, the truth was hardly ever the real truth.

"The message said, 'Get out of our town.' Spooky, ain't it?"

My father nodded frantically: yes, yes, yes, of course, yes. He agreed with everything silently so he could never be taken for his word. "Well, every town has good and bad people."

Rutgers shook his head. "There are no good or bad people, Mr. Ostrander. Only people."

"Yes, of course. Yes, yes." I did not understand why my father seemed so nervous next to this man who looked like an insect.

"I used to live here. Not *here* here, in this house, but in this area. My parents owned a house out in the country, secluded without being too far away. We used to play in the woods behind my house. We pretended the trees were so many things. Now it's just half a suburb."

"Towns change. Life changes. Strange, isn't it?"

"Yes, well, thank you for the exquisite tea. I must go now. Like I said, a lot of new residents moved in recently."

With a curt handshake, Rutgers walked stiffly back to his car and drove away.

Because the house made me claustrophobic, as if I were a mouse navigating a maze. I launched out the door and walked down the street. My father sat at the kitchen table, reading over papers with font so small it should have been illegal. The Halloween party was tonight, which meant seeing Cass.

Cass would stand there and drink and talk with us. But she never spoke directly with me, not since the night we spent together near the Red Hole, where I felt maybe I had made a connection. Whatever had been built faded with each new conversation, like she was getting bored with me. Maybe she was. Maybe I had no more personality than what I put on. I couldn't fake being good at talking to girls. Somehow, Cass no longer looked at me as romantically viable—even after she broke up with Justin. Afterward, she'd grown closer to Blaine. Now they both treated me like the weaker species, the docile koala who might have been cute but never sexy. Maybe I had tried too hard, pursued Cass too strongly, and now she had mired my efforts in the friend zone.

Once downtown, I spotted the black-scorched hill where a purportedly haunted house once stood. All these people who would come to the party might have once ventured there, all these teens with the same story. The default childhood experience. In their midst, I felt unbearably isolated like a caveman floating in an iceberg for centuries, melting into existence among earbud-wearing hipsters. An anachronism. A misquoted line from a movie that was not well known. But this didn't make me unique, just alone.

I thought of Aron, Blaine, Cass, and even Elijah. They reacted to each other in practiced ways, conditioned to assume certain roles. Where had they learned this sense of place and identity? Who had established these characters in this theater production that was my life, me an absurdist main character, the stage spinning around me? Scenery rushing by, all the characters fleeting and minor and forgettable. Even the main character had no significant lines. Wearing a different mask during each act. Who were these ghosts that haunted my life, these people whose names I would not remember in six months?

They were the eternal teenagers. All that came before and all that followed merely derivatives of what they were. Generations of shadows.

The teenagers of this town were addicted to upholding the illusion of perpetual ecstasy, youth that would never fade. Cass surprised me most of all, becoming rapturously drunk on weekends and dancing at four in the morning with abandon and then appearing on Sunday with perfect makeup, attentive and awake, her image and southern-belle manners wholly intact.

But the semirural South offered little alternatives to the young, restless soul, to the eternal teenager, and I would be drawn into this lifestyle by some inescapable, glazed-eyes gravity.

Most of the guests donned uncreative costumes thrown together from household clothes. Aron, in a red jersey, dressed as Ronaldo, the Manchester soccer player. I couldn't discern Charlotte's costume, which included a lacy black corset that thrust her breasts forward and a satin ribbon tied in a delicate knot around her neck. Others like Blaine wore plain clothes, while I felt ludicrous in clanking plastic armor and carrying a shield bearing a vague dragon insignia. After twenty minutes, I gave up continuously pushing up my visor and chucked the helmet into the bathroom.

I ambled tirelessly through the house, grimacing at the vast awkward silences that bloomed in my presence. Sitting down next to a girl in a massive peacock costume, looking equally depressed in her giant, fanning, glittering tail and intricate eye makeup, I pulled out my phone and pretended to text while instead playing Snake.

Finally, a black boy sat down near me, shuffling some white powder on the surface of his phone with the edge of his credit card. "You want any of this?"

"Um, I'm OK."

"It's not coke. Don't worry."

"I'll be fine." He took a long, exaggerated snort, just like Scarface would do, and he then he made a pained face. "You OK?"

"Fine. Just tastes like—like nasty is all. Tastes disgusting— shit drips down your throat. Do I know you from somewhere? I'm Cory." He promptly shook my hand.

"Probably not. I'm new here."

He shrugged. "Yeah? Well, yeah, me too. Just moved here at the beginning of the school year. Fucking weird place. I go to Exeter Academy, and those guys—well, at least they know how to party, but—they're crazy, you know?"

I nodded, as if I did know, and then he clapped me on the back as he disappeared back into the party.

<hr />

I stumbled onto the porch to find the sky coughing up gallons of water. Rain pooled in the front lawn and flowed up Cass's driveway. Cass and Blaine sat speaking quietly on the seat swing that hung from the edge of the porch. For a moment, I did not want to approach them, they looked so enrapt. So intense. Sitting so close, their noses almost kissing.

"Declin," Cass said. "You're not drunk, are you?"

Truthfully, I was not drunk, but I felt dizzy.

"Do you need something?"

"You can drive?"

"Drive *where?*"

By now, I should have been soaking in the party atmosphere, which should have invigorated me, electrified my lungs. But my lungs were a void, my senses dulled and burned-out.

As we piled into the car, Aron called to us. "Where are you headed out to?"

Cass explained, "We have to go buy some more weed. We're running low."

"You are a fucking gracious host—anyone ever told you that?" He seemed a little drunk, but not half so bad as Blaine, who mumbled to himself and preened his hair compulsively. "I need to get away from here. Charlotte's probably looking for me." He climbed into the back with Blaine, Cass up beside me in the passenger's seat.

As I weaved Cass's car through Golden Oaks, Blaine related to me how the wind from the storm had scattered the weed. All those drugs lay somewhere in Cass's front lawn, sopping wet and lost, while those porch-bound initiated, in Blaine's words, a great search for the elusive bud. They found nothing. He rambled like an Arkansas plain, and when he finished, I had left Golden Oaks and drove through downtown. I swear he paused more often than Christopher Walken either for dramatic effect or because he was too stoned.

We drove past midnight in a screaming storm to buy illegal drugs, accumulating bad omens.

Blaine's directions, though sparse and annoyingly incomprehensible, led us east out of downtown. The streets were flooded in places, and I slowed the car to ease through the shallow water.

This was a strange part of town I had never traveled to before. The houses shrank in size considerably, squeezing closer together. The windows were broken, missing, the wooden sides of houses unpainted, the roofs largely replaced by patches of frayed tarps. The ghettos stretched for about three miles, the houses sprawling farther and farther apart until they became trailers. The trailers sank deeper into pine forests until nothing remained but trees. Lickskillet hosted different communities immured in poverty, though black and white poverty was clearly divided, a now-defunct train track cutting through the ravine that physically separated the regions.

"We're almost there," Blaine announced as we passed a yellowed cow pasture with a small church at its far end. "Turn down this road, here."

The lonely road warranted no name, a dirt thread that weaved through the field into a thicket of trees. The pines rose before us ominously. Then, we saw the sign: Pepper Plantation.

"Is this where you buy drugs? It looks so—it's dead and creepy." Cass wrinkled her nose as we entered into the absolute darkness of the forest. Rusty trailers stood far back into the trees. This had been where my father had been going, this hillbilly hellhole.

"Don't worry. It's pretty legit. Park the car, Declin. I'll go find my man." I shut the car off but kept the keys in the ignition just in case. Blaine bolted from the car and sprinted away into the woods.

The trees were farther apart here as if they had been cleared away. Most of the residences were dark trailers so dilapidated that it did not appear anyone could live in them. I squinted through the rain, trying to make out shapes among the trees. I imagined Pepper from school holed up inside one of those strange, broken homes. In the distance was a larger house, its lights glowing dully. I itched to leave, but Blaine had not yet come back.

"Can you believe that people even live here?" asked Aron.

"It's so—sad, really." Cass did not sound sad, just drunk. She leaned against the window and stared pouting at the nearest trailer. The linoleum panels were black, perhaps from a lightning strike or unfinished paint job.

We spotted Blaine creeping through the dark, crouching and attempting to roll and failing to roll properly. When he clambered into the car breathless, I shot out of there, back through the woods, down the dirt road, and into town.

"What did you get?" Cass pawed at Blaine nervously. He produced a brown paper bag for Cass and leaned back sighing.

"I think he was angry about being woken up. But I swear that whole family is crazy. I suppose that's a good asset, though, for a drug dealer. But still, damn. The whole family is crazier than those fucking dog whisperers on TV. You know the—what the hell?"

I glanced into the rearview mirror. An almost blinding light illuminated the road behind us. "Dammit," I said. "Why can't he turn off those lights?"

"Fucking idiot," Blaine mumbled. Then, he rolled down the window to yell, "Fucking idiot!"

The truck behind us sped up, its front bumper dangerously close to our back. We sped, zipping down the dirt road, faster and faster—the truck accelerating behind us, some drunk asshole swerving and causing problems for us, both racing, racing, racing.

"Who the fuck keeps flashing their lights? Drive faster." Blaine karate chopped my shoulder.

Then I saw the stop sign and pumped the breaks. The truck halted too, inches behind us. Cass showed her middle finger through the rearview window. "What is wrong with this asshole? Get out of here."

As we waited for a split second, the door of the truck swung open. They were coming to get us. I stomped the pedal and sped off.

We reached the outskirts of the city, the truck driver zigzagging across the road. Blaine's weight shifted the car as he leaned out the windows, shouting curses. "Fuck you!"

Cass pulled him inside, and I stepped hard on the gas, reaching downtown. When we were past the first light, I looked behind us. Our pursuer was mere feet behind us, taunting us, blaring his horn and his radio, flashing his lights on and off and on and off—

"Is he following us? Who is that?"

Blaine punched me this time. "Look at the road, idiot."

Turning a corner—the first red light, green, yellow, red—

Cass screeched something I could not hear.

We were about to cross the line, but the light turned red, so instead of using the brakes, I pushed down hard on the gas—a light from our right, blinding. A horn, deeper. I knew: we would crash.

But then suddenly, we were clear, alive.

I stomped on the brakes, and the car swerved and turned. When we stopped, we faced the intersection. Metal crunched into metal, the eighteen-wheeler smashing the smaller truck, pushing it up onto the sidewalk. The truck that had followed us spun wildly, the chasse folding upon itself like a toppled house of cards, its roof a broken jaw, its metal sheared teeth. Everyone breathing raggedly, we stumbled out of the car.

Blaine: "Man, we need to get out of here. The cops will come. The cops."

The cab of the truck had caved in, and the glass lay strewn across the street. The eighteen-wheeler squealed to a stop a hundred yards away. Downtown stood quiet, ghostly. "Let's leave. Get in the car."

I numbly climbed in and started the car again, accelerating as we fled. "We're murderers."

"What the hell are you talking about?" Blaine beat my shoulder again. "I think I bit my tongue." He dabbed his fingers on his tongue and inspected them.

"We killed that guy."

"He was drunk, trying to run into us. That guy was crazy. He deserved that. There's no need for us to stick around. Let's just get back to the party, OK?"

Cass sank farther into her seat, shaking her head. "Cass," I said, "are you crying?"

She nodded mutely. "Get back to my house. We need to call an ambulance for him."

Blaine shook his head. "Hell no. We don't even know that guy. Probably a psycho serial killer."

"No, that was Justin's truck."

CHAPTER 17

ARON KING

We had been dating a little more than two months when she insisted we meet each other's families. What I felt for Charlotte wasn't exactly love because maybe love was too serious for what we were. Maybe there existed some relational affection between just liking someone and being in love. Whatever that feeling was, I felt it. But I never meant to actually care about her. Already I knew we would break up before summer.

A long, stiff tablecloth draped over our laps as we sat underneath the stark oaks circling the church. The church stood behind us, its white paint flecking and beams creaking each time a breeze shuttered through its walls. Inside, pews hewn of unpolished wood faced a sturdy oak podium over which hung a cedar cross. Once prayer broke, my family members sliced into the plastic wrappings covering potato salad, plates of ham, bowls of banana pudding, and heaps of turkey drumsticks.

She looked like a marshmallow dropped into a barrel of raisins. We were the dark backdrop of her white peculiarity.

Dark like it was Sunday, and we ate a lunch after church at a long picnic table. Dark like your grandma pinching your cheeks and then looking at your dad, saying, "He doesn't have that much black in him, does he?" Dark like "Hallelujah!" to what the preacher said, like two hundred years of bad history finally turning bright, like every clash and angry conflict embodied in a family member who sits at the table with his strange pale girlfriend. Dark the way I could never be.

Including the children of Aunt Georgina's first husband, a car salesman she divorced a long time ago to remarry a man who owned a strip club, I had seventeen cousins. My great-grandmother, who sat at the head of the table, presiding over the food and holding the power to single anyone out to give the blessing (which had a required time limit about at least three minutes), was skinny and frail with jowls that hung to the tops of her breasts, which hung to the tops of her knees. She looked like someone dipped a stick figure in tar, the goop still dripping when it dried. I nearly gagged thinking that she had birthed eight children.

Those children had had their own children, one being my father who had sex with my mother. They must have stayed together for a couple months, maybe even a year. But she got fed up putting up with me, my dad always being at work. She left us both, returned to Washington DC. I learned to take care of myself.

At church that Sunday morning, Charlotte had watched with a stupid, open mouth as my grandmother writhed on the floor. "What's happening?" she asked.

"She's possessed by the Holy Spirit," I said. This was not an unusual sight.

In the rapture of such glory and praise, some members of the congregation fell upon their knees, screaming sounds they claimed were other languages. They trapped themselves in the ecstasy of their fervor. The Holy Spirit of God clutched them, filling their blood with fire, making them dance and sing and scream. These seizure-dancing devotees of something they doubted, something they proved by going mad once a week. I always closed my eyes and braced myself for the same spirit to fill me, to throw me onto the floor, to overwhelm me and teach me the awe and power of God. But God never seemed to want to touch me, and I only stood by as the others lay claim to their beliefs.

Charlotte leaned across the table, clutching her fork dripping with creamed corn. "Are you any good at soccer? Aron is amazing at soccer. You know, he's the captain of the team."

Smiley grinned at this, his big, square, white teeth gleaming. "She's kidding right?" Charlotte had been at this for minutes, praising me for everything I did right, and Smiley, two years my senior, reacted by ignoring her and addressing me. "No real black guys play soccer. I did play ball in school, though."

I nodded, my lips pressed firmly together. My entire family played basketball: Smiley and his brother Austen, and our cousin Jason. Then there was me, a pariah of another sport. Charlotte kept munching on green bean casserole, oblivious to the stares that traveled down the table.

"Yeah, well, I don't. Actually, I have practice later today." A lie.

"Practice?" Smiley was incredulous. "Aron, it's Thanksgiving. Don't you want to spend it with us?"

"For a while."

As we stuffed our faces with gravy-drenched stuffing, I thought about how my family treated my father. When he first announced he was going to law school, they derided him—why did he want to be so much better than everyone else? But then he helped keep Joey out of jail, and they valued him. But they never forgave him for sleeping with a white woman, never for having me. The great embarrassment of the family.

"Charlotte, you ready?"

Still eating, she looked up at me and dropped her fork. "Fine."

Before driving away in my truck, we lined up to talk with my great-grandmother. She smiled with bright-pink gums and then tightened her arms around my waist before turning to Charlotte. Squinting up at her, she rested her thin fingers on Charlotte's hips. "She's a skinny one. Won't be able to make much chaps."

"Yes, I know."

Maybe she was blind, or blind enough, but she said nothing about Charlotte being white. Then we shuffled across the grass to a gravel lot where my family's vehicles stood in six uneven lines. Once I closed my door, Charlotte chuckled. "That was fucking awkward."

"I didn't ask you to come along. They're so—they're—"

"They don't respect you. I'm sorry."

She grasped my hand as I drove away and felt a stab of regret.

⟞⟝ ⟞⟝

I parked outside of my house. My father was supposed to visit the courthouse to review witness testimony with Barnaby Rutgers after the Thanksgiving lunch. "You ready to go inside?"

We had decided finally to do the deed—sex. Up until now, we had done everything but sex, and she told me again and again she didn't want to be used. She wanted to have sex with someone who cared about her. I didn't love her, but I felt something for her. I had invested time in this girl, and now she'd give me a reward. Relationships were ambiguous transactions in which each partner put forth something the other wanted. Ever since I met Charlotte, she wanted a boyfriend, and eventually we started dating. Since we started dating, I wanted to have sex, and now we climbed out of my truck and snuck inside the empty house.

When I pushed open the door, I called out, but no one was home. "Let's go upstairs. You sure you still want to do this?"

"If you want to, then I want to."

We crept upstairs and into my room, which smelled like dirt and legal paper. "Do we need a condom or something?" she asked.

I shook my head. "I don't know. I mean, you don't have any STDs, do you?"

"No," she said meekly.

"And you said you're taking birth control?"

"Yeah, of course."

"Then—then it won't matter. Don't—don't worry." I laughed to break the tension and stepped forward.

She pressed her hand against my face. "You think I'm pretty, don't you?"

"Yeah, sure."

"But—"

"OK, you're pretty. I'm just kidding." Already, I was thinking about the girls I could sleep with once we broke up.

We kissed, falling back onto the bed as we stripped off our clothes. "You sure your dad won't come home?"

"Just relax."

"I can't just relax. I—"

"Shhh. Don't worry." As I ran my hand through her hair, I felt something almost like affection for her, and it scared the shit out of me.

I stared at the ceiling and pulled the blankets to my neck as she dressed beside the bed. I didn't know what to say. She leaned over and kissed me on my forehead.

"That was nice," she said.

The whole evening felt rushed, felt anticlimactic. Maybe I was expecting something more. She didn't seem too impressed either.

When we first met, we had been passionate and wanting. Now we were only awkward. The sex had been too calculated, marked on our calendar like just another holiday to spend together.

"Are you OK?" she asked.

I didn't want to think of myself as the type of person who used girls for sex. After all, I dated her. I entertained her. I bought her ice-cream cones and movie tickets, and didn't I deserve something in return? Thinking like that made me a little sick.

"You're coming to meet my parents, right?"

I nodded vigorously. "Yeah, sure, whatever."

⇥ ⇤

On the way to soccer practice, I felt absolutely lousy, still like something illicit had happened. Maybe because of how she insisted on looking me in the eyes when we had sex, staring into my eyes as if that could form a bond and not simply awkwardness.

I shoved the images out of my mind to think about soccer. About dribbling and scoring and tackling and soccer balls, round, voluptuous soccer balls, and breasts, great bouncing breasts, and about how great it would be to fuck her again—about soccer.

Nothing made sense anymore.

Winter break drew nearer, which meant exams, which meant that feeling of a train crashing through your head. Soccer practice just made it worse, though I'd thought that after I made the state team things would quiet down. They didn't. Instead, the coach realized my talent and put me doubly to work. I already had enough troubles: Charlotte grew more clingy with each passing day.

The team was already running laps when I arrived. While I slipped on my cleats, the coach waved me over from his fabric throne. "You're late again. That's not something I'd expect from someone who is going to get a soccer scholarship. This season will be over after December, but then I guess you're on a school team? Yeah, and where are you going to college?"

"Well, I haven't thought about it. I've started applying to a lot of places, but—"

"Well, you're obviously running out of time. You have, what, two months to decide? You need to apply everywhere possible. And in soccer season, your money will pour in. Given it any thought?"

"Might stay in state. I do want to stay near. Anywhere in the South, I guess, is fine. I've applied to—"

"Applied anywhere up north? California?"

"Why would I? It's just more money."

"I figured since you're black, you're probably liberal. It'd do you some good to leave the South. Get to know some other cities. You know, I went to college in Chicago and loved it."

"Why would I want to go north just because—I'm not even—"

"Just think about that, OK, David?"

"OK, but—"

"Go run some laps. You're behind, and we have a game next Friday."

Charlotte asked to come over on Thursday; I had an essay due Friday that would never get done.

Charlotte wanted to have sex again. I wanted to have sex again. But I didn't want to see her, speak with her, and pretend to love her.

I ran behind the other boys, my chest pounding harder than normal, as if Thor's hammer were beating my rib cage into shape. Maybe the coach was right, and maybe I could leave the South. Were there decent soccer teams on the West Coast? I imagined there were better teams, sweltering in a heat that wasn't compressed by pine trees and racism. A heat that invoked palm trees and movie stars and fancy tropical drinks you could only order at the beach without seeming suspicious.

Perhaps the world orbited like that, not just turning and circling the sun consistently but also turning upside down. Every now and again, the earth trembled off its precarious axis, and the world would cast everything you've ever known into orbit. Black boys would play soccer. Football stars would fall into a coma.

I recalled the evening of the crash. One moment we were sailing drunk through the city, almost gleeful that some maniac was terrorizing us, but then the sobering crunch came. The truck flipping over, the windows shattering, the chasse tightening like someone's stomach when a person feels self-conscious.

The eighteen-wheeler screeched to a stop. Blaine was bleeding from his mouth, Cass was sobbing, and suddenly Declin was stomping on the gas to get away. We sped back to Cass's house.

So surreal, stumbling back into the party after witnessing the potential death of our school's star quarterback. Everyone still stumbled around or pretended to be friends, but we knew the horrid truth of death, and it would not leave us but instead cling to us like the scent of Mexican food rotting. Even Blaine, who had probably smoked enough weed to sustain the economy of Colombia for a year, seemed the soberest man in the world.

Charlotte disappeared, and I walked into the cold with Blaine. Cass shooed people out the door. We returned to find the house emptied out but still loud. Cass was shouting at someone in the basement. Declin had already slipped away. Blaine searched for Elijah, but maybe Elijah had already gone home. We drove back to our respective houses, and when we fell asleep, the town was still untouched by tragedy.

By the next morning, the newspaper had written up a two-page biography of Justin Ferrara, who had won far more athletic scholarships and accolades than I imagined. The driver of the eighteen-wheeler had not expected anyone to be driving, much less running red lights, while drunk. Blaine theorized that Justin had been watching, waiting. He had been stalking Cass out of loneliness, and seeing her with another man, he became enraged. Of course if Blaine meant him or—well, I did not know.

Cass took it particularly hard and visited Justin in the hospital nearly every day. Her fault, she kept saying, as if these were magic words. She was responsible for Justin following us, for getting too drunk to think right, and for getting into that crash. He had broken many bones, fractured three ribs, and possibly sustained brain damage. The doctors would know the extent of his injuries when he woke up, if he woke up. And if he woke, what would he tell them? That we had lured him through the intersection, that we had forced him to speed drunkenly past that white line?

For days, we were numb, not speaking. But we had gotten used to the idea of sharing this tragedy.

I pushed my body, my legs pumping harder, my feet moving faster. My breathing building, each inhale a crushing tidal wave of air. My heart pounded. I needed this, to think and to not think at the same time. I needed too much, but most of all to right the world, to turn it right side up and make it make sense once again.

Maybe I needed to tell her the truth, that I never lover her or meant to hurt her. I only wanted to express that I had not known what I was doing at that party in the summer.

I needed to find a way to break up with Charlotte.

I remembered being in bed with her, her body heaving beneath me. I closed my eyes and pressed my lips against her neck, pretending to be floating in space. Pretending that we were both someone else, both strangers, and I was not even present. Just breathing and sighing and sliding against her.

I could push myself harder, to run faster, to breathe with more purpose. Breathing in and out though each rush of air was a bulldozer pureeing my heart.

In the aftermath of the accident, the night kept us together. After the accident, the night tore us apart.

"Aren't you excited for winter break? I'm excited as hell. I mean, won't we be partying? What about New Year's? That should be a lot of fun, don't you think?" Declin grasped desperately to start a conversation among the dead. "At my old school, this one time at this party—"

"No one cares, Declin." Blaine sighed. "I mean, you can just stop going on and on with this bullshit. You're pathetic."

"I—what are you talking about?"

"What am I—look, I don't give a shit about you and your fucking girlfriend and your fucking old friends. If you liked them so much and if they were so much fun, why didn't you stay in California or Wisconsin or wherever it is you're from? Not that anyone can believe half the things you say—it's all a bunch of bull." Blaine appeared especially bedraggled, his eyes drooping and his face pale. He snarled. "You've probably never even kissed a girl."

Declin turned horseradish red and then stood up in a snapping motion. "Hey, fuck you guys. At least I'm not rotting in the asshole of the universe like you bastards."

As Declin walked away, I shouted, "Look around. I think you've reached the asshole."

Sighing, we watched him go, and Cass said, "Don't worry about him. He's selfish and full of himself, can't stand that no one's showering him with attention anymore." But an uneasiness settled over me until I stood and exited the cafeteria.

I could hear the bathroom door slam closed and followed Declin inside, where I heard something burst from him like a cracking trumpet. He had locked himself in the back stall and was sobbing. "Declin, you OK?"

"Go fuck yourself."

"Don't take it so personally. You can't take everything Blaine says so personally. We've been through a rough time—we all have, you know that?"

"How long have you known?"

"Known what?"

"Well—what Blaine said."

"You're a bad liar, but we're all liars, aren't we? I mean—I mean—" I struggled for the words. "Charlotte? You know Charlotte?" A mumble of assent. "I hate her guts. I keep pretending like I love her, but I don't. It's just convenient—that's all—and now we're sleeping together. I don't know what to think."

"Oh."

"Don't tell anyone, especially Blaine. Anyone. It's complicated."

"OK."

I pressed my hand against the door and sighed. "Come back out soon." I waited but heard no reply. "Because it doesn't matter who you were. It doesn't. It only matters who you are, who you'll become." Silence from within. I left him with his thoughts.

⚒ ⚒

Standing outside of Charlotte's house, I checked my reflection in the glass of her front door. A button-up shirt, ironed, and a tie that felt too tight around my neck. Lex Luthor and Grown-Up Cheerleader answered the door, and the shock on their faces could have powered the electricity for our entire city for at least a month. Her father, tall and shiny bald, gripped my hand, crushed my fingers, and directed me inside. Her mother resembled Charlotte only in her buoyant boobs, which she had trapped in some sort of magical Wonderbra that caused them to levitate above her stomach.

While I waited awkwardly alone, Charlotte's parents disappeared. I noticed the gun strategically placed on the couch, its barrel pointed toward the ceiling. Lex Luthor must have left the weapon in a conspicuous space, the quiet threat of a southern father.

She wore dark-purple lipstick and a studded bracelet on her wrist. I wondered what they did for family game nights, whether during Monopoly she ever tried to call on spirits in a séance or made blood sacrifices.

Her parents reentered the room, shifting around the table as if I were some wild animal that had broken into their house. "So, your name is Aron? I'm sad to say Charlotte has told me little about you."

Lex Luthor spoke with a low drawl, his words abbreviated and squat, each sound a bullfrog's croak. Ominous scars traced his lower neck, disappearing under his collared shirt.

"I'm a senior."

"As in high school, right? Well, then—you're going to college? Do you know where yet?"

"Well, no, not yet. I don't know."

"Where have you applied to?"

"Well, I haven't actually applied to—"

"But Aron is going to get a soccer scholarship, won't you, Aron? He's the absolute best in soccer. He even made the state team." Charlotte said all of this in a voice I'd never heard before, almost exuberantly. I was thinking, what the hell?

"That is very nice, Charlotte," said her mother. "Now, would you like to say grace, Aron?" She raised her arms like a Buddha, clutching Charlotte's and her husband's.

"Grace? You want me to pray over the food?"

"Yes," said Grown-Up Cheerleader. "That's what *grace* means."

Even snarky, her voice was mellow as honey, that sort of southern woman's magic that could soak into your skin like summer sweat, could convince you to do anything whether it be climb beneath her car or buy her shots of sweet-tea vodka or shoot the next-door neighbor.

I bowed my head, took Charlotte's hand, and allowed my other hand to be crushed by Lex Luthor. "God, will you please bless this food for us this evening?"

Decent start. Now I just had to combine the remnants of blessings my grandmother had given into a single conglomerated prayer.

"Please, watch over Charlotte and her family and give them—well, happiness. And safety. And your will so they can, um, do it. Please also allow this food to nourish us in—well, a way that would benefit our bodies to—better serve you. Our Father, who art in heaven, hollow be thy name. Send the Holy Ghost to fill our souls and to watch over us and to, um, keep this food nutritious—again. Amen."

When I finished, I lifted my head and plowed straight into the food. Grown-Up Cheerleader tittered away, slicing individual spaghetti strands, Lex Luthor didn't touch his food, and Charlotte gave the look one should give a suicide bomber terrorizing the "intimate apparel" section of Walmart.

"So," Charlotte finally said, "you guys wanted to ask Aron a few questions?"

Here it came. Grown-Up Cheerleader half grimaced and half grinned at Luthor and then said, "Aron, how do you like school?"

"Um, well, there are better schools. Lickskillet is a bit dirty and run-down, but I mean—the education is one of a kind. The same unique education you'd get at any public school in the state, so no fears about Charlotte going. Even with the drug raids and occasional car thefts, I don't think Lickskillet High is a bad place at all."

Grown-Up Cheerleader nodded. "Drugs? In Lickskillet? You don't do that stuff, do you?"

"Me? Not at all. I'm not a bad influence."

Charlotte scoffed. "Like I need him telling me what to do? I could do drugs without his influence."

What the hell was she talking about? I shot her a dirty glance. "Charlotte—"

"No, really. I could." She beamed at me proudly, sliding her hand across my crotch underneath the table. "Aron and I have a mature relationship, Mother. We're adults."

She narrowed her eyes. "Well, *she's* only seventeen."

"But I'm plenty old enough to decide for myself if I want to smoke or drink or fuck."

Lex Luthor paused with a piece of garlic bread half in his mouth. "You did what?"

"What the hell? No—I mean, Lickskillet High."

"Of course we had sex," Charlotte interjected. "We can do whatever we want, because we're in love."

Even I had to snort at that. "Look, maybe you're exaggerating."

"No, Aron and I are in love. You're just angry that I fell in love with a black boy."

"I'm not even all black, only—"

"If you touched my daughter—" Lex Luthor stood up suddenly, rounding the table. Almost too late, I stumbled to my feet and began inching away from him. "I will break your nigger neck!"

Now that we had introduced racial slurs to our dinnertime conversation, I felt the boiler pot explode with pressure. "Why exactly did you invite me here? Just to piss your parents off?" One look at her, and I knew. "Isn't that the only reason you wanted to date me in the first place? To rebel against these assholes."

Luthor puffed up his chest and stood up. "Get out of our house. You'll not be seeing our daughter again."

"Yeah? That's fine with me." I stormed from their house, pushing open the front door and stalking back into my car. I fumed as I drove away, and then I abruptly stopped. I sat dazed and somewhat relieved, feeling oddly as if I had just lost something important.

⚊⊰⊱⚊

She called six times, and I ignored each ring. She sent me texts, but I deleted them. She had used me. She knew her parents were racist hicks deep inside, and she needed me to bring those tendencies out. She used me. I used her. At least now she taught me how it felt to be reduced to a trophy, to be less than a person. Must have been how resuscitation dummies felt after receiving mouth-to-mouth, still lifeless and placed back in the closet after being kissed so dispassionately so many times.

⚊⊰⊱⚊

Declin invited me to the courthouse to watch the trial. I had purposely avoided downtown since the trial officially began. News crews had returned to document the witness-stand confessions, Matthew Pepper's guilty face, and the protestors. I parked my truck far down the street and walked with him up Main Street. White vans mounted with satellites created a barricade in front of the courthouse steps. Crowds of people stood outside.

On one side stood black men in suits, silent and reverent, holding signs that read Justice for Francis Jameson. On the other side of the steps stood a mass of men bearing white masks—I had never actually seen them in person. They looked like people dressed up for Halloween but with terrible taste. The Ku Klux Klan. Holding signs, reading Free Matthew Pepper, Matthew Pepper Is Innocent, and Stand Up for White Values.

"Shit, this place is a circus."

Declin nodded. "Yeah, my dad's been bringing me up every now and again. Today, they're supposed to be looking at the autopsy reports."

The Ku Klux Klan was adept at staging nonviolent protests, inciting riots, and seeding anger in the public. This required only their presence, robed and hooded, each braced for the public to take action. They supported other discriminatory groups in a show of solidarity, including the Hammerskins and the Knights of Southern Heritage. Two years before, I remembered reading in the paper about a counter-protest they held in Arlington against the Westboro Baptist Church. They complained that the funeral protestors were hate mongers, disrupting services that were meant to be reverent, though their presence drew national media attention, camera crews flooding the cemetery to watch the groups square off. In America, tragedy was never private.

Almost an hour later, we found seats inside above the sea of curious spectators. High-school teachers, PTA leaders, real-estate agents, civil-rights lawyers, coffee baristas, and tattoo artists had all crammed into the small Lickskillet courthouse to watch the trial. According to Declin, the audience of the trial grew every day. Currently, the Lickskillet Justice Department was negotiating a contract with several of the news stations who sought the rights to broadcast the trial. When the judge entered the hall, the murmurs ceased, and we stood up.

My phone buzzed in my pocket. I grasped its outline through my pocket.

My father and Barnaby Rutgers sauntered to one side of the courtroom. Declin's father approached the defense table. The bailiff escorted Matthew Pepper into the room, garbed in orange. His bright-red hair shocked me. He looked just like his sister. I scanned the crowd to find her but could discern no one's faces below. As Matthew Pepper sat down next to Roscoe Ostrander, a few jeers erupted from the Klan members.

Their presence unnerved me. Growing up in the South, I always knew they existed but had never seen any of them. I had never realized their numbers were so great.

Declin had told me that Matthew Pepper entered a plea of innocence at the onset of the trial. But why would he claim innocence? He could have faced a less severe prison sentence admitting his guilt, could have avoided this absurdly melodramatic trial. When I asked Declin whether he thought the defendant was guilty, he said, "Well, he had the motive. They're still having trouble linking him to the actual scene of the crime, though those who can provide his alibi are racist hicks. And he's a racist hick. Even if he didn't kill Francis Jameson, he's guilty somehow."

But I wanted to watch the trial for myself. The notion that someone could be guilty for simply being some way made me uneasy. I wanted evidence, wanted reasons to cement his guilt. After all, I knew what it was like to be assumed guilty for the crime of what others thought of me. Every time I stepped into a gas station, the cashier watched me closer. Police cars slowed down as they passed me on the street. For them, every cigarette looked like a joint and every soccer ball looked like a bomb and every bulging pocket like a gun. For them, every black boy looked like a criminal.

After a few minutes of preliminary preparation, the Lickskillet County coroner climbed onto the stand. They set up a projector in the middle of the room and displayed photographs of the victim's body. The coroner pointed out the bruises along the ribs, against his legs. Jameson, he concluded, had been severely beaten before being murdered. When they removed Jameson from the tree, the coroner determined his blood alcohol level to be dangerously high. Whoever had killed him could have done so easily because of Jameson's incapacitation.

My phone buzzed again in my pocket, and I reached inside to turn it off. Charlotte was calling again. I silenced the phone.

The coroner spoke at length about the lacerations on Jameson's neck, and each word felt like a noose tightening. This could have been me, could have been anybody. My face could be projected on the back wall of the courtroom, bloated and purple—the strangest fruit you would ever see. I swallowed.

Six texts from Charlotte, my phone said. I opened the first.

Charlotte: Call me now.

I ignored the text.

As the coroner continued, Matthew Pepper looked like death.

I scanned the crowd and wondered how many of these men in white hoods could also be Matthew Pepper, could be monsters dressed in human skin. Under their masks, they could be teachers or PTA leaders or real-estate agents or civil-rights lawyers or coffee baristas or tattoo artists. Anyone could don a white robe and become a ghost, become the specter of this black boy's nightmares.

I looked to Declin beside me, whose father now stood to cross-examine the coroner. He too was a liar. He too wore masks. I thought about Charlotte, how she had assumed we were in love. Maybe she only believed this because I pretended it was true. I pretended to love her and care about her. I too wore a mask and could be someone's nightmare.

They could stand in their Klan regalia and strike fear into my heart. I could stand in my own skin and strike fear into their hearts. Stripped of his lies, Declin didn't seem so interesting.

Stripped of a white uniform and burning torch, Matthew Pepper didn't seem that intimidating. He just seemed like another man afraid of dying.

I looked into my lap and opened the rest of Charlotte's texts.

Charlotte: Call me now. I need to tell you. I'm pregnant.

CHAPTER 18

THE JOURNAL OF ELIJAH RODRIGUEZ

November 8

Even though Blaine drugged me at the Halloween party, I have still been sitting with him and his friends during lunch. Quentin, I must say that my silence seems marginalized next to their silence. This entire week, they've been mostly quiet, just eating their food. It's really sad. I think everyone is still real shocked about Justin getting in a car wreck on Halloween. No one knows what happened except that he was drunk and ran an intersection. A semi smacked into his truck, destroying it. But everyone is sure he'll wake up soon.

I visited him today, which is what I want to talk about. Aron and Blaine came too. Cass sat beside his bed just watching him. When we came into the room, Blaine joined Cass. He put his hand on her leg, a little too far up to be friendly. When you're an observer, you notice the things other people overlook. Like hands on thighs and medical charts. I read the chart as Aron said something to the unconscious Justin, perhaps giving his condolences.

Both arms broken. Left leg shattered. Three ribs snapped. Ruptured gallbladder, removed during emergency surgery. Major possibility of permanent brain damage with little chance of recovery. Intermediate possibility of long-term vegetation. Small possibility of death.

The words made me shudder, the beep of the machines echoing my heartbeat. He laid upright in the bed, tubes poking out from his chest and sliding down into his mouth. Fluids moved through the tubes from IV bags dangling from metal contraptions above his head. He was attached to so many wires and chemicals he could have passed for a cyborg. His face was fixed in frozen shock, like Mario's when he accidentally runs right into a walking Koopa as his invincibility star is wearing off. Such a surprise that, yes, you too are just bones and blood and guts, so pathetically mortal.

I can't stop thinking about what it would be like to exist without living. To live by simply breathing, because your body keeps pumping blood. But his brain? It might not even be coherent any longer. It seems pretty harsh punishment. Like when the Marvel villain Thanos was sent by a personification of Death to destroy a universe where Death was dead, only to be rendered immortal and then trapped inside the universe as it collapsed.

I'm sorry, Quentin: I know you don't read comic books, on account of you're just a journal, but bear with me. Basically, torture without dying.

School has been going swimmingly well. I invited Declin to come play *Dragon Sphere* with me one Saturday, and he said, "Yes, maybe." Not much else has occurred.

November 23

I love the smell of old books. I love their feel, how fragile and old their pages look. I like how if you ruffle the pages of an old book, all the pages flutter down like dusty moth wings, almost tearing but still managing to fly. Even just float, for only a second.

I've been bringing my journal to the library more often, because it's easier to think here. It's quiet. Out there, outside this place, there's just too much noise. If you go to a café and drink coffee, don't you dare write anything in a journal (especially if it has Diary written across it, which mine does). Not with the other kids from your school looking at you and laughing at either you or some joke you'll never be told. There's that cackling. And there's music so loud that it defies its own "ambient" nature. The clinking of bottles, the grind of the espresso machine. Too much noise for the writer to think.

In a library, you're alone, confronted only with a polite and short cough. Or the overzealous ruffle of book pages. Or the squeak of book carts as they wheel by. The library is a place where I feel safe.

I am not at the public library because that's crowded as well. The public was allowed access to the school library at Exeter Academy, which held twice as many books of much older and rarer origins.

At school, sitting at the lunch table by myself or in class quiet, I used to like to write things down. I'd like to record everything just as I saw it, like a human mockingbird, only I'd write the words down. Pen the movements of the body, each elbow twitch or flutter of an eyelid. Aron and Charlotte don't sit together anymore. Charlotte has been consumed by a new horde of friends, fellow black-lipstick wearers. Declin and Blaine sit with Aron now, and Cass sits there too. Maybe because Justin is gone. In a coma or trapped in a collapsed universe.

Now that I sit with them, I see more. Blaine attends to Cass so carefully you'd swear they were together longer than she and Justin. If they are together, which I think they might be. They pass glances back and forth, not exactly loving, but imbued with want.

I can't write about all of this at school—everything that happens. And at home, it feels so strange to write anything. The poetry I've written—just a few verses—I write in the depths of the stacks, sitting at a little wooden cubicle.

I love old books, the smell and feel. I like reading the names on receipts, the names of people who read these books before me, held these books before me. I've been flipping through the pages. Moth wings

November 23—continued
I can't go back. Not safe.

Trying to write something when they walked in. Crouching in the little booth in the nonfiction section. When they walked in, I could see them out of the corner of my eye. Floating down the aisles like identical ghosts, in blue blazers and leather shoes. I could hear their shrill laughter, feel their malicious attention, directed toward me.

"What the hell are you up to, faggot?"

One of them swaggered forward. Slick hair, demon eyes. I tried to stand, but my knees felt too wobbly. "I—I—" I burped up the words timidly.

He squared his shoulders, smirked. "Shut your little faggot mouth, faggot. Rhymes with *maggot*, doesn't it? You're a little faggot maggot." He really seemed to enjoy using that word that made my jaw lock with fear.

Eyes gray, crimson cracks zigzagging across the whites. He leaned toward me, and I tried to get away. The aisles were all empty. If only I could just run. But his fists wrapped around my shirt, almost picking me up. He pushed me back against the wall. Slumping down the wall, staring up at the ceiling.

He smirked. They floated away, and quick as they came, they left. Like death. I sat on the floor, looking down the aisles at where they might have gone. I don't understand what they wanted, why they had come at me like that with such loathsome zeal. I guess some people just enjoy how power tastes trapped in their vicious jaws.

I snatched up the journal and came home.

CHAPTER 19
ELIZABETH PEPPER

A patrol car sat parked across the street, a uniformed officer watching as I entered Southside Seafood. They would be keeping tabs on us, Dylan told me, and not only them but federal agents as well—they had arrived, dressed in conspicuous black suits and unstylish sunglasses not long after Dylan announced his newest business connections. Inside the seafood shop, it smelled like grease and something distinctly chemical.

I marched straight to the counter, looked the owner squarely in the eye, and told him what Dylan had instructed me to say: "The blue-crab special, please."

He chewed his lip, glancing out the window and then back at me. "Uh—we don't have that on the menu."

I sighed—because I was a girl, most likely. "I said, I'd like the blue-crab special."

"But—OK, follow me." He stepped forward and drew his curtains before leading me into the back. He pushed buttons furiously next to the industrial dishwasher, and then a great mechanical churning broke out beneath us as the dishwasher slid from place, gears whirring, revealing a set of metal stairs. Once we stepped through, descending the stairs, the dishwasher slid loudly back into place. "Dammit, Lemire didn't say he was sending some little girl."

"I'm almost eighteen." He didn't comment on that but instead directed me down a dimly lit corridor that ran beneath Southside Seafood, leading to an adjacent bowling alley. Dylan had informed me about all of the particulars. "I mean, I cook this stuff. I'm the one doing all the—"

"I don't want to know. I shouldn't." He cast a fearful look. "The less we know about each other, the better, understand? Now, up here we go." A similar staircase stood at the other end of the corridor, and we climbed it into the abandoned bowling place that had closed down five years before.

The alleys lay cast in shadows, behind rolls of dusty marbled balls with various finger-hole sizes. Behind the counter where they kept the shoes stood a towering, scar-notched man with a wispy beard and cruel eyes, my cousin's business associate from Charleston. "You're the one that little fucker sent?" He growled over the counter, slamming his hairy palms down. "All right, tell him this might be the last order." He smelled like cigarettes and sewage.

As he shuffled through his bag, I piped up. "Last order? What do you mean?"

"I mean, you have a rat. A mole. The FBI jumped on your family as soon as we started doing business with you, and we can't risk them tracing your little operation back to our own. So you're cut. It's business, kid—just business."

Felt like a stab in the heart, but I couldn't argue—this would mean I could venture outside the cramped cooking trailer, stop working nonstop up to the crackling light of morning cooking meth. Maybe I could have a life; briefly, I wondered about the college acceptance letter stuffed in my sock drawer.

"Tell Dylan to make four pounds. If there's any excess, he can sell locally. But warn him he'd better be careful because someone's been snooping—someone's watching." I nodded. "Understand?"

I nodded again. "That's it. I don't—"

The man sighed and then removed a silver briefcase from behind the counter and set it on the table. When he undid the latches, I saw stacks of hundreds, Benjamin's face staring nobly at me. Enough money to buy a house or enough money to buy all of Golden Oaks sitting in that briefcase. Damn, we could use that money, needed that money more than we needed anything before. The partner divided out a few stacks of the bills and pushed them across the table to me. "Go out the back. Don't be seen. I hope he's giving you a pretty decent commission."

Stuffing the money into the bag and remembering his new demands, I fled from the back door, running and then slowing down once I slipped through an alley. Strolling casually.

In downtown Lickskillet, there was this strange coffee shop called the Rise and Shiner. On weekday mornings, it served espressos and frozen smoothies to new-in-town yuppies who lived squeezed together in the downtown suburbs, what Daddy called "rattraps." On the weekends, starting Friday, the café became a Roller Derby ring, home to Lickskillet's Heartless Harpies. I slipped into the alley to enter the side door, hoping the men in suits would stop watching me. Their presence made me nervous.

In the back room, I sat alone among the circular tables with flour sacks as tablecloths. Along the wall hung drug-inspired artwork and racks of Rollerblades and helmets. Beyond a curtain at the back of the room was the ring, dark and smelling like blood and sawdust. I thought about the envelope I had opened a week earlier, right here, at this table: that single piece of paper that changed my life. Then my heart dropped when I thought about what my father would say when I showed it to him. Pride, anger, disappointment? Or when I told him that I would leave our family behind in a manner of months?

When I began to walk home, I looked curiously into the houses I passed, once past the suburbs and into the projects. A lot of black kids lived here, in the place the white kids caustically called the ghetto, where the duplexes all had the same grimy red doors and broken window blinds and empty garages. I walked past the overflowing Dumpsters, never tended to. I walked past the kids at school I never talked to because they were black. The Peppers didn't talk to black kids. They lived lives we could not understand in places we only walked through, only saw glimpses of. No one ever told us why they lived so separate—in the same town, of course, but separate.

Then I thought about how these houses came to be, back when the mills was still running, though the mill had been knocked down a generation ago, replaced with shopping malls and fast-food empires. The houses spread out from the mill, sitting in sad rows owned by the same families for generations, and when the mill closed, the families drifted apart, either into the suburbs or into the woods. My ancestors had once worked for the mill, and before that they worked as sharecroppers at the same plantation we now somehow owned, but that was a long time ago; we hardly ever spoke of that version of the past.

My entire life my family had told me to stay away from here, saying the word *black* with pointed tongues. What a strange habit down south, whispering the word *black* or instead strangling out the phrase *African American*, as if it pained people to say it. I didn't understand what was wrong with the word *black* itself—was it some dirty, unholy word for white people? Even the teachers at school—their predisposition to political correctness was questionable. They talked a lot about a different culture, a different America, a different people, as if they were not a part of our America at all, and most likely I couldn't judge that because I never learned about it. What we never learn about, what we don't know, was what we became the most afraid of.

At the edge of downtown, there lay a chasm where a train once ran through, though the tracks rusted over years ago. Metal bridges continued on the few roads that joined these stark places, but we crossed them only out of necessity. Even as I thought that perhaps we lived in the same strange state of confusion, in dilapidated residences surrounded by people unrelated to us whom we called family for the sake of having one, we were separate.

I walked down into the wall of woods that signified the border of Lickskillet, where the potholes overwhelmed the asphalt enough that stone melted to dirt. I could walk down this road back to the plantation, but I had work to do. Beyond the apartments that lined the roads, the duplexes and liquor stores, an army of trailers nestled in the shadow of downtown.

Dylan's trailer looked strange parked among these others instead of crushed between the two oak trees where it had been for the past four decades. Though most of the homes on our property were mobile, I often forgot that fact. Knocking on the door, I waited, watching behind me for anyone approaching. Not even the men in suits followed me, though. Dylan opened the door, even grislier than before. He had, for as long as I could remember, worn a white scar down his face. Now his nose looked misshapen as well, and he sported one black eye.

"Did they follow you here, Elizabeth?"

"They never crossed the bridge. Did they do this to you?"

He smiled, revealing gaps in his teeth. "Who? The agents? No, if they caught me, then we'd be over. I wouldn't be here talking to you. Did Lemire deliver?" I reached into my bag and removed a mass of bills, the most money I had ever held in my life, but once I handed it to Dylan, he looked disappointed.

"This is all he gave you? And how much does he want?"

"Four pounds?"

"Four pounds? What the hell? How on earth—well, we'll have to spend the money just on the materials to cook four pounds."

He grimaced and then swung his fist at a wall. "Can you cook enough?"

"I need to go to school; this man keeps visiting Daddy, telling him if I don't go to school—"

"Ah, fuck school. If we make this much money a week, you'll never need another dime again, and who needs school?"

I bit my tongue rather than tell him it wouldn't matter if we made that much money a week, since we would apparently also need to spend it. But Dylan did not often think, only acted on instinct like an animal in a forest. He spat on the floor and then looked mournfully behind the ragged curtains that blocked the sun. "You know, I'm real sorry I can't go see Matty tomorrow. You know, those men know who I am; I've got a record. That's why I need you."

"But why me? I mean, I—"

"Who else, Elizabeth? Who else can save this family? Me, I'm stuck in here, and your brother's stuck in jail, and your daddy—he—well, that damn Yankee lawyer's got him wrapped around his finger. I can barely drive my truck, barely conduct business in this town without someone trying to tell me something, but I don't need none of it. I know what I know, and that's all." He snorted. "I need your help."

He dug through a pile of clothes and found a bag of crystal meth, which he placed gingerly in my hands, as if I had never seen the damned stuff before. "I need you to make a delivery, a delivery to this local—his sales make decent money, maybe some money we can use on the side to help pay for that lawyer or to get one of our little cousins some braces or—he's a seller for us. Name's Cain. All I want you to do is give it to him."

I nodded. "I can do that."

"That's all, you understand? Don't say a word to the little bastard—just take the money and go. Don't go with him anywhere, and if he tries anything, come tell me so I can kick his damn teeth in."

The thought of speaking to a boy at all made my muscles clench up, but I only nodded and pushed back the desk so I could sprint through the maze of trailers and into the woods where I was safe. As I reached the dirt road again, the sky turned black 'cause it was November, and the sky grew dim quicker. When I had dragged my sore feet up the road many miles, I finally turned onto the road that weaved into our property, our mythical place in the woods.

When I was smaller, Daddy once told me our land was special land, property our family had owned for years 'cause over generations our blood seeped into this soil, making it special for us. We could prosper here, be safe here. Somehow, I had always believed that we would be forever isolated and protected as long as we continued to live on this hallowed land, but then the cops showed up to arrest Matty. They pulled him right out of the house, slamming him against the hood of the car, tightening the cuffs on his wrists. That was when I realized that we were not ever safe, and we would be safe nowhere.

Our land, our trees, our place. Sing me a lullaby, trees, I thought, so that I may fall asleep in your arms. Sing me a lullaby and give your protection. Watch over me. And as the darkness closed in, I truly felt that the trees were watching.

⌐+ +⌐

The buildings framed the streets like metallic Popsicle sticks from an elementary-school history diorama. We used to make those in the third or fourth grade, all sorts of things. Native American villages, the wooden sticks bound with twist ties to form wigwams. Little Popsicle cities that we dyed silver with hand paints. Other kids would bring custom-built exact replicas of the Empire State Building, all steel and soldering. My projects were all Popsicle sticks and Elmer's glue.

Breakfast at a roadside Waffle House before the sun eclipsed the horizon. Chewing omelets in somber concentration, sipping scalding coffee. My father drank four cups. My father never drank coffee; he said it was unhealthy because of the caffeine: a crystalline xanthine alkaloid that stimulates the central nervous system to induce alertness.

When we parked outside the prison, I already regretted not finishing the greasy hash browns. We limped together toward the fenced entrance.

In my dreams, I sometimes imagined Matty at the prison, chained to the wall while rats nibbled at his toes. It stood, a dreary citadel, on some cliff far away where storms brewed in the sky year-round.

But the prison in Columbia looked anything but medieval, an abstractly concrete cube, all steel and soldering.

Concrete: 50 percent tricalcium silicate, 25 percent dicalcium silicate, 10 percent tricalcium aluminate, 10 percent tetracalcium aluminoferrite, and 5 percent gypsum.

⛓

Even inside, it was strangely cleaner than I had imagined. The floors and ceiling all concrete, the bars separating us from the prisoners merely metal. After a security guard patted us down and took our belongings—the keys and cell phones and wallets— he directed us through the prison.

In movies, the men always beat at the bars whenever a woman entered their presence, but they just sat on cots, watching languidly as we passed by. "Spooky, isn't it?" said Mr. Roscoe.

"Yes," I told him as we entered into a smaller visiting room.

Matty sat behind a glass screen with a mesh hole in the center, trying to smile. He lifted his raccoon eyes to us as we entered. My father sat down in front of the screen and I close behind him;

Mr. Roscoe folded his hands and stood next to the prison guards lining the back of the room.

"Little sis, how've you been?"

"I've been great, Matty. Great. Is it depressing, staying here?" Dad scowled.

"It feels strange. I shouldn't be here. You know that, don't you? You know that I didn't—I didn't—"

"I know, Matty. I know you didn't do it. I've been trying to tell everyone at school, but people just can't think. Nobody can think right, because in their minds, they know you did it."

"As long as you don't think that."

Stepping away from the window, I allowed Daddy to greet his son. "How are you holding up?"

Matty shrugged. "Could be better. How's the family business?"

"Oh, well, you know—you being in jail, no one wants to come to us. Some people—they think you're a murderer, Matty."

"No, they wouldn't want to deal with a crook, would they?"

"There's more than that. We've got a problem. Snakes in the grass." The code phrase meant that our operation was in trouble from the law. "Now, we've brought Mr. Roscoe. You know we go back to court in February. Prepare yourself." Daddy nodded and stepped away.

"How've you been doing?"

Matty shook his head. "Not well. But I'm ready to get back. Have you changed any minds?"

"Well, I mean, if anything—they don't exactly have any real evidence against you. Just little coincidental things like that you punched him in the face and that you had motive because he slept with—um, your girlfriend. Oh, and, well, calling him a—well, in court, a—"

"A blue-gummed porch monkey."

"Well, you can see that they hate you."

"Have you seen what they've made of it? Some sort of circus." He shook his head.

"But what about the truth? As long as we convince them you didn't kill anyone, we'll, um—" Mr. Roscoe looked pained.

"The truth doesn't matter to these people. They want someone to blame. I'm their scapegoat. I'm their sacrifice to the gods of entertainment. They want someone to hate, so that's me."

"Right, well, I'll keep looking at things. I think maybe if I, well, if I find something concrete, something that will pin this whole thing on someone else. I mean, well, figure out who actually committed the crime. Since it wasn't you."

"Five minutes, guys," the guard said.

"Come here, Sis. I need to tell you something really important." Daddy and Mr. Roscoe floated toward the wall, and I came forward. "I know you're special, OK? You've always had something—great about you. Something that made you better than all of us. And no, I never resented that. You were meant for big things, so remember, when big things come, don't be afraid to accept them. Ride the wave, kiddo. And keep safe, too. Snakes are in the grass, remember. What with the trial going on, I can't imagine what they're saying at school. But it's almost over. I never even made it out of high school—dropped out. But you—just keep safe and do better than I did."

The way his eyes, ringed in black, shone so sincerely, I wondered if he knew what letter I had sent off months ago, that I'd been accepted early into college. Smiling, I nodded and backed away. The guard escorted us out of the prison.

—≺+≻—

My father sat at our kitchen table, scraping his fork against an already-empty plate. We ate venison for dinner, as we did almost every night in this season. I pushed the manila folder across the table. "What's this?"

"Look at it."

"Is this from a college?" He removed the sheet and read it for too long. His face blank, his eyes no longer scanning the page, only staring. "Well, I didn't even know you—applied. This is certainly—"

"I'm sorry."

Daddy smiled. "About what? You got into college. So, you need some money, but—this is good."

"You're not mad?"

"Why would I be mad?"

"I just thought—I would have to leave. You'd have to get along without me."

"We'll be just fine, you hear?" He stood up and wrapped his big arms around me. "I want you to go. I swear we'll find a way to get you there."

I didn't say anything because I had lost the ability to do so. He said, "But I have something else to ask of you, though I fear I always ask too much. Your cousins, both those named Pepper and those without names—I want you to watch over them. As vigil as trees watch over us, watch over them."

"I will. But why? Is something bad going to happen?"

"I'm not sure. Mr. Ostrander may save us yet. If something bad does happen, I want you to make sure they're OK. And once you do that, don't stay here. Get far away."

"Yes, sir. What about Matty?"

Daddy sat for a moment, fingering the edges of the letter in his hand. "Matty's fate—what happens to him could change what happens to us."

"I don't want nothing to happen to us."

Daddy nodded. "Just know that, no matter what, I'm proud of you. Whether you go to college or stay here, get married or don't—I know you'll make the decisions you'll have to." He embraced me again, rocking on the balls of his feet with me in his arms just like we once had done when I was younger and we danced.

When I pulled away, he was crying, and politely, I walked upstairs.

⇌ ⇋

School ended Tuesday, and I did as I was told. He stood like some tall reptile in a blue blazer and mirrored shades. Even in the parking lot, the suited men were watching. I wasn't sure whether they were observing everyone or only me. I walked right toward him, pulled the bag out, and tried to push it into his hands. "Put that away. They're watching." I knew that as well, but I tried only to do as I was told. "Put it away."

"Take it. You'll make a scene. Just—please, take it."

"We'll make the exchange elsewhere. Pretend like I'm picking you up. Climb in."

I remembered what Dylan had said but only took a deep breath and climbed in. Cain didn't say a word as he started the car and pulled out of the lot. The car purred wonderfully beneath us, zipping smoothly through downtown. "Just leave the bag in the car, OK?" I placed the bag on the back floorboard and turned toward him.

"What now? Can you take me home?"

"I can't just take you home; you think I'd be seen there? Dylan told me all about the agents, about the police—what was I thinking? What did I do?"

"You do? We didn't do anything either. You're just as guilty as we are."

He beat the wheel, turning down the radio. "Look, my brother didn't fucking hang a man."

"He did not."

203

"You don't think he did it?" I shook my head meekly. "Wrapped that rope loop around Jameson's neck? Beat the shit out of him and lynched his black ass? If so, you think I care? Just tell me the truth—the guy was a disgrace. You should have heard my dad talk about him. Before he left office, he was planning to bring this city to its knees. Make it a Yankee paradise; expand these suburbs to the max. So, really, we're both on the same side of this fight. If your brother hadn't gotten to him first, I may have fucked that guy up. At least then, my dad—well, my father—he deserved to die, you know. Your brother did the right thing."

"I don't think he deserved to die. No one does."

"Well, life isn't fair, huh? And rarely good."

"Just let me out here. I don't want to talk about it."

He pushed down harder on the pedal, ignoring me. "Parents and teachers and priests want to claim we've grown up in a violent culture, affected by video games and gory television and R-rated horror movies. That's not the truth: we're a violent species. We always have been, before we could let a four-year-old simulate stealing cars or stabbing hookers or blowing up Nazi zombies. Before all that, we were running around, caving each other's heads in with hatchets and swords. Ain't no evolution, just a continuance of the violence we've always been prone to."

"Let me out. I don't care. I don't care what you think."

He slammed on the brakes, looking at me bewildered, and I realized no one had ever probably told him that: they didn't care what he thought, about the endless stream of lies flowing from his lips. "Don't care? Well, get out then. Go back to your fucking hut in the woods."

I climbed out, slamming the door shut, huffing away as I marched up the road where the woods began; at least he had taken me this far. I stood at the edge of the forest, exposed, and walked slowly into the mythical protection of our trees.

Except from Lickskillet County Court Transcript: The Trial of Matthew Pepper
Charged with Murder of the First Degree, Hate Crime, Disruption of Justice
November 30, 2013

{Witness Marlene Wanda Frell takes stand, called by Prosecutor Barnaby Rutgers. Places hand on Bible. Honorable Judge Andrea Jackson addresses her.}

> **Judge Jackson**: Do you swear to tell the truth, the whole truth, and nothing but the truth, so help you God?
> **Frell**: I swear.
> **Judge Jackson**: All right, Barnaby, you can begin.

{Rutgers approaches witness stand.}

> **Rutgers**: Ms. Frell, were you in a relationship with Francis Jameson before and during the night of his murder?
> **Frell**: He asked me out a couple of times. I went with him to the movies, out to bars, but we weren't in a relationship.
> **Rutgers**: But you were seeing him?
> **Frell**: Yeah, you could say that.
> **Rutgers**: How did Matthew Pepper react to you "seeing" Mr. Jameson?
> **Frell**: Matty? He was pissed off. Still is. Matty thought I was his fucking [redacted] property. I broke up with that fuck [redacted, man] almost a year ago, and still he tries to come over and talk to me every time I walk in somewhere.
> **Rutgers**: Did Francis Jameson and Matthew Pepper have any sort of contact before the night of Jameson's death?

Frell: Them? Sure, they hated each other. Like I said, I was at the movies with Franky, and Matty comes up to us, and he says—well, sir, I'm not sure I can say it in court.

Judge Jackson: Repeat what he said. We won't judge you for it.

Frell: Well, he said, "I can't believe I stuck my cock in a damned nigger lover like you." He said a few other things, but I can't remember.

Rutgers: Would you describe their interactions as "violent"?

{Roscoe Ostrander objects to the question, and Judge Jackson forces Rutgers to retract it.}

Rutgers: How would you describe their interactions, Ms. Frell?

Frell: Well, pretty violent. Not that they actually fought each other until that night, but they certainly traded a few words. You see, Franky was in the real-estate business, and he wanted to buy up the Pepper property, turn it into a new subdivision. Even when I was dating Matty, he hated Francis Jameson for that. He told me he'd never let some—pardon me—some "Yankee niggers ruin his family land."

Rutgers: I see. So, they engaged in a physical clash the night Jameson died. Could you describe that to us?

Frell: Sure, I could. I came in with Franky to Ford's Bar, and you know, I'm not sure why we went there. Just a bunch of racist rednecks hang out there, so I'm not sure why Franky would want to go. Anyways, I see Matty with his cousin Dillon and one of their friends—Robbie, I think. They're ignoring us at first, but then Matty comes over, starts bothering Franky.

Rutgers: Can you tell us what they said?

Frell: I don't remember. But Matty started to get real mad and then punched Franky in the face.

Rutgers: Matthew Pepper initiated the fight?

Frell: Yes, sir.

Ostrander: Objection, Your Honor! This isn't about the fight. It's about a murder.

Judge Jackson: I'll let it stand. Continue, Ms. Frell.

Frell: Huh? That's all. They fought, and then we left. Franky dropped me off at my house an hour later, and I—I never saw him again.

Judge Jackson: Mr. Ford, the owner of the bar, testified that Matthew Pepper threatened Francis Jameson's life.

Frell: I don't know. He may have, but he may not have. I don't remember, like I said.

Rutgers: He didn't say, "I'll kill you."

Frell: Look, I don't even remember. I'm sorry. I don't know whether he did or not.

Rutgers: All right, well, I think that's all. Ostrander, you ready?

CHAPTER 19

DECLIN OSTRANDER

The truck crumpled. When the metal crunched, it made a sound just like when someone steps on an aluminum can. A fire bloomed in my rearview mirror as I sped away. Hyperventilation spread through the vehicle like a plague. These dreams often melted into scenes of humiliation: standing at the front of class as my fellow students threw insults and balled-up paper in my direction. "Liar! Fake! Loser!" Then I would wake up.

On Sunday, the alarm on my phone refused to sound. At noon, I rolled groggily out of bed and found my cell phone dead under a pile of clothes, which due to the fact no one, especially I, ever washed them, should have been putrefying. After salvaging my phone, I tiptoed downstairs. The house was unusually quiet.

Sunday, my father could not be at court—maybe he had visited the Peppers. I tried feebly to imagine what strange religious traditions they practiced. Perhaps sacrifice of some black-furred animals to expel Yankees from Lickskillet. What more could you expect?

I sat down at the table while a bowl of Easy Mac revolved inside the microwave. Eating on the weekends became much like eating on weekdays: fifteen minutes of solid silence, an iceberg of silence. Lunch was torture, but at least less so since Charlotte had abandoned us. First, she had thankfully traded bitchy trash talk for bitchy silence; a few days later, she disappeared from our lunch table. The rest of us still sat together, even Cass, who in the absence of Justin seemed deflated. We counted down the seconds until we could stop trying to not look into each other's eyes.

The accident had done something to us, frayed us like lightning might a tree. How fast could we be scattered by a truck? Aron, Cass, Blaine, and I had nearly died that night, but instead Justin had been hit. His truck had been crushed in on the passenger's side, so fortunately, he had not died. Almost worse, he had been dragged from the car unconscious and broken. He had not yet awoken. This was the sort of thing that could make lunch unbearable, that secret hanging above our collective heads, that shame and responsibility.

We were bound together by proximity. We were bound by flimsy bonds, what classes or streets or restaurants or lunch tables we shared. We were friends of convenience.

The pronoun *we* seemed gratuitous, though. I would never be part of a *we*, just forever an outsider looking in. A strange cowboy riding into town with a mask and no name.

Maybe the others thought I was too foreign to truly share this blame. "We don't even really know you," Aron had said one day. This was after Blaine outed me as a liar. I hated him. If he had really seen through the lies, he could have at least been nice about it, not such a dick. I hadn't even realized he noticed anything or could be empathetic to people's discrepancies as he could. He spent our classes together completely stoned, somehow still managing to pull off passing grades. Everything he said, he said too fast, and none of it made much sense.

Even stuffed with gelatinous cheese, my mouth felt dry.

As I dumped the bowl of Easy Mac into the already-overflowing sink, my father hurried into the kitchen. "So," I said, rubbing my forehead, "how are things?"

"Huh?"

"You know, with the case and with the Peppers and the racism and that dead black guy?"

My father slumped into the chair where I'd just been sitting. "Just went to visit Matthew in prison this morning."

"And?"

"Just, I thought he should know that he'll probably end up on death row. And he's probably not even—not even the murderer. I mean, the boy is rather rough. And—well, he had the motive. But I don't think he ever killed anyone. Then again, you always think about that, don't you? I do. Thinking everyone's a saint, as if everyone hasn't got a smudge on their records. Not true, though, is it? He probably strung Francis Jameson up in a tree, and I'm just being played like a banjo. I—well, that's how the case is going. I've got nothing."

"But you said he probably didn't do that. How do you know?"

My father looked dismally at me. "A hunch, Declin. That's all I have to go on. I don't see how this case will hold up for much longer, not without any evidence. I'd give it till March before we're humping back down to Alabama or—wherever. I just—I'm sorry."

"I—you know you don't—you know, have anything to be sorry for. I mean, I'll be all right. And you'll be—fine. And you know, maybe this case—it—"

But it wouldn't become anything. He'd lose. Matthew Pepper would fry in an electric chair, his eyeballs popping out just like in the cartoons. I wanted to tell him I would not disappoint him, but I would. I wanted to tell him he had never disappointed me, but he had.

Suddenly, I felt the immense pressure to do something important. Without realizing it, I had felt this pressure my entire life: to avoid becoming a failure like my father. If only I turned out to be successful, maybe he could feel like he had done at least one thing right in raising me.

For hours, I had looked through college websites online, but I had applied nowhere. I could only fill in my name, but once it came time to talk about myself, I had nothing. Everything interesting that had ever happened to me had been made up. I lived the most boring life imaginable, so there was nothing to set me apart. My test scores—those were fine but not spectacular. Even if I got into college, even if I could pay for it with scholarships I also hadn't applied for, I didn't even know what I wanted to do.

I didn't even know who I was. My life had been a well-crafted lie, but not until you begin to fictionalize yourself do you begin to understand your past. I had begun to understand.

Standing in the kitchen, watching my father brood, I wanted to say all this, scream all this. Reassure him that all would be OK and berate him for not making things better. We both had so much to say, and all these words, these bold exclamations, in the end—they added up to silence.

⟞⟝

By Wednesday, the hardest exams lay behind us. We could taste winter break approaching like snowflakes that would never fall on this town. Like marathon runners, we were ready to collapse, stumbling out of the school, shielding our eyes from the bright sun. Cass lingered in the parking lot, digging through her purse.

"Cass, how about that English exam?" Immediately, I felt so stupid. After two weeks of avoiding her, avoiding the question of when a certain someone might wake up, I began with English. She only shrugged.

"Hey," I said, touching her elbow. She pulled away, sighing. "Are you OK? I mean, you just—you've been so offish. You've been acting so differently. Are you sure you're fine?"

"Am I fine?" She stared blankly at me as if she did not understand the question. "Am I fine?"

Cass looked at me, her eyes reflecting the crushed metal ball that had once been Justin's truck. Her eyes screamed, "Go! Go!" The squeal of my wheels as I cleared the intersection. And then Justin in that hospital bed.

She visited him every day, I'm not sure why or how. After the accident, for a week, we had all visited him. The entire school—hell, the town—had visited him, to wait for him to wake up. To finish out the football season after this minor setback. He'd wake up like after suffering a mild concussion, and then he'd get a scholarship. He'd win a state championship for Lickskillet High. He'd play for Clemson or USC or somewhere out of state. We shared a communal dream.

But then he never woke up. The machines kept beeping, and we stopped visiting. I could not sit in the room with him without feeling an immense guilt. But Cass—she still went every day. She sat beside him, waiting.

"Just—you seem so obsessed with Justin, what's going to happen to him. And I thought—well, I just thought—you guys had broken up, so—"

"I was with him. Two years. I can't just—it wasn't. I forgive him."

"Why? Because—" I bit my lip. "He's a creep, Cass. The only reason he got into that crash—you know it's not—not my fault." She said nothing. "He was following us, and he was drunk. He made those choices."

"It's not your fault. It's mine. If I hadn't broken his heart, he wouldn't have been pushed so far, to such extreme—"

"What the hell are you talking about? He cheated on you, remember? He deserved this."

The slap stung, coming so fast I collapsed. She screamed, "No, he deserved me. He deserved to play ball and go to college and live. But now he's going to die, and that's not going to be on me. I can't—I did this to him. He followed us because he loved me. Because he didn't want us to ever—now I have to stay with him. I love him."

I felt so shaken, squinting up at her from the ground. "But you—what's going to happen, then, if he dies?"

"Then maybe I'll die too. My life—his life. Now his life is ruined, and yes, Declin, it's partly your fault. So get the fuck out of here. I—please."

Whatever I'd hoped for, that maybe I could rekindle some romance with her, was over. In the end, Cass didn't even exist. Only Justin existed. Now that he was in a coma, Cass had ceased to be a person. She was a ghost. A breathing vegetable. And until he woke up, I doubted she'd be a person ever again.

Pissed off and stewing in the anxiety inherent to sanity, I marched off. This was echoing in my head: Cass is not even a real person. Cass wasn't even herself, just a shadow of someone else. Justin's girlfriend, not a full person. An accessory. It made me want to rip her head off, how dependent she was. She was lying, and what was worse than lying?

I stopped suddenly, my throat feeling drier than before. Lying: you could not be a real person if all you did was lie. Never could I feel like a real person.

Blaine had revealed that, that I was nothing but a fucking fraud. A sham of a person, a hodgepodge of made-up stories that made me into some mythical being. No one could know me, not even me. I was a surfer, an Aborigine, a Spanish bullfighter, and a liar. Mostly just a liar. Who I wasn't was Declin Ostrander. Declin Ostrander didn't even exist.

⬛⬥ ⬥⬛

When the weekend came, the exams finally over, Aron and I decided to spend the night shooting the breeze, pointing the barrel of a gun toward it and pulling the trigger.

I recognized the dilapidated church at the edge of the Peppers' property. I craned my neck out of Aron's car, staring into the night, and asked, "Where are we going?"

"Somewhere they won't hear the gunshots." He smiled. Something about the way he said this made me squirm. I had never shot a gun before.

After a few moments of silence, I said, "Winter break. That's great. Don't you have soccer practice?"

"Not for a while, no. We finished out the season last week. Trained all through November, trained hard. And our school soccer team—that'll be starting up in February. I've got about a month and a half of reprieve, only in January, I'll have to travel to Washington, DC, for the national tournament with the state team." He said all of this matter-of-factly, like he was rattling off directions for how to properly change a tire.

"Well, that's nice. I guess you have a lot of free time, then—to, um, shoot guns. And do other things you like." Forever, I had thought shooting guns at nothing had been a purely redneck pastime, but when Aron asked me after school to come along as he went shooting, I abruptly changed my mind. As we drew closer, I wondered if he had different intentions, to perhaps kill me. "Without soccer and without—well, Charlotte—"

"Right, her," Aron said curtly. "Well, I guess it's good she's gone, right?"

"I admit, she was annoying. What happened between the two of you? Just—well, didn't work out?"

The rest of the drive remained nearly silent until Aron pulled off the road and idled the truck. "Look, Declin. I brought you here for a reason—to talk to you in private. To talk and tell the truth. And no, not just because I have a gun in my hand. If you want to know anything, sure, I will tell you, but promise me you'll be honest with me."

"Why?"

"Why what? Why would you want to be honest with me?"

"No, why do you care? What is there to talk about?"

"Let me start. Charlotte and I broke up because we were never really together. I wanted to have sex with someone, and she came along wanting to date me. Expected me to date her. Turns out she just wanted to piss off her racist parents by dating me, and I—well, I wasn't much better. That's something to admit, don't you know? Sometimes, that you're not being true to yourself."

"True in what way?" I asked.

"That's not how this is going to work. My turn to ask the question. Why did you piss off Cass a couple of days ago? She was really—what did you say?"

"Me? I—I didn't say anything. I just wondered why she was so obsessed with Justin."

Aron said, "*Maybe* because he's dying. *Maybe* because she needs something to hold on to and doesn't know how to let go yet. It's more complicated than you think. You don't even know her."

"Well, that's the problem, isn't it? I'm the new kid, still. Everywhere I go, I'm the new kid. I'll never get to know anybody, and even when I think I do, I get driven out to the middle of nowhere, questioned at gunpoint, and told I don't know jack shit."

"I didn't mean to point the gun at you. Sorry."

We climbed out the car, advancing toward the forest. I asked, "Why do you like shooting a gun, anyways?"

"Well, if you're implying it's because I'm black—"

"Look, lay off that. I thought you were being truthful. So, out with it."

We stopped, and Aron loaded the gun, holding it up to his face. "See that tree?" He pulled the trigger, and after a bang that made me jump, the bark on the tree exploded. Aron fished a Coke can from the ground and set it atop a branch. "Declin, you've basically lived in the South your entire life, no matter where you've moved to, right? Your dad ever teach you to shoot a gun?"

"No, he's always been too busy, and anyways, it's not really his thing."

"Yeah, but in the South, that's something dads teach sons. They shoot guns and hunt and go fishing. And you know, your dad and my dad—they're about the same. In fact, we're the same. Only I'm half-black, and you're not. That's a major difference, mind you. Means when you get pulled over, you don't get pushed against the ground. My name is Aron; yours is Declin. You see? Our fathers are both good guys, just fighting for different sides in a war that doesn't make much sense."

"Yeah, I guess."

"So, I wanted something. Something I couldn't do with my dad. Something that would calm me down. And hell, soccer just fires me up. But shooting stuff—that makes me feel pretty damn calm inside."

He missed the can and handed the gun to me. "I guess it's time for you to ask me another question, then."

"Who are you, Declin Ostrander?"

The bullet pinged off the can, and I whistled, smiling. "Well, what do you think of that shot?"

"Good. It's good. But you're stalling."

"Who am I?" I scrunched up my face. "Hell if I know. I'm just a teenager. Even teens who don't spend their childhoods zipping around the Southeast with a deadbeat dad don't know who they are. Do you know who you are?"

"No. I guess we're in the same boat. But that's what I'm getting at. We're the same. Everyone is. No one is sure about who they are or who they want to be. And you act like some martyr, as if you're the only one confused."

"Well, you know, excuse me if I feel entitled to uncertainty. You're anything like me? You're a hotshot soccer player, and yeah, you're probably going off to a really nice university to play. You've got at least that figured out. And I'd bet you at least know what you'll be majoring in, am I right? So yes, I think my problems exceed yours by just a bit."

"Thanks a lot for really showing how you feel." Aron, bitter, snatched the gun from me. He shot erratically at the can but missed each time. He reloaded and emptied the gun again. "I just—look, we're more similar than we are different. I just thought maybe if I was truthful with you, you'd be truthful with me. I don't think you're that alone, and you're not the only person who has ever lied about yourself. Hell, what do you think the Internet is for? And you know, my mother—she left when I was really little. Moved to New York, hardly comes to visit, and sends shitty gifts. And your mom—she's not around."

I took the gun, shot at the can, and whistled. The can popped high into the air and clattered back down through the tree branches. "Well, what do you think of that shot?"

"What I think is that you shouldn't be complaining your little ass off about not knowing anything about anybody if you don't let anyone know anything about yourself."

"Well, great analysis, Sherlock. You've really got this nut cracked, haven't you? I'm just a lost soul, begging for someone to understand me. For your information, I didn't ask you to try to get to know me."

"Well, that's because you haven't even bothered—"

"My mom's dead, OK? Is that what you wanted to hear? At least your mom has the decency to stay alive, to at least be somewhere out there in case you ever really need her. But when I was a kid, my mom hated me. She was afraid of me. My mom was crazy. Is this what you want to hear? Really, Aron, is this it? Because, you know, fuck you. She thought that I was there to ruin her life, and she heard voices. Yeah, we're so much alike. And then, you know what? When I was four, she drank a Drano cocktail. Mixed that shit with wine and drank it. So yeah, your mom killed herself too because she was too stressed to take care of you, right?

"And your dad—he's exhausted because he had to quit his job and move away from the town because he was so ashamed? And even then, he never got to take care of you? Don't pretend like you know me, like we're just carbon copies of each other. We don't share the same story. We don't share anything." I dropped the gun. "Let's just—let's leave."

Until we reached downtown, Aron stayed deadly quiet. But I didn't feel guilty. He had asked for the truth, and if the truth was too much, that was too fucking bad. "I'm sorry," he said finally. "I didn't know. But I'm glad you told me."

I nodded. "Well, I've never told anyone that before. I—I saw her die, and I guess—it's not something I ever talk about."

"I guess not." A minute of silence, that familiar iceberg floating between us. "Well, anyways, you're a really good shot. Better than me, and I've been at it for years."

"Well, I guess that's—well, solace. I'm sorry I was such a jerk. I just—sometimes—I guess we do have some stuff in common. I just overreact. I'm no closer to figuring out anything. Who I am or who I'll be."

"Yeah, me neither. Don't worry about it. We've still got time on our side."

As teenagers, we were allowed to be directionless, clueless. The teenage life was simply a prologue to what came after. The story of what happened before anything really happened. Nothing too interesting occurred, except for stupidity and experimentation. Because everyone kept changing who they were, it would be impossible to keep all the characters in such a story straight. We were the eternal teenagers.

CHAPTER 20

MR. PEARSON

Principal Reiser ignored me for a few minutes while he furiously checked his e-mail, his fingers tapping with the vigor of a trained assassin, and then he glanced up over a stack of forms and books and framed photographs of his pet iguana, Sandy. "You wanted to speak with me, Pearson?"

I hefted the history textbook onto my lap, flipped to the chapter entitled "War of Northern Aggression," and then slid the book across the table to him. "It's barely two pages. Don't you think we should be teaching...well, more about this?"

After a moment, Reiser closed the book firmly and smiled. "About what? We chose a book that covered the first battle in Charleston—Fort Sumter. The chapter on the Civil War explains the contentions of states' rights and even describes a few battles. It's embarrassing for our country to bring up all those horrors that led up to the war...The world wars—now those were important—those really showed the world what a spectacular country we lived in. What our boys could do."

"But—but—considering we live in South Carolina, wouldn't it be important to learn about how the war affected the lives of slaves?"

"Slavery? These students know about slavery. You grow up in South Carolina—it's slavery this, slavery that. They're just trying to get you to feel—I don't know, guilty? But on top of that, slavery's brutal. Over the years we've received calls from parents complaining that what we were teaching students just went over their heads. How should they understand slave ships and beatings and fieldwork? How alien a concept—they wouldn't even understand. Such conversations just make kids feel uncomfortable about the privilege of their lives. You understand?"

"I don't understand. To me—well, to me, it seems extremely important. Why choose a book that just glosses over these things, these ugly things? Perhaps kids might feel uncomfortable, squirm in their seats, but don't we need to feel uncomfortable? Sometimes, don't we need to be jolted out of our cushiony lives?"

Reiser cleared his throat. "Due to extenuating circumstances, we found it best to choose reading material that would prevent any upsets within the community."

"But these kids need to know about the atrocities—"

"Don't worry. The subject won't appear on the state-issued exam. If it's not on the exam, why would they need to learn about it at all?" He gave a brief smile and then began pecking at the computer. "Is that all?"

"I—I—I'll just go to lunch."

Without looking up, Reiser muttered, "We'd prefer to stick to the curriculum, Pearson. Everything runs smoothly. I'll make sure the superintendent stops by your classroom, to show her what an exemplary teacher you've become. Please, don't disappoint us."

Two weeks later, when the students were slated to learn about slavery, I entered the classroom, and a prim young woman introduced herself, clipboard in hand. My blood felt rusty, felt wrong, as I began a PowerPoint based on the history book about how the South lost its God-given rights.

CHAPTER 21

THE JOURNAL OF ELIJAH RODRIGUEZ

December 13

Most people are happy that winter break is here, but I'm horrified. I'll have to eat lunch alone for two weeks. Even if they're silent and sometimes they shout at each other, they're my friends.

I know now how a butterfly must feel trapped because of its beauty, forced to suffocate in a mason jar because someone could not share that beauty with the world. My parents don't understand. They might not believe me anyways. How soon that butterfly is going to die and then be pressed into a book. A sort of token to keep forever.

He followed me to school. The Exeter boy from the library. Stepping out of the building, I saw him. He had been waiting on me, standing by his car. I'm not sure if he had been waited particularly on me, but I felt it. I don't know what he wants with me. As soon as I saw him, I knew he had come to get me. He will torture me forever, maybe, because I amuse him. And keep me in a glass mason jar until I run out of air.

Sometimes, people don't seem to notice I'm there. I could stand directly beside someone, but they'll talk through me as if I'm some ghost. I overhear a lot I'm not supposed to know because of this. Like how Justin Ferrara was supposedly taking steroids before his crash. And how Blaine and Cass are sleeping together.

But the Exeter boy doesn't act like most people, doesn't just leave me alone. I think he thinks it's fun. He's just taunting me, waiting for his chance. Ever since he found me in the library, he has wanted me. For something, though I'm not sure what.

Today is Friday the thirteenth, and I'm not superstitious, but I don't feel safe.

December 14

With only Josh as my companion, I keep getting creamed in *Dragon Sphere*. Even though the Dragon Master says I'm getting better, I feel like I get eaten by dragons at least once a week. I'm starting to wonder if maybe Greg the Devil Dwarf was right. Maybe *Dragon Sphere* really *does* have too many dragons in it.

We played all day. I felt very safe being indoors. As long as Nick is around, I really doubt Cain will mess with me. I told him I was going to bring a friend, if I could. I knew I could maybe convince Declin to come with me.

December 24

When we left my grandfather's house for Christmas Eve Mass, I slid into the passenger's seat of my father's car. We followed a procession of our family's vehicles—crammed with young cousins, uncles, aunts, and my gnarled and Puerto Rican grandfather. He didn't speak English very well, and I couldn't speak Spanish very well. We rarely spoke, except to greet one another with mutual disgust.

"Did you see that girl's ass? The one Julio brought along? Must be getting some sort of ass from that bitch." He guffawed and then peered over at me. I did not laugh. "Ah, straighten your tie, Elijah. God wants you to look good when you enter his house. But that ass, though."

We drove to church in silence and then filed out to enter the massive cathedral. My grandfather still attended Mass every Sunday like a good Catholic at a Spanish-speaking church, and every Christmas my father dressed in a suit, moaned the repetitive slogans, and pretended he too was a good Catholic. Outside stood a nativity scene, Latino faces peeking out from beneath heavy blankets-made-robes, a plastic baby doll propped in the pig-feeding trough.

The church opened its maw as we entered, the interior walls decorated with depictions of the Gospels. Overhead I spotted Jesus on the cross, his thorn crown hung low over his brow and his bleeding hands midtwitch. Along the sides of the church stood various stations for saints—Saint Agatha and Saint Thomas and Saint Francis of Assisi. We could pray at these stations, hoping the saints would convey our desires to God. *"Bienvenido."* A greeter furiously shook my hand and patted me on the shoulder.

At the head of the church stood a pulpit rising like a horn from the marbled floor. To the right of the priest's pedestal, a small wooden closet stood in the corner. I remembered the confessional booth well from my youth. When I was six, I didn't mind confessing my sins, whether it was stealing candy or thinking bad thoughts about my grandparents, though as I grew older, I also became more reticent at that partition screen. Turns out, good Catholic boys never watched porn, and all the other boys never told.

The church slowly filled. I strained to recall the rituals, crossing myself as I saw my mother do before she sat down. I snatched up a program from the pew and began reading, calculating how many hymns I would have to pretend to sing before going home. My body ached exhaustion. The congregation began to stand, and a portly man in white robes ascended to the pulpit. He called out, *"El señor esté con vosotros."* We each made the sign of the cross. I stared straight forward, ignoring my father, whose eyes drifted to the pew in front of us where Julio's girlfriend bent over to pick up her fallen program. I held my breath and then opened my mouth to sing.

⭐ ⭐

Around two in the morning, we returned to my grandfather's house, where my family began to drink and dance. I plopped into a foldout seat in the corner, isolated from the action. My grandfather hobbled around the room, kissing people on the cheek and speaking very fast. I took three years of Spanish in school, but even after that instruction, I could not understand my grandfather's accent. When he stood in front of me, he bid me stand up, and I did. He poked my ribs and clutched my jaw, his eyes level with mine. *"Débil,"* he muttered, which I understood clearly.

My father hovered behind us on the couch, laughing at my grandfather's remark. "Well, I try and try, but he's such a— delicate boy. His mother doesn't want him to get hurt."

Nodding, my grandfather patted me on the shoulder and then shuffled back across the room. My uncles cracked beers, teasing me with open bottles. "You want one? No, you're too young to drink."

My father took Mary by the arm and pulled her into the middle of the floor, and he danced like an octopus having a seizure. Somewhere outside, fireworks popped sporadically, the lights fizzling through the window. Mary sat down, and my mother joined my father as he stomped across the floor. The living room became a frenzy of flailing limbs and sliding feet.

My family continued to dip, bend, and sway to the mambo. They circled the living room like writhing nightmares, rising and crouching in accordance with the crescendos and decrescendos. The trills and scoops electrified some staccato soul. The music possessed them and drove them to the precipice of sanity. The colors of my father's culture lived not on any canvas but rose up from it like some vibrant, soulful sculpture—a sculpture that could dance.

I stood up, slipped out the back, and watched the bursts of color erupt above the horizon of pine trees. I felt terribly out of place. My father always regretted not forcing me to learn more Spanish in school; instead, after three years, I began taking French because I fancied one day I might go to France and explore the cities. My father, though, said the French were all homosexuals.

—❧ ❧—

The party ended too late, and then we drove for nearly an hour home.

My family's Puerto Rican Christmas Eve probably wouldn't interest anyone. That's why I'd make a terrible fiction writer. If it were my job to come up with plots, I wouldn't know where to begin. I suspect I could write fantasies, since I like fantasies. Not those trashy, dumb fantasies chock-full of clichés. Real, epic fantasies that would inspire people. Like Tolkien. I always liked some science-fiction writers, especially Bradbury. Sometimes, I'd reread the same books.

It's difficult to write any of this in the back of my dad's car as we ride home since most of the roads are dirt paved and strewn with rocks. South Carolina isn't known for its decent infrastructure.

I sometimes pretend the floor of our car is transparent so I can watch the road racing away beneath us. My parents sit in the front seats, bobbing their heads to "Rudolph," "Silver Bells," and "Sleigh Bells." My parents do not talk to each other often. They do not talk to me often either. We sit like a gang of polite strangers on a train, silent and cautious of each other's gazes.

December 28

He followed me home more than once before school let out. Eventually, I stopped noticing him as he hid behind his shades. I never told you until that last day when he deliberately waited outside of school. He wanted to be seen.

One day as I walked home, he called out to me from ten paces behind. "Faggot maggot," he called, snickering to himself. I imagine that, under his shades, his eyes burned demon red. He leered at me for a moment, waiting for me to retaliate. I kept walking.

Waiting. Waiting for me.

The boy's name, I learned today, is Cain. Whenever I saw him with a gang of others, he wore his Exeter uniform. The trim fitted jacket and navy-blue dress pants. The uniforms unnerved me as well because the boys looked like part of some private-school infantry. Carrying books instead of guns. Driving BMWs instead of tanks. Shooting words rather than bullets. Whenever Cain surrounded himself with others, he did not acknowledge me, though I could tell he watched me from under his shades. He wore shades too often, I felt. I began trying to remember what his eyes looked like underneath; I saw them in the library. But the color, shape, and gleam—nothing. I wonder if he has eyes at all.

They roamed down the streets of downtown, where fortunately I never go. I walked down the blocks only to get to school. Once break began, I only spotted Cain a few times quite by accident. At the mall or gas station or while out to dinner with my parents. Almost as if he were a ghost following after me. Today, I saw him again.

Cain stood on the street corner out of uniform, wearing jeans and a hooded sweatshirt too shabby for his surname. Again, wearing glasses that reflected back everything he stared at, which made it look like he never blinked. At dusk, I walked downtown because I could not stand the house. Once, I had been able to sit in my bedroom, fiddling with video games or drowning in books. Now, however, the stale air inside suffocated me. I needed a place to breath.

Beginning down one street, I saw Cain in the distance as I turned a corner. He idled alone against the brick wall of the drugstore, lazily smoking a cigarette. I recognized him only because of his sunglasses, which were unnecessary as dusk crept upon us.

Another man approached him from across the street, signaling his attention with a slight nod. The two bustled into an alley near the Dumpsters behind the coffee shop next door. Nothing pulled me into the dark faster than curiosity. My tormentor's private life hid at sundown behind the Dumpster.

Peeking out from around the corner, I could see and hear them clearly. Cain did not speak with the same high, haughty voice he used to mock me, instead speaking in low tones with false gangster language. Every few words I heard were *man* or *bro* or *brother*. The man opposite stood a head taller than Cain, and up close I could see a massive scar that cut from his right ear across his eye to the corner of his mouth. His head was buzzed, though the jagged fuzz was a cartoonish orange.

They spoke harshly, but I could not make out their words. The older redhead grabbed Cain's arm, his face screwing up. I recognized him now as one of the Peppers. Must have been related to the guy who was arrested. After a few exchanges, the Pepper grew more agitated.

He lunged forward and knocked Cain roughly to the concrete. The hood fell back from his mop of hair, and the sunglasses slid off his nose, shattering under both their weight. The man pinned Cain's arm on top of the broken black glass and snarled, poking the point of the blade at Cain's chest. The blade hovered closer to Cain's body; the man then grazed his shirt. Like a tongue seductively traveling up his body toward his face.

He dug the tip lightly into Cain's shoulder until he drew blood. Such violent acts right here. I could hardly stomach it and considered running again. But Cain's embarrassment held me fast, rooted me to the ground. I wanted to watch this happen. The act repulsed me and attracted me.

The man finally closed his knife again and smirked as Cain trembled pathetically beneath him. Fat tears rolled down Cain's naked face. I stood on my tiptoes, almost begging the man to hurry and kill him. I admonished myself for wishing his death, editing my desires to "severely maim." Instead, he gripped Cain's pinkie and cleanly snapped it. Cain cried out, baring his teeth at the sky.

The man growled, exchanged a few more words, and fled. He jogged down the alley in the opposite direction from me. Cain lay still sniveling in the alley. I turned and ran all the way home.

I'm sometimes not sure whether to be shocked at human suffering or delighted by it.

CHAPTER 22

DYLAN PEPPER

A few days after Christmas, this kid texted me that we had to meet, like I was supposed to be at his beck and call, like I was some fucking servant. So he stood on the street corner, arms crossed, trying to look intimidating, but no matter how much he bunched up his face or squared his shoulders, he looked like a pretty boy to me. Looked like some sixth-grade punk tryna impress his date to the Valentine's dance. Smoking cigarettes. Spitting the smoke through his nostrils—shit, I shoulda beat him then, slit that little fucker's throat, but I was feeling good on account of I just popped a bunch of oxys and felt like I was floating across the street, and my face felt numb as hell. Felt like my veins been pumping in my head, like I was invincible. So I started walking on toward him, and he nodded at me like he knew what was coming.

I parked my truck across the street. He probably would look for a gun, so I kept my shirt hanging below my waist. He squirmed to see and then retreated into the alleyway. Kid wore a gray hoodie and ripped jeans, the sort of costume an undercover cop would expect a teenager to wear.

"Where you been?"

"The fuck you mean where I been? You don't know where I been—you haven't noticed?"

He paused and swallowed. "The cops in town—those agents—they're for you. I—I thought you skipped town, man. I thought you just—bro, I'm real sorry. I didn't know."

Clenched my fist. "Listen, tell me what the fuck you know about what's going on."

He sighed. "My—my dad says, well, they're trying to catch some local dealers. They think there's some supply coming from here."

"You fucking—what? Dad? Your fucking father is involved with that? God Almighty, why did I ever talk to a little shit like you? What do they know?"

"They suspect—well, they suspect it might be your family that's supplying a crime syndicate out of Charleston. I—I don't know what to think. I didn't know. Things were going great. I'm pushing as much as I can, and you just disappear—man, I don't—"

Clutching his arm, I leaned in until I could see sweat leaking from his face and feel the increasing tempo of his heartbeat, thudding through his arterie, where his fear rose to the surface, embossed with tattoos. He couldn't look at me, couldn't look me in the eye. Probably didn't want to glance at the ugly scar, cutting through my face like a tributary.

"Listen, you little fucker. These things don't just happen. Someone has to blab. Someone had to bring them here. If I find out it's you, I'm going to take you into the middle of the pines and bury you up to your neck in dirt. Then I'm gonna take a baseball bat, and I'm gonna smash it over your head until your head looks like a piñata."

"I—I didn't say—I didn't."

"Then you're going to tell me about all the Exeter boys you sold to. Did they know who you were getting—"

"No, they don't know anything. I haven't said anything. Please, please—"

"Don't fucking beg me for your life, kid. 'Cause you should be praying I kill you. You won't like what will happen if you're lying to me."

"I'm not. Never." He quivered, shrinking against the wall. I pushed him to the ground, and he yelped like a puppy whose tail I'd trod over. "Please."

Then the kid, quick as shit, pulls out a gun. Well, shit, I grab his arm and pin it behind his back. "What you tryna do with that little piece, boy? What you tryna do?"

"I thought you would hurt me. I—my dad gave me that gun."

"Fuck your dad."

Removing my knife from my pocket, I flipped it open. His sunglasses toppled from the face, shattering beneath him, and I pushed him down on top of their remnants, poking his chest with the tip of a knife.

"Are you afraid of me, boy?"

"Well—"

"Good. Because that means you going to do what I say." A moment passed before he nodded. "I'll find you from now on, you understand? You come here, and you give me the money." Digging through my jacket pocket, I removed a pouch. "You keep peddling to your friends. But if I hear one word about you talking to these agents, I'll give you a scar worse than mine."

I dug the knife into his shoulder and drew blood. Warm, fat tears rolled from his eyes while he watched helpless, and I still felt so invincible, smirked, and then flipped the blade closed. "You're going to remember what you promised, won't you?" Ain't it easy to scare piss-poor the trembling ones, the ones who puff up their chests and jut out their lips like they gonna do something?

"I will. I will."

"You will."

Grabbed his hand and pulled his fist toward me, took his fingers between my knuckles, and held his pinkie taut. *Snap.* Before he could scream, I had pressed his finger as far back as possible, until his nail kissed the back of his hand. Cried, cried, cried. Gave him a firm kick, dropped the gun on the pavement beside him, and then left him there alone.

⊫ ⊨

I parked my truck in front of Papa Pepper's house. The wild dogs in the forest kept barkin' and squealin', watching me from far back. Hopped out the truck, walked right into the front door, and swung open the screen door. He sat in his new Sunday clothes, his hair neat and combed. Didn't even look up when I walked in but said, "Dylan? Wasn't expectin' you. Going to the courthouse with us? You look a little—dirty."

Dirty? Fuck yeah, I felt dirty. For four weeks I lived in a trailer pissing into beer cans cause the plumbing never worked, and I stacked 'em in pyramids and towers impressive as ancient cities, piled against the windows. Four weeks of sweatin' through my skin, leaping to the window, prying apart the blinds, peering through. Expecting the feds to swoop in any moment, break down the door, and shoot me dead while I been shittin' in a bucket. The whole place looking like a failed science-fair project, broken beakers and snarled plastic tubes dangling from the ceiling.

Dirty, he calls me, the savior and prodigal child. "That's all you got to say? That's what you got to say while you sit on your ass while the family falls apart. You've given up, haven't you? You don't even know what you doing anymore."

He put down his fork. "Listen, I'm trying."

"When was the last time Elizabeth went to school? You've had her cooped up."

"And you've had her running errands she has no business running. You're putting my daughter in danger. Get out of my fucking home."

"So you can continue to stuff your face with bacon, get diabetes, and die?"

"Don't you dare speak to me like that." His chest grew big. "I can't help it. Diabetes is genetic and runs in my blood."

"Bacon grease runs through your blood." I spat. "You're pathetic, and you don't even know it."

When he looked me in the eyes, I felt I might be swallowed by the sky. "Now, you listen to me, Son. We all have our addictions. For some, it's bacon, and for others, it might be crystal meth. But just hope your addiction doesn't kill you before mine kills me. You have no idea what you're doing, what danger you're putting us in. We don't need this."

I backed away from the table. Clenched my fist. "You have no idea, do you? I'm the only one holding this family together."

"Holding it together? You sold this family off. Every other day, there are different men in suits coming to my door, threatening me at gunpoint. Don't think I'm afraid of you." When he stood up, his stomach pushed the plastic table back. "You're just a boy. You don't know what you've done."

"I gave us a chance. If I hadn't saved us, we'd not even be here right now. The police would have come to fuck us all. The only reason they haven't is because of what I did. I made these connections, something you could have never done. Because you've always been unwilling to do what's needed."

Papa Pepper threw up his hands and began to stalk out the door. "Get out of my house, Dillon. Go back and hide in your little hole. You think you're some sort of savior, but you've damned us. Ever since you prostituted this family to that damned man from Charleston, you damned us."

I nodded. This was what he believed, and I couldn't believe it—made me sick. "OK, fine then. Fine. Just don't expect me to save your ass when everything crumbles onto *your* head."

As I sped from the property, I kept checking my rearview mirrors for any suspicious cars. Every day, I didn't wanna open the door, flinched every time I opened my eyes. They were coming for me.

Papa Pepper made me damn sad 'cause he gave up, and the world had begun to rot, and some days I felt like our family stood to decide earth's fate—whether we went to heaven or hell. But shit, life was disappointing, just like when I was a kid and my mother told me we'd go to Myrtle Beach and instead drove to Walmart: "We can't afford it but can afford milk."

These days, the world was different. Our president was black. Heathens taught evolution in school. Homosexuals were trying to get married. Christianity had been abandoned, all morals flushed down the fuckin' toilet. America had become a dustbowl of dumb hippies and political correct bullshit. The future of this country scared the shit out of me. I felt angry and fearful and a bit helpless.

CHAPTER 23

BLAINE MOREAU

A nother Monday loomed ahead and maybe five hours of possible sleep. When I climbed in through my window, I cursed myself for being so stupid and not sleeping sooner. Another night I would not sleep, but at least I had a remedy.

When my alarm clock began to scream, I forced myself to sit up fast, which felt like being plunged into ice-cold water. Digging through my sock drawer, I removed a tiny plastic baggy that looked empty. After flicking and pinching the bag between my fingers, a few crystals of Molly sprinkled onto my bedside table; if I didn't take some as soon as I woke anymore, I felt like total shit. The first day I went without it, I plunged into a moody depression, a sulkiness that lashed out at everyone. I even told Cass to fuck off and then berated Declin for lying so fantastically every day.

But I felt better now, happy, fulfilled.

I studied the empty baggy, shaking: empty. Where could I get more of this? Maybe if I told my parents I needed gas for my car, they would give me money; I couldn't tell them about the drugs because they couldn't understand. They never understood anything I did, anything I wanted. The fad of this generation was to scorn the traditions our parents adored: team sports, higher education, and abstinence were generally mocked.

As my heart began break-dancing, I peered into the crumpled bag. Nothing remained. With eagerness, I had consumed so much in the past months that it was gone. And usually, this stuff was more expensive than Siberian tiger cubs. I had gotten a deal, but to get more I would have to talk to Dylan Pepper again, who actually scared the shit out of me. I would have to ask Cain.

In the shower, I scrubbed my body raw and felt like living and dying all at once. Passing shampoo over my bald head, not able to remember when I'd shaved it all off. I set off from my house like a firework.

⚒

"Blaine, where are you going?"

I looked up from my feet. "Huh? Me? I'm just—the—" The class was still sitting down. I slunk back to my lab bench next to Aron. Ms. Schall continued giving me a weird look but sat down, probably supposing it wasn't worth it. Already, three people had walked outside to vomit while we watched a human-penis dissection video.

"She is quite the trip, right?" I smirked at Declin, who avoided eye contact. Ever since I revealed his secrets, he'd been pissed. And now winter break was days away, but he still would not talk to me. As if everyone had not already seen through his stupid lies. All of his stupid stories about his stupid fake girlfriend whom he had stupid fake sex with.

If only he knew what Cass and I had done, what would he think? Maybe he knew, and this thought gave me such satisfaction, I began tasting hot chocolate. I began to laugh, and even Pepper watched me warily.

When the bell rang, I stumbled again out of the classroom, feeling suddenly dizzy. Aron caught my arm, asking, "Blaine, are you all right? Are you OK? Are you OK? Blaine? Blaine? Blaine? Blaine? Blaine? Blaine? Blaine?"

He pulled me up from the floor where I had slumped over, and I mumbled, "Fine." But he shouldered me in the stomach, lifting, and then there was a blur; he plopped me onto a wooden bench. The bright sun hurt my eyes, so I recoiled against the brick wall of the school. "Why the courtyard? I have statistics to get to."

"Well, didn't you know that seventy percent of the time you're being an asshole, and the other thirty percent you're too high to remember your name?"

"My name is Blaine. Name is Blaine."

The slap tasted like white-lemon Italian Ice. "Delicious," I told him, smiling stupidly up at him. While I was collapsed against the wall, Aron looked like a giant, like the Marshmallow Man, only dipped in caramel.

"Blaine, what's wrong with you? How much have you smoked today—and hell, how much do you smoke every day? Maybe it's just caused some sort of permanent damage. Maybe your brain is all—"

"My brain is perfectly fine. You're overreacting. I'm tired; that's all."

"Blaine, it's only Monday morning. Where did you go last night?"

I only grinned because I guessed he probably knew. "Nowhere. Look, man, don't worry about this."

For a moment, I thought he was going to walk away, give up, but instead he pinned me down. His hot breath in my nose felt like Mike Tyson's left hook. "Blaine, I am going to worry about it. We're almost done, right? We've been doing this together for years, ever since we were kids. So, don't go screwing around now when everything—"

"You think I can't graduate? Aron, I'm a genius"

"You're such a dick. You don't even appreciate—look, you have this amazing talent. And you're so high, you're near collapsing. You can't even function. And when is the last time you even slept? Blaine, this isn't good. You have a responsibility to do something with your life."

"Don't throw that Spider-Man shit at me."

"Yeah, well—" Aron stood up, letting me stand and breathe as well. "I just want to help, OK? You're meant for more than this."

"More than what?"

Aron paused. "I know what you've been doing, Blaine. Just, I had to—I had to say something. When you get back from winter break, be better."

"Yeah, I'll be fine."

"Promise me."

"Promise you what?"

"You'll do better. Really, try."

"Yeah, sure." As I said it, Aron nodded. He walked away. I hustled off to class.

━┼ ┼━

My tutor grabbed my wrist. "Blaine, are you even paying attention?"

"Yeah, I—well, uh—I've got this."

"What answer did you get?"

"Answer?"

"Have you even been working on this problem?" We looked down together at my piece of notebook paper, which was blank.

I looked up at the problem on the board. Just numbers at first, but then they came to life. I fell into them, the nines rising up around me like tall skyscrapers, the threes all hobos, the summation signs zigzagging trams. The equation became a city in my mind, the answer waiting somewhere to be found, flashing in the Manhattan-like lights that blinded me. With the drugs, the buildings were wonky, off-kilter. I did not recognize the numbers as well as I once could, but I struggled through the haze, the numbers spinning. A storm above my head, spinning, spinning, spinning.

Thinking used to feel like speeding in a race car, the wind pounding my face in exhilarating fashion, but now it sounded like two bagpipes playing out of tune.

"Well, I've got two hundred six over seventeen. That correct?"

The tutor sighed. "Yes, but—we're supposed to actually work out the problem. Then we can move on and do better, bigger things."

"Why? No one uses this math. Even Einstein didn't do this stuff. Only me, because—"

"Because you're a synesthete. But if you bothered to learn the process the right way, to make it make sense, you could—"

"Why is there always a right and wrong way of doing things? If we both get the same answer, what's the point? Life is just an equation that we all go through differently to arrive at the same result."

"But even though you're—well, there's more to it. If you don't understand the math, really understand it beyond a step-by-step process, you'll never find a real career."

I hated my tutor for this, his condescending glares. As if he could do half of what I could. Even after years of studying, he knew nothing. "And what do you know about real careers? You know all this but get stuck tutoring me. You're a washed-up fuck."

He tightened up, his mustache contracting like a furry spring. "But wasn't given the same opportunities you've been given. I wasn't born with your gift. That makes everything so—effortless.

You have to do something with that gift. But you don't understand, because you're such a"—like venom—"genius. You never have to work for—"

Something overwhelmed me. Perhaps his voice, his face, the drugs pumping through my veins. Leaping to my feet, I pushed at his chest. I bore down on him, clutching his lapels in my balled-up fists. Then I cocked back my arm and smacked him in the jaw. "I didn't even ask for this. I don't have to do anything. I'm more than just a freak math genius. You don't understand—what it's like. For—for everyone to expect so much from you when you can only give them, well, nothing."

Once I said it, I deflated. He was stronger than I thought, taking the punch and then rubbing his chin. Saying nothing, only staring at me. "Well, I guess I don't understand all of your—niceties. Good luck, you little shithead."

As he stormed out of our school library, I doubled over laughing. As if he had taught me anything, the old fucking fraud. If anything, this just gave me extra free time after lunch.

⇒⊹ ⊹⇐

My parents sat around the table like torturers of the Spanish Inquisition, or maybe Nazis waiting patiently in the dining room of a Jewish home. Between them sat a manila folder. I crossed between them, eyeing the letter. "Is that for me?"

"It looks awfully thin," my father said. "Look at the address."

I did. Michigan Institute of Technology—no big deal.

Ripping open the envelope, I pulled out a single piece of paper, which was a universal sign for rejection. "I'm sorry to inform you," I read, and I swear my parents deflated like Mylar balloons at an archer's birthday party, "that your son was actually accepted to our crummy school, and we're duly impressed with his intense talents and achievements." They screamed so loud and hugged me so tight I figured they didn't even notice that I had botched the words.

"Blaine, this is fantastic. You can finally go where you've always wanted."

"But I never—"

"We're so proud of you. Know that, OK?"

I nodded, dizzy and high. With the envelope in hand, I headed upstairs. I laid it on my desk, sat down, and watched it. My mind churned and crackled.

What if I did go to college, get a degree, get a job? Would that ever help? What would I even do? I felt like some freak science experiment, like the Hulk, ready to be shipped off for government experimentation. But here I was, breaking the fingers of the hand of fate. When I began digging through my sock drawer, I remembered that I threw the baggie away—no more Molly.

Uncertainty tasted like the oil of a gun dripping onto your tongue as the coldness of the barrel presses against your throat.

I collapsed onto my bed when I realized it was nearly midnight, but I could not go to sleep. The letter kept me awake, or maybe it was the beginnings of withdrawal. When I was a kid, in the doctor's office, my parents seemed so proud to have this freak son. This son who could just look at numbers and delineate the secrets of the universe. But that had never been what I wanted. What I wanted—I didn't want anything. I had never asked for any special treatment from God, but he had given me this burden anyways. As if I was supposed to do something with it. Well, I figured, fuck everyone.

Sitting up in bed, I watched the sun rise and wondered why my parents had not even called me back downstairs for dinner. How removed was I from them that they had stopped noticing Blaine their son, just talking to Blaine the genius? I thought of Aron and my tutor and even Cass, who sometimes hinted at what money I would one day make. Not one fucking person cared about me. They only cared about what I could do, how I could help them or society or humanity or their companies. But no one deserved my help. No one ever deserved anything.

⊷ ⊶

As we walked from our last class to the parking lot, I approached Cass, sliding my hand against her back and then downward.

"Stop that."

"We're going back to your house, right?"

"I'm going to visit Justin in the hospital."

Even when we reached her car, she hadn't registered my incredulous look. "Again? Cass, he's in a coma. He won't even know if you're not there." I tried to push her against the car and press my lips against her neck, but she pushed at my chest.

"Fuck off, Blaine."

"Was it something I said?" She began to climb into her car, and I grabbed her arm. "I'll see you tonight?"

Sighing, she slammed the door and sped off—a yes, I presumed.

⊷ ⊶

It seemed strange to me that we lied to children as they grew up, about Santa Claus or sex. Then we also impressed upon them to trust what adults say: don't cross the street, don't touch the stove, don't run at the pool, and don't question me, because I'm right—that's why.

How fucking contradictory. You inject an incredulous strain into an otherwise perfectly uniform education, and then when that child grows up, adults worry why the child doesn't trust them. Of course they don't—they spent the first nine years of their life believing in the stork and the Easter Bunny. Punished for impudence but encouraged to think outside the box. In my opinion, we needed people willing to break the rules, challenge the status quo, talk during the movie, and never use signal lights when changing lanes; if everyone always did what they were told, we might never have made any progress.

And if no one ever bothered to lie to us, then we'd never have learned to be distrustful.

"What do you mean that wasn't Molly?"

The truth screamed from my bones, like a spell that had been etched there before I was born. Cain shook his head, snickering, but then covered that up. "I mean, some of it was Molly, but it was cut with meth. I thought you knew."

"I want more."

"Molly or meth?"

My cravings had wrapped securely around the base of my spine, spiraling up into my brain stem and infesting my mind. The thought of giving up and rejecting his drugs—that now seemed insane.

"Well, well—how much for—um, some meth?"

"We can call it Molly, if that makes you feel comfortable." I sat beside him in his sleek Porsche. He munched lazily on trail mix while fiddling with the radio knob, caustically oblivious to my needs.

"You've got money, right?"

"Eighty dollars."

I passed the wad of bills to him, waiting with fidgety anticipation for him to count them. "Take this. If you want more, I suggest you start looking elsewhere. Dylan wasn't too happy to take your order."

Opening the bag, I breathed deeply. "This is—um, less than—"

"This ain't cut Molly; this is the real deal, pure. Before, I gave you a helluva a deal. Consider yourself a friend for that. So, you can take that much or leave it. Your choice."

"And what do you mean look elsewhere? Are you not cooking?"

"The Peppers are going to be stepping out of the business, so to speak. Me too. After Matthew Pepper was arrested, people started watching us." Cain's eyes scanned the woods momentarily. "They're going to give him the death sentence."

"Right, unless they find him innocent."

Cain snorted. "Does it really matter if he's innocent or not? If they kill him, that's just doing society a service."

I nodded. "Yes, yes, yes. Of course. I guess I'll, um, see you around." I stumbled out of the car. Cain sped off, and dust clouded around me as I stood alone beside the church.

Once he disappeared, I removed a small crystal and crushed it with my fingers, lining it up clumsily before rolling a dollar bill and snorting—that rush, potent as a bullet to the head.

⊷⊷

By the time I reached Cass's house, my entire body was shaking. Sweat pouring down my face, I walked through the front door. "Oh, shit. Frank, shit, shit, shit." Cass's mom slapped the man in the face, and he finally looked up and dismounted.

The man whose name was Frank blushed, pulling a blanket over himself. "And you are?"

"Oh, sorry. Here to see Cass. Is she—?"

"Blaine, come up here." I followed Cass's voice up the stairs. She sat on her bed, working delicately at her nails. "You look like you saw a fucking zombie. Well, I guess you did see Frank's dick. Saggy old bastard, isn't he? Almost as old as my grandfather, actually."

"Your mom is cheating on your dad."

She smiled. "Yeah, but at least she has good business sense. My dad is fucking some hippie yoga teacher. Frank down there—he's my parents' boss."

"Right. Well, sorry about that."

"Don't worry about it. I just wish they didn't have to do it on the couch, right next to the door. I think my mom's hoping my father will catch them."

"But they would get divorced, wouldn't they?"

Cass shrugged. "Maybe. But imagine the material it will give them for their radio show. It would definitely increase listenership."

How *totally* fucked up, I thought, almost as fucked up as us.

I pulled off my shirt, wiping my face with it. "I've wanted you all day."

Cass pushed me away, smiling. "Oh, you see Frank and my mom fucking and you get all aroused? You need to cool down."

"But—" I swatted her hand away and fell on top of her, but my lips missed hers, landing somewhere on her hip.

"Get off of me, you fucking—"

I hit her so hard she rolled backward, tumbled off the bed, and sprawled across the bedroom floor. "Fuck," she said. But I was on her, kissing her, biting her lip, my fingernails digging into her upper thigh. Whether the next "Fuck" was angry or euphoric, I couldn't tell. But then she kneed me in the balls. "Get off of me." Her nails, much longer than my own, found their way between my legs and dug in.

"What's wrong with you? Why are you acting so fucking—"

I swung at her face.

This time she was ready, grabbing my arm. "You think I don't know how to fight, you fucking asshole? You think you can come in here and just—" She was smiling and crying at the same time. Then a surge of pain shot through my entire body, my limbs going rigid. She had kicked me hard right between my legs; she was wearing pointed heels.

As I crouched cupping my balls against any further attacks, wondering if I even had any genitals left, she paced her room and gave me another kick, in the center of my back, for good measure. This time I was the one yelling "Fuck." Even the pain seemed somehow enjoyable, that savage and pleasurable white-lemon taste filling my mouth like blood.

She buckled as she sat on the edge of her bed, bending her head painfully toward her knees. "Please, just get out." When I recovered, I stumbled to my feet and limped down the stairs. As I left, Frank and her mom didn't even bother to pause.

⟩⟨ ⟩⟨

I began to worry when I spent New Year's Eve and the next two days sleepless, trailing after Cain from party to party in a perpetual haze. Boredom wasn't even the enemy any longer. I faced myself, the broken-mirror version of myself staring back at me. I wasn't worried, though, not at all.

Anxiety had that bitter taste, but I didn't experience anxiety anymore. Everything I tasted was sweet like white lemon.

The Swag Boys traveled in a pack, each cocky and cruel and entitled. Each laughing, each wasting his life like me. Fuck fate, they seemed to say, whatever circumstance had brought. All the money and privilege and status—none of that meant shit. The only thing anyone truly owned was power. And now I felt powerful, perhaps for the first time ever. I felt invincible.

No one could decide my life for me. Nothing, not any untold entity floating above our heads, could control us. If someone in the sky was trying to orchestrate some greater plan for my life, I was doing my best to fuck it up. To burn everything I or anyone had ever done. The weeks were a haze, an endless series of fuckups that added up to my life. My life that was such an equation, so easy to calculate, to weigh and count and multiply, until the final product was zero.

None of this worried me; it empowered me. Even when I returned to school to find Cass still wearing her black eye, I didn't taunt her. I didn't care.

Shoving bits of windowpane up your nose would not provide the same exhilarating, pounding, wild sensation that meth did.

This drug belonged to a new level, another plane of smashing the palace of reality. If synesthesia made my senses tweak out, meth made them enter an entirely different dimension. Cain sold me an entire eighth for sixty bucks.

A mistake perhaps, but for me a mind-numbing, mind-expanding mistake.

When Declin stopped talking to me for outing him as a deceptive virgin, I could not have given less of a shit. Or Aron, who abandoned me to focus on soccer—fuck him too, I thought. Even Elijah was still holding a grudge against me for drugging him at the Halloween party. What a boring bunch of self-important children.

Winter break ended, and nothing slowed down. Not until I stood in the restroom one day, and my left canine fell out. When I was a kid, my first tooth became loose, and I felt myself growing toward adulthood; even in the car-surfing accident, I had felt the joy of debauchery, but now I only felt death impending. With this lost tooth came a feeling that I was a machine falling apart, the gears becoming too rusty to work right. Bent over the sink, I couldn't help it. Something broke inside of me. My chest filled with unsettling sobs that poured from my throat unbidden.

"You can't control it."

I looked up, but no one was around. I was alone.

"You think you're in control, finally, but you're not."

Reaching into my pocket, I removed a film capsule where I kept the glass. If I took some more, I wouldn't feel this anymore. I could go on feeling like I was plunging my hand into the molten core of the earth.

"Because it controls you. Because you can't help but take more and more. You only have the illusion of control."

Now hearing the voice clearly, I kicked open the stall doors, roaring. But I found again that I was alone. Everything fell quiet. I said, "You can't control it. You're addicted. You always thought this was just for fun, but now you can't even stop. And you're not that person, that person who is imprisoned."

No, I thought. I pulled at my hair, leaning against the mirror. Blood and spit dripped from my lips. The tooth lay near the drain, the roots black and corroded as a car bumper. I kept saying to myself, I'm not this person.

I cannot be controlled.

Nothing controlled me.

Not my parents. Not my friends. Not God. Not Cain. Not drugs.

Nothing.

—⟨+ +⟩—

How much time passed, I wasn't even sure. I opened my eyes, and the fluorescent lights in the bathroom nearly blinded me. I was still alone, my head resting against the bottom of the urinal. Somewhere, the smell of shit and vomit stirred. My own vomit, and probably my own shit too. My mouth was dry except for the ooze of blood from where my tooth had been.

I peeked out of the bathroom to find empty hallways. Class had resumed without me, but I couldn't go, not like this, so I retreated back inside. As if I belonged here in the stench, in the grime, in the lurid reflections of these dirty mirrors. Pushing the tooth into the drain, I sighed and picked up the film canister from where it had fallen. This was possibly the worst first day back ever, what with the sickness, loss of a tooth, and existential despair.

I needed it—I could feel that even my veins needed it like a flower needed light, that my bones wanted it lustily, that my soul screamed from some dark pit for reawakening.

So I rubbed just a dab of the glass into my gum.

CHAPTER 24

CASS TERRIES

He twitched. He gasped. But he didn't wake. I sat beside his bed for two and a half months, and each time his body jerked involuntarily, I stood up to observe. Images of his truck folding like a Coke can smashed flat by a train kept haunting me. His blood-alcohol level was twice the legal limit. He must have followed us, spotting Blaine's car that every day he saw next door to him. He lay in a coma now, and we didn't know when he would wake up. All this was my fault.

When I first started dating Justin, I knew somehow this love had been fated, that we should date because the stars demanded our togetherness. We courted the notion that life had been a book prewritten, and we were simply omniscient narrators watching the lives of our characters unfold. But who had written this book, had told the tale with such an unhappy ending? I wanted to be a fly on the wall, to sit in the theater of my skull and distance myself from the action. I didn't want to believe that any of this was real.

I wanted him to wake up. I wanted him to die.

Everything felt so pointless. A few weeks before, I started sleeping with Blaine. He had been in love with me since the first time I knocked him down on the playground in the second grade. Maybe he thought he was romantic, but I always closed my eyes to kiss him and pretended to be anybody else. I wanted to be nobody or at least not myself. Justin lay in bed in a tangle of tubes, reminding me of my grandfather. Even this strong boy could die, could be made mortal by a semitruck, a bottle of Jack, and youthful stupidity.

One day, I would die. Justin would die, would become nothing more than worm food.

Everything I wrote—even now, it would crumble and be recycled into toilet paper. Everything we had ever done would be forgotten, wrought meaningless. In old age, even I would not be able to recall these events that I felt impacted my life so greatly. By then, none of this would matter.

What we learned would be forgotten. All those dollars we fought and bled to earn would be worth nothing one day, replaced by some other currency. Even memories faded. Even I would be reduced to a pile of ashes or maggot-digested dirt. Forgotten.

The truth: we faded faster than Internet fads.

We were the viral videos of human existence.

From nothing, we became nothing. All that dust-to-dust crap. All that ashes-to-ashes bullshit.

⊷⊶

His breathing quickened. Justin's eyelids fluttered, and his fist clenched. I stood up, swallowing bile. "Nurse—nurse, he's awake." The scrubbed nurse rushed into the room, slicking down his hair.

"You saw him wake?"

"Yes, he woke up. I saw him open his eyes." The nurse leaned over Justin, opening his eyelids gently.

"He's gaining consciousness, yes. Mr. Ferrara? Can you hear me?"

No response.

"Mr. Ferrara, do you understand what I'm saying? If you understand me, please nod your head."

At first, he only shivered. Justin nodded and opened his mouth and moaned, his entire body jerking. The sounds erupted animalistic, almost savage, but I thought they might have said, "Yes, I am awake."

⚊⚌⚊

The doctors made me wait in the frenzy of the hallway. I buried my face in my hands. Finally, a white-coated man strode out, rubbing his cheeks. He warned me, "He could have sustained serious injury to his brain and memory. He may not remember anything. It will be months before he will ever walk normally again. Until then, he'll have to use a brace. Just don't have too high of expectations. It won't be pretty."

At school the following day, the teachers announced Justin's waking, apparently relieved not to have a student die on them. Two years before, a local gay boy had jumped off a downtown bridge onto a train track and died; half the town mourned, while the other half conversed dejectedly about why he should have never come out of the closet in the first place.

I remember my tenth-grade chemistry teacher lamenting, "Like, no one even liked him, you know?" She liked to use slang to foster closer connections with us—rookie mistake. You could only respect to a certain degree a teacher who used the phrase *trippin'* to describe any student making less than a C.

I passed through classes silently. Aron asked me what I would do now that Justin was awake. I didn't know; I didn't know anything. Before Justin woke, I thought things would be better once his eyes opened. Now I wasn't so sure.

Indecision froze me, left me feeling hollow.

I stopped sleeping with Blaine, ignored his texts and phone calls. His addictions worried me. I hadn't seen him sober in weeks. He had been acting crazy. A few weeks before, I woke in the middle of the night and found him crouched in the bathroom, shearing his hair with a jagged razor, tufts of his hair fallen at his feet. His eyes popped from his face menacingly. He didn't look human. When you spend every day a living corpse, you fail to notice when others fall apart.

He told me, "Nothing's wrong. Can't sleep right now. Figured I'd just—"

I drew back the curtains, crouching low against the linoleum. He rocked himself in the tub, wearing loose boxer shorts. Strands of hair dangled from his mangled scalp. Switching on the buzz razor in his lap, I pressed the blade against his head until each strand fell dead on his lap and he sat folded, pink, and shorn.

I lay in bed, sprawled on my back. I wondered whether his presence would help me forget about Justin. Now I could only feel the indent both boys had made in the bed, feel the sliver along my spine where someone else's heaving chest should have been.

Two weeks had passed, but Justin could barely speak, barely move. Even when he managed a few words, he spoke few to me. He didn't bother offering an explanation, only shrugged when I asked him if he remembered what happened. He remembered who I was.

Tomorrow, I told myself, I would return to the hospital again. He would be better. The doctor told me he had already made incredible recoveries—the glory of the young brain, the doctor said, which could rebuild itself even after serious damage. Tomorrow, I would confront him and comfort him.

⋙⋘

The nurses were absent as I bustled through the hallways. After a few weeks of intense physical therapy, they had moved Justin to a lower floor, his room shared by two other patients. They could release him in less than a week, they said, after he learned to use arm crutches. Outside his door, I pressed my ear to the wood and listened. I could hear only shallow breathing and the persistent bleeps of out-of-sync heart monitors. I cracked the door open and slipped inside. Justin was awake, though his elderly neighbor slept, his lips trembling with each thunderous snore. A ten-year-old boy lay at the far side of the room, facing the window.

"It's you," he said. His voice was strained and stilted.

"You still remember me, right?"

He gritted his teeth. "I'm having trouble remembering a lot, but I remember people. I still can't recall a lot of school, but—"

"But you mostly slept through class or skipped," I finished. "Yeah, I know."

I laughed, but the sounds felt forced, like high-pitched hiccups karate chopped from my throat. Justin struggled to sit up, his eyes locked onto me.

"The nurses said you came every day."

"I did. I wanted to be here when you woke up and—"

"Why? You broke up with me. Don't you remember that?"

"But—Justin, it's not that I want to get back together, only that—"

254

"Well, I don't want that. Look at me. I can't play football. My arm lost so much muscle mass when I was asleep. I can't even walk. Fuck. I can't even walk."

"I'm sorry." I crossed over to him, wrapping my arms around him. He had always seemed so big, so powerful, so bursting with life. But now as I hovered over him, he was frail and emasculated. I pressed my lips to his. He pushed me away.

"No." He grimaced, tightening his lips until they disappeared.

"What? I thought—"

"What did you think, Cass? We broke up, didn't we? Or is my memory that fucked up?"

"I—I just thought that was a fight. But I've gotten over that. There are more important things. After the crash, I sat here every single day. I was just waiting for you to wake up, but—I realized that—"

Justin shook his head. "You had to freak out and throw a party without me. So it's your fault I ended up here. You were the one who pushed me away." He paused. "You didn't even come back for me. You were in that car, and you just drove away. I remember because I saw you. You wanted me to die."

Somehow, I knew he was right, but I just shook my head, starting to cry. "I loved you."

"But I never loved you." He said this with such malice. He brewed blame in his gut, and now this ugly truth spewed from the lips I once loved.

I stood up. "Well, fuck you too."

I tore out his IV.

"Fuck!"

The old man startled awake. The nurses in the hallway stumbled in, grabbing my arms and pulling me off of him. I began to scream, hysterical and staccato.

"And, well, you won't be fucking anyone but cripples in physical therapy, you lousy fuck. You missed the end of the football season, and—you're not even going to college." The nurses stopped holding me, looking at each other awkwardly. I broke away and shouted louder. "Not that you'd do anything with useless arms and useless legs—a useless fucking life. If you're lucky, you'll end up a bag boy forever."

When I stopped, the nurses said nothing. Justin said nothing, staring holes into my head.

"Yeah, but that was always what was going to happen. I'll be the once-great quarterback of Lickskillet High. At least people will respect that." He screwed up his face. He had been rehearsing these lines in his unconscious head. "But you, you fucking bitch—you'll just be known as the once-great quarterback's slut of an ex-girlfriend. You'll never be anything more."

How long had he rehearsed this, his mind building animosity as he slept? Or had he believed all of this before he ever got hit by a truck?

I nodded. "Well, good luck learning to walk. I'm glad you got hit by that truck. You deserved it." As I left, he looked so calm, so resigned, not at all the boy who had just lost his entire future. Our entire future.

And maybe that was all; he could come to terms with everything that had happened. Maybe he actually believed he deserved it. Maybe I actually believed I deserved him.

>—‹‡ ‡›—

The indent in my bed disappeared. I didn't need Justin, didn't need anyone. I wrapped my arms around my shoulders and held tight.

>—‹‡ ‡›—

"Well, this is nice, isn't it? To have the family together like this, just like we used to when you were a kid." My mother smiled at me as she sliced her green beans into eighths. I racked my brain for the memory she referred to, eating together years ago, though we only ate together for holidays, and even then I was forced to be quiet, speak softly, and practice manners while their friends and employers filled the house with festive drinking and conversation.

I nodded but continued my vigil of silence. My father spoke up. "So, your mother and I were at this Drake concert last night. And I swear I've never seen so many blunts lit up in public before. As if just because we came to see a rapper, it was fine to just toke right there." He laughed from a tin, hollow gut. "You remember when you used to tag along? Remember when you were six and got lost in the crowd at a Blink-182 concert? Next time, we're bringing you. Definitely bringing you."

"Why are you home? You're never home. Why are we having dinner together? I don't think I've sat in this seat for eight years."

Again, me being the blunt bitch, the mean girl to root against in a classic eighties romantic comedy. Like I couldn't even have a fucking opinion without someone calling me a bitch. I was still seething about what Justin had said at the hospital and wanted to show him differently, that I was somebody, that I didn't need him.

"Your father and I want to just—we thought it would be nice to sit down, catch up. It's been so long since we've just talked and eaten a good, home-cooked meal."

I looked her in the eye. "You just bought vegetables from the fresh market and brought them home in a bag and put them on the table for us to eat raw. But—"

My mother broke in, "How is Justin? We haven't seen him in so long."

"We broke up. Not to mention, he was in a coma for the past few months."

"Oh, yes, I read about that. Tragic. Isn't it?" She touched my father's hands and shook her head.

"Tragic," he agreed.

"Seriously, what's wrong?" Eating dinner together—this was red-alert abnormal behavior.

My mother swallowed. "Dad died last night. Or maybe the night before. I'm not sure when last time anyone checked on him."

"Oh." Neither of my parents said anything, shaking their heads slightly as if to convey my grandfather's death was typically tragic. "Well, that may be for the best. He hasn't been himself ever since—" I paused. "I'm sorry." I forgot sometimes that my parents and I were related.

My mother stopped furiously cutting up her vegetables, sighing deeply. "You're right. It was his time. Only, it never seems to be. I just wish—we were away, and he never got any recognition. People never do get their due, not until death. And by then, usually, it's too late."

Strange how something like that, which should have scalded my insides, hardly affected me. Strange to think how for months I had already considered him a corpse whose ass needed wiping. Strange how now someone so great and smart and fascinating would become a morsel for worms.

"We'll need to have a funeral, I guess," I said. "So he'll get his due."

CHAPTER 25

DECLIN OSTRANDER

We stood awkwardly in stiff suits at the viewing while a dead body lay in a casket at the head of the church. We arrived just as people flooded in. When I found Aron, he asked, "Have you seen Blaine?"

"Don't think he was invited. Justin either."

Blaine had been acting strange for several weeks, missing school for weeks at a time. Reportedly, he had fired his personal math tutor and the same week received three full-ride scholarships, but he never acted like a person with a future, or even anyone intelligent. Some days, he rocked back and forth, murmuring, "Hungry, hungry." Another day he came to class with his head shaved, and he never explained why. In biology, he wasted time asking inane questions like, "If the first thing that develops in a fetus is the anus, does that mean all humans start off their lives as little assholes?"

Aron and I stood making noncommittal eye contact with each other, wondering whether we should step up to inspect the little stick man in the cedar box. "He was a music innovator. He owned an entire record company, and when he sold it, he made a fortune."

"Right," I said. "So that's why Cass lives in such a big house."

"She never told you what her family does?"

I looked at him and smiled. "Sometimes, people just don't talk about their families."

Cass embraced us both, kissing us chastely on our cheeks. "I'm glad you came. Sorry if it's a bit awkward. I guess you don't know anyone else here." Then she looked to Aron. "There's someone here you might want to talk to."

She indicated the palest girl in the room, whose black dress was half-tulle. Distinctly Charlotte. Aron looked like he was choking on a black eight ball. "Why did you invite her?"

"Thought you guys may want to talk, OK?"

Aron shook his head. "No way. She—I need to go to the restroom." He stalked off with his head bowed like a prisoner approaching the gallows.

Cass turned to me. "And what about you? Any exes you need to make awkward conversation with?"

"Ha-ha. Very funny. Obviously not. I mean, you know I was—"

"You don't have to confess to me. No hard feelings."

I pressed my lip into a hard line. "Were you and your grandfather close?"

"Well, the last few years, he's been living with us. He—I don't know."

"It's OK. The things we never talk about are usually the things we need to talk about the most. It's our pain to never say anything directly, to always talk around what we feel we must say."

"Declin—"

"Talk about it. Otherwise, you end up crazy, bouncing around the walls, curled up on the floor talking about your childhood with your dogs."

"He was a great man. And he had Alzheimer's, so I took care of him. I'm not too sad, really. He was far, far gone. He was already gone a long time ago."

"That must be strange, losing yourself like that. Waking up one day, not knowing who you are." Cass nodded, but I wondered if she understood. She, like I, had forgotten momentarily who she was.

The church would be packed the following evening, Cass assured us. Tonight only family and friends were allowed. But the businessmen of music would fly in for the funeral, to show respect for the man. Before I left the funeral home, I finally approached the casket.

Every court case my father fought involved death and funerals he would awkwardly attend. But not me, who had not been to a funeral since my mother's. I could still remember parts of the service, but mostly I remembered the confusion. Too young to realize what had happened, I clung to my father, wondering why these people around me were crying and what lay in that closed box up front.

The man lay with his arms crossed at his chest, a single rose poking through his bony fingers. Something regal resonated from him, though his body looked frail. His face was composed for eternity in resigned determination, and I realized I did know something of this man, the small parts of him that lived on in Cass.

⚔

I had been coming to the trials as often as I could. Usually, I didn't care what happened, but now I wanted to see the trial's outcome. I worried about my father, who every day faced a trial he could never win.

When Matthew Pepper took the stand for the first time, I realized why people had been so quick to name him killer. He was haggard and sneering, sporting two black-ringed eyes and wild red hair. He collapsed into the witness stand, chewing his lip and running his fingers through his stringy scalp. After he took a nervous oath, he looked out blankly at the jury. My father approached him.

"Now, Mr. Pepper, I'd like you to tell the jury what you told me about where you were that night. Everything about it." He turned toward the jury. "We've already established that there was certainly a feud between Jameson and my client, and you've heard his father testify about Mr. Pepper's whereabouts at the time of the murder. Now, if you'd please, listen to Matthew's personal testimony about what happened."

Matthew started, pausing every few words to take deep breaths. "I was at the bar that night. I was with people."

"Where? And with whom?" asked my father.

"Right. I was at Ford's Bar. My cousin Dylan and my friend Robbie were with me. We were minding our own business at the same place we ate every night. I was a little drunk, but not too drunk. Just feeling very good. Then Francis Jameson walked in, and who's he got with him? My girl Wanda. Was my girl, anyhow, till that bastard stole her—"

"Please, calm down. Tell us what happened." The judge was short-tempered and unusually bored with the court's proceedings.

"Well, he swaggers in there. And he's looking at me, all smug. I shouldn't have, I know that. But I walked over. And I says, 'What do you want?' I only asked what he was doing in our bar, so he says it's a free country and he can go where he pleases. And I say I don't like him being there, and he says he'll kick my ass. So I punch him in the face."

Mr. Rutgers, the prosecutor, stood. "Excuse me, but he's leaving out some very important information. May I, Judge?" She nodded, and he approached. There were two prosecutors, Mr. Rutgers and a bald, older, black man. "Mr. Ford, the owner of the bar, told us you threatened his life."

"Not literally. Just metaphorically."

"I'm not sure you can metaphorically kill someone."

"I'm not sure you know how metaphors work. You can do anything—"

"That's not important," the prosecutor said. "What I mean is you threatened to kill him. So you had motive. But you want us to believe you didn't kill him that same night?"

"Well, I didn't."

"All I can promise is that justice will be served, and whoever did kill Mr. Jameson will face that justice."

"May the defense continue?" Clearly, my father hated Rutgers with the deep sort of passion Carolina and Clemson fans hated one another. "All right, what happened after you left the bar?"

Matthew paused. "I took a ride home from Dylan. He dropped me off at my house. I felt lousy, so I went to sleep. So, see, I wasn't even in no Golden Oaks."

"You've done well. That's all we need. As you can see, yes, my client engaged in conflict with Jameson but could not in his state execute a murder of such detail." My father sat down, but I felt by pulling Matthew up to the stand, he had lost more than he had gained.

⊨✦⊨

On the courthouse steps, I idly played with my cell phone and eavesdropped on conversations.

"You must be Declin Ostrander." I straightened up, eyeing the boy who addressed me. He wore a fancy button-up shirt with a striped tie, a small emblem pinned to the lip.

"Do you know me? Who are you?"

"Me? I'm friends with your friends. I know them. Cass. Blaine. Even—do you know a kid named Elijah?"

Thinking of Elijah made my stomach churn. Every time he hung around us, I felt both sorry for him and repulsed by him. He said nothing, which should have meant he never annoyed me. But something about the way he followed after us reminded me too much of something familiar. "Yeah, what's your name?"

"Your dad—he's the defender, right? Interesting, bringing Matthew to the stand. My dad swore up and down he never would, what with the Peppers saying every racist thought possible. But he did. I guess that's sort of brave."

The way he praised my dad confused me. "Your dad is the prosecutor. Mr. Rutgers?"

"Of course. But I guess you've always known the prosecutor's son." He grinned but didn't explain. "Actually, I wanted to ask you about something." The way he smiled, he seemed too much like a tittering clown with cold eyes. "Is Cass single?"

"What? Cass? Well, I think so. Technically, she and Justin—after the wreck—"

He nodded solemnly. "Well, yes. I met her once or twice, and I can't be blamed for wondering. I would love to get to know her. Word is she and Justin are done for good. They ended it after Justin woke. So, I figured—I know you're her friend. And maybe you could—" He paused, probably at last noticing the look on my face. "Oh, do you guys have a—thing?"

"What? No, not us. We're just friends. And we won't be anything more. I'm not going to—"

"Because you could if you wanted to. I'm sure you could. That's how I know your name. I talked to her, and she mentioned you. But if you're only friends."

"Sure, I'll talk to her. Of course."

The boy looked at me, squeezing my shoulder. "Only if it's OK with you. My name is Cain, by the way."

"Nice to meet you, I guess."

"Sure, of course. Good to meet you as well." He melted into the downtown crowd that poured from the courthouse.

Matthew Pepper's trial had drawn the interest of the entire town. Even the folks from the nursing home, who spent their weekends playing bingo, tuned in to watch the man's fate play out. But a hate crime, a murderous treachery—this stirred up the talk. Men and women pushing walkers rolled out every time court came into session to watch what would happen next. *The Jerry Springer Show* was getting old.

I stopped and looked up where a large sign hung above me: Lickskillet Gnome Emporium—World's Largest Collection of Unique Garden Gnomes.

Every time I had been downtown, I had never seen any great prestigious museum of garden gnomes, but here a sign pointed down the alley between the Rise and Shiner Café and a flower shop.

If Cass were single, completely free of Justin, I was the only thing holding myself back from dating her. When I arrived in Lickskillet, that had been all I wanted. Someone to call my girlfriend, someone to brag about sleeping with. But thinking about it made me feel cold.

Down a staircase, a door opened into a small room like a theater kiosk. No one was around. I pushed past the next door and walked down a long hallway. On either end, the gnomes stood with chipped porcelain and faded paint. They stood as sentinels with their spades raised high, their eyes glimmering with painted cheeriness.

"Huh."

This place was horror-movie scary. After everything I'd heard about the gnome museum being the prime tourist attraction in Lickskillet—this was it?

No big show, no colorful lights, and no curators rushing about polishing their eyes. Not even placards about the statues or museum, just a crammed collection of creepy, little porcelain men.

I quickly retraced my steps out of the strange corridor, up the staircase, and out of the alley. There must have been something more in Lickskillet that drew people here, not just a collection of a few gnome statues that Portland would soon make look like a doll collection.

Even great gnomes could be dwarfed, and things could change.

The gnomes made me think of my father, his ideas about himself. When, if ever, had he been proud of himself? He could never win a court case, and losing this one would mean nothing to him. Losing would only reaffirm his ineptitude But if he won, maybe he could do something, even if it were small, even if it would save the life of one morally repugnant, racist, innocent man.

⚔⚔

As school skated into second semester, I one day felt deeply uneasy after seeing a junior march through the hall to the gymnasium with a floppy banner exclaiming, Buy Prom Tickets Here. Only a little more than a month away, the exalted social event eluded me in purpose, but also frightened me. I wouldn't have a date or even a car, and I'd end up sitting alone in my bedroom trying to ignore the throbbing loneliness that had settled in my spine.

The impending reality depressed me, the thought of tulle dresses, elaborate corsages, and surreptitious drunkenness in the presence of teachers. After lunch, I commented on the banner, and Cass sighed as well. Only Cass and I and Elijah remained, the rest of our group having spun temporarily out of the loop of gravity.

"Prom sucks," Cass said definitively. "I mean, it's a whole bunch of traditions no one cares about when we could be doing anything else."

"Yeah, I guess. I've never been. I just thought—well—"

"What?"

"Nothing."

"You wanted to ask me?"

"No, I know you—it's OK."

"I'll go with you."

I looked up from my Nutella-and-banana sandwich to stare at her. "Really? I mean, that'd be really nice."

"No funny business, though."

"No, OK, of course not. I—"

"And you have to do something for me first. Have you ever seen a Roller Derby match?"

⊷ ⊶

Nick eyed me uneasily as if I had just eaten his holographic card collection. "Have you ever played *Dragon Sphere* before?"

I shrugged. "I've never even heard of *Dragon Sphere* before. But Elijah says you need an extra member, and here I am."

How this adventure began: Elijah invited me to play some weird game with someone named the Dragon Master. At first, this seemed like the absolute last thing I would ever do on a Saturday. But this was the third or fourth time he had asked and I had rejected. He shrugged, and I asked him about the game. As soon as I did, he hopped in his seat like Frankenstein shocked to life. He told me about how, in a special realm, they ventured into mountains, across deserts, and underneath the oceans, acting as goblins, wizards, and dragon slayers. I told him I would come check it out. Now I seriously questioned my decision.

"First you have to choose what sort of character you'll be. Your quest already has the red wizard—Elijah. And there's Josh—he's a woods elf. Maybe you can be a thief, so you have special powers to steal things."

"Elijah mentioned I could be a dragon slayer. I mean, in a game called *Dragon Sphere*, what else would I be?"

"A slayer, then? Very well. That was my choice when I first began playing the game. But be wary. The path of the slayer is riddled with grief and great opposition."

"Well, that sounds thrilling. Where's the board?"

"We don't need a board. We have a stack of cards. We draw cards to reveal elements of a scenario. Then I decide what else to include. Then you must figure out what to do."

"Good. Let's get started." I felt antsy, ready to leave this creep's house. He sat in a cradle gaming chair like it was some throne, munching on cheesy puffs. His face was a mask of orange powder.

He drew the first few cards and smiled wickedly. "You are traveling to retrieve the gem of Allek. But it lies in the center of a rancid swamp where the bone dragons live. While traveling through the swamp, Josh the woods elf is caught in a bog, slowly sinking to his death. Save him."

"We can do anything?"

"Yes, use your imagination. Like a story," Elijah said.

I nodded, grinning. "All right. Elijah, break a branch overhead from one of the trees. If we're in a swamp, there must be trees."

The Dragon Master shrugged. "No problems."

"Now extend the branch to Josh," I told Elijah. "I'll help you pull him out of the bog."

"A bone dragon attacks," Nick said.

"What's a bone dragon?"

"The wrong question to ask in the face of death, don't you think?"

"Right. Elijah, help Josh. Use your magic or something, if you're a wizard. I'll fight the dragon."

Elijah grabbed my shoulder. "Declin, you're a first-level slayer. You're not experienced. You don't even know how to kill—"

"A dragon? Right. I'm going to leap and stab it in the heart. Or cut off its head."

"You can't do that. The bone dragons have no hearts. They're just skeletons."

"Well, I'd knock my sword into its legs. And neck. That way, it couldn't pose a threat."

"The bone dragon fell apart. And Josh is saved. Good job. Except," Nick smirked, "bone dragons cannot die. They are zombies."

"Elijah, how are we supposed to defeat something that can't die?"

"The bone dragon knocks Declin into the bog, where he begins to sink."

Josh bit his fingernails. "We have to save him."

"Too late. Dragon ate his head."

"What? That's not fair. I didn't have time to think. You're just mad I chose to be a slayer."

"I told you the path would be fraught with misery, young one."

"Right. Don't grasshopper me, you asshole."

"Declin—"

"No, what the fuck is this shit? I was doing great. He made me lose because he can't stand someone outsmarting him."

"Well, you did very little of that, so no worries."

"Who the hell do you think you are?"

He rose from his throne, dropping the cheesy puffs onto the carpet. Clenching his fists, he bellowed, "I am the Dragon Master. I know kids just like you, people who don't appreciate genius, who complain when things don't go their way. Well, stop acting like a little, immature kid. You don't need friends like this, Elijah. He's just as bad as the rest."

"What are you talking about? Elijah, let's go." I pulled Elijah up off the carpet by his elbow and began marching toward the door.

But Nick proved quicker than I had thought. He tackled me, and we tumbled down together, his weight suffocating me. "You don't deserve to play the game. We only accept the strong. Are you a bone dragon? Do you re-form when you die?" His pudgy fingers pressed over my throat, and he squeezed.

With a great thrust, I pushed him off of me. He toppled over. I scrambled to my feet, saying, "Elijah, where did you find this freak?"

Again, I underestimated Nick. He stood and calmly approached a cabinet I had not seen before beside his *Dragon Sphere* promotional poster. Inside a glass case stood many medieval weapons: a mace, a long sword, and even a faux-crystal ball. But Nick drew a short sword from the bottom shelf, the type a ninja uses in movies. With mind-blowing swiftness for someone of his girth, he began to slash the sword through the air.

I threw up my hands, backing away into the kitchen. "Don't you dare leave," Nick screeched, catching Elijah by the arm and pulling him closer. The blade pressed lightly against Elijah's throat.

"What are you doing? It's just a game, OK? Can't you calm down?" Josh approached Nick, but slowly. "Seriously, man, remember what happened last time you freaked out and tried to kill somebody?"

"This happens more than once, but you're still friends with him? What the hell is wrong with you people?"

Trying to be a good person never seemed to work out for me.

"You didn't do anything, Josh. You just watched. I got kicked out of school, you know." He pushed Elijah into the corner and pointed the sword at his face. "But you, Elijah—you're going to be just like me. You have to finish what I've begun. But you have to choose something better."

"Elijah, don't let him—what the hell am I saying? I was just saying you were being unfair." I had never had a sword at my neck, and I had no real experience being brave, but I just said, "Be brave, Elijah."

Nick lowered the sword a little. "It'll be fine. I won't hurt you. But you've got to stop hanging around with these people.

"They're my friends."

"Elijah," I said. "You stood up to Justin. You don't have to take this guy's shit. He's a jerk."

Before Nick could react, he sank to his knees. Josh continued to clobber Nick's head with the nunchakus he had snatched off the wall. "Sorry, you guys. He's usually pretty cool. But he gets— he thinks—I'm not sure. Just come on; let's get out before he wakes up."

In the sunlight of Nick's front lawn, the entire day seemed too strange. "Did all of that just happen, or did someone put LSD in my Froot Loops this morning?"

Elijah nodded. "I think so. I'm sorry he acted like that. He's usually fine. He's my friend."

"Maybe you need new friends."

"Well, now you sound just like Nick." Elijah and Josh stared at me for some time. "Anyways, I'm sorry I invited you. Are we going to do anything?"

"Best not to. Just don't come back, Elijah. These games are over. The Dragon Master—he's gone for a little while."

Even people like Nick could have friends, like Josh who was concerned for his well-being even after knocking him out with nunchakus. If someone could care about Nick, then maybe everyone was close to someone. Even serial killers had family. Unless the serial killers ate their families and used their skins to make lamps.

But I realized, in this moment that Elijah was my friend.

Even before getting to know me, he had been the one to stand up for me. Aron had at least tried to reach out. Even Blaine, beneath his drug-addled consciousness, liked me to a certain degree. Too long I had been exhausting myself to pretend to be something I was not. Whatever I pretended, that was what I became. But I didn't want to be a bullfighter or surfer or even a ladies' man. Not anymore. I just wanted to be a good person.

"Elijah, I'm sorry your friend turned out to be a megalomaniac psychopath."

"It's fine."

"I'm sorry for ignoring you, about letting Blaine drug you. Just about—I mean, you stood up for me. Not just once but twice now. You're brave."

"No, I'm not. I sometimes wish—well—" He hesitated, as if he wanted to tell me something but decided not to. "I've got to get home."

Even though I wasn't sure if I could live up to this promise, I told him we would spend time together again soon. We parted ways.

＝‡‡＝

Soon after Cass's grandfather's funeral, Aron took off for a tourney with the state soccer team. But he would return on Monday morning, which gave me some hope for normalcy. Cass had partially descended from her spiral since Justin's awakening. Blaine—I wasn't sure he was ever sober around us any longer. He had taken to keeping a flask in his book bag and hanging out with the Exeter prep kids on weekends.

My father took the afternoon off from working the case to watch war movies on cable. My dad slumped on the couch, reaching for his beer bottle but growing too exhausted. He had become so tired of his job, of his life.

One night, as I visited the bathroom past midnight, I found him asleep in the kitchen beside a bowl of milk, no cereal. Going crazy, like my mom had. Maybe everyone ended up mad but our madness symptoms were different.

Blaine took drugs.

Cass refused to talk.

Elijah played *Dragon Sphere* with sadistic weirdos.

Aron slept with girls too young for him.

I pretended to be someone I was not.

My father watched shitty television.

My mother killed herself.

When I was a toddler, I waddled into the kitchen, where she had been scrubbing as adamantly as Lady Macbeth. On her palms and scarred knees, she pressed a sponge against the floor.

"If you get this fucking floor dirty, I'll cut off your earlobes," she told me. This was before my father caught on that his spouse had a fatally degenerative mental illness. My father never paid us any attention in those years, consumed in his courtroom work.

Her eyes red and swollen, her hands calloused and coated in chalky white, the air putrid with cleaning supplies.

"Where's the doggy?"

We had adopted a dog—my father's idea. The day we picked up the furry mutt from the pound, I held it in my arms. My parents let me name it, which turned out to be a bad idea, because I called it "Woof."

"Mommy, where's Woof? You let him out?"

She gave me a deathly stare. "He made a mess of the floor." She swallowed. "So, I'm cleaning it up."

"But Woof, Mommy."

"We let him go. He's gone."

She told my father Woof ran away, but I wasn't completely stupid. I found the turned-up spot in the backyard where she'd buried our puppy. That was after she committed suicide, though.

⇥⇤

Even before, it could not have been peaceful. Not when my mother, bug-eyed and scratching the skin off her arms, called me "evil, evil, evil little boy." Even as a toddler, I knew her sadness was somehow my fault. She was ashamed of me.

Maybe trying to care for me, she had gone crazy. But you couldn't just go crazy, could you? She'd been addled before that and just imploded.

Sometimes, you'd wonder if you might turn out the same way: insane, suicidal, unable to cope.

If one day you'd end up just as unhappy.

You'd wonder if you really had a choice.

CHAPTER 26

BLAINE MOREAU

When I reached the gate of Golden Oaks, I leaned forward, my foot stomping the pedal, the car lurching. The security guard dropped her cane, leaping into a bush. As I barreled past the guard booth, the gate arm caught in my fender and snapped, pieces of red and white wood slapping across the Mustang's front window. Galloping over the speed bump, the entire car shuddered and then screeched forward and around the bend.

Cass would be sitting in her house like a princess waiting to be saved. Justin would prowl her lawn, her evil dragon sentry. An evil dragon hobbling on crutches. We would duel, perhaps to the death. I carried a long hunting knife on my passenger's seat in case he stood in my way, and I would gut him and, this time, kill him. The strength to do this surged through me, filling me with anticipatory glee. It felt like a needle sliding across your wrist, never puncturing, only teasing.

Some people would call my adventure rash, as if I had suddenly climbed into the car buzzing with energy and power to win back my girl. But I had not slept in five days, and bent with the iridescent ecstasy of living like no one else on earth, I calmly approached this drive. Planned to run the guard down and save the day. If Cass rejected me before, she could no longer, not after I showed her I was the hero. In my story, I would be the protagonist, the one who raised his banner and got the girl in the end.

Navigating the streets, I knocked down only four mailboxes.

—<—— ——>—

A week earlier, Aron visited my house before he left for the tourney. We stood in my room for a long time, with him telling me about Charlotte and his plans for the future, though I could barely pay attention.

Aron eyed the bed and then sat down on it. I asked, "How long will you be gone?"

"About a week. I am travelling to DC."

"You look a little sick. Will you win?"

Aron shrugged. "You look haggard yourself. When is the last time you slept?"

Maybe I looked calmer than I felt. My heart shuddered with each breath. "I've been studying. Sending out college applications. Though I'm pretty sure I'm going to go to MIT. That's where my parents want me to go."

"Free is free. Damn, I'd go anywhere if they paid for me. You're so lucky, with your—well, you're luckier than you realize."

"Thanks. I will keep that in mind. I'm sorry I freaked out or have been freaking out. I've been—" He nodded as I talked, as if he knew, but he didn't know. Not yet. His eyes hung like a hangman's noose, dark as coal.

Aron said, "I know there's something going on. When I came over last weekend, I found something."

"After the funeral. I never went. I wish—no, it wasn't right. I couldn't be there."

"You can still talk to her. But you—Blaine, you attacked her. She thinks you're crazy. I mean, you are. What is that in the paper bag?"

"What? Paper bag?"

"This." He leaned down, rummaged under the bed, and held the bag to my face. "Is that—"

"I don't know what that is."

Inside the bag was something much like rock candy, only clear and more jagged. Aron said, "I haven't seen you so fucked up. Have you looked at yourself lately?"

I did, and if I thought Aron looked like a melting wax figure, then I looked like I had been slapped in the face by a sledgehammer. "I—I—this doesn't really have anything to do with you." I stood up, snatching the bag away. I rolled the bag carefully, concealing the little I had left from the last purchase.

A pointed silence filled the room as I lowered the bag to my side.

"You should go. You'll be late."

"I'm not leaving till tomorrow. I wanted to talk—"

"Get the fuck out of my house, OK?" A surge of anger swelled in my stomach, rising like bile in my throat. He wanted to take the drugs away. I couldn't let him take that feeling away from me.

Aron swallowed, begging with his eyes for something I couldn't give him. But I was invincible. I felt in control, and he could never take that from me. "I just don't want you to mess up so badly you end up—broken."

Thinking, I stopped and shook my head. "Life is a broken roller coaster, right? Sure, it's broken, but don't spend your time repairing the track. Just ride it and hope you don't die too soon. Sure, you're going to die at some point. But up until that point when you spiral down onto the amusement-park cement, try to have some fun."

He did not try to take the bag from me, and if he had, I might have wanted to kill him. I felt the absurdity of saying farewell. I was losing something, something I wasn't sure was there. "Fun," he repeated, glancing from the bag to me. "We can talk more about it when I get back. For now, you'd better get rid of that."

When he left, I peeked inside the bag. Only a little remained, and I thought, Yes, when you return, it will be gone. Then what?

⊨⊧ ⊦⊨

Whenever I closed my eyes, I imagined Cass naked, except not with me. With him—with Justin, with the boy she had always wanted.

Ratcheting up the first slope of that broken roller coaster, I made a pipe to smoke the rest of the glass. I was done, though. This would be the last. I kept telling myself these things like prayers, not knowing how true they would prove to be.

Then five days passed without Aron or Cass or even Declin. In the cocoon of suffocating isolation, I was waiting for a moment. Every day, I felt better until I believed I would always feel this high, a bird whose wings could stretch over continents.

⊨⊧ ⊦⊨

Crashing through rich residential streets, destroying private property on a quest for love—that shit woke me up like snorting wasabi. I was the emergency and she the fire ax shattering the glass case, spewing extinguisher foam onto the flames.

Stumbling onto her front lawn with bloody elbows, I wondered briefly where my Mustang had gone from beneath me, the entire chasse gone. A moment passed before I remembered parking it on top of the fire hydrant. Her front door hung ajar, beckoning to me, but only after I kicked it open. Something cracked. I stood in the doorway, the passing woodsman posed to find a cross-dressing wolf in Granny's bed, snacking on Riding Hood's calf.

"Justin. Come out. I know you're here."

From far away, there was an echo: "Go away. Please, go away."

I limped toward the stairs, asking, "Cass?"

"Don't come up. No one is here. I don't want to see you here."

"Where are you? I'm here to save you."

"Just go away."

"Come down. I've come here for you. I wanted to keep you away from him."

At the top of the stairs, I heard her approach. She stood silhouetted by something holier than the moon. "From whom? Justin? We're over."

"But he's awake."

"He's still an asshole. Just like you. What are you doing here? I heard the crash." She paused, her eyes watering. "What happened to you?"

"But—come here." I crawled up the stairs painfully, as if all my brittle bones were breaking in millions of places. She faded back into her bedroom, the door slamming closed. I threw my body against the door, scratching and pounding like it were the entrance to heaven and, any minute now, the cartoonish trapdoor to hell would drop in the cloudy carpet, sending me spiraling into the pit.

I did not connect the sounds of sirens to my own actions until much later. I was the hero.

My fists were pistons of steel against the wood, which seemed like it would yield but never did. Then it opened, and Cass watched me resentfully as I swatted at air. But something more— fear. Maybe she was afraid. Of me. But she carried the aluminum slugger in her grip, and she swung.

The clomp of boots downstairs. The hollow aluminum-on-skull knockout. Tumbling down the stairs. My heart gasping. Shadows.

⇥⇤

I woke from my fever dream in a room without stimulus. The walls white, blank, and the air quiet and stifling. If this were another dream, I willed myself to startle awake. But the night sat heavy on my chest, my heart sputtering like a lawn mower running out of gas. Everything was bright and sterilized. My fingers felt rubbed raw, but the tips were black. Fingerprinted, I realized. I was in a police station.

After some minutes in purgatory, I finally stood up, shaking myself from sleep, if it were sleep at all. My head still throbbed where the bat had struck. I massaged my forehead where someone had wrapped a bandage. Something occurred in the room like boredom or pain or something else we could only taste.

I searched the room for dust, running my fingers over the walls. So clean here, so perfect, so unsettling. As I came down from the high, I figured they would come soon. They were watching me, I knew. They would knock on the door to take me to a grimier, crueler place. Where the other boys lived. Or maybe first I'd be brought to court. When would I get to talk to my parents about this? Had they even been told?

Who was even keeping me here?

The room had no windows, only one door that had no doorknob on my side. No way to tell the time, to know between day and night. The first few hours, what might have been hours but could have been eternities unto themselves, passed. No one came, not even to give me food or water. The bright lights blazed above, illuminating every bit of the room equally. Crouched against the wall, I tried to sleep it off. But I could not sleep.

There was no toilet, only a hole in the floor I kept pissing down into. I wondered if I could balance long enough to shit accurately without splattering the perfect floor. But I never needed to shit because I felt hollow, gutted out as if with a torch.

I began to wonder if an entire day had passed or if even the days had blurred into one another. "I'm not high anymore," I said to no one. No one listened. "You can come get me now." My sober scratched at my spine and swallowed my senses. "Shit," I muttered, pacing the room. I beat the walls as I passed them, in a circular pattern. "If only she—Cass. Bitch." Grasping at my hair, I slumped against the wall.

Her fault. Back in her empty house sleeping with that asshole Ferrara. I hated her.

I began howling, clawing. Why had she gone back to him? If he hadn't been there, this would not have happened. But he hadn't even been there, had not wielded the bat. She had been alone. My memories arose jumbled from the hissing pit of my subconscious.

How long had I been here? "You can't leave me to die in here, you know. Habeas corpus and all that shit."

Maybe I *was* dead, I considered. The idea drifted up through the thick smog in my head. Maybe this really was purgatory, and I was waiting here for my sentence.

I was no longer high. My hands ceased to shake.

How long had I been there?

Too long. For years. I groped at my face to check for a beard. Coming down from that high tasted like drinking curdled milk.

Eternity. Forever, trapped between the four white walls. Were there four? I could not quite make out the corners, so I crawled to each.

Where had all this started? Cass screamed in my head, "What happened to you?"

What happened to you? What happened?

Drugs kept me sane. Before I began taking the pills, I could hardly talk to anyone. Shyness and anxiety strangled my voice, making me mute. Somehow the drugs swam through me, making me live. But now I was here, alone. Nothing to lift me from the reality I sank down into. Reality—it gripped me like a creature's icy claw. They left me here to die.

The white was not a number, not like other colors. Red made me feel a bit angry, or more like turned on, and made me think of the number nine. Blue shocked me whenever I saw it, like a tidal wave washing over me. But I grew used to those feelings.

Not white. My ever-logical mind could not grapple with white. It meant nothing. I stared into it and felt nothing. White was emptiness. White was sobriety's revenge.

White, like eternity, could not be understood. Time could not go on forever. But it could never end either. When would time end, drop off its own history like a barrel over a waterfall?

But what if death was not like white at all, not sleep but constant wakefulness? I could not sleep. And in such consciousness, what dreams may come?

Our eyes worked, though our eyelids stayed shut. We could feel every incision the morgue worker made. Filled up with stinking juices to keep our flesh from rotting prematurely. To stare up helpless from a casket while one by one each relative and friend walked by to kiss you or spit on you.

Forever awake in a dead body. I was *dead* already. I could feel the knife, the hot glow of the heat lamp.

I began to scream, beating against the wall or walls, depending on how fuzzy the corners became. Only the screaming was in my head. Shrill and terrifying, ringing overhead. Whose voice is that, I asked, not aloud. And yet I heard my own words, tumbling from my lips like the maggots that would devour my tongue after death. Trapped in a casket as worms squirmed through your skin, eating away the rottenness. The delicious rot of our lives.

———

Time passed; I no longer could tell how long it had been.

It could be worse. What if we were cremated? Our conscious agony would go on forever. Worse than hell. What was the point of pretending morality when something worse than hell awaited you after death?

Why not enjoy myself? Why not smoke, drink, and fuck? These things gave me pleasure, and perhaps if I died, and God indeed did exist, I would burn in hell. If he did not, what did I have to lose?

Eternity. It tasted like whiteness.

You could spend your whole life wondering if you've died. Crumpled in the corner, shaking, wondering, is it over yet? Is this over yet?

This was what sober felt like to me, coming to terms with consciousness. I needed drugs, needed blur and confusion and colors to distract me from the torturous truth. Whenever I felt the sober biting at my heels, I caustically sighed at other people, how easily they could forget their mortality.

They stared into computer screens, ignoring the truths that exploded so violently around them. All my friends concentrated on insignificant worldly things, never considering eternity. Never fearing death, but wasting life. I knew what eternity meant, knew how the notion of infinity could wreck the mathematical mind.

Sometimes, people woke up, startled from sleep, wondering what was real and what was a dream. Most people, though, lived their entire lives like that.

This lurid acknowledgment of our existence dragged us from our beds and tasted sour like the blade embedded in the Halloween candy apple. Even stumbling around like a doped-up zombie, I wasn't truly dead. We were simply underwhelmed, these zombies waiting for someone to put bullets in our heads (or decapitate us, depending on which undead mythos you subscribed to).

Scream like you mean it, I heard myself say.

Consciousness bore down like a razor-edged pendulum.

I began to scream, reaching my arms into the air as if in the agony of a firestorm. "I can't go on."

This was what sober felt like for me. Everything you've ever despaired over attacking you at once, leaving you a husk of yourself, staring blankly into the white abyss.

The door opened, and I sat up. Had I been screaming? I heard only silence, and silence tasted like papery Communion crackers you ate at church that signified the body of Christ.

"Blaine, come with me."

Someone set me free.

⚔

The light swung above us, illuminating his gaunt face in brackish light, the intervals of the swings extended with each creak of the wire above.

He shuffled a file of papers aimlessly. "I believe we've met. You're a local here, right?"

"You—you don't look like a police officer. Huh. What day is it?"

"It's the afternoon. What do you mean?"

"How many days was I in there? You locked me up."

"Not me. And only for a night and half a day. Calm down. Your name is Blaine Moreau?"

284

I tapped my fingers against the table and looked around. The interrogation room proved a huge improvement over the cooldown room. "I want a lawyer. I won't speak until—"

"I am your lawyer."

Licking my lips, I sized him up. He was a thin man with thick glasses perched on a cherry nose. "I didn't hire you. Who are you?"

"My name is Barnaby Rutgers. I'm the best thing that ever happened to you."

A mirror loomed to our right, unnerving me. People stood on the other side, watching me squirm. I asked, "Who is watching us?"

"No one is watching. Just you and me."

"Bullshit. There's always someone watching. In case something illegal happens. Like, if you try to let me go." My body shuddered. I wanted something to drink, smoke, hit—whatever. But the dim lights offered no escape from my skull.

Rutgers smiled. "Why would we not let you go, Blaine? You haven't done anything wrong. In fact, you've done us a great service. We found drugs in your system. Drugs we've been searching for, that the US government has been searching for."

"A service? What did I do?"

"Nothing. Yet. But we need you. And when we're done here, you can leave. Go home. Take a shower. Never let us bring you in again. Go home and be a good boy. Understood?"

I nodded. "What do you need?"

"I don't want to see you get into trouble, Blaine. There are certain people, though, who might conspire against someone of your—well, status. Do you know what sort of people? Wicked people. Our town is infested with wickedness, and all I want to do—all I have ever wanted—is to get rid of the wickedness. And that sounds nice. But soon, new plants open down here. Plants for energy that will destroy our forests, pollute the air, and over-run us. That will bring people down here to suffocate us, bring their own ways along. We have to build more houses to accom-modate them. And they're bad people who want our ways to die. But we will not die. We fight back.

"And there are others who we considered friends who are evil too, who spread their ideologies and thoughts into the air like gas fumes. Well, pretty soon there'll be a spark. And then what? Explosion. But I don't think you're a bad kid, Blaine. You grew up here. And I've heard all about your special skills. The truth is we want people like you. Especially if you're willing to help?"

"You want me to tell you whom I got the drugs from?" The realizations came in waves. I could go home. I could be safe.

"Something of that nature, yes. I knew you were a smart kid. If you tell me now, I'll convince the judge to reduce your sentence to simple PTI—pretrial intervention. You'll have to do commu-nity service and take drug tests but—no jail. The names?"

"His name was Cain. He sold to me. He actually sold to me the first time, and I didn't even—"

"Do you think this is a joke?" His face collapsed angrily, his voice hinting at gruffness. "You're going to have to tell me the truth, Blaine. Who sold you these drugs?"

"Cain. I swear that was his name. And he is a Swag Boy. And he goes to Exeter Academy and—"

"Do you know who I am, Blaine? I know who you are. I know that for the past few weeks you've been having sexual relations with Cass Terries, daughter of the Terries music jockeys on chan-nel 104.6. I know that your father works at an office out of town, though *office* is a big word for the cramped cubicle he sits in. Runs numbers for a living. Can't believe he still holds on to a job at that firm after the invention of—well, computers. Basically useless. And your mother—she's the one with the money, though she's not worth anything anyways. Inherited it all from her father who died when she was young. A great and shifty stockbroker. And those two insignificant people made you. A worthless worm.

"Also, you're lying. Cain is my son. So give me another name or—"

"The Peppers. The entire family makes the drugs. They sold it to me. A guy named Dylan Pepper. That's the name, I swear. They're making meth, all of them. Even the young ones—even the girl who goes to school with me. They're all crazy hillbilly meth dealers." I gasped. The confession spouted out like a prophecy, the last desperate breath for air. I didn't want this man talking about me or my family, didn't want to know what I already knew.

Rutgers gave me a hard stare. "I have suspected this for some time. We've been watching. The whole FBI has been watching. Justice, true justice, will be done. You did such a wonderful job. That—that was everything we needed."

"That's it? I waited eternity for that?"

Rutgers stood up. "Follow me." He led me out of the room into the adjoining room, from which we could see the table. The room was empty save for dubious-looking machines. A moment later, and we stepped into the sunlight. When my eyes adjusted, I realized we stood behind the police station downtown. Placing his hand on my shoulder, Rutgers leaned down.

"Remember what I said? If you touch any of this again, we'll come for you. We will watch you from now on. Your parents will likely want an explanation as to why the police raided your house. Stumble on home. And arrive in court on the sixteenth of next month."

He left me alone in the alley, and I was not sure whether to feel relief or horror.

CHAPTER 27

ARON KING

As I collapsed onto the bench, collecting articles of clothing to rub against my numb legs, I was absolutely convinced that until now no one had ever truly frozen their balls off. I pulled my arms into my shirt and cradled myself against the bitter air.

"Are you frozen, King? What the hell do you think you're doing out there?" Coach Goodman loomed over me, but I could not even look at him. I needed to smoke a cigarette; I hated smoking cigarettes, but the anxiety churning in my stomach inspired smoking. At halftime, our team could hardly move through the slush of hard-packed ice—ice the opposing team didn't seem to notice (boys from Wisconsin). We never experienced ice or snow down south, and now the weather immobilized us.

When halftime ended, we hustled onto the field but could not ignore the brush of cold wind attacking our genitals. The grass crunched as we fell over each over in attempts to steal the ball. But five minutes later, I was again shivering and miserable. The sky bled into night, the game winding down. Once we caught a whiff of losing, we slowed down until we were overwhelmed one to six by game's end. After clapping the hands of the opposing team, we slunk dejectedly onto our bus and returned to the hotel. The South Carolina All-State soccer team dissolved once again into just another group of listless boys.

Both nights before, we celebrated after victories. Many of the boys harbored water bottles sloshing with vodka that they passed through rooms, everyone becoming ethereally drunk. No one celebrated this night. We soberly filed into the hotel, departing into the elevators. We would return home tomorrow, and though we had grown close in the past few days, I realized I would not remember the names of these boys. In two weeks, their faces too would fade like the names of books you loved as a child.

In the wake of failure, we sat up silently in our hotel rooms. We were staying in a very lavish suite, even for DC. Two beds stood in a small bedroom; two more could be made from pullout couches in the other. We even had our own fridge, though no food to keep in it. While I lay on my bed, studying the ceiling, the other boys watched a documentary about strip clubs in which all the strippers wore those black electrical-tape Xs over their nipples while being interviewed. One boy complained that it was absurd to learn about strippers if the audience could never even see their nipples.

I wondered whether this tournament meant anything to any of the boys, if any had planned to win, or if like me each counted on colleges offering scholarships in the future. We would scatter from South Carolina across the nation, kicking balls and pursuing degrees in *whatever.* The thought made me sick, though I didn't know why—how people could come together and then disperse and forget each other.

Charlotte swam through my mind like the night we met. No one would understand that I could watch her drown with a clear conscience. No one could understand how easily I intended to let go. Each time I imagined her, I could visualize my future as a ship capsizing in the Pacific. She became like a balloon, her secret swelling inside her stomach until it spilled out for the world to see—my child.

"It's not my fault. She came on to me," I had told Blaine when I first revealed the secret.

Though I thought he had not been listening, caught in his habitual haze, he responded, "Came on to you? Like, what, she forced you?"

"Not like that. The way she dressed—she asked for it. She wanted it. It's not my fault."

"It's the twenty-first century. You can't blame short skirts and push-up bras for your indiscretions. It's not only fucking sexist but also ridiculous. Men in this culture can't take responsibility for their actions. It's her fault, her mother's fault, her skirt's fault. Well, she's pregnant now, and I think we both know whose fault it is."

Sometimes, I too easily forgot that Blaine was not just an idiot but actually also a genius. Never before had both identities seemed so strongly represented in a single person.

—◁+ +▷—

As we rode the charter bus back to South Carolina, leaving behind the monuments, politics, and strange American-flag apparel of DC behind, I checked my phone. Blaine had called sixteen times. By five in the morning, however, the calls had stopped coming. I texted him to tell him I was returning but received no reply.

As we crossed the state line into North Carolina, I fell asleep.

—◁+ +▷—

I sat in a funeral service. A boy lay in the casket with his arms folded. From far away, I barely recognized him. As the preacher finished his prayer, he closed and locked the lid. For a moment, I wanted to run to the front of the church and reopen the box, try to recognize this boy. Whoever he was, I felt he had been my friend for many years and we had shared so much, but I could not even remember him. In the reflection of stained-glass windows, I looked so much older, but the boy did not. He should have been dressed in callous clothes, dirty and smiling. Instead he wore a starched tuxedo and a grim frown.

A baby began screaming, as babies tend to do in serious moments. Looking down, I found the baby in my lap, its arms groping at my face.

⇥⇤ ⇥⇤

I woke up in a sweat, other boys shuffling past me. I sat up in my seat and fell against the window. Almost home.

After retrieving my luggage, I stumbled into a Columbia afternoon. With my bag slung over my shoulder, I walked a few blocks to the garage where I had left my car. Something bore down on me, an ominous prickling.

When I found my car, my phone began to buzz. Cass.

"Hello?"

"Aron, where are you?"

"Columbia. I'm returning from DC today, from the tourney. What's wrong?"

"Nothing. Well—something. When you get back to Lickskillet, come see me. We need to talk. About a lot."

The prickling increased. I hadn't been able to contact Blaine, and now he had done something.

"Is it Blaine? What did he do?"

"Just come right away."

⇥⇤ ⇥⇤

I checked my watch pointedly, in that exaggerated way actors do in a film, holding my wrist aloft and scrutinizing the broken device on my wrist. A scream of sirens seared through downtown, several police cars speeding past the Rise and Shiner Café.

Cass appeared from the crowd holding a cup of coffee. "I don't think I've actually ever witnessed a Roller Derby match here, you know?"

I stood up from my seat, feeling my stomach rise toward my throat, and then I sat back down again. "Roller Derby?"

"Yeah, they do Roller Derby in the back." She gestured toward the back of the café and sighed. "Declin promised he'd go to a match with me one of these days, if I agreed to go to prom with him."

"Right, prom. OK." I had forgotten that prom was only a month away, but it hardly seemed important anymore. "You said you needed to talk to me about something."

"Blaine?"

"I—I'll tell you in a second. I want to talk about Charlotte."

"What about her? When did you talk to Charlotte?"

"She was at the funeral, remember? Did she tell you?"

"She texted me, but I haven't talked to her yet. I just don't want to—I don't want to see her."

"She doesn't know for sure if she's pregnant. She told me she took a test and it read positive, but we're going to the doctor. We're going to find out for sure." She paused. "She wants you to be there, Aron."

"I can come. I mean, at least I can be there."

"But really, Aron, she needs that."

"I will be there. I promise."

"If she's pregnant, do you know what you want to do?"

"I have no clue. I mean, I don't know anything." I took a long gulp of coffee. "I just need time to think—I need—have you seen

Blaine? I've been home for a whole day, and he won't return my calls. Where's Blaine?"

Cass looked down into her lap, biting her lip. "Blaine's in rehabilitation for the next three weeks. He's—well, he went crazy. He got himself arrested, and now his parents sent him to drug rehabilitation, took him out of school."

Shipwrecked. Capsized. My heart was ready to rupture. "I—I knew—I could have stopped him. I told him—what do you mean he went crazy?"

She trembled. "Aron, he attacked me. He came to my house in the middle of the night. I had to call the police. He ran right through the arm guard at Golden Oaks—they still haven't fixed it. He went mental."

The air smelled like sawdust and coffee beans. We both exited the cafe and stood on the street as more police cars streaked by, heading out of town.

"Something's happened," said Cass.

I watched two more police cruisers speed by, the town erupting into an orgy of sirens. I swallowed and prayed they had not found another black man hanging in a tree.

CHAPTER 28
CASS TERRIES

Aron told us he would wait on the curb outside of his house. He would ride with us to the women's health clinic in Columbia, the place girls went when they didn't want their parents to know about indiscretions. Declin and I huddled in the car warming our hands over the heat vent, peering through the melting gaps in the window's frost. But Aron's house was dark, his truck missing. After a few minutes, Declin said, "Maybe he just forgot."

When I shifted into drive, Declin sighed. "He meant to come. Maybe he overslept. Maybe he—"

His voice trailed. We drove toward Charlotte's house, cruising slowly through the tidy suburb, the morning sizzling with silence. He would come with us, had promised. Now I imagined Charlotte's soft surprise. "Where is he?"

⇥⇤

They called Charlotte's name, and she rose to discover her fate. She held her stomach like a ticking bomb. We could still hear the grizzled protestor screaming outside. Because the center ran one of the only abortion clinics in the state, each Saturday this man and sometimes others marched and screamed outside the doors. He did not discriminate between women, whether they were here for checkups or operations, whether they were pregnant or not. As we approached the building, he crossed the parking lot to bellow at us.

"Jezebel! Whore of Babylon! Murderer! Repent for your sins, you murderers!"

The silence inside of the clinic waiting room allowed his voice to carry through the walls. Some of the older women eyed me, maybe blaming me. They thought I was pregnant, here like so many other teenage girls to deal with an indiscretion. But I was thankful it wasn't me. I didn't want to lie down on that table while the doctor poked around inside me and prepared the news.

Declin finally broke the silence. "I got accepted into college, even with a scholarship. I might stay." He slouched in his chair. "Feels like the uncertainty's just lifted. Do you know where you'll be going?"

I nodded. "Clemson. Always planned to go there, where we hoped Justin could get a football scholarship. Strange, actually, to think I'm leaving, and he's left behind." At school, Justin hobbled with walkers attached to his arms, making him look like a crippled robot. "I've got no clue what I actually want to do, what I want to study."

The clinic smelled like vinegar. The future felt like a sucker punch. A surprise party you've expressly declined to attend throughout youth.

Charlotte had been back with the doctor for forty-five minutes.

Aron never arrived at the clinic, never answered my texts. The future for them—what did they plan to do? We had forgotten to ask ourselves the important questions. Our lives were the failed experiments of a generation. For years, we watched movies and television shows in which teenagers lived without consequence. They drank and had sex and never slept. Carefree lives were the norm because the producers would never make an episode about characters dropping out of college or living alone or confronting adulthood. We devoured these lies, thinking we could live that way and not worry about anything. We knew that everything would resolve itself in the end, and during the next episode, we would not even remember our tragedies, escaping to some new plot thread. We wanted that glamorized failure, that hollow hedonism, not realizing there might be something more.

"Excuse me," asked the nurse. "Are you two here with a girl named Charlotte? She's ready to go."

"Yes, how is she?"

"She's been through quite a shock. She's not pregnant, just thought she was. I mean, those tests don't always work. We get more girls in here than you might think who assume they're pregnant but they're really worked up over nothing."

"So she's fine?"

"You could say that. When I told her, she had a slight flight of hysteria and started breathing very heavily. I told her to lie down. That's why she's been back there so long."

Charlotte emerged with her head bowed. She didn't say anything to us as we left the clinic. We slipped through the back door. We could still hear the protestor screaming at women as they arrived in the parking lot.

"Murderer! Baby killer! Sinner! Sinner!"

I sent Declin to drive the car behind the clinic, and then we set back to Lickskillet.

———

"Where were you?"

"I couldn't come." Aron hung his head between his legs, perched on the edge of his stool in the cafeteria. The scrape of forks, the belch of human guts, and the murmur of conversation ricocheted off the high ceiling. He looked sick. "Is she looking at me?"

"She's not looking at you. It's fine. It's over. She's not even pregnant."

"I know—I know—but I was so afraid that she was, that she would expect me to—it wasn't my fault."

I straightened up, glancing to my side to address Aron. Strange to find Blaine's seat still absent. I wanted to miss him, but I couldn't remember him as the boy I had been friends with, only as the meth-addled lunatic.

"It's not just your fault, no, but not her fault either. You share the blame. What did you want to happen? You would do nothing, let her raise a baby by herself or deal with whatever decision? Sometimes, we have to take responsibility for our actions, Aron. It may not seem fair, but it's what's right. You can't get crushed by the weight of your decisions. You just deal with them. It's part of growing up."

Aron nodded morosely.

"When Justin crashed his truck, I thought maybe—maybe it was my fault. Maybe I owed him something. That we were bound. That what happened to him happened to me. But I don't want to just be defined by another person. I don't want to be anyone's girlfriend. I accepted my part in his accident, but I didn't blame myself. I'm not defined by what happened one night. So you can either deal with Charlotte or not deal with her, but it's better to confront her now. Make amends. Put this all behind you."

Declin did not speak, his face drooping. Exhausted, he asked, "Are you still joining that Roller Derby team?"

"It seems like something I should do. I mean, I don't exactly know how to Rollerblade like I used to, but I could learn again. There's always something more."

Our lives could not be contained like books, plays, or soap operas. Each time we reached an ending, we looked into the abyss of something new. The least we could do was learn to stop regretting and looking back and obsessing over things we could never change. While you may not be able to change the past, you could change the future. Our stories never ended, and our sequels were endless.

⸺⸱⸱⸺

When I was nine years old, I forced my mother to buy me roller skates. Skating would be even more impressive than riding a bike because I'd zip up and down hills in Golden Oaks, gliding like an angel above the asphalt with my knees slightly bent.

Perhaps because other girls in my neighborhood asked for ponies, my mother was happy to bestow small pink skates. After three months, I lost interest in skating and pushed them into the back of my closet. They collected dust under the shadow of Barbie's Dreamhouse, next to a broken Hula-Hoop and an impressive collection of Beanie Babies.

When at eighteen I tried the skates back on, they suffocated my feet.

Strapping them on tighter, I hobbled to the edge of my driveway and perched awkwardly on the peak of the hill before rolling forward. I accelerated faster than I had intended. The wheels shook as the skates scooted me forward and down until—a rock. I flipped once and skidded halfway down the asphalt slope on my back until finally I rolled to a stop. I felt like a meteorite plummeting from space to earth.

Despite having bruised my arms and scraped the skin from my knees, I went that same weekend to see my first Roller Derby match, Declin in tow. If I had felt even more confident, I would not have invited anyone, but having Declin along felt right—besides, he had promised to join me if I went to prom with him.

"The Rise and Shiner Café? But that's closed this time of night. It's a coffee shop. Anyways, I thought we were going to—well, what are we doing?"

"It's not only a coffee shop. Have you never seen the rest?"

His eyes grew. "You don't mean—why are we going to a Roller Derby match, exactly?"

"I've never seen one. I wanted to. Maybe I'll join the team after I figure out—"

"It's violent. Girls get hurt. Is this is about Justin—"

"These are not girls, obviously—"

"Or Blaine—"

"These are strong women who don't buy into all this bullshit." We paused to pay the cover charge, slipping into the fray of shouting, bustling spectators. I never before realized the sport was so popular. "It isn't about anyone but me."

We entered through the coffee shop's back room to access the arena.

The first round was about to begin, the derby girls skating into the rink. In the center of the large cement room, we gathered around the hardwood track. The girls, their hair dyed with streaks of pink, white, or purple, dressed in deadly fishnet stockings and hot pants and leather corsets, took their places on the track. "Those in the front—they're the blockers. And the big group behind them is the pack. Last two are jammers. Point is jammers try to pass the pack and the blockers, and each opposing team member passed earns a point."

"Sounds simple enough."

"It isn't."

"Why do you know so much? Are you planning on joining? I don't think you'd make a very good—"

"Yes, I know I'm rather—top-heavy. But who doesn't want to do that? It's pretty fucking cool."

An announcer broke in from above. "Welcome first our local team, the Lickskillet ladies, Heartless Harpies. And coming all the way from Georgia, the Soul City Sirens." These girls too entered the rink, grimacing and tensing. They wore different costumes with accents of blue and purple. "Now, you ladies know the rules. No hitting or tripping—no, wait, definitely do those things." The announcer snickered, and the girls rolled their eyes in unison. "Now on your mark—"

When the girls shot off, they were rockets. Their legs pushed, muscles tensing as they began to skate. Once the pack was half-way around the track, a double whistle blew so that the jammers could race after them. It took maybe twenty seconds before the jammers lingered at the back of the pack, and then one scooted through the crowd, elbowing a black-clad girl, coming out in the lead. The clash continued.

"And you want to do this?" Declin watched me watch them, and he must have seen something—the elegiac longing like Narcissus staring at himself in the river. "This isn't you. You're not—like them. It would be great if you were, but you're—"

"So what? You'd prefer *what* exactly? I just wanted to show you something, something that would make me feel alive. Don't be such a git about it. Watch."

A Siren blocker spun, elbowing the Harpy jammer in her face, sending her sprawling across the track. Blood spurted into the crowd, and the cheer went up raucous and savage. The girls orbited the track with wicked grins. They could, I realized, probably kick my ass; that exhilarated me. I needed practice riding on skates, though. These girls curled around corners smoothly, rolling swifter and smaller when they wanted to and then occupying the air with two outstretched arms to block and zipping and whipping across each other like human checkers.

Declin finally stopped talking. We fell into comfortable silence. He too was in awe of this bloody, wonderful spectacle. This, I thought, I could do. I would join up, as soon as I practiced and maybe worked out more often. I didn't need boys; I craved violence.

In a world where things were always ending, monuments we thought would last forever crumbling under the power of bulldozers, where great men died in fits of lunacy hallucinating past lovers with electrical eyes, all we could count on was violence. Violence was the great constant in this world, repeated acts throughout history and into our gory future.

When the first round ended, we stepped outside for a smoke break. I had begun smoking cigarettes not long after Justin crashed his truck, mostly because it made me feel more grown-up. That was what I needed—a false sense of maturity to compensate for how much I felt ready to fucking freak out all the time. The smoke rose from my mouth in thick plumes, and I imagined this looked sexy; Declin did not watch me, likely because he found it to be the opposite of sexy. Then again, maybe that was what I could strive to be: the opposite of sexy.

We watched the rest of the game, and I returned home in a gleeful fervor.

When the weekend ended and we returned to school, Declin did not say another word about visiting the Roller Derby. All Sunday I did push-ups in our living room, skating outside in the interim of workouts, because those girls had bulging biceps. Their growls and the announcer's words and the crowd's cheers repeated in my mind in a cycle of mindless mantra. I wanted to be a Heartless Harpy, an angel of death, a sawdust ballerina—graceful and destructive.

Your tits could be an asset for only so long before they became the only thing other people cared about. I didn't want boys like Declin to drool over me because they entertained the tantalizing thought of having sex with me, how sex had always been the only act boys expected of me. I didn't decide to stop having sex and swat off men and suddenly feel ashamed of my body, only that sex was not my sole power.

Not a girl who rolled her eyes when a boy refused to open her car door or bring her flowers, but instead the girl who bought herself flowers and put them in a vase in her bedroom, and it didn't fucking matter that no guy bought them for her, because she fucking deserved them anyways.

I wanted to throw fists, curses, and elbow jabs. I wanted violence. I wanted change.

CHAPTER 29

BLAINE MOREAU

Each time I took a drag from my cigarette, it crackled like a campfire. I liked smoking for its symbolism, its thematic properties. Cigarettes reflected the American desire for death, the necessity of it with our lives. Without death, we would not be able to justify our wasteful lives. If we were to live forever, then we would be forced to do something, but death had become our ultimate cop-out, our greatest excuse for failure. I tried, we would say in whatever afterlife existed. I tried to do something good and impactful, but I didn't have enough time. Death caught up with me before I could manage anything significant. I also liked smoking because it was something to do when there was nothing to do.

The enemy had won, I mused: boredom had conquered me. After transferring to a new school, I found myself unbearably isolated. At Exeter Academy, the boys my age belonged to a cliquish gang who called themselves the Swag Boys, and even when I attempted to talk to those who had previously sold me drugs, I confronted silence and disdain. I was an outcast, a nobody.

I tried texting Aron again, and I again received no reply.

To Aron

Me: Hey, Aron, what are you doing tonight? Doing anything interesting? I'd be pumped to come see you play soccer. When's the first game?
Me: Maybe you didn't get my last text. Are you busy tonight?
Me: I'd kill for something to do. Maybe we can get drunk, knock over mailboxes with a baseball bat?

To Cass

Me: I'm really sorry about what I did. Really, I am. I've been attending rehab every day now. I'm getting better. I'm changing.
Me: I understand that you don't want to see me, but won't you at least talk to me?
Me: I'm sorry. How many times do I have to say that?
Me: Please...

To Declin

Me: Hey, man, what's been happening?
Declin: I'm busy. Sorry.
Me: I just want to know what's been going on.
Declin: I'm doing homework.
Me: It's a Friday night. You're not going out tonight? Are you seeing Cass soon? I want you to pass on something for her.
Me: Declin, it's been twenty minutes. Talk to me.
Me: Are you there? Did your phone die?
Me: Declin?
Me: Hello?
Me: Well, fuck you too.

To Cain

Me: I know I don't know you, but I'm bored as hell. Are you and your gang doing anything tonight? I have a bottle of rum.

Cain: Meet me at the train tracks, under the bridge downtown. Be there at 11:00 p.m.

Me: Cool, cool. See you there.

CHAPTER 30

ELIZABETH PEPPER

It was a cruel indecency that I had to find out from the state paper, hours after the judgment was passed, two weeks after the majority of my family was sent to jail for making and distributing meth, that my brother Matty Pepper had been found guilty and sentenced to life in prison.

They considered killing him as well, keeping him imprisoned until the state saw fit to electrocute or inject him. But there would be no appeals, not with all the Peppers facing their own heinous charges, Dylan on the run down to the gulf, and me trapped in another city far away.

My foster parents, the Hendersons, were not so bad but nothing like what I expected. Usually you imagine foster parents to be warm and endearing, acting in the stead of real parents both practically and emotionally, but those more attentive parents must have been reserved for toddlers and babies.

I was brought to live with three other children, one my little cousin, under the care of an elderly couple who did not seem to notice the fifteen-year-old Andrew (who had lived here two years) smoking weed in the bathroom.

They did take care of us, though, buying us microwavable meals or fast food. Except for the fact that my entire family was imprisoned and my brother sentenced by a court who believed him a racist murderer, life was going great.

The dreamless sleeps and the lightless days—this was existence on the fringe. As I fiddled with a pencil, preparing to finish the meager homework my chemistry teacher offered, Andrew walked into my room, leaned against the door, and crossed his arms. His eyes bloodshot, his mouth curled too tightly, he watched me.

"Wherever you come from, they don't have pencils?"

"Yes. They do."

"It's true, isn't it? About your family? I wasn't sure, but your last name is Pepper. We saw it on the news, and you cried. That man they gonna kill, that's your brother?"

"Yes. He didn't do it."

"So your family is filled with crazy, racist assholes, right? That must be a trip. Did you say you were seventeen? You don't look like seventeen. You look twelve. I mean, I know girls a grade younger than me with bigger tits than yours."

"I'm trying to do my homework."

He rested his hand on my shoulder, the fingers sliding down. As a smile crossed his face, I whipped around, slapping him in the face. This stunned him, his face contorting, twitching. Time enough to sink a fist into his stomach. Like the first deer I ever killed, he fell and jerked, his eyes wild and fearful, spinning.

"Fuck off. Next time, I'll make sure to knock your nuts into your skull." I remembered Dylan once saying this to a bald man, and the bald man never messed with Dylan again.

Daddy always said, "Don't let any man mess with you. If you never asked him to touch you and he touches you, kick his ass."

When I left the room, Andrew doubled over, clutching his stomach. Not much remorse.

My cousin Natalie played with a thirteen-year-old girl named Kate, which unsettled me because Kate never spoke. Andrew told me on my first day that she was a "certified cutter" and had tried to kill herself four times since she started living with foster parents. The old couple bought her long-sleeve shirts, and Kate wore them sullenly, silently. She never complained or sulked or talked about how shitty her life was, but you could tell by the way she never tried to interact with anyone that she probably wasn't the happiest.

My cousin Natalie was seven, accustomed to life in a trailer. They played a game where you stacked blocks, taking turns removing blocks from the wooden tower until someone knocked it over; I had never heard of it before, but I didn't see the point. You meticulously constructed a tower just so you could eventually destroy it. I passed them without a word; neither Natalie nor Kate looked up at me.

Outside, I felt better and could breathe and move and pace and rub my face raw. Inside the house, I felt too stuffy, like I was working in some noisy factory, machines churning above my head as I slept. These unnatural sounds made me nervous, and perhaps I felt uncomfortable inside only because I had been taught for years to never stay in the trailer where we cooked. If you did, breathing those fumes, you would get ugly, maybe even die.

There were not many trees to watch over me in this neighborhood—only the decorative palms people planted in their front lawns that did not seem as powerful as the oaks, pines, and cedars of my home.

The night I killed my first deer, I promised to prove Matty innocent. Though Mr. Ostrander was paid to do it, he somehow couldn't. Perhaps it took someone who truly loved Matty to find the truth, to uncover what happened. When I began to see the men in suits, I thought I was one step ahead, so smart for finding them. I could stop them, I thought.

But then the arrests happened fast, one night when the Knights of Southern Heritage met. They were meeting about the possibility of adopting a highway, another of Mr. Ostrander's ideas to revamp their public image, as if this could change minds about Matty's fate. The Pepper arrest only hastened the jury's decision, illuminating us in a lurid, evil light.

Two boys rode by on bicycles, one shouting at the other to slow down so he could catch up. When I was five, I had asked for a bicycle for Christmas, but Daddy told me no, because we didn't have enough money. By my birthday I had forgotten about the bicycle, but he gave me one anyways. He had saved up enough money to buy me something nice. Matty tried to teach me to ride it, except he had never ridden one before. I was the first in the entire family to do so.

⊷⊶

After a dinner of store-bought fried chicken, I retreated to my room. Andrew did not reattempt his failed seduction, which left me alone for a couple minutes. The door swung open, and Natalie stood watching me.

"Hey, how are you doing?"

"Well, Kate and I—we played Jenga today. It was OK, I guess."

I nodded, standing up and closing the door. "Do you like Kate?"

"I guess I like her because she's nice."

"Is she? Good. Can't you sleep?"

"I can sleep. I just wanted to see you. Kate said you were leaving. She said she saw you packing last night."

"Kate spoke to you? She never—"

"She talks to me. She's just shy." My cousin plopped on the bed, all red hair, freckles, and innocence. I tried to remember when I had ever felt that blameless and perfect and unsullied. "Are you leaving?"

The bag with my clothes stood in the closet, ready to be thrown out the window. "Maybe. I don't belong here. I need to be back home with our family, with—"

"You said that—that the bad men took everyone away. They're gone."

"Yes, they are. But—but there's still a place for us there. You can come too, if you want to. Do you like it here?"

She sat up, regarding me with eyes that now appeared too old; how much had she aged in the past weeks? "I guess I like it. I don't mind."

I nodded. "You know, it's probably for the best that you stay here now, OK? I've got to go back to Lickskillet. Stay safe, OK?"

"Are you leaving right now?"

"Tonight. I'll wait until everyone goes to sleep. If they ask, tell them I said I was headed to Charleston. Taking a boat to Mexico or something," promise?"

"OK, I promise. Are you coming back?"

I swept down and kissed her forehead, just like Daddy used to do whenever I was afraid. "I hope so. Be good for everyone. Do your homework, eat all your vegetables, and—"

"Blah-blah-blah. You're just like my mom."

Her mom was in prison, though, and would probably stay there at least fifteen years. A lifetime to some people and an eyeblink to others. "And don't trust Andrew. Stay away from him. Promise me all of this, OK?"

"Fine, I promise. I don't want you to leave."

I didn't say anything. Sometimes silence wasn't just about embarrassment or hatred or awkwardness, only a love that had no words.

⟞⊹ ⊹⟝

That afternoon, a steady rain had wet the streets, and despite it being already March, despite living so close to the coast, a town near Edisto, I shivered. With a rucksack snug on my back, I stumbled down the road.

The lights off of the highway blinded me as each car shot past. My thumb ached from reaching into the air for so long. Wearing jeans too big for my legs and a shirt that draped over my waist like a dress in bad taste, I trudged on.

At the tourist information center a few miles up the road, I took every map of South Carolina and studied it. When I walked in, they stared at me warily but said nothing. Outside at the picnic table, I traced the highways back to Lickskillet.

One hundred twenty-six miles. Could I walk that far?

On the side of the highway, I dragged my feet through the sodden roadside grass from exit to exit. The morning came cruel and bright.

Each McDonald's sign rose as a beacon in the distance, but once I reached each waypoint, I still had miles to go. I wore only a backpack and regretted now bringing so little. Most of my clothes, though, were still stuffed in drawers in a house in Lickskillet.

A van bumped over the side of the highway and stopped. It took me a moment to realize that they had stopped for me. I rushed to the van as the side door slid open. Inside were three young girls in sparkling tiaras. "You lost, girl?" The speaker was a long-faced woman with black hair that looked like it was falling out.

"I'm on the way to Lickskillet."

"We're headed to Columbia."

With thirty dollars in my pocket (that I borrowed from the Hendersons), I could maybe buy a bus ticket into Lickskillet. It ran through downtown once a week to take old people with revoked licenses to and from major cities.

I climbed into the van and squeezed into the backseat, where one of the girls sat. They were triplets dressed in sweaters, wearing frilly pink tutus and silver tiaras. "We're playing princess," the girl beside me said, leaning in and whispering as if it were a secret. The van lurched forward. I sank back into the seat.

After an hour and a half of listening to why Diane's magical unicorn was prettier than Wilma's imaginary mermaid friend, I climbed out of the van and thanked the frazzled mother. She smiled nervously and turned the radio back up, the speakers blaring jams from Disney stars.

The bus station smelled like feet and Doritos.

Almost noon, the bus to Lickskillet had already departed, and I waited into the afternoon. Propped against an advertisement for some cable company, I began to dream.

Of trees and the animals rustling in their branches. Of torches and how they resembled lightning bugs in the distance. Of cooking and its simplicity—how I felt so proud to be wonderful at something. Of bruises and scraped knees. Of bees in the spring, packs of wild dogs all through the summer, wild hogs in the autumn, and crows in the winter. Of leaves both green and dead, blooming and falling.

Of collard greens and paper plates. Of grasshoppers and rocking chairs. Of Coca-Cola and tall grass like Mother Nature's stubble. Of the pond and swimming naked there alone at midnight, the coolness so natural on my skin. Of the men in hoods and the men in working clothes. Of the women in hoods and the women in pressed Sunday dresses patterned with flowers. Of Daddy telling stories, spreading his wisdom, giving us advice as if he had lived thousands of years.

Of the trees, of the trees, of the trees.

At four, the bus driver had the courtesy to honk me awake. I climbed on and gave him my ticket, which had cost me half my funds. The bus brimmed with bad smells and strange men. I sat near the front alone, trying to sleep but not wanting to.

We rolled into Lickskillet an hour later. Everything the same, yet everything different. Like that moment when you come home, when the carpet smells the same, the windows have the same dirty smudges, and nothing has been moved, yet you feel a momentous difference, a change you soon realize was actually you. The bus stopped next to the library downtown.

The stores were preparing to close, owners pulling the recycling bins inside from the street. I would have to walk, as I already often did, through downtown, through the ghettos, through the woods, past a peach orchard, and onto the Pepper Plantation.

Not too far, considering the distance I had traveled since the previous night. I began walking, and soon the trees came into view. I knew soon I would be home.

Some of the nicer trailers had been towed away. The less livable ones stood still cradled by trees, moss, and weeds that had encroached their windows and doors. Our house static with emptiness, I could not walk through without holding my breath. Once

I found the property vacated, I felt hopelessly lost, wondering why I had escaped in the first place.

Before arriving in the forsaken woods, I had not formed any plan. I could not ever free my family from prison because they were guilty. Matty, though he might not have been guilty, would never be free. After everything that happened, no one would believe a Pepper.

Every person involved—my father, the aunts, the uncles, the cousins, and the elderly who only adopted our name because their own families had died—they were all in prison. All the children had been taken that night and sent to foster homes. I wondered why I had not been arrested as well, being almost eighteen—how I had possibly seemed innocent. It would have required every single person arrested to deny my involvement.

Almost eighteen. I checked my watch and then closed my eyes. Today was my birthday: I was eighteen.

The trailer we used to cook had been bound in yellow caution tape I tore down.

When I finished surveying the house and the surrounding trailers, I picked one to sleep in. Dylan's old trailer would do until I could find something more permanent. I stashed the acceptance letter to the state university, still propped on my nightstand in my bedroom, in Dylan's kitchen. Then I crept out to the edge of the forest to find my bow.

Everyone was gone, and I was truly alone. But I was an adult now. I didn't have anything to prove to anyone, but I needed to eat.

CHAPTER 31

ARON KING

They streamed Matthew Pepper's conviction on all news stations. Finally justice had been served in America. On live television, my father clapped Barnaby Rutgers on the back like they were friends. Like all the tension in our skin had been released. Most people had been crossing their fingers for Matthew Pepper's death. But I didn't want him to die, even if he was guilty, because his death couldn't bring back Francis Jameson. His death wouldn't fix anything.

Guilty of first-degree murder. Guilty of a hate crime. Guilty of obstruction of justice.

Matthew Pepper hung his head, covering his face with his hands. Only a few weeks before, most of his family had been arrested for running a meth ring. Because Matthew had been in prison at the time, he couldn't be connected to the drug charges.

Finally, I said, "I'm sorry your father lost the case."

My father won the case, but it didn't make me feel any better. The man who killed Francis Jameson, embittered by hate and jealousy, would face justice. But it didn't make me feel any better.

"Yeah, he might not take it well."

"What happens now? To you?"

"Me?" Declin didn't seem to know. "What always happens—I guess I might be moving soon. Not immediately. I'll figure out what to do. Anyways, I'm accepted to the state university, and if I am, I guess I'll stay in South Carolina. And my father—what about you?"

For me, it didn't change anything. People would crouch over their televisions and applaud the court for sending such a terrible man to prison for life. They would cheer for him to be strapped into an electric chair, that unholy throne. That was how we operated—watching the battles of the good against the wicked. And then when the bad guy received what he deserved, everything ended. We went back to our lives satisfied the system worked exactly as it should have.

Except not for everyone—not for me. He looked so guilty, but I didn't think he was guilty. It seemed too simple, the story that everyone wanted to believe.

Hours after Declin left, I tried to study for a biology exam. Our finals were a month away, but Ms. Schall had already begun assigning endless reading each night. After school, soccer practice, and the final knowledge that I didn't know anything, reading about mitosis didn't seem so bad. Around eleven, my father stumbled in, shouting good-bye to whoever had dropped him off.

He smelled of whiskey and walked like a lion on its hind legs. "Did you see? We won. We won. We won. That bastard had it coming too. You know, after this—well, I don't even know. Maybe things will get better, and I—I'll be pretty damned important now. Mr. Rutgers has got to see that, hasn't he? How I took this entire case and—" He made some sort of animal noise while gnashing his teeth wildly and then began laughing. "Oh yes, I won."

"I saw on television. Good job. What ended up winning the argument? What did you end up using as evidence?"

"Evidence? That man hated Jameson. Obviously, it was won before we even began."

"Do you think he killed him? What's going to happen to him now?"

My father eyed me strangely.

"He'll go to prison. Might die—if Judge Matheson gets his way. That's—that's the way it works. Justice, I mean. I did my job; the jury did theirs."

"What do you think happened? I just—I felt weird about it."

"He had enough cause, and his alibi was only backed up by convicted drug dealers. How more clear-cut could things get? This was a bad person."

"Well, maybe not. You keep saying justice is all about separating the bad people from the good people, rooting out the wicked. But what is that supposed to mean? Who really has the right to judge someone else? Yeah, Matthew Pepper seemed the worst. A low-life, racist asshole, but he never had a chance in that court. You know it."

"Of course I knew it. But that's not the point. It's not so much about whether or not he killed anyone—"

"No," I said, my own voice surprising me, "that's exactly all that should have mattered."

It occurred to me suddenly that the case against him had been wrong all along, that there must have been some mistake. I didn't know why I knew this, but I did. I thought about Charlotte in the clinic, doubled over at the news of her nonpregnancy. Surprised that she didn't need to have any procedure and horrifyingly guilty that she'd considered it. On Channel 7 News, Matthew Pepper never looked like that—distraught, maybe, and cruel, maybe, but not guilty.

This should not have affected me so much, but in the midst of considering Charlotte's almost pregnancy, the verdict seemed another indecency heaped onto our lives. In the end, cruelty seemed to be the fate for everyone. Maybe not forever, but at least temporarily. Tragedy took the time to track each person down and shit on his or her life; unfairness became our common trait as human beings, the one fucked-up rope that tied us to the same stake to burn together.

⊷ ⊶

At school, I avoided Charlotte. No one talked about the verdict of one of the best-publicized trials in the past decade. No one seemed to care that the redheaded kids from our school had simply disappeared. The first game of the soccer season was on Friday, my first chance to show off, and everyone cared more about the soccer game than what happened to Matthew Pepper. After Justin Ferrara fell into a coma and corrupted his football team's chance at victory, the student body pegged their hopes at a state championship on my rising star. The first college recruiter would come to the game to watch me play.

I was all exposed nerves and trembling veins.

⊷ ⊶

Outrage had always been a coping mechanism for not getting what we wanted. That was why, the night before, I acted all pissed off when Matthew Pepper was sentenced to life in prison though I was more than halfway sure, despite my qualms about the justice system, that Matthew killed Jameson.

In a way, it made complete sense, and my grumbling never accomplished anything. Even my father forgot we had fought about it when he sprang awake, somehow miraculously hangover-free, to go to work the next morning.

What was the purpose, I thought, of winning such a big case if you still had to wake up at five in the morning to go to work, not getting home till late at night? Just like despite the fact that some kids made straight As, they still had to go to school every day.

In biology, we sat at our designated tables to complete the exams. Two holes burned in our group like piercings in our tongues. Blaine, studying at Exeter Academy. Pepper, whisked away someplace after her entire family ended up in prison.

When I turned in my test, I noticed Declin looking at me. After class, he approached, hopping. "I'm staying in Lickskillet. It's official. At least until the school year ends. My dad has to go to Tennessee, but we're keeping the house off the market just until I can move to college."

"Awesome."

"Yes, yes, yes. I don't think I've ever spent an entire year at one school before. And graduation only in two months."

"Yes, soon."

I tried to cheer myself up, even joking with Elijah, who had become a permanent awkward fixture at our table. After Blaine left school, Cass joined us again. Before she ever dated Justin, it used to be like this. Blaine, Cass, and I, middle-school rebels fighting the system together, as if that meant anything.

"You're going to kick ass Friday, right, Aron?"

"What?"

Cass laughed. "The soccer game. First one of the season. Who're you playing?"

"Lousy team. We'll knock 'em out fast. I almost forgot."

"Damn. You can't be so—you're so depressing lately. All this talk about death and dying and bullshit. I mean, don't you guys remember when we used to be fun? Even in a town as boring as this, we found a way to have a good time."

"Well, you seem—happy," Declin said. He looked to me. "That's different."

"Exactly," she said. "And why not? I know I was trudging through the mud for a while, but hell—shit happens. And I feel—I feel better. How about when you win this Friday, we'll throw a party?"

I looked up. "Oh, those. I almost forgot what one looked like since—"

"I know. Turns out no one gives much of a shit around here about having a good time except me. But that's fine." Cass raised her head high. "I suppose I must bear the burden of having all the fun by myself. So Friday, my house. Invite—well, almost whoever. That's how it goes, right?"

Declin even laughed. "She's right. We've been—tense. It's time to let things go."

I nodded. "Sure. That sounds fine."

⋙⋱ ⋰⋘

By Friday, the fever of spirit had spread like the flu. I walked down the corridors ribbed with blue-and-gold streamers hung across the ceiling every fifteen feet. Consumed with secondhand fervor, the janitors had taken their annual initiative to sweep the floors and even pour bleach into the browned toilet bowls. After a football season marked by the star quarterback falling into a coma, hopes at Lickskillet High could not be higher for soccer glory. My glory.

We stood in some polluted snow globe, the dome above us glowing greenish blue like the bottom of an aquarium. As the horizon gnawed on the sun as if it were some dripping papaya, my nerves kicked in. My heart became a jackhammer, slamming full-force against my ribcage. Confidence flooded my blood. I could taste in the sweat that dripped from my forehead the premature taste of triumpth.

I swayed as I walked onto the soccer pitch, and the students jostled in the stands, maybe calling my name. Maybe loving me from afar.

We assembled in loose war positions, bending our knees.

I sprinted.

The ball glided gracefully between my feet, and I forgot myself. I forgot everything but the present moment—here on the pitch with the ball, the players, and the heavenly lights blinding me. *Dribbling up, then back, and then around the oppossing players' careening bodies, I advanced toward the goal. When I launched the ball, it bounced off the corner of the goal. A swarm of opposition carried the ball away, but I followed closely after them. The faces from the stands blurred. The stampede of feet had become deafening. This made me feel so alive, more alive than anything else.*

When the game ended, I hardly had time to collapse onto the bench and take a swig of water before the students poured onto the field. My peers clapped me on the back, and the team as well, screaming victory. All this because of me. We won seven to two.

Hands clutched my armpits, lifting my body into the air until I sat on a throne of shoulders. However long this lasted, it did not last long enough. The adrenaline carried me through. Once the crowd began to dissipate, wandering off to parked automobiles like lost dogs, a man approached me. I knew exactly what he wanted.

"I'm from Irwin University, located in upstate. I came down to see you, and boy, I'm impressed. Do you think you'd like to talk sometime? Tomorrow, maybe I can come by to speak to your parents. Irwin would love to have a young, talented athlete like you on our side."

"Thank you. I'll give you my information."

He would come, and Dad would be ultrapolite, but what did it matter? There would be more next time from bigger schools, other schools that would outdo previous offers. They came here specifically for me—Lickskillet had seen football recruiters but none for university soccer teams.

By the time we finished our conversation, most of the students had driven away, likely headed toward Cass's house for the party. Declin and Cass waited by the gates to escort me out.

Cass threw the party at her house, where I found Charlotte cross-legged on the couch. This was the couch where we first met.

Charlotte.

She no longer sat with legs splayed wide, her eyes seductive. Instead, she carried her fists clasped in her lap, the holy burden of painful clenching. When I entered the room, she didn't look up; she heard my voice and glanced away, her bottom lip stuck out.

"Charlotte, you—you're, um, looking better." I lowered my beer and sat down, but she only scooted to the other side of the couch. "The game tonight—we, uh, won." The words tumbled feebly from my tongue. "Are you OK?" I reached out to grasp her arm, and she flinched.

"Don't fucking touch me. Get away from—just don't."

"What?"

"Don't sit there and try to apologize like you mean it. Don't keep on making boring small talk, like anything matters, and just—I'm fine, but I don't need to talk to you about this."

All of my apologies threatened to explode inside of me. Atonement caught in my throat, a grenade I could never pitch back from my demolished gut. "Yeah, I guess I know you don't want to talk about it, but—"

"What don't you get? You hated me. You fucking hated me. So what? And I was stupid enough to believe you actually cared, at least enough to find out if I was pregnant. Now you're ready to acknowledge I have feelings? What exactly do you want to hear?

That it wasn't your fault? Well, it wasn't your fault. There. Do you feel absolved?"

I wanted to reproach her—she got pregnant, not me. She couldn't swing back at me with the consequences, though I still felt them. "How do you feel?"

"I had to find out all by myself, and you—you weren't there for me. In some sense, maybe you weren't supposed to be. I just wanted to feel important to someone, and I wanted to feel like I was an adult. But now—shit, I don't know what I want." She stood up from the couch. "I don't know what I'm doing here, so I'll just go home. Enjoy your party, Aron."

"Wait. Look, I was wrong, OK? I'm at fault, too. I kept thinking you were the one who was maybe pregnant and you used me, but it's not like that. I'm sorry. Even saying that, it feels so empty, like I should have learned something about how to be better or how to treat people. But I feel like I haven't learned anything, that I'm the same asshole as before."

We spent too much of our lives wandering around at parties, searching out someone to fuck as if that one-night stand could change our lives, cure our insecurities, and heighten our social status. But in the morning when the other left, we discovered we were still alone. The foolish game we played, that yearning so long for a few minutes of ecstasy, still left us lonely. "Maybe under different circumstances—"

"Aron, don't do that. Don't say that, like you care. Please, just—I'm going to leave." I watched her leave, unsure of when I'd ever see her again, unsure whether I wanted to, repulsed by my own impulses.

"Look, you don't get to act all high and mighty. You used me." She nodded. "And you used me. So what does that make us?"

Now I remembered the things Blaine always said, how he took pills to stop feeling, to plaster the wound's cracks. I was wrecked, absolutely wrecked—so I tipped the bottle back and started to drink.

⤜⧓⤛

The night wore on till nearly five. Even Cass rose from moroseness. I spotted Elijah talking awkwardly with a group of other juniors, and I wondered when he ever got any friends besides Declin. He too joined our party, jolly at the thought of staying in Lickskillet for the remainder of the semester.

"Aron, I need to talk to you. Top secret."

"What's up?"

We leaned over Cass's couch, whispering. "Well," said Declin, "I have a brilliant idea. I know what with everyone leaving—getting ready for college—that we're busy. Well, we have yet to leave a mark on the school. Every class does—some indelible mark on the history of this town."

I wondered if he meant the senior gift. Each year, the senior class reluctantly left behind something for the school, whether that be planting flowers in the bus lot or repainting traffic lines. The wicked smile on his face told me he didn't mean this at all. "You mean the senior prank? Well, I hadn't been thinking about—"

"Well, I have. Cass told me all about what the kids did last year. Removed all the doorknobs in the school. Brilliant. But I have—I have an idea, and it will blow that out of the water."

He told me, and the scheme shone with such brilliance I stumbled around the rest of the night blind. When we parted, we promised to meet back up soon to draw up a plan.

Something else bothered me, a nagging in my ear. An omen. As if something bad were about to happen. I had to ignore it because if I thought about the future, I'd be a goner. I was happy. I had my future planned out perfectly, even if I knew it could never turn out exactly how I wanted. But still it would be nice to be able to pause life, to freeze-frame the brink of adolescence when we were all still full of hope and optimism.

I thought about what Blaine could say about this—all of this happiness. Maybe he would compare it to math. Thinking about him made me slightly sad.

He would say life was a parabola. On one side, there was happiness, joy, and on the other misery, sorrow. Life was a balancing act between the two extremes, everyone a dot racing up and down the slope of that line. And each mistake we made boosted us up the wrong side, heading toward negative infinity, but gravity brought us to equilibrium, balanced everything out.

Maybe as far as math was concerned, the bigger the mistakes we made, the better things got once the disaster dissipated. Now, in this moment, the world careening in such a way that I could only barrel back into misery, I thought, Well, at least everything has the possibility of beauty. Despite being in messed-up situations most of the time, some of us, through perseverance, luck, or fate, got to experience something wonderful.

Better things were coming. We could escape from this static town, this southern doom.

What beautiful mistakes we made.

CHAPTER 32

BLAINE MOREAU

I walked through the same hallways I had during summer, dressed in that blue uniform with starched blue pants and fancy-ass sports jacket. Walking down the halls to the library that housed more books than our public library, passing sconces with torches on the wall, dressed like a fashion-forward, metrosexual gentleman, I felt like a mannequin sprung to life.

At Exeter, new students felt like T-bone steaks dancing into a lion cage. Or an anorexic model, rib cage jutting out, attending a Weight Watchers class. Out of place, vulnerable.

In my first class, Advanced Calculus, I nearly laughed at the formulas written on the board. Even remedial Joe Bubs could understand this shit, and here were the future leaders of tomorrow (reigning with the power of the dollar), but they had, by March, not even gotten past learning integrals. When the others entered, I recognized only one, a Swag Boy named Cory. He did not pay any attention to me.

"Hey, Cory."

He regarded me silently. "I'm sorry. Do I know you?"

"Yes, that time you—well, I know you. I know Cain as well."

"Cain? Yeah, well—good for you, man."

Now I knew how Declin felt his first day of school, overwhelmed by the novelty of each interaction.

⊷⊶

Usually my parents purposefully ignored my bad habits, the nights I never came home, the funky marijuana scent of my bedroom, the empty vodka bottles in my closet, stacked as if in decoration, but after being arrested, they paid a little more attention, at least enough to force me to leave public school and enroll at Exeter Academy.

I came home to their decision, which they gave too calmly, as if they still harbored the fucking stupid dream of me going to Yale and becoming the next Albert fucking Einstein. On most days, I could tell my mom, "I'm taking your car tonight to hotbox in, OK?"

She would reply, "Yes. The flowers are lovely, aren't they?"

Now a simple "I'm leaving for school" constituted an inquiry that lasted for hours.

Moving to Exeter, however, did not improve my relationship with drugs. The boys there simply took more refined and expensive drugs than the public-school students. On one of my first days, I walked into the bathroom and found Cain snorting coke from a toilet seat.

"What the fuck, man?"

"Blaine," said Cain so calmly you'd swear coke didn't powder his nose, "come here. Try this. Had this before?"

"I haven't. I can't. I have a math exam."

"Good. This'll help." His hand on my shoulder forced me to my knees as if he were preparing to give me a swirly. "Try it."

You didn't contradict Cain: the invisible hand with strings tangled around each knuckle. I needed to lean down farther, and I nestled the bill in my nose, breathing like a vacuum.

Too long out my mind, dealing with the cold sweat of soberness and the teachers' watchful eyes. The pitiful release: I needed this.

Slurp.

Imagine the highest you've ever been while fucking a porn star, and right as you orgasm, someone electrocutes your ball sack: that was cocaine.

Like if everything you saw in life became binary, and everything made perfect, computable sense. Logic that floated through the air like the numbers during my math exam. I finished so fast I should have entered the Olympics for elementary calculations. Numbers whizzed by, hurricanes, flurries, tornadoes that sent up Kansas houses, and I snatched equations from the air greedily.

"What are you doing tonight, Blaine?"

"I'm not sure. I guess I have to go home, but I guess—"

"Meet me at the library around closing time. Eight. Can you manage that?"

Fuck no, not with my parents breathing down my neck like they're rottweilers salivating over a ham hock. "Maybe, if I can get away." I needed this, and I felt I needed to go. Otherwise, I would continue the strange outsider existence where everyone I thought I knew ignored me. But Cain seemed friendly—I needed something.

The same night, I texted everyone I could think of. I asked to do anything; I asked for them to save me, but no one could. Hearing back nothing, I finally caved and texted Cain.

⚔ ⚔

At seven thirty, I convinced my mother I needed to study for biology with a friend, and I drove to the library, jouncy, nervous, palms leaking. My mouth as dry as ham on rye and my fingers as jittery as an eighth grader's while unhooking a bra. Pulling in to the library, I saw Cain's car idling, and I slipped out of my driver's seat into his passenger's seat before he roared away.

"We're not staying here, so why meet here?"

"Because it's a surprise, Blaine. Cory, blindfold him." Before I could protest, hands from the backseat pulled my face against the headrest and then bound a cloth around my eyes, fastening me to the seat as well as obscuring my vision. "This will be your first night of initiation."

⸻

Cain paced along the rail of the bridge, uncannily balanced, strikingly poised. "The Swag Boys is more than a gang or some bullshit boys' club. We're a society that stretches back generations, having assumed many different names when our fathers, brothers, and even grandfathers wore these uniforms. We're the finest, bravest, strongest, sexiest males at Exeter Academy, and we prove that we kick ass.

"Which is why we're asking you to leap off this bridge onto the train. Every night at midnight, the train comes. Land on it and then dismount some time later, and we'll know at least that you have some balls. Do you accept this challenge?"

"The Swag Boys? You want me to jump onto a train so I can be in your what—the Swag Boys?"

I should not have offended his stupid gang, but the whole history and name sounded phony.

"Believe me. Not every guy at Exeter gets this opportunity, and not every guy makes it through initiation. So think of this as the first step to becoming someone better. Someone you never knew existed inside your before." Cain smiled. "When I was a sophomore, I was initiated by Harrison Yeltin. You know he rows for Harvard now? He showed me things—that we belong in something bigger. Something more prestigious. This is a group of fine young gentleman who will inherit the world."

The train ran through downtown, passing under a number of bridges. We stood on an arched wooden bridge, and I could hear the locomotive whistling in the distance.

Donny clapped my shoulder, shoving a handle of whiskey into my hand. "Be courageous." I took a hefty swig and then mounted the rail next to Cain. When he leaped down, the wooden supports shook, and I almost lost balance. Steeling myself for the jump, I felt ready. This was not so bad—not as bad as being alone when everyone thinks you're an asshole, when even your best friend since childhood refuses to speak to you because of stupid mistakes. And you realize in that moment of desperation you didn't have a choice in the first place.

The train rolled underneath the bridge, not moving incredibly fast but still chugging, chugging, slicing the tracks—I jumped.

The wind whipped my face as I fell, my surroundings melting into a colorful blur. And then *smack*—my body hit the train car, and I bounced up, my fingers digging at the metal to find a grip.

I hung from a handle, dangling off the side of the train as it steadily plowed forward. My arms shook as I attempted to lift myself onto the train's roof, but I managed it, collapsing on my back, both fists gripping white-knuckle on separate handles.

The boys on the bridge faded out of view, but I could hear them whooping like natives practicing a deathly, delicate ritual. I rolled to my side and collided with the ground, my knees cheese-grating against the gravel, my face slamming into the dirt. But as I dusted myself off, I counted myself lucky to be alive.

Cain, Donny, Brad, Rick, and Cory—the Swag Boys—tumbled down the slope to congratulate me, laughing and sloshing the vodka onto their clothes. They looked too pedestrian without their uniforms—almost like other kids. But before coming to

Exeter, I had heard stories—these were not normal kids. They lived the teenage lives you aspired to, the perfection of hedonism you slaved to grasp.

Cory pulled me off the ground, handing me the bottle. "Damn, you just fucking—committed. Just leaped on there and—" He burst into fresh laughter.

I rubbed my elbows and wrists. "Tasted like white-lemon Italian ice, honestly. So, what's next?"

⟥⟤ ⟥⟤

When I was very young, before the doctor delivered the grave, miraculous news to my parents that I was special, I competed with Aron in everything. But because I had not yet cultivated, through years of tutoring and practice, a proficiency in math, I envied his excellence. Someone who at six could play every single possible sport, always being picked first for flag football, always last to be tagged in dodgeball, should not have also had such decent grades.

At six, we played together on a local recreation-league soccer team, and at this age, our coach recognized prematurely that Aron had a knack for handling the ball, for curving his kicks past the heads of first graders into the goal.

How we played, the kids ran in a thick mob behind the ball handler as he or she dribbled up the field with sloppy feet. Whenever the person in front faltered, we swarmed violently, desperate to kick the ball away. Very little did it matter which team held the ball, but which person—that mattered to us and became a matter of childish pride. Aron often raced forward with the ball across the pitch as both teams alike hustled after him.

Tonight, the players did not resemble a stampede, yet Aron still dribbled around them with ease. Hovering over the grass, he controlled the ball with such dexterity I suspected he might be capable of telekinesis. Leaping over the leg stretched to trip him, spinning to avoid the attacking player, he shot the ball like a bottle rocket into the upper-right corner of the goal. A bounce, and the roar rose. The score ran six to two already, Aron having scored four of his team's goals.

I craned my neck to survey the crowd, searching for the college scout. He would be sitting away from the crowds, with an air of pretentious significance, likely holding aloft a fancy clipboard and studiously training his eyes on Aron. The first scout would be here, furiously noting Aron's skills, his finesse. Preparing to offer him as much money as possible to lure him to a particular college. The way these vultures preyed on athletes made me sick and jealous; no college scouts ever peered intensely over your shoulder during a calculus quiz. Before I spotted anyone who looked that right mixture of aloof and fascinated, I spotted Cass.

She stood on the second row from the front of the stand with the rest of the students. I avoided that area and sat on the opposite end of the stadium bleachers.

I promised him months ago I would attend the first game of the season, so here I sat, watching him kick the other team's ass just like we all knew he would. Not even showing my face to them, incredibly shamed.

Cass watched the game carefully, cheering at the appropriate moments and keeping up conversations all around her, meticulously avoiding my gaze.

Such a terrible thing to pay the price for something you thought was free. Such a terrible thing to continue pursuing that exorbitant passion, that cruel, draining need. Such a terrible thing, something only an addict could understand, to chase so fervently something that would one day kill you.

Aron bounced the ball off his head, and it spiraled down in front of his teammate's feet. The teammate wound back a kick and rocketed the ball into the net.

Seven to two.

The game ended soon after. My classmates—no, not mine—those students who still attended Lickskillet High without me—stormed the field, whoops rising up into the night. The opposing team slunk back onto their bus while the students embraced the soccer players. I made my way down from the stands to the edge of the field, prepared to speak to Aron again.

How would he respond when I finally faced him? Accusation for halting all communication with me after the arrest? Apology for what happened with Cass? Happiness as if I had never been taken to be interrogated, never been caught? Fondness?

Once in the seventh grade, he and I clashed severely over a video game that he accused me of cheating at. Of course, I hadn't cheated and was simply better than him, but Aron was too accustomed to being the best at everything, always winning. We did not talk for three days straight, three agonizing days of summer I spent alone at my house, until Aron pedaled his bike over and asked to play the game again. We never discussed this brief rift in our friendship, and perhaps (excluding the weeks of soccer-themed summer camps Aron visited) this was the longest time we had ever not spoken to each other. Until now, until I broke into Cass's house tweaking on meth, until—

The others lifted Aron onto their shoulders, carrying him away. He surfed atop them, pumping his fist. I idled awkwardly, avoiding eye contact with the people who used to be my friends.

"You. I didn't know you'd be here."

"Declin, I haven't seen you since—since I left school. How has everyone been?"

"Everyone has been fine. I thought Exeter boys were supposed to wear their uniforms twenty-four–seven or something. They're always prancing around in those stupid blue jackets."

"Well, it's not really my style." Declin's face seemed so blank that I could not tell whether Declin sympathized with me or despised me. "How's Cass?"

"Fine, I guess. A little bit crazy. She actually—well, she's fine." He didn't want to talk about her, I could tell. "I heard about what happened the night—well, that night. You know the one."

"With Cass? Yeah, if you see her, tell her that—I just—I lost it. I couldn't—" But Declin didn't seem too interested and kept peering over my shoulder. "What is it?"

"Did you want to say something to me?"

I turned. She faced me with the expression of a girl at a club you're trying to ask to dance and know will reject you. "Yes, I wanted to—apologize. Where's Aron?"

She pointed to the corner of the field where Aron crouched with a gray-headed man in a fedora who must have been a recruiter. "Oh, all right. I just wanted to—yes, apologize to all of you. I know I've been a little less than stable lately, but I—" What could I say—that I had been doing better (drugs)? Cocaine as a replacement for meth and weed throughout the day? That I had replaced my friends as well with the Swag Boys?

"We know about the drugs too, all of them," Declin said suddenly. "And the shitty thing you did to the Peppers. You sold them out. They'll spend forever in prison now—"

"Wait, what? Is that what you're pissed about? That I helped put drug dealers in prison? Seriously? Or that some murdering, racist redneck will fry like an egg? Seriously, that's the dumbest shit I ever—"

I usually liked to claim that I never underestimated people, but I did not expect Declin's fist to meet my face so fast. A pain shot through my jaw, and I toppled backward, drooling blood. Declin stepped over me, red-faced. Cass didn't say anything else, looking at me now with disgust and pity. "I just can't—I can't talk to you anymore." As she walked away, I remembered how she looked the night I broke into her house—so afraid.

Every plummet had a pit to fall into, and here was the bottom, spitting out blood and another tooth. My mouth would soon look like a checkerboard. I stumbled to my feet, shaken. Obviously I had underestimated how pissed off my actions made people, and maybe coming back here to the old alma mater too soon had been a mistake.

I fumed, wondering whether Cass had simply moved from Justin to me to Declin in a succession of using men, and this pissed me off as much as when I first saw them together at the Red Hole. When I searched the crowd for Aron, I watched him walk off the field toward Declin and Cass. They attacked him joyfully, hollering in celebration, and then marched toward the parking lot.

Here was my pit; had I always been the pendulum cutting my own neck?

⚔ ⚔

"The next stage of your initiation will not pose any danger but will require a strong stomach, which is why we've had you take plenty of—um, vodka shots. Those. And now I'm done cooking this delicious, um, entrée." Cain grinned warmly, presenting the frying pan to us. On it was perhaps the most disgusting confection of cheese and puke I had ever seen.

"What is that?"

"Well—the plan is that we all get so drunk we get sick, except you, and then mix some of our own—well, bile with cheese and eggs. Included bacon too, since bacon makes things better." Cain seemed to consider this for a moment. "I present you with our creation—the vom-lette."

When he set it on the table before me, I studied the culinary creation closely. We sat in the kitchen of Cain's immense house in Golden Oaks; driving there, I passed Cass's place, where no lights were on. I slowed down, waiting to see any movement, and then drove on.

Cain lived in a similar palace, both historic and outfitted with technology I had only seen in science-fiction films.

"Wait, you want me to eat this?"

"That's the idea. Eat it, and then you'll only have one stage of the initiation left."

I smiled and picked up my fork and knife. "Well, it smells fucking delicious."

They pressed in close, their eyes widening as I calmly cut the vom-lette into strips and lifted the first to my mouth.

Having consumed in my short life many various drugs and likely enough alcohol to get Godzilla drunk, the taste of vomit was not one unfamiliar to me. As I ate, I heard the screeching of crows and tasted the vomit. I swallowed as quickly as possible, shoving the next piece into my mouth, and then began cramming the chunks through my teeth, trying to avoid placing it directly on my tongue. But in under a minute, I finished and burped loudly and took a long swig of vodka to burn away the taste.

We celebrated my achievement by getting blackout drunk and drawing dicks on Donny's face when he sprawled unconscious on Cain's kitchen floor with a hand stuck down his pants. We shotgunned cans of beer, and I proved myself mightily worthy of their drinking ranks. Even Cain slumped over before I did. So high on the excitement of the night, the freshness of talking to people who did not quiz me in math or talk endlessly of scholarships, I could not help but smile.

"You're going to fit in well," Rick said. "Man, you're going to love it. Party with us, and we'll show you a different way of living.

How we party—that's a whole new level. We live like everyone else dreams of living." For some reason, he found this hysterical and could not stop laughing.

"So, what's the final stage of initiation?"

Rick shrugged. "Cain will decide that. We all did what you did when we first got in, but the last stage—it's unique. We go on a bit of—a mission to do something we've never done before. You'll see that you truly are—you're a better person than others. That's the whole point. We have something other people don't; we live with inherent greatness others clamor after their whole lives. We were born into this world not simply human, but better. And there will be—be something to prove that."

I smiled at that, liking the sound of it: *better.* Of course I ended up here, being as talented as I was. My condition caused me to view the world, experience everything, on a higher plane than anyone else I knew. Maybe I had no prowess at soccer or suaveness with the ladies, but I belonged among the Swag Boys.

I was better, and it was time people acknowledged that.

⚔

Halfway through class, I raised my hand to ask to go to the restroom. For a moment, the teacher turned purple, ready to snap. But teachers paid special attention to the Swag Boys, tiptoeing around the students as if we were time bombs. "Go."

Though we had thirty minutes of school left, I slung my bag over my shoulder and rushed for the door. I hurried down the hall into the parking lot where the other Swag Boys waited—not that I was a Swag Boy yet, but I would be after the final stage of initiation.

I tingled with anticipation for a feeling of belonging. Too often I felt my skin and bones were not my own but instead a disguise for my soul.

"Blaine, ride with Cory. You can help him find your old high school, can't you?" I nodded, of course. Cain's mouth stretched an animalistic length, his teeth bared. "Let's go."

Cory did not appear as thrilled as I climbed into his car. "You seem nervous. You've done this before, right?"

He looked at me as he turned the key in the ignition. "This was my—my least favorite—I only did it once. I mean, I was the latest initiate. I only joined this year in the fall. Selling drugs to you—that was one of my stages. We had to do—well, there were a few more rituals I had to go through before—I think Cain likes you a lot. He wants you in."

"Oh." I wasn't sure how to respond, not sure whether he was jealous or simply angry. "Well, I'm sure it wasn't too bad. He—"

"Do you even know what you're talking about? You're as dumb as fuck as the rest of them. Do you want to hear about *my* initiation? You didn't do shit. You got off fucking easy." As the other cars veered to the right, Cory drove in the opposite direction. "You should thank me. I'll tell them you pussied out and refused to do it."

"But I didn't—I don't even know what I'm supposed to do."

"You're supposed to beat the shit out of someone. A stranger. I'll drop you off or something—"

"Wait, why? Why would we do that?"

"Because that's what we do. The Swag Boys are better than everyone else; it is our right to do as we please. And there is a boy Cain has taken a particular disliking to—his name is Elijah—"

"Wait, him? I know him."

"Yes, Cain has been—he tracked him. We're supposed to meet him outside the school and—and—and—just kick his ass. But Cain never stops at that. He's so—look, I'm not going to let you hurt Elijah."

"You know him?"

I placed my hands on the dashboard and turned in my seat. Cory had seemed so silent before, so complicit in Cain's plans that I couldn't imagine his life outside of the Swag Boys. Once you become one of them, you remained a unit, thinking together. You would begin thinking as Cain thought about the world. Where had Cory met Elijah?

"I—well, I don't really know him, but I *feel* like I—just, listen, get out the car now. You won't regret this, this giving up. Not everyone makes it through initiation. You begged me to drop you off somewhere, so I did. Go back to your old school. Forget Cain. Forget everything about this fucked-up place. You don't want to be a part of this."

"Why are you freaking out? It's only a little good-natured hazing."

We parked beside a closed, boarded-up video-rental store. Cory eyed me squarely. "You don't know what any of this is about. You just want to be part of the gang, but you're in over your head. Cain is out to kill; he's a psycho. Today, we kick the kid's ass, maybe rough him up a little. That's nothing. Cain never stops there. He's a psycho."

"What do you mean? He seems fine."

Cory took a deep breath. "Well, fuck it. Let me tell you about my initiation. It may be something you want to hear before making your decision."

CHAPTER 33

CORY JOSTIN

When I moved into the neighborhood in the beginning of July, I felt like I didn't belong. Not in the massive house overlooking a golf course where retirees drove white comets over the hills while telling each other stories about how things used to be different in Lickskillet. Not down the street from the towering clubhouse that held the Golden Oaks offices, a full gym with a running track, a banquet hall, and an expensive grill and golf store. Not among these kids who threw lavish parties.

In my first few days, I explored the town by myself. I walked downtown where no one recognized me, and in a way, there was a power in not being known. No one expected anything of me. I sat down in a café called the Rise and Shiner by myself, sipping a latte. The city did not promise anything until Cain showed up on my door holding out a plate of cookies.

I sat in our new living room watching our new flat screen. All of this merchandise courtesy of my father's new employer. He would be helping run a local plant a few miles out of town that manufactured and bottled over-the-counter medicine.

So that new diet pill that became all the craze lately—that bought the leather living-room set that made it impossible for us to ever buy a pet. The heartburn medication you've seen in commercials—that made it possible for me to watch *Leave It to Beaver* in any room in the house.

"You must be Mrs. Jostin. My name is Cain. I work at the academy over the summer, meeting potential students. We received your son's application and wanted to meet him. The administration finds him highly qualified. Also, we made you these."

I turned to peer over the couch, trying to see his face. "Why, that's lovely. Yes, Cory is planning on attending Exeter Academy. His father says it's one of the best private schools in the state. What do you think?"

"If Exeter has taught me anything, it has been the value of honesty, ma'am. Exeter is a fine school that turns out fine men. You know, most of the teens that come to our high school end up making six-figure salaries or more. Of course, we used to be an all-boys school, but we have accepted some exceptional girls as well, though not many. Is your son here?"

"Cory, come here. Come meet your future classmate."

I stood and approached him, extending my arm in formal fashion. He grasped my palm enthusiastically. "Ah, you'd make a wonderful addition to our lacrosse team. Ever play lacrosse?" He inspected my calves and biceps with clinical interest.

At my old school, there had been a lacrosse team, a group of boys who liked to terrorize me. Not that they openly mocked me, but the way they ignored me and delicately reminded each other of parties I was never invited to while I sat between them— I knew they hate me. But because of our school's strict bullying policy, they never touched me. Not that I didn't know they called me a faggot behind my back.

"I don't like lacrosse. Your name's Cain? And you go to Exeter?"

"Yes. I'd love to show you around sometime."

He was taller than me and very attractive with skin that seemed to glow golden and gray eyes as cool as Siberia. "Sure. What sort of cookies did you bring?"

Mom shot me a mean look, but I ignored it, reaching for the plate. They were made with some sort of nut. "Pecan," Cain said, pronouncing *pecan* like "pee-can." I almost laughed but stopped myself.

I would have to get used to how people talked down here. Maybe everyone speaking in deep, slow voices would make me feel more self-conscious—my voice had always been comically high for my size and sex. But maybe southerners would suspect my accent was merely "Yankee."

Cain continued, "Well, if you can't swing by the school, maybe I can show you around the town. I know it's difficult to make friends in a new town."

All of this made me very nervous. No one acted so nicely to me when I first met them, but maybe people down south were genuinely friendly. I nodded and said, "Sure. Sounds great."

"Well, you can meet me tonight at my house." He gave me the address, and I committed it quickly to memory.

<hr>

Summer nights never seemed to begin, so when I walked to Cain's house three blocks away, the sun still hovered above the horizon. I wore cargo shorts and a T-shirt but was sweating. When I saw Cain still dressed in a button-up shirt tucked into khaki pants with a tie around his neck and loafers on his feet, I knew he had to be a psycho. I wasn't far from wrong.

"So what the fuck is wrong with you? You fucking weird or something?"

I stopped, my mouth open. "What?"

"I mean, you're not a weirdo faggot, are you? I just figured since you acted weird at home. I don't want to hang around, well—you know. You're cool, right?"

His question caught me off guard. All day I thought about Cain, how easily he wanted to befriend me, believing perhaps the South wouldn't be too bad.

"Yes, I'm normal. I'm just new here. I don't know you."

"Everyone knows me here. Soon everyone will know you too. That's the shitty thing about this place. People know people, and nobody gets to be anonymous, not in this town. So, your name's Cory?"

"Yes. That's my name. What are we doing tonight?"

Cain shrugged. "You're cool, right?"

I should have told the truth, told him I wanted secretly to rip his clothes off. But these weren't things I even told myself. "I'm down for anything. We're going to a party?"

"Exactly. A party."

We cruised in Cain's Porsche to another boy's house. His name was Donny.

"This is Cory, a new recruit."

"For the Swag Boys?"

"What's the Swag Boys?"

"Not yet," said Cain. "I meant he was considering coming to Exeter. And then maybe—well, we'll see what he's made of before inviting him."

"Wait, what's the Swag Boys?"

"We're a sort of gang," said Donny. "Not like street thugs, but we—we do things together. A boys' club. A society."

"Oh. Well, that sounds interesting. And tonight. What are we doing? Is there anything to do in Lickskillet, South Carolina?"

We arrived next in a clearing in the woods where clay dunes rose around an indent in the earth filled with clear blue water. "The Red Hole," Cain called it, sliding out of his car and retrieving a bottle of booze from the backseat. Other boys waited in their own cars, following us farther into the woods when we climbed out.

"Here. You drink?"

No. I took a large gulp from the bottle anyways.

That night was the first of many strange fever dreams inhabited by strange, southern rituals that echoed through time, memories of people who lived long ago transplanted in our heads. In the familiar strain of the southern teenager, we became sloppily drunk until we could not walk, our legs having betrayed us. Whenever we stood, we tried to lean against something to support us. This had not been the first time I ever drank alcohol, but never before had I indulged in such sick-sweet irresponsibility.

"Do you find this boy worthy to join our ranks?" Rick bellowed and raised his arms in mock sacrifice. "Why this pussy? Though there is something in him yet. He may become one of us."

"That would be—be nice." My lips felt so numb I could not form a sentence.

"But it's no easy path," Cain whispered cryptically. "When we first began this gang, we wanted to set a standard. We're not street thugs. We're teenage angels of death. We are gentlemen courting debauchery."

⭃⭤ ⭤⭅

I never had to jump on any trains. When I came to Cain's house, I gladly wolfed down the vom-lette. We would do anything happily if Cain asked us to. We relished being spectators of our hero's endeavors. We worshipped him as if he embodied all we ever hoped to be: the smart, savvy, cool prep kid. We were all ecstatic participants in his life. As if it were a privilege.

When I finished the last bit of egg, I began to vomit as well, my vomit tasting doubly like vomit. But they clapped me on the back and congratulated me. I would soon be one of them.

⇥ ⇤

My indoctrination did not take long. I had always wanted this. I had always wanted to be part of something.

⇥ ⇤

"The next phase is simple," Cain explained. "And I promise to make it very easy on you." He dropped a ziplock bag full of weed on my lap.

I picked it up, sniffing it cautiously. "I've never smoked before. Do you want me—me to smoke all of this?"

He began to laugh. "No. That's an ounce of weed. Cost me about three hundred bucks. I want you to sell it. Not all of it. That'd be daunting. Just one sale. A guy hit me up a week ago—wants to meet me tonight downtown. Go meet him and make the transaction. Twenty bucks for two grams."

I smiled. This would be easy. "Sure thing."

⇥ ⇤

At midnight, I snuck out of the house and drove to the library as instructed. Blaine, blazed and giggling, waited for me in his totally inconspicuous yellow Mustang, revving the engine for fun and blasting the Bee Gees. "Blaine."

"Hey, man, you must be Cory. Cain said you were coming to hook me up. Wanna get high?" He placed his arm on the windowsill, a smoking joint in hand. "This is the last I got, so I hope you brought more."

"Are you crazy? Turn off the car."

"Huh?"

I glanced over my shoulder. Cars passed us on the roundabout. The police station was only a block away; it would take thirty seconds. I braced for lights and a siren. "Turn it off. Someone's going to hear. You're sitting at an empty library at midnight in the middle of downtown smoking weed. Just—"

Pushing his arm out of the way, I leaned through the window and turned off the ignition. The engine died, the music faltering midway through "How Deep Is Your Love?" I snatched the joint from his hand, snubbing it out on the roof of his car. "My paint job," he muttered.

"OK, listen, let's do this fast. Have twenty bucks?"

I waited as he stared up at me. "Um—what?"

"Do you want weed?" I showed him the nugget wrapped in saran plastic.

"Oh, yes. I want that." He groped for it.

"Come on. Twenty bucks. Please. Hurry. This is illegal. And I've got to get home before—"

"Right. I have to pay." He began rummaging in his pocket and handed me a ten-dollar bill. "That's all I have."

"Well, this costs twenty."

"No, that's a rip-off. Ten, and we're done." After a moment, he began giggling. "OK, well—half."

I didn't know how to weigh drugs. In the movies, dealers used scales with precise measurements. Cain had told me to sell all of this. "Give me ten more dollars."

He opened up his change drawer, counting quarters. "Shit. There's a fiver in here." He handed me that as well and then took an excruciatingly long time picking out eighteen quarters and five dimes. With cash and change in my pocket, I tossed the baggy of drugs into his car and sprinted back to my car. I peeled away just as the Bee Gees songs commenced.

⇒⊹ ⊹⇐

"Let us celebrate this momentous occasion tonight. Cory becomes one of us. Once tonight is over, he will forever be our brother. Right?" Cheers of assent, and my heart sprang giddily.

The final initiation. I knew how rich white kids' clubs worked, about the exclusion inherent in their choosing of members. I knew this but still clamored to belong.

We drank shots of vodka off Cain's dining-room table. "Go walking at night," Cain suggested. We drove to the edge of downtown and dumped Cain's Porsche in a shitty back parking lot where people would smash in the windows to steal his change. We walked three blocks, began to stumble, and threw the bottle against the concrete.

Everything became a haze. I had only begun drinking heavily three weeks earlier, at the beginning of the initiation. The alcohol did not burn anymore, but I felt disoriented. I wanted to fall over and sleep on the ground where there was no chance of me falling. Then we saw him, reeking of booze and dragging himself up the street.

"Shit, who gave you that black eye?" Cain approached the man, kneeling down and rolling him over onto his side.

The black man on the ground mumbled something.

"What's that?" Cain stood and then kicked him hard in the ribs. "Know who the fuck we are? You don't come around this shit anymore. Fuck you." He kept kicking. "Cory, your turn."

"Do what?"

"Show this guy who we are, how powerful we are. We want them to fear us."

"Who's *them*?"

Cain kept kicking the shit out the man and then dropped to his knees, pressing his fingers around the man's throat. "Well, come on."

But Cain was attacking this man, and I wanted to be just like him.

Then we fell on top of him, kicking and punching. Blood pooled around the man, bits of teeth floating in gelatinous red. Only a minute in, we stood back in horror to see what we had done. Cain kept slamming the man's face against the asphalt.

"Stop."

"Fuck. That felt good. And that's it—we're done."

I shook my head. "What the—the fuck did we just do?"

"Survival of the fittest," Cain explained. "Whenever we see someone weaker, we crush them. If he could have fought us off, he may—he may have deserved to live. Well—do you know who this is?"

Brad said, "I think I know him."

Cain nodded. "Shit. Let's get him out of here. Quick, hide him before anyone comes. I'll run and get my car." Cain sprinted away; we dragged his body out of the street and behind a Dumpster, where we covered him with cardboard boxes. Donny began to hyperventilate.

"Is this what you do?"

Everyone shook their heads; we were accomplices to murder.

Cain squealed up in his Porsche and waved us over; the man's body was heavy as we carried it back into the street, pushing the corpse into Cain's trunk. A slam, and we were off. Only blood left to signify our sins.

At some point, we should have stopped, should have done something, but we trusted in Cain's better judgment. Only in him did we invest any faith.

Our breathing was audible, and we listened to nothing else as we sped through downtown, zipping under stoplights burning red.

Rick gurgled, pale. "What just happened?"

Cain replied softly, "Rick, we killed someone. Quit acting like it is some big fucking deal."

Donny broke in. "It is—you killed someone. He's dead—he's in the fucking trunk."

"He already had a black eye. They won't think it was us. They'll think—he was mugged. They would never suspect us. Hm—what if we sent a message?"

The elderly guard smiled amiably as we sped past, a body growing colder in our trunk. "What the hell do you expect to do?" I asked. "Bury him in your backyard?"

This was too much. I had never meant to become a part of this, but now we were bound by this sin.

"We're not hiding him. That would be idiotic. They'll come looking for him."

"Why would they? Wouldn't they just check the ghettos? Where we found him?"

Cain turned to give me a curious look, parking his car. "He lives here. Do you know who this is? He's not just some random drunk. This man used to be the mayor of Lickskillet."

When we dragged the body from the trunk, he was still squirming. I said, "Fuck. He's still alive."

"He won't be for long. Cory, get the rope. Do you know how to tie a noose?"

"What the fuck? We're going to hang him?"

"Yes. Look. I know it's barbaric. That's the point. Trust me. By tomorrow—we'll be clean."

No one asked why Cain carried hemp rope in his trunk, almost as if he had planned this. He took us along with the intention of forcing us into conspiracy. Before I got kicked out of Boy Scouts, the noose was the only knot I'd learned to tie— besides the square knot, but everyone could tie a square knot.

The man was still alive. He began to groan, his eyelids fluttering, his palms turning up. Cain tightened the loop, tossing the rope over an oak-tree branch. And we wrenched him off of the ground. And we grasped the roped and pulled like a team in tug-of-war. The man clutched at the tightening rope, gasping, his body scraping against the ground until he balanced on his toes. Another tug, and he dangled in midair, writhing, twisting.

He went limp, purple hue creeping across his cheeks. His eyes strained against their sockets, his mouth gaping wide, wide like a giant trying to swallow a mountain. We drove away slowly without the pomp of newly minted killers; we held a secret.

I was a Swag Boy. I would always be a Swag Boy. What I had always wanted. What would haunt me until I died.

CHAPTER 34

BLAINE MOREAU

In life, some mistakes we make; other mistakes make us. They transform us until we are quivering on the ledge of sanity, clinging to anything that makes us feel alive—whether drugs or nature or soccer or lying or sex or some stupid role-playing game about dragons.

"What's going to happen? They're just going to scare him."

Cory shook his head. "No, they might hurt him. I'll go. I'll make sure nothing happens—nothing too bad."

I couldn't breathe, couldn't speak—every time I tried to inhale, oxygen became needles in my throat. "You killed him. I thought—I thought—"

"Matthew Pepper." Cory nodded. "Cain is clever, a genius in a way. He knew who would be blamed. Maybe he thought it was a fun game to terrorize Francis Jameson. Now he's dead, and another man will suffer because of what we did. You can't tell anyone. You can't."

"I won't. How did they never find out? It would be obvious."

"No one wanted to find out. What if Cain's father had an inkling of what really happened? Would he accuse his son of murder? Never. People needed the Peppers to leave—they were old-fashioned, worn-out. Maybe forty years ago, there was some use for them, but people don't give a shit anymore. You can't tell anyone. I just needed to—you can still be saved. You can still leave."

"And go where? I've—I did this. They could kill him if they wanted."

"I will say you ran away, wimped out."

"You can't do that. I spent too long—I don't have anyone else." I felt desperate, would hurt anyone if that meant being accepted. I would do anything just to be accepted again.

"If you spend your whole life only trying to get people to like you, doing whatever is necessary for their acceptance, you will never be able to live with yourself. Now get out my truck."

I stumbled out, and he drove away without another word. Collapsing onto the pavement, I began to sob.

Alone again.

When I reached home, the house was quiet.

What I needed was an escape. I climbed upstairs, pacing around my bedroom. What would Cain do tonight after he found out I had not come? He would come after me, know that I knew what they had done. He was not afraid to kill people; he was psychotic. The truth played through my mind again—they killed Francis Jameson. They beat him and hung him in a tree.

Even as I contemplated this, I wanted to please Cain, to force him to like me.

I began hyperventilating, clutching the edge of my dresser for support. Escape—I needed escape. I could not live like this any longer. My entire life I had been running from what I feared becoming, but here came the choice, divisive as a guillotine.

My father kept a gun in his closet.

CHAPTER 35

THE JOURNAL OF ELIJAH RODRIGUEZ

April 5

Today was not a good day, Quentin.

This week was not a good week. My mother brought me the notebook in the hospital, even though my dad raged when I asked for you. I needed to write things down. It makes my head clearer.

Sometimes, I think things cannot become truth until we verbalize them. We might have ideas or opinions we don't accept until we say them aloud. Events might occur that make no sense until we put them down on paper. Even our maddest dreams can seemingly become reality when we pen them in solid ink, making them visibly real. That's all I need—to reaffirm my own beliefs. To counter what I have seen, what happened, with what I can write.

I'm sorry. I didn't mean for there to be tears. Your pages get soaked, and I can't help it. I don't know why he came—I thought he was gone, but he came. They came. They all did, just like in the library. Tomorrow I am going to leave the hospital; I'm not sure I want to go home. My dad will just call me a faggot for not beating them. But I couldn't. I can't. I'm not.

The nurse wants me to sleep. I need to tell the story, and it bubbles at my lips, but I can't. I still haven't told them exactly what happened. They think still it was just some misunderstanding. Like a football game gone wrong, something innocuous. Who gets two teeth knocked out, blood choking them, an arm broken, playing friendly football?

Sometimes, I think they purposely ignore the signs because they don't want to accept that their son is a failure. I just watch them, as expressionless as Rorschach, knowing they might never bother to find out the truth.

CHAPTER 36

DECLIN OSTRANDER

Blaine's absence became a missing front tooth, too painful and obvious to continue to ignore. We convened on a balmy early-April afternoon, one month after Blaine transferred to Exeter Academy. Planning the senior prank without him felt like running Camelot without King Arthur, but he left us, we remembered. We attempted to remember why.

No one from Lickskillet High had yet visited my house, and I felt queasy when they began pulling up in the front lawn. I stepped out of the house as Aron walked toward me. "Is your dad in?"

"Well, he's clearing things up at the courthouse. Running into a bit of trouble getting paid for defending Matthew—what with his entire family in prison. The Knights of Southern Heritage are supposed to pay him for his legal help, but they're almost broke running advertisements in an attempt to recoup their public image. How are things?"

Aron shook his head. "Declin, when was the last time you saw Blaine?"

"I haven't really—I mean, he was at the soccer game."

"Soccer game? My last one?"

"The very first of the season. He was there. We didn't tell you. We didn't want to—"

"We?"

I opened my mouth to speak, but he cut me off.

"You haven't read the newspaper, have you?"

I did not entirely care for current events, not anymore. They depressed me.

When I followed him inside, he placed the front page on my kitchen table. "He was declared missing three days ago. And this is the first time we hear about it. So he's been gone five days."

Aron nodded. "Look, Cass is pulling up. I'm sorry. I just thought you should know. I guess he must have taken off—skipped town. Ran away from home."

"Why would he do that?"

"You didn't know him very well, but he hated this place. He hated school. He didn't even want to go to college. He just wanted—he wanted to own a farm. Work out on a farm where his head could be clear, where he could think and breathe and—not exactly a farm, but—Cass?"

She looked drastically different with purple hair—a change she made to complete her Roller Derby persona. "Did you guys hear?" She shook the same leaf of newspaper. "Apparently, his parents are looking for him. Might as well not waste their time, huh? Declin, you said you had a plan."

I waited for her to mention Blaine again, to express some wish to find him, but she never did. We walked inside.

"Yes. I've been thinking about how to top last year's prank. I know you guys want to do something memorable."

"When I was dating Justin, that was possible. We could have gotten half the school body involved. Had a flash mob. Something unforgettable."

"Well, we can still do something. Just us. And it can still be legendary."

Aron nodded. "Legendary. I like it. You know, Blaine used to really like pranks. He went on and on about how we were supposed to leave our imprints here. We would go on to do huge things with our lives, and people here in Lickskillet would still talk about us."

Both looked at me, waiting for brilliance. "Where's Elijah?" I asked.

"He's supposed to be coming?" Aron looked out the window.

"He's small, inconspicuous. He's invisible. We need him. Well, I'll debrief him at school this week. We have a week. That's when the school holds its spring fair every year, the Saturday before prom. Students, parents, alumni, half the population of the town—they'll crowd into and around the Lickskillet gym. That's where we strike."

"And you still haven't told us what we're doing."

So I did.

—≺‡ ‡≻—

Our first operation would be scouting out the gnome museum. For the prank, we needed to acquire thirteen gnomes, a table, a banquet of food, and gnome-size clothing. Cass joined me at the museum on Wednesday after school.

"Have you talked to Justin much? I hear he's still struggling with the physical therapy."

Cass shrugged. "I don't take responsibility for it. Not anymore. I bet he'll go to tech school, take up welding maybe. Good for him. I'm happy."

"For him? Or you? You look pretty bruised up."

"I've been practicing. The girls—they'll let me on the rink, but I'm not good enough yet. Now, look here—there's an alarm on the door."

"And there are two security cameras." I nodded at them as discreetly as I could. "I guess people are proud of this place, so—we can't just steal the gnomes. They'll see us."

Cass nodded. "We'll have to figure out something. Apparently, a few years ago, this group of teenagers raided the place and stole a few gnomes—kept them hostage. After that, the city began investing security in the last vestige of legacy it had. Look, that gnome has a mustache."

He stood with as much elegance as a gnome could muster wearing facial hair reminiscent of Salvador Dalí. "Have you heard anything about Blaine?"

"No."

"I just thought—maybe—I mean, if he talked to anyone—"

"He didn't say anything to me. The police are tracking him. Might as well not waste their time in my opinion. He's—he's just—we used to have something, you know? Not me and Blaine. But all of us. Aron, Blaine, Justin, me, everyone. We all sat on these thrones thinking no one could hurt us if we were so high up. We thought we were better than other people. That's all I thought when I first met you, how much better than you I was. Hanging out with you, I was doing you a favor. We were stupid. And we've been friends since the first grade. You know how we met?"

"No. I mean, I thought it was a bit weird—you being friends with them."

"We were six. We went to the same elementary school a little ways out of town, and our playground was surrounded by this wire fence. Blaine and Aron grew up together, and if Aron weren't half-black, I'd say they were brothers. They used to dare each other to climb over the fence, go into the woods, and bring something back. They used to dare each other to do the stupidest shit. They would see who would go farther, risk more. And one day, I watched them. Well, I called them stupid. They were stupid. It was a stupid game—so they asked if I would ever go over the fence. Because I was a girl, they thought I might be too scared.

"I did. I climbed that fence and ran as far as I could. You know what? I never turned around. I ran all the way downtown. This was when the Rise and Shiner first opened, and people used to drop their coffee cups into the garbage outside—we didn't pretend to care about the environment then.

"Well, the teachers called my parents because I never came back. My parents weren't furious; they never cared enough to be angry at me. But I did get grounded. When I came to school the next day, I showed them a coffee cup I had taken from downtown, to prove how badly I had beaten them. We've been friends ever since."

I nodded. "I'm sorry."

"For what?"

"Just—for everything fucking up, for people fucking up. For the world—you know, fucking up. I never really had friends growing up. Maybe you guys are the best I've ever gotten. I—I didn't really like Blaine, but at least he saw through the bullshit. My bullshit. And you guys—everyone had something. But it got blown away, like some tornado ran through our lives. I'm used to things always changing, always losing people. But I don't know what it is like to lose someone I actually care about."

She just looked at me. "Come on, we'll go find Aron. We'll figure out a way to get the gnomes."

⊷⊶

In seventh-period psychology class, Elijah was absent for the third day in a row. Sometimes, after school, I walked with him to the edge of town. I knew vaguely where he lived. I vowed to look up his address when I got home.

"Cass said the museum has cameras and security alarms. The gym has nothing. Only a lock. So we pick the lock and carry everything in. Simple."

I turned to Aron as we walked toward the parking lot. "Just pick the lock? How exactly is that going to work out? Do you know how to pick a lock?"

"No, but maybe we could get some keys. Pay off a janitor."

"Who would snitch us out in a second? We need to steal them. Aron, what about the soccer coach? Distract him a bit, talk him up, and then snatch the keys when he's not looking. We'll get them back by the next morning."

"I can't just steal his keys."

"We only need one key. The door to the weight room. Then we can carry in our supplies through there into the gym. It's perfect. Have you heard anything about Elijah?"

"No, I haven't seen him."

"What about Blaine? Any word?"

Aron stopped. "He left—he just left, you know that? He didn't secretly tell me where he was going. Damn, I wish I knew where he went. Sometimes, well, people fuck up. We all do. But he runs off like we can never forgive him, like we can never make it right."

"So you really think he just—he ran away?"

Aron nodded. "Skipped school, skipped town, and got the hell out of here. I've got to go. I have soccer practice."

On the way home, I called Elijah's cell phone, but he didn't pick up. The mover's van waited in our front lawn, men carrying the few boxes we owned out from the kitchen. As I entered through the living room, I found the house empty; he had left the television for me.

I stomped up to my room, which had not been touched. All else had been cleared out in a little less than an hour—my father talked to the movers in the kitchen when I came down. "Declin, you're home. We're just—well, I'm leaving."

I leaned against the counter. "Yeah, leaving."

"Well, um, keep safe. I won't see you until—well, probably graduation. Duty calls. More cities to visit. More people to defend. Cases to—well, frankly, lose."

"You don't lose every case, Dad."

"Maybe not every case. Anyhow—ah—this is good-bye for some time. You'll be staying here. I might not be back for certain—"

"It's OK. I'll be fine."

"I will come back if I can. It's a long drive, but maybe—yes, I think I can come. I'll see you very soon. In a little more than a month. Don't destroy the house. Don't—just make good decisions, OK?" He slung a duffel bag over his shoulder, glancing toward the door. "I love you, know that?"

"Thanks. You too. Bye."

He nodded and followed the movers out the door. In a few minutes, the house fell quiet again.

⌲

When I knocked on his door, I could hear his parents arguing in the kitchen. "—will cost fucking six thousand dollars for a few days. Those damned greedy bastards. We ought to burn that place down. Those doctors are a bunch of faggots railing—honey, do you hear that?"

The door swung open, and I felt guilty standing on their front porch so brazenly. Elijah's father looked like a grumpy Puerto Rican walrus as he eyed me. He wore a police uniform, the buttons undone. "You'd better not be here to sell me any Girl Scout Cookies, boy. Or your wacko, homosexual religion."

"Is Elijah here?"

His parents exchanged looks. Apparently, Elijah did not get many visitors. "He's upstairs," said his mother. "He may not be up for anyone visiting. He just got out of the hospital."

"Why was he in the hospital?"

No answer—only empty stares, anger, and resentment. His father retreated behind a closed door into what looked like a cluttered office, while his mother led me, as if she were ferrying me across the River Styx into Hades, up the stairs and to Elijah's room.

He lay propped up in bed shirtless, his pale skin covered with wicked bruises and Frankenstein stitches. On his arm, he wore a clunky cast clean of signatures. A glossy *Fables* comic covered his face, but he lowered it to peek at me as I entered, his swollen face forming some expression that lost its meaning in his disfigurement.

"What happened to you?"

"I-gah-freig-ho."

"Are you OK?"

He wrenched blood-soaked cotton balls from his mouth and gasped. "I fell down."

"You fell down a mountain?"

Elijah looked at the floor. "Don't worry about it. I had an accident. How is everyone?"

I waited until his mother left and then burst into my proposition.

"You disappeared. I needed to know—look, Elijah, we're planning a prank. I know you're not a senior, but we could use your help. Once you feel better, get back on your feet and all. We got it all planned out. All you have to do—seriously, what the hell happened to you?" I noticed how his face accumulated bruises, marks like fists across his cheeks and jaw.

"I can't—I don't want to talk about it."

"Are you coming with us? For the prank? We have everything ready. The plan—well, we need you probably." Beside him on a table beneath a stack of comics lay a journal. I had seen him carrying it with him at school, stuffing it into his bag, and scribbling in it whenever we watched 1970s informational videos in Psychology.

I said nothing, snatching it out of his reach. He groped after me as I perched at his desk across the room, flipping through the pages until I found the last entry.

"That's personal."

"Is this your diary?"

"Well, not a diary, but—"

While he protested weakly, I stole his secrets.

———

When I finished, I looked up at him, dropping the book at the end of his bed. "Well, I'm sorry. We will—I will—this won't happen again."

"How can you promise that?"

"I can't, but—did you see Blaine? Was he with them? Did he attack you?"

"Blaine wasn't there. They said he ran off. He refused—they said he was gone because of me."

"When you return to school, I'll bring you up to date on the prank. Project Gnome. These guys—they're pathetic. People won't remember who the Swag Boys ever were. But us—kids will remember us forever."

CHAPTER 37

THE JOURNAL OF ELIJAH RODRIGUEZ

April 7

I am not ready to tell anyone what happened, but I am prepared to share the story with you, Quentin.

Every Friday, I stayed behind after school to talk to Mr. Bradley. He often had harsh criticisms for my poetry: it was too sentimental, too safe, too boring, or too lousy. He once published an anthology of poetry in college, which according to him became a series of thinly veiled plagiarisms of Ginsberg, Kerouac, Whitman, and occasionally Eliot. My poetry, however, he quoted as "drivels of a euthanized loser with anemic word choices."

Despite his smarminess and obvious relish for criticism, I enjoyed it—he turned out to be helpful. Things were looking better for senior year. I had friends who weren't seniors, who weren't leaving. One of them was named Alice, and I think I was starting to like her even though she had no curves to speak of. She would not fit well in a rap music video, but maybe in a library—maybe.

And there was Hank, the palest Asian kid I've ever met, who was the only person trumping me in class ranks. Cass didn't even mind when I invited them to her party.

Usually, I walked home with them. Sometimes, Declin walked with me since he too lived without a car. My house only a few blocks away, on Friday, I walked alone. Things were going well. I had not seen the boy named Cain for several weeks, believing he must have been preoccupied.

They must have waited outside of the school, following me from a block away in their caravan of cars. Only a block from my house, they began bleating their horns, whooping, getting closer. I walked a little faster, keeping my head down. Then something knocked me over from behind.

Faster than the Flash, I slammed into the pavement, pain shooting through my body. My back and face scraped the cement, bleeding. I tried to sit up, but the scene became immediately blurry, my arm aching. The Swag Boys climbed from their cars; Cain had driven the car that had hit me from behind.

"You fucked up my paint job, you useless faggot maggot." He kicked me hard in the chest.

I coughed, unable to breathe. In the hospital, they asked what happened. I told them: an accident.

"Look at this fucking kid cry." Another Swag Boy, a big one.

I trembled but lay as paralyzed as Barbara Gordon after her run-in with the Joker.

A truck pulled up from the other side, and I prayed for salvation. I lifted my head. Another member of the gang stepped out of the truck.

Cain asked, "Where's Blaine?"

The black boy shrugged. "I told him what we were up to, and he—"

"He was never going to make it. I knew it. He didn't have what it took. Will he show his face at school? I hope so, and we can—"

His foot came blasting toward my face. There came a point after the third kick when I could only taste blood, and the pain left me numb. My eyes hazed by tears, by screams. Everything terrible and real and present.

It becomes now not so much my story but a piecing together of what happened, an investigative probe into the events that occurred. I lost two teeth; my left arm fractured, so I have to wear a cast. That must have been from getting hit by the car. All else I remembered was pain.

"Cain, we're done. He's down."

"But he's not dead."

I heard more shouting. Someone pushed Cain away from me. "We can't kill him."

"Then you do it. Do it."

Another last jab of pain as a shoe made connection with my chest. I blacked out.

＊＋＞

There it is, the whole story as best I remember it on paper. I'm sorry for being so pathetic. I'm sorry.

CHAPTER 38

ELIZABETH PEPPER

I crumpled against the wall, clutching my face, the debris piled around me. Once when I was eight, we experienced a tornado that tore through the plantation, shifting and flipping trailers, uprooting trees, and destroying our lives. We rebuilt our homes and our lives, but now as I searched through the Pepper Plantation, I found no one to help put things back the way they were, the way things should have been. Everything lay in sad disarray while I perched in the center of the chaos. When I walked back into Dylan's kitchen, I looked at the shitty Tupperware I had gathered and carved with hunting knives into makeshift chemistry beakers. The milliliter marks scribbled in Sharpie had smeared while I tried to work.

I ran out of pseudo days before, and the boy refused to go into town and buy it. He refused to leave his trailer most days, and all of his pent-up teenage anguish was starting to piss me off. He had never experienced what I had—my entire family beaten into submission, crammed into squad cars, and whisked away behind granite walls and my brother sentenced for something he never did. No, not Matty, he would never kill anybody.

Instead, the boy was going through withdrawals. Not sure what all he had been taking—meth and coke and booze and weed and ecstasy—but now he had nothing, shaking sweating in his bed with his forehead burning furnace-hot and his arm twitching. I couldn't sit there and watch him suffer, and instead I worked. Climbed into the trailer and got to work on rebuilding our family's business.

Lunging forward, I knocked the slapdash meth outfit to the linoleum floor. Most of the pieces shattered on impact into shards of clear plastic. All we had left of our efforts—nothing. The police had hauled away the setup we operated with before, and we were forced to cook with homemade half-assed equipment. I needed to keep the business alive; maybe Dylan would return from wherever he had escaped to. Maybe my father would come out of prison proved innocent, and maybe, maybe—I needed air.

I burst out of Dylan's trailer and collapsed onto the ground, rocking myself until I lay utterly still.

My face pressed against the dirt so that the grit nearly pierced my eyelids. The sun made me dizzy after days in the dark, long hours of failing at something I once had been so good at, once had done so expertly. Something my family praised me for, the reason they all loved me, wanted me, the only people. So I couldn't just stop—even after the raids and arrests and storm. Sometimes certain acts defined us, and if we ever ceased them, we would no longer feel like ourselves.

"Are you awake? You're alive, right?"

The boy prepared to kick me until I lifted my hand, wiping dead leaves out of my hair. "I didn't find anything," I said. "Nothing we could use."

"Well, I guess that's it. What do you plan to do with what we've made?"

I stood up, biting my lip, gathering my courage to speak. "First off, there's no 'we.' You assisted; I cooked. Secondly, that's not even meth. It's—it's terrible. When Dylan was around, we had all these glass beakers and tubes, and it was easy to understand. Things made sense. But not anymore."

He didn't say anything for a long time and then sucked in his breath hard. "I want to ask you something, Pepper."

Sitting on the concrete steps of Dylan's trailer, I twisted leaves of grass between my knuckles. "Yes?"

"I think I need your help."

"Why is that exactly?"

He hesitated. "I just need to say good-bye is all. I'm planning to leave in a few days. Thanks for letting me stay here with you— it's been great. But I, well—every time I see Lickskillet, hear Lickskillet, smell Lickskillet—all I feel is—maybe it's the sound of a car wreck or nuclear bomb exploding, the taste of death or spoiled milk—but all I really feel is how much everything hurts, that I really can't live here anymore. I need to leave." He paused, reaching almost too tenderly to brush the dirt from my arms.

I nodded. "Then pack up your shit and leave. See if I care."

—⟨+⟩—

I met the boy from school—his name was Blaine—a week earlier when I almost skewered him through the neck with an arrow. Crouching in the brush, I waited for any movement.

Hunting seasons did not exist—I followed the laws of the hunger that kept me coming out to hunt every night, every morning, whenever I could find time. After I dropped out of school, I got lots more time. Bent over with an arrow notched, I heard something moving loudly through the forest, something too big to be a deer or small rodent. I thought maybe a bear had wandered south.

When I stood up, I drew back my bow, and the arrowhead leveled with his Adam's apple.

He froze, struck with an expression of horror.

I lowered the bow, releasing the tension on the string and saying, "I could have killed you. I would have had to bury your body out here."

He didn't say a word, only trembled.

"Well, what the hell are you doing out here?"

"I'm lost. I—ran away. You're the girl from my biology class. We share a lab table, and we—your name is Pepper. Your last name, I mean. I thought you all disappeared."

"Like the dinosaurs? Like Elvis? I'm afraid some things keep coming back. We're a resistant strain of human DNA. You're the boy who gets high all the time. You're an asshole."

"I know. I know. I'm sorry." He paused and then glanced at his feet. "I—I have been out here for two days. Do you—well, do you have a place to stay? Are you living out here?"

Many trailers stood empty on the plantation, and I could use his help hunting for food. But that would mean feeding another mouth. After what Andrew tried, I hardly trusted males at all; if he tried anything, I would probably break all of his fingers.

I explained all of this to him, and he agreed, clutching his stomach. I led him out of the woods to my house; he would stay in my great-aunt's trailer—she had owned a flat screen but never a satellite connection. Then we sat down to eat roasted raccoon with bits of the fur still stuck to it.

⇥⊹⊹⇤

When the police came looking for Blaine the missing math prodigy, I felt smug that they would not come onto our land. Though we still owned it, most of my family resided in prison, and my existence needed to remain secret. They scoured the trailers and ran dogs through the woods who followed the zigzag paths of Blaine's scent from whenever I had taken him hunting.

Meanwhile, we waited miles away on the back of a peach truck headed out of town. We waited, two bedraggled and dirty teens, in a Waffle House, watching the search unfold on live TV. He had some money to spare, so we bought a motel room for a night with two separate beds.

The police never found any sign of Blaine around Lickskillet and vowed to expand their search. But they would give up, Blaine knew. He assured me of this as we lay in the tense darkness of the room.

I had never shared a room with a male before overnight, not anyone who wasn't family. The experience felt strangely scandalous. As he told me how his parents would figure out that he had simply run away and could do nothing about it, I thought I heard choking, as if he were crying. All night in the lurid stench of the room, he trembled in his bed. Every time I gave him water, he puked it up and moaned; he could hardly move. He couldn't sleep either and just stared up at the ceiling like he were dead or something.

I turned away from him, pulling the blankets tighter around me to give him some dignity. In the morning, we would return to my family's plantation.

⚔️⚔️

We hid in the woods with self-made wooden bows and arrows while a low rider pumped its music through the trees. They tore apart Dylan's apartment, but they found no one. Surely they knew our operation had been shut down, but these men still looked pissed.

We watched from underneath the towering power lines that led into the city.

For a moment, I felt sad remembering that it was what I made that reached so many people, and the ridiculousness of this made me feel ashamed, that I could be proud of producing drugs. But once the men left, I knew we had a void to fill. Not only in the city, where these men sold our product. But for me. We could keep cooking if we wanted, build back what our family had lost.

Blaine was a terrible cook partner and took direction poorly. I asked for supplies I needed as he too often dumped the wrong chemical into the wrong vial. After a week and a half of work, I had run out of pseudoephedrine and had produced something that looked so impure we wouldn't even be able to sell it to prostitutes in Atlanta. The glass looked brown, stained.

We were finished.

Blaine pulled me off the ground. "So what, the whole product's ruined? We tried everything we could, and now it's over? Just like that?"

I smirked. "You've never done anything like this before, have you? Look, I've been around this ever since I was ten. I had a natural affinity for this. But it's OK—you'll leave. I'll press on. It's what Peppers do."

I began to walk back into Dylan's trailer, but he pulled me back. As soon as I felt his hand on my shoulder, I twisted and slapped him hard across the face. He stumbled backward, and I rushed him, landing a fisted punch just under his rib cage. On his back, he stared up at me as I placed a boot firmly below his neck, bending down.

"Don't ever touch me. You're not in control here. Maybe at school—back at Lickskillet, you're such a big deal. You think you own the world. But out here, you would have died if not for me. I fed you. I gave you my cousins' clothes. I tried to teach you, but you were too stupid to even comprehend it. And they call you a genius. Out here, I'm the only one who survives, who understands. What exactly do you need from me?"

I released him, and he rolled forward, clutching his chest, gasping. "What are you going to do? Make meth the rest of your life? I've seen you in action—you belong in NASA or some shit like that. This—you're wasting your talent."

I helped him to his feet, watching him carefully. "This is my talent. My family has a trade, and we live in harmony. We're happy. We—"

He screwed up his face, trying not to say what he wanted, but he spewed out the words like vomit. "What family? Pepper, they're all in prison. I came out here only because—damn, I thought I could live out here alone. But you've been hiding out here, away from anyone. You've turned into an animal. Look, your family pushed all this drug business onto you. But they're gone. I'm really sorry, but they're gone. You don't have to pay anything back to them. You've given them your entire life, your childhood, but you don't have to give them your future. It's over."

I began to speak, but he cut me off.

"I know what that's like, for someone else to choose your future for you. I was born with a gift I never asked for. All my life, everyone has told me how great I'll be one day, but I don't even deserve it. I never worked for any sort of success; I never wanted it. But my parents, my teachers, my friends—they all thought I would grow up to be someone I was never meant to be.

"I'm done listening to them. I feel so pressured to do everything at once, and so far—I've tried to reconcile this by destroying my life. Knocking down all the walls. But that ended up hurting people other than just me. So I'm going to start over. Maybe move out west, work on a ranch, and breathe in the fresh air. I won't have to worry about what people expect of me, because in the end, I can be anyone I want.

"And your family—they expected you to make their business flourish. Maybe twenty years ago, they sold to a few bikers to keep their heads above water. But you came along and changed all that. If what you say is true, maybe you do have a gift. But your family exploited that—"

"My family loved me—"

"Look, I understand about family. But just because someone loves you, it doesn't mean they can't look at you as an opportunity. I'm sure the others were great people—are great people. But they're gone, and everything they expected of you—that's gone. You don't have to be tied down to what other people want. You gave a lot to them, I'm sure, but now who are you doing it for? Yourself? Is that what you envision for yourself? Living here your entire life, being some old-hag meth lady?"

"I can't. I can't get into college. I haven't even finished high school. I wanted to be a chemist—work on something important. Something that could actually help people."

"And who says you still can't? We always tell these stories to ourselves about how our lives should turn out. We rehearse them until they seem real, the words already written. Sometimes we forget that we can change the plot, that we can scrap the ideas completely and start over."

⊰ ⊱

Before Blaine left, he needed to see his friends one last time. At least this I could understand: the desire for finality, closure. While we trekked through the forest toward town, I imagined my father waiting on his court date, my brother locked away alone, waiting to die, and how I'd never see either again.

"What do you want me to say?"

"Just make him promise that he won't call the police—or my parents, for that matter. That he'll stay silent on this. I only want to talk to him, to tell him good-bye."

An hour later, we walked through Blaine's old neighborhood. He insisted on rounding the block to avoid his parents' house. I approached Aron's door while Blaine stood by a tree across the street. Three knocks, and then the door opened. Declin stood, regarding me with a mixture of horror and interest.

"Pepper, you—what—"

"Is Aron here?"

"Aron, you'd better come down here. Um, it's Pepper. Remember, from school?" He held wire cutters that he quickly placed on the floor as he beckoned me in. "Are you OK? I'm sorry about your family. You disappeared after—"

"I wasn't the only one to disappear. Blaine wants to speak to you. Both of you."

Aron, coming down the stairs, said, "Blaine? You know where he is?"

"Yes. I might. But you can't call the police. Or his parents. You can't tell anyone he's here. Do you agree?"

He paused, fumbling for words. "Of course. Where is he?"

I stepped out and gave the signal. Blaine trotted across the street, keeping his head down, and then clomped up the porch steps. He pushed past me and wrapped his arms around Aron. "I'm sorry. I'm sorry. I'm sorry. I've been such a—an asshole. I meant to tell people I was leaving, but they—the Swag Boys would have come after me."

Declin coughed. "The Swag Boys? They're psychotic. Cain is psychotic. What were you even doing with them? They put Elijah in the hospital."

Blaine trembled. "The hospital? Fuck—I should have done something. I could have. But I was too—and I just ran. I knew what they wanted to do, what they wanted me to do, and I ran." He seemed on the verge of saying something else, but he stopped.

"What happened to you? What did they do to you?"

"I wanted—I wanted to be like them, be a part of them. But what they asked was too much. I ran away. Not just to get away from Cain and his gang, but—I needed to get away from everything. I want to start over, somehow, in a city where nobody knows me or hates me or expects me to be some freak genius. Because that's not all I am." Blaine turned to look at me knowingly. "I've wanted to do this a long time, but I've always been afraid to act. The only thing I'll miss—well, Aron, we've been friends a long time. I hope you understand."

He nodded slowly. "Look, next year I think I'm—I'm headed north anyways. I was offered this scholarship for soccer, but I—I haven't really told anyone. I think I'm going to leave Lickskillet, leave South Carolina. In a few months, we would have parted ways regardless, so maybe it's better like this."

"Is Cass OK?"

Declin said, "She's doing better." A long moment of silence that pierced us all. "Blaine, I know you're eager to leave, and—I respect that, but can I ask you a favor before you go?"

"What exactly?"

"Well," he said, picking up the wire cutters he had dropped earlier, "we need to break into a gnome museum. But there's an alarm. Not to mention the camera. We figured we'd break the lock and try to shut off the power from the inside before the alarm sounded. We don't want to cause too much physical damage—in case we get caught, we want to play it off as a prank."

Blaine looked stunned. "The senior prank. I almost forgot." A wicked smile crossed his face. "What exactly do you have in mind?"

"Well, we need your help breaking in and stealing gnomes. If only there was some way to cut the electricity from the outside. Do you—"

"I know a way," I broke in. "There are power lines on the Peppers property that send electricity to the whole town. They'll be in chaos trying to fix it, the whole town dark, and you can do whatever you need just fine."

"The entire city dark," Declin muttered. "That would be drastic, but it would work."

"Good. Good." I smiled.

Aron and Declin turned back to Blaine. "You're really leaving?" Aron asked.

"I may come back one day, when I get things straight. I'll hitch-hike out west until I find—well, until I find whatever it is I'm looking for. Not that there's some answer waiting out there for me, but maybe—just maybe—I'll find something almost as good."

They embraced with embarrassing affection, and I wondered briefly how differently high school might have been had I made friends. Blaine promised that once Aron texted on the night of the prank, the power would go off. All we needed to do was figure out how.

I pointed the bow into the sky, aiming our missile toward the power lines. Blaine stood beside me, holding a cell phone over his head for better reception. We had played with the idea of attempting to slice through the cables with a sharpened arrow, but using a lit bottle rocket seemed more straightforward.

"He says go." Blaine flicked open his Zippo to spark the fuse. I pulled back the string and let go, the sparkling fuse whipping past my face. Halfway to its target, the rocket spurt fire, exploding upward, striking the wire. A shower of sparks erupted above us as we ducked, the dangerous high-voltage lines crackling and falling.

After a few moments bent down in the forest shrubbery, the phone buzzed again. Blaine said, "Well, according to Aron, apparently it worked."

Blaine left early one morning. We stood by the side of the road at the edge of my property as he shuffled his feet and tightened the straps on his bag. I convinced him not to carry his gun so openly, instead stashing it in the front bag pocket in case he ever needed it.

"Thanks, Pepper. I—I'm sorry I was always such a jerk to you. You helped me when no one else would, and—I should tell you something, something bad."

"Bad?"

"Well, never mind—it won't ever help—it won't." He glanced away, his eyes trailing the forest. "It's time I walk down this road and wait till a car picks me up. From there, I'm really not sure where to go. And Pepper?"

"My name is actually Elizabeth."

"Elizabeth. That's a nice name. Well, Elizabeth, I just think—maybe even though you could stay here forever, maybe it's time you move on too." He smiled grimly and then shuffled forward to embrace me awkwardly. Tapping my back once, he backed away, skirted down the road, and disappeared around the corner.

That afternoon, I walked the perimeter of the Pepper Plantation.

I touched each tree as I went by. Here I would be safe. I could hunt to feed myself, and my future was certain—at least as certain as it would ever be.

But with each step, I remembered my family and that they would never return to this hallowed land. I escaped their fate only out of sheer luck, but now fate had nothing to do with it. I loved this land, loved my home, loved this city, and loved my family. Sometimes love, however, could be a crutch, an excuse for not pursuing something more. I always wanted to go to college, to do something good.

My family—they no longer needed me—never again, not truly in the way they had once. We had lost the war, and I was the only warrior left standing. A crow who had lost her flock.

I could find no point to keep struggling. I could leave. I could find another city, and then I could be anyone—not Pepper but Elizabeth. Pepper was a curse, a burden I carried with me throughout my life. But Elizabeth didn't have a past, a reputation—she could be anyone she chose to be.

CHAPTER 39

CASS TERRIES

Sitting in Aron's truck across from the museum, I strapped on the skates. Aron closed the cell phone.

We waited. "You know, you don't have as many bruises. Getting better?"

"At Roller Derby?" I shrugged. "I—well, I quit the team. They're too violent, honestly, and that's just not me. I saw how powerful they were, and sure, I wanted to be like that, but that's not really who I am. Besides, at the last game, a girl punched me right in the tit."

For so long, I believed there to be only two forms of power: sex and muscle. But power could not be deemed either masculine or feminine because there existed so many other forms of strength that we each possessed in varied forms, power that had nothing to do with our genders.

The first streetlamp flickered out, and then a wave of darkness descended on downtown. Midnight struck. Our night began. I pushed open the door and launched into a sprint, silently sliding across the pavement on my skates.

I skated down the alley on the left of the building, bending low to round the corner, barreling toward the exit door, which

I hit at full force. The door opened when I pushed against it, the electronic locks disabled. The alarms never rang, and the cameras hung dead above me. I scooted through the hallway of offices in the back into the main exhibit, where gnomes stood watching me.

Unzipping my book bag, I snatched and stored the gnomes—exactly thirteen—and then skated back toward the exit. In twenty-six seconds, the heist was complete.

Aron propped open his door; he had pulled over to the opposite side of the asphalt. Out of the corner of my eyes, I could see people milling in the street, trying to decipher the power outage. Already, we were gone, speeding toward the school.

All night, I kept thinking that graduation waited for us in just a few weeks. We would put on the glitzy mantle of adulthood and pretend we belonged in a world ruled by those who had their shit together. But we would not—would probably never—have anything figured out. We would change and grow, maybe even become bitter, but tonight, we were the purest versions of ourselves we ever were, doing exactly what reckless teenagers were meant to, becoming legends unto ourselves.

CHAPTER 40

ARON KING

We skirted through intersections, fearing headlightless cars colliding with us from the side, each stoplight reflecting nothing as we passed under them. Cass untied her skates, tossing them into the backseat, and I pressed the accelerator pedal into the carpet so forcibly it left an imprint. We carried thirteen illegally obtained garden gnomes in a bag, speeding through the darkened city to make our mark on Lickskillet history.

When we parked beside the high-school gym, we unloaded the gnomes and rushed them to Declin and Elijah, who had already set up the next phase of the plan. We carried the gnomes through the weight room and into the gym. All around the edges of the basketball court were tables set up for tomorrow's main event, a spring fair that annually drew hundreds of Lickskilletans to Lickskillet High to celebrate history and clean, family fun.

Each year, families milled outside for an hour or more. Preparations had been made the day before, so they needed only to open the doors. No one would be inside yet to discover what we'd done.

Morning would come. Our work would be revealed to the public. I smiled at the genius of it.

The banners, the reflective spiraled ribbons, and the unidentifiable papier-mâché objects courtesy of the local elementary school: these we expected to be there. A full feast-size table laden with a Thanksgiving's worth of food and cups filled with Kool-Aid to resemble wine: that even took me by surprise.

Snagging the keys to the workout room wasn't as hard as I expected. With each new, highly generous scholarship offer, my coach adored me exponentially more. While he waited out on the field during a practice for the team to get dressed, I simply walked into his office and rifled through his key ring until I found the right one. I had handed off the key to Declin at school on Friday. Our preparations were worth it.

Thirteen gnomes now sat around the table. We turned off the lights. When next the room lit up, it would be too late for the administration to remove our gnome-inspired rendition of the Last Supper from the high-school gym.

We climbed into my truck, and as I drove out of the lot, the streetlights flashed back on.

CHAPTER 41

THE JOURNAL OF ELIJAH RODRIGUEZ

May 3

When the power cut off, Declin sprinted across the parking lot, keys jangling in his hand. I realized too late we were in a hurry and raced after him, heaving the sack full of fruit and bread over my shoulder. When I reached him, he had unlocked the door, and we carried our supplies through the weight room as quickly as we could.

A crash beside me. Declin sprawled across the ground, grasping his groin. "I ran straight into the lifting bench." I helped him stand up, and we navigated more carefully through the weight room, edging around the elliptical and hopping deftly over the florid yoga balls. I wondered whether football players ever actually used those.

According to Aron, no one would be in the building until they opened it to the public Saturday morning. Tomorrow.

As tradition mandates, once the decorations are set, no one is allowed in the gym so that the theme for each year's spring fair won't be spoiled. Lickskilletans wait hours just to usher their kids from dunking booths to apple-bobbing stations to face-painting tables. This year, they will receive an extra, divinely designed surprise.

We hauled a table out of the gym annex, one that might have been meant to collect tickets, and draped it in a long, black tablecloth that barely skirted the linoleum. Then we set up the feast for the gnomes, delicately stacking fruit, apples posed atop pineapples. We arranged the meat slabs as if a family were preparing dinner for the in-laws. We placed silverware at each spot to insure absolute inauthenticity. We did, however, pour plastic goblets of red Kool-Aid, the blood of the messianic gnome.

When Aron and Cass burst into the gym, I nearly broke into a run, expecting the police or, worse, Principal Reiser. They carried gnomes, which we placed around the table. A brief debate broke out about which gnome best resembled Jesus, but in the end, we decided we didn't have enough time for small details. We finished setting the scene, right down to the single gnome kneeling beside our centerpiece savior.

Clearing out of the gym, we hopped into Aron's truck and drove slowly away.

We will stay at our own houses tonight, meeting back up the following day at the spring fair to inspect the outcome of our crimes. Despite everything that has happened, tonight was the best night I have ever spent with friends, knowing we are rewriting our own stories, preparing to be known as the teens who pulled off the best prank the school had ever seen.

May 3—continued

Tonight was a success, and though I'm incredibly happy, I cannot sleep. Perhaps it is the pain still in my arm, which is difficult to move in the cast that I still have to keep on for a long time.

I think I hear someone outside my house—maybe Declin.

CHAPTER 42

CORY JOSTIN

Cain's vendetta against him and my crush on the poor boy did not begin to grow until the day Blaine abandoned us, until I told him the truth about us, about what we did to the ex-mayor.

"You little piece of shit," Cain spat through gritted teeth as I delivered a kick to Elijah's chest. His body fell limp, but I kept kicking. If I stopped, Cain would attack me next. He would push me down and beat me unconscious. Elijah's body flailed as the other boys joined in, pummeling his face with knotted fists.

This was the pain of evolution, of becoming the fittest that needed to rid the weakest. First, we evolved from apes, and then we started to keep apes in cages. Then we put humans in chains. We would always be fighting to be ahead of the curve, to seem to one another like we've reached the next step of evolution. But the truth: evolution's next step was self-immolation. There came a certain point when creation became destruction.

"Hey, what do you think you're doing?" An elderly man hobbled toward us, wielding his cane.

"Let's go before he calls the cops." Cain did not move quickly, however, strolling toward his car, his eyes spitting venom at the intruder. The man started toward Elijah, but Cain snapped out at him, kicking his cane away, tripping him. The man fell onto his face, and we left him trembling on the ground next to the boy we had beaten unconscious.

═╬═╬═

No mention of the attack in the newspapers, meaning Elijah knew what would happen if he talked. Cain still fumed over Blaine leaving us on the night he might have been initiated, but he relished that Blaine had not returned. During lunch, he told stories that Blaine had probably joined some hobo camp or shot himself in the mouth or become a male prostitute in Atlanta.

Donny tripped over his feet, landing on his teeth at the foot of the stairwell. Cain lurched down behind him, squealing and kicking Donny out of his way. He dropped a mostly empty beer bottle onto the marble floor, and it shattered, shards sliding under the carpet, below the table.

"What are you doing—you hanging around?" Cain tried to stand but stumbled. "Have a drink."

A crash from the other room; Cain and Donny didn't seem to notice, collapsed on the bottom step. I brushed the glass away with my feet and peeked into the kitchen, where Rick was sprawled on the counter like a dead spider.

"Anyone else in the mood for fast food?" Rick lifted his head and looked at me. "You don't seem too bad off, Cory. Drive us. Come on."

We gathered outside, piling into Cain's car. He sat in the passenger's seat giving me directions with a trembling finger while I drove to the nearest McDonald's. We pulled through the drive-through, ordering our food through the scratchy loudspeaker around back. The clock blinked a minute closer to midnight, and Donny slumped over, snoring.

Cain leaned over me, fumbling with the change in his car console. "Want to see something fucking hilarious?"

He pulled a gun from under his seat, a small silver piece of work with a six-bullet chamber that he spun playfully. The car jerked up to the first window, and we dumped a pile of cash in the worker's lap before screeching forward. "Wait for it," Cain said, steadying my hand on the wheel.

Some young girl, red-eyed and pimpled, leaned out to hand us our food, and Cain's fist appeared under my chin in a flash, fingering the trigger, pointing the barrel into the girl's face. "Don't move."

"We only carry fifty dollars in the cash drawer," said the girl, as if rehearsing from memory. "And I don't know the combination to the safe."

"I don't want cash. I want to play a game. There is a bullet in here." Cain removed the chamber and spun it before clicking it back into the gun. "We'll see if you're lucky."

Click.

She gasped, staggering away from the window, and I stomped on the gas pedal. "That was—Cain, are you OK?"

He was only laughing. "That could have messed up the paint job even more." When he grinned, he reminded me of a demented Cheshire cat. "She got lucky, though."

His arm hanging out the window, he shot again. This time the bullet rang out and smashed through the golden arches, yellow plastic raining down on our car as we sped away.

⇥✢ ✢⇤

I pointed the gun at Cain's temple now. We sat upstairs at his house with his parents asleep below us. Like followers of some cultish religion, we sat in a circle of chairs in Cain's bedroom, which was big enough to fit three of my bedrooms inside of.

Click.

I imagined Cain's brain flopping like a plate of spaghetti onto the floor. He took the gun from me and in turn pointed it at Rick, who smiled drunkenly. No one questioned this game because questioning this would make us seem weak, and we were not weak.

Click.

"There's not really a bullet in it, you know. You don't have to flinch like a little bitch."

Cain played with the gun, weighing it delicately in his hands. "Well, this was fun."

Click.

⊱✦⊰

Bring the spray paint, Cain had said. I parked beside him, and he climbed into the truck with me, shaking each canister and sniffing the nozzles. "Good, good, this should be enough."

"Where are Donny and Rick?"

The power had been out for more than an hour, every streetlight dim.

"Not here. Remember that time we went to McDonald's and I threatened the window clerk?"

He said this just like he might have asked if I remembered the time Donny got a match stuck up his nostril.

"They broke out an investigation on us. Someone called the house earlier, looking for me. They might know." He looked straight ahead, down the street. "But they won't find us. And if they do, my father will take care of it. I think I know a certain drug addict who recently skipped town, who had a history of breaking the law."

He meant Blaine—he had to. I said nothing but began driving around the block. "That house—that one." Cain pointed it out, the house with no cars. The power remained off. We sat silently in our car, waiting for something I knew nothing about.

We will write Faggot across the side of his house, Cain said. Simple enough, not too violent, just me and him armed with spray-paint cans. Somehow, it did not seem like a big deal, as long as no one got hurt. Even though I felt sorry for the kid named Elijah. Something about him attracted me.

The lights flickered back on, exposing us on the street. Whatever problem the city had been having with the electricity, someone had resolved it.

As we prepared to climb out the car, another truck pulled up, stopping in front of the house. Elijah climbed out, hobbling inside.

"He never told anyone. He hasn't said a thing. He will, and— the drive-through. They may know something. But if we scare him—"

Cain trembled, caressing something in his pocket.

I wondered if people went to hell for doing evil things or simply for not preventing them from happening.

———

You spend your entire life painting yourself as the hero, writing the story in your head so it makes sense, but in the end, you figure out you've been wrong all along, the antagonist to yourself, the one nobody roots for.

He crumpled on the sidewalk, his eyes rolling back.

We the aggressors, the villains. I the aggressor. I the villain.

He put the gun in my hand and said, "We'll play the game with him. We'll—"

This time, the gun did not click but exploded with sound. A gun going off in your hand sends a jolt through your entire body.

It felt strange. Brains look less like they do in movies—not pink coils but more like blood-soaked sponges.

Cain fell onto the pavement, blood pooling at my feet.

I spun the chamber, inspecting. Five bullets—Elijah was never meant to live. I put the gun inside of my own mouth.

Click.

CHAPTER 43

DECLIN OSTRANDER

We heard about the murder first from the newspaper and later from Elijah, who had been there. Who had rushed downstairs once he heard the gunshot though every fiber of his body told him to stay upstairs. Cain Rutgers died immediately from the bullet wound in his head. Elijah found them, the boy with the gun slumped over the dead boy's body. In the wake of the murder, Principal Reiser rescheduled the spring fair, finding the idea of celebrating inappropriate. The gnomes were removed without serious comment and the gym redecorated for the following Saturday. Over the course of the next week, the truth came out about what Cory and Cain had done. Cory confessed to aiding in the murder of Francis Jameson.

The following day, my father arrived at the Lickskillet courthouse to begin the appeal process for Matthew Pepper, who, despite being (at least in my eyes) a despicable racist, never actually killed anyone. Once the truth came, no one truly understood or believed the events that had happened. Guess that sometimes the stories we told ourselves were easier to digest than the stories we heard, like sometimes we had trouble believing that other people were people too, just as wicked and wonderful and strange and unpredictable as ourselves.

⇥ ⇤

Cass insisted I go stag to prom, though she danced with me throughout the evening. We drove together, Elijah and Aron in the back. We arrived at my house at around two in the morning after a late-night Waffle House dinner, stumbling across the lawn in stiff tuxedos. My father had helped acquit Matthew Pepper, who was being investigated for matters related to his family's meth-production business. Because of his actual absence during the raid, my father believed the prosecution had little evidence. Once the court dropped murder charges, my father packed the car and moved to Jasper, Alabama, where a member of a white nationalist group had reportedly fired his shotgun into the dome of a local mosque.

The house had not, however, been empty. Friends came and went, and on this night, the house shook with an energy that almost made our residence distinguishable from those of our neighbors. When I brought out the pot brownies I had bought for the night, Aron groaned. He still had to be drug-tested for his college soccer team. We squeezed together onto the living-room sofa and began watching late-night infomercials, breaking the silence with stories.

Cass told us about a time when she was fourteen, when she stole her father's car and drove to the Red Hole alone. She decided to go swimming, and when she climbed out, she realized another car had parked farther away. At first, she'd dashed to dress herself and then realized the car was rocking back and forth. She banged loudly on the window. A college couple was having sex in the backseat. Cass wanted to go to Clemson to study nursing.

Aron reminded me about our first day together at school, when he thought I was half-crazy in biology class. He also reminded me that our final was in less than a week. In the past month, Aron had finally accepted a scholarship offer to play soccer for Chapel Hill.

Elijah's date, Alice, remained reticent, but Elijah yammered about how he would miss us, though thankfully, before he could start crying, the pot brownies kicked in. He fell asleep on the floor.

I enjoyed listening to their stories, though I felt a slight pang that I couldn't share any of my own. Somehow I had never really experienced anything I found notable, not as myself but only as my fake selves. But these fake selves remained skeletons I had buried and would try to forget. I wanted to feel real, wanted to know the world through my own eyes.

As a lifetime liar, I recognized the value of the truth. Not just the *truth* truth but our own personal truths, the ones we chose to believe because those are the only ones that made sense. Sometimes, we learned the truth about ourselves, about others, or about humanity, but deep down, the truth became subjective, just a story we told ourselves. All of human history, everything we claimed as fact in our textbooks, in our documentaries, began as stories.

I looked forward to college, to leaving Lickskillet, and to finding new friends. I would remember these people, these winking heathens, like I had remembered no one else. Maybe I would have stories to tell—the botched murder trial, Nick the Dragon Master attacking me with a flail, or even Elijah's bullying. I smiled to have memories I could share, though already they felt like memories. Already, prom night seemed like just another story we'd tell ourselves so we could remember how alive we felt. Our lives were not exactly the stuff of legends. None of us won Nobel Peace Prizes or became president or anything extravagant like that. We came out only kids, still dazed and unsure where we were headed. Shedding old skin, walking with feet we recognized only as our own.

Science taught us that the universe was broken into components. The world was made of atoms, but that was not all; the world was also made up of stories, our stories stitched together so intricately they blended together. The catalog of human experience made up existence, reality, or whatever you wanted to call that beating that started in your heart and vibrated your eyelids every morning you awoke. All those treacherous confessions whispered to ourselves in our own heads at night when the entire world fell quiet and we began entertaining eternity—those were the most important stories to tell. Because they were the truth, and though the truth might not have been believable, it made for a damned good story.